DRAGON WYTCH

YASMINE GALENORN

BERKLEY BOOKS, NEW YORK

THE BERKLEY PUBLISHING GROUP
Published by the Penguin Group
Penguin Group (USA) Inc.
375 Hudson Street, New York, New York 10014, USA
Penguin Group (Canada), 90 Eglinton Avenue East, Suite 700, Toronto, Ontario M4P 2Y3, Canada
(a division of Pearson Penguin Canada Inc.)
Penguin Books Ltd., 80 Strand, London WC2R 0RL, England
Penguin Group Ireland, 25 St. Stephen's Green, Dublin 2, Ireland (a division of Penguin Books Ltd.)
Penguin Group (Australia), 250 Camberwell Road, Camberwell, Victoria 3124, Australia
(a division of Pearson Australia Group Pty. Ltd.)
Penguin Books India Pvt. Ltd., 11 Community Centre, Panchsheel Park, New Delhi—110 017, India
Penguin Group (NZ), 67 Apollo Drive, Rosedale, North Shore 0632, New Zealand
(a division of Pearson New Zealand Ltd.)
Penguin Books (South Africa) (Pty.) Ltd., 24 Sturdee Avenue, Rosebank, Johannesburg 2196,
South Africa

Penguin Books Ltd., Registered Offices: 80 Strand, London WC2R 0RL, England

This is a work of fiction. Names, characters, places, and incidents either are the product of the author's imagination or are used fictitiously, and any resemblance to actual persons, living or dead, business establishments, events, or locales is entirely coincidental. The publisher does not have any control over and does not assume any responsibility for author or third-party websites or their content.

DRAGON WYTCH

A Berkley Book / published by arrangement with the author

PRINTING HISTORY
Berkley edition / July 2008

Copyright © 2008 by Yasmine Galenorn.
Excerpt from *Night Huntress* by Yasmine Galenorn copyright © 2009 by Yasmine Galenorn.
Cover illustration by Tony Mauro.
Cover design by Rita Frangie.

ISBN: 978-0-425-22239-3

BERKLEY®
Berkley Books are published by The Berkley Publishing Group,
a division of Penguin Group (USA) Inc.,
375 Hudson Street, New York, New York 10014.
BERKLEY® is a registered trademark of Penguin Group (USA) Inc.
The "B" design is a trademark belonging to Penguin Group (USA) Inc.

PRINTED IN THE UNITED STATES OF AMERICA

10 9 8 7 6

To all you sensual men
who make us hunger for dark knights
in a garden strewn with rose petals and thorns.

ACKNOWLEDGMENTS

Thank you to my husband for being such an inspiration, in so many ways. Thanks also to my agent, Meredith Bernstein, and my editor, Kate Seaver. I also want to thank my cover artist, Tony Mauro, whose artistic talents bring my visions to life. Thanks to my Witchy Chicks, the best blogging group on the Net and a supportive cyber-family. And thank you to my friends for supporting me through the ups and downs of this career.

To my cats, my little "Galenorn Gurlz." To Ukko, Rauni, Mielikki, and Tapio, my spiritual guardians.

Thank you to my readers, both old and new. Your support helps keep us in ink and fuels our love of storytelling.

You can find me on the Net at Galenorn En/Visions: www .galenorn.com, at MySpace, and you can contact me via e-mail on my site. If you write to me snail mail (see Web site for address or write via publisher), please enclose a stamped, self-addressed envelope with your letter if you would like a reply.

Power Play: Bid for advantage: an attempt to gain an
    advantage by a display of strength or superiority, e.g.,
    in a negotiation or relationship.

—MICROSOFT ENCARTA 2006

The secret of success is learning how to use pain and
    pleasure instead of having pain and pleasure use you.
    If you do that, you're in control of your life. If you
    don't, life controls you.

—TONY ROBBINS

CHAPTER 1

There was pixie dust in the air. I could feel it seeping in from under the door of the Indigo Crescent, my bookshop, as it wafted up to tickle the back of my throat. There was no mistaking the stuff; it was different from just about every other manifestation of Fae magic there was. Sparkling, the dust shimmered on the astral, hovering in that in-between place. Not quite physical, not quite ethereal. And yet pixie magic had more effect on humans and the human realm than it did on anybody else.

Curious. The fact that I could sense it all the way back in my office meant it came from a pixie with strong magic. *Otherworld* magic, if I wasn't off my mark. I hadn't seen an Earthside pixie near my shop since I'd been here. Or at least, I didn't think any were around. The creatures usually gave me a wide berth, partly because I was half-Fae and partly because I was a witch. Either way, they didn't trust me.

A number of witches back in Otherworld made a habit of trapping pixies to harvest their dust. The pixies weren't hurt, but they took a severe blow to the ego during the process, especially when some of their captors sold the dust for profits that would make even a leprechaun blink. Of course, the pixies didn't get one penny from the transaction, and sometimes they banded together to raid a shop with some success. But for the most part, they just tried to avoid us altogether.

Of course, *I* didn't trust *them*, either. Pixies were born troublemakers, and they enjoyed every minute of it. They weren't usually dangerous, not in the way your average pain-in-the-neck goblin was, but they were trouble all the same.

I finished counting the receipts and tucked the money from the cash register into a strongbox, hiding it in the bottom drawer of my desk. So much for another slow day. The Indigo Crescent was having an off month. Either nobody was reading, or I wasn't moving in enough new stock to draw in new customers.

I gathered my purse and keys. My sister Delilah was already gone for the day. She ran a casual PI business upstairs from my shop, but she'd been out on a case most of the day and hadn't bothered with more than a quick check-your-messages pit stop this morning.

Glancing around my office to make sure everything was in order, I slipped on a light capelet. My tastes ran toward bustiers, camisoles, and chiffon skirts, not exactly weather-appropriate wear, but I wasn't about to change my style because of a few storm clouds.

We were nearing the vernal equinox, and Seattle was still chilly and overcast. Roiling gray clouds seeded with fat, heavy raindrops had moved in from the ocean, opening up to splatter the sidewalks and roads.

Granted, the trees around the city were vibrant with budding leaves, and the moss gave off a rich, loamy scent, but spring in western Washington was a far cry from spring back in Otherworld. By now, the skies over OW would be stained with thin rivulets of gold from the setting sun, creating a watercolor wash as they blended into the indigo of the approaching twilight. The warm blush of the waxing year would encourage the night-martins to sing every evening, and the smell of Terebell's flowers would permeate the gardens around our house.

Sighing, and a little bit homesick—memories were all we had of our home in OW right now—I set the alarm system and locked the door. Tired or not, I'd better find out where the pixie dust was coming from. If a group of them had moved into the neighborhood, *all* the shops would be in for trouble.

As I turned toward the sidewalk, a whinny caught my attention, crowding out any idea of tracking down the wayward pixie. I glanced up the street and froze. *What the hell?*

A unicorn was heading my way. He passed Baba Yaga's Deli, which had moved in next to my bookstore, and then stopped, close enough for me to feel his breath on my face.

With a nonchalant bob of the head, the unicorn said, "Good evening, Lady Camille."

I blinked, wondering if I'd been working a little too hard. But no, he was still there. His coat shimmered with that silky, luminous white that only adorns magical creatures. His eyes glinted with intelligence, and his horn sparkled a lustrous gold. That's how I knew he was a male, other than the obvious anatomical signs, which were most definitely in attendance. Female unicorns have silver horns.

The more I looked at him, the more he reminded me of something out of one of those ethereal perfume commercials— the ones where I was never sure just what they were advertising until they splashed the bottle on the screen and the announcer warbled something lame like, "Magic—experience the thrill."

I blinked again.

He was still there. Clearing my throat, I was about to ask him what he was doing meandering through the streets of Seattle, when a noise from up the street startled me. As I turned, a goblin, a Sawberry Fae, and a bugbear emerged from a nearby alley and started our way. They looked pissed.

I know, I know. A goblin, a Fae, and a bugbear wander into a bar where they meet this gorgeous wench with her boobs hanging out . . .

My train of thought stopped in mid-joke when, in a matter of seconds, the situation deteriorated from a whimsical *what the hell is going on* to *oh no they can't really be planning to do that.*

The goblin held up a blowgun and took aim at the unicorn.

"Hand over the pixie, Feddrah-Dahns, or you're dead!" The bugbear's voice was guttural, and he spoke in Calouk, the rough, common dialect familiar to most Otherworld citizens. The words were garbled. The threat was clear.

Cripes! Without a second thought—unicorns were dangerous and beautiful, but goblins were just dangerous and stupid—I closed my eyes and whispered a quick chant to the wind. My fingers tingled as a thick bolt of energy slammed through me, gathered from the gusts blowing steadily in an east-northeasterly direction. As the rippling force raced down my arms, I focused on forming it into a ball in my hands, then sent it tumbling toward the goblin.

Please don't let my magic fail me now, I silently begged. A lot of my magic went haywire because of my half-Fae, half-human blood. Call it faulty wiring or even just plain old bad luck, but I was never quite sure when a spell would take, or if it would take right, or if it would slam out of me racing ninety miles an hour like an express train out of control. I'd already ruined one hotel room this year playing around with lightning and rain. I wasn't keen on the idea of possibly tearing up the pavement and having a city street crew cussing me out.

This go-round, the Moon Mother smiled on me, and the spell held true. The bolt hit the goblin square in the chest, knocking him off his feet before he could shoot his dart at the unicorn. The spell didn't stop there, though. After it KO'd the goblin, the magical gust of wind ricocheted off the side of my bookstore and bounced back, slamming into the bugbear, sending him rolling into the streets like a trash can on a windy day.

I stared at the chaos I'd managed to wreak in just a few seconds, caught between mild embarrassment and intense pride. I was getting pretty good! I usually didn't manage to pack that strong a punch, especially with wind magic. Maybe a little of Iris's skill was rubbing off on me.

"Youch!" The tickle of a lash licked my arm, sending a white flame through my skin and jerking me out of my self-congratulatory mood. "That hurt, damn it!"

I turned to see the Sawberry Fae was bearing down on me, whip in hand. Scrambling a few steps to the side, I said, "No thanks, I'm not interested in your kinky little games." Maybe I'd better focus on the here and now. There'd be time for patting myself on the back later.

He licked his lips, drawing back the whip once more. *Eww.* I had the feeling this dude was enjoying himself just a little too much. Apparently the unicorn had taken notice of the fight. The gorgeous stallion galloped past me, horn lowered, and skewered the Fae in the shoulder, tossing him three feet into the air and five feet back. The screaming man hit the sidewalk and lay there, bleeding like a stuck pig.

The carnage continued as a speeding car screeched around

the corner and ran over the bugbear. Splat. Flat as a pancake. The Porsche—at least it looked like a Porsche—sped off before I could get the license plate.

I shrugged. I had my sincere doubts that the bugbear would have wished me any better luck, so I wasn't going to waste any tears on him. I turned back to the mayhem on the sidewalk.

"Well . . ." There wasn't much else to say. It wasn't every day a bunch of Otherworld creatures got themselves mowed down in front of my bookstore.

The unicorn trotted over to my side. I glanced up into his face, mesmerized by the swirling vortex of colors in his eyes. Pretty. Very pretty. And, unless I was off the mark, he looked a little bit pissed, too.

"You might want to call a constable," the horned horse said, sounding mildly concerned. He nodded in the direction of the flattened bugbear. "Somebody could slip on that mess and hurt themselves."

He had a point. The sidewalk looked like a scene out of *Pulp Fiction* or *Kung Fu Hustle*. I could hear Chase now. He was going to just *love* getting my call. He'd been swamped lately, trying to keep up the facade that we were still on the official up-and-up with the OIA—the Otherworld Intelligence Agency—and not running the whole show ourselves. Cleaning up after a trio of Otherworld thugs was probably the last thing he wanted dumped on his plate.

I let out a long sigh. "You're probably right. Would you like to come in while I make the call?" I motioned to the shop.

If unicorns could shrug, this one would have. "All right. You wouldn't happen to have anything to drink, would you? I'm thirsty, and there don't seem to be any public watering holes around."

"Sure, I can get you some water. I'm Camille, by the way. Camille D'Artigo. I'm from Otherworld." I unlocked the door and punched in the security code to turn off the alarm system that I'd just armed.

"That's rather obvious." The unicorn's words rippled with a droll tone, and I realized we weren't speaking English. We'd automatically switched over to Melosealfôr, a rare dialect of Crypto that all witches who were pledged to the Moon Mother learned during their training. "I know who you are. You stand out in the crowd, my lady. How do you do? I'm Feddrah-Dahns."

"Feddrah-Dahns, eh? You're from the Windwillow Valley then." Something about the name rang a bell, but I couldn't quite place it. I *did* know that every unicorn coming out of the Windwillow Valley assumed Dahns as their surname. The area was teeming with Cryptos, and there were rumors that huge herds of the horned beasts roamed the plains, nomads who migrated across the vast valley during the summer months.

"You know your geography, Camille D'Artigo."

"Yes, well . . . What about the pixie? Where did he go? I noticed pixie dust a little while ago."

"I hope he'll be all right. He retrieved something from the bugbear that belonged to me. Technically, he was simply reclaiming stolen property, but the bugbear and his accomplices apparently didn't see it that way." Feddrah-Dahns blinked those beautiful big eyes of his.

I grinned. "Thieves rarely understand the concept of ownership, be they bugbear or human." I opened the door as wide as I could. As the unicorn cautiously stepped over the doorstop, he bobbed his head, a curious glint in his eye. Life in Seattle might be gloomy and wet, but nobody could ever convince me it was boring.

CHAPTER 2

Before Chase and his team arrived, the wounded Fae managed to crawl off, leaving a trail of blood spatters that disappeared into the alley behind my building. I had glanced down the gloomy passage, but it was too dark to see to the end, and I had no inclination to wander down there by myself. Chase and his men could explore it if they wanted to.

I did, however, decide to drag the unconscious goblin inside, into the room next to my office. He stank, which was gross, and his clothes were greasy, which was even worse, but I finally wrangled him into the back where I hog-tied him with some strapping tape. He woke up and glared at me as I was wrapping the clear tape around his wrists and ankles.

I immediately slapped a piece of tape across his mouth before he was able to speak. Nasty looks wouldn't hurt me, but whatever came out of his mouth just might. Some goblins used magic. And they were all dirty, filthy little liars.

The bugbear, on the other hand—or what remained of him—could stay right where he was. Way too nasty. No way I was going to clean up a slick patch of roadkill, especially not while wearing velvet and lace.

Ten minutes later, Chase leaned against the counter, staring at the unicorn, while Sharah and Mallen scraped the bugbear off the road. I had to hand it to them. The two elves looked ready to gag, but they finished their job without complaint.

Feddrah-Dahns was busy drinking his water from a bucket I found in the back. Iris used it for cleaning, so I rinsed it out and filled it with fresh spring water from the water cooler. He looked about as contemplative as I'd seen a unicorn look. Not that I'd seen too many unicorns, even back in Otherworld. They usually preferred the company of their own kind.

A few of my regular customers who'd been passing by noticed the open shop door, and they wandered in to see if everything was okay. Eyes wide, they immediately glommed onto the horned beast, surrounding him as if he were some sort of god.

When I thought about it, in a way he *was* a god. Few unicorns had shown any interest in coming through the portals, and the Earthside species seldom showed themselves. Considering the wonder with which they were revered in human legend and mythology, it didn't surprise me that people immediately opened their hearts to him.

Henry Jeffries, one of my best customers, gently reached out to touch the wild mane that cascaded down the ridge of the unicorn's neck, a look of wonder rippling across his face. Feddrah-Dahns glanced at him, gently whinnying. Henry shuffled over to me and rubbed his hands across his eyes. He looked teary.

"I never thought I'd live to see the day. Do you think Mr. Beagle ever really met a unicorn?"

I frowned. It was unlikely that Peter S. Beagle had even believed in the creatures when he wrote *The Last Unicorn*, but then again, who knew? "I'm not sure, Henry. You never can tell." I flashed him a smile, and he mirrored it back to me, then returned to Feddrah-Dahns's side.

"Camille? Camille? Did you hear what I said?"

"Huh?" I turned around. Chase had been talking to me at the same time as Henry. "No, I'm sorry. What was it?"

He sighed. "This is the third report of Cryptos on the loose that I've had this morning."

Chase was suave. Less lecherous than when we'd first met, he was a damned good detective. I'd gone from disdaining the dude to actually liking him, as long as he kept his eyes off my butt and boobs. Oh, now and then his gaze still wandered into forbidden territory, and he still smelled like spicy beef tacos a good share of the time, but at least he was polite about the occasional peek show. And most importantly, the scent of cigarettes was long gone. My sister Delilah had him on the nicotine patch, and he was faring remarkably well. Of course, he had incentive; she refused to kiss him or touch him if he smoked.

"You make it sound like they got loose from the zoo." I sighed. "Chase, babe, you've got to get over the idea that two legs equals intelligence."

He snorted. "Don't give me grief, woman. You're from Otherworld, you're half-Fae. You've been here, what . . . a year now, isn't it? The portals have been open about four—maybe five years, right?"

I nodded. "That's about right."

"In that time, a number of Fae have crossed over to visit Earthside. And the Earthside Supes have come out of the closet. But we've never had a run on Cryptos before. Not that I can remember. Now, they're everywhere. Portland's reporting a significant increase in sightings, and they've been spotted all over western Washington. What do you think it means?"

I had to admit, he was right to be concerned. While Otherworld Fae still weren't commonplace, and we tended to settle around the West Coast, we were no longer the novelty act that we'd been when the OIA decided to open a few of the interdimensional portals.

Since they'd reestablished the lines of communication that had been shut down during the Great Divide—when Otherworld had split off from Earthside—we'd become increasingly accepted in human society. And over the past month or so, a home court renaissance of sorts had sprung up. Earthside Supes were quickly becoming the flavor of the day.

After the first shock waves settled, we'd been welcomed with open arms. For the most part. There were still a number of factions who thought we were evil incarnate and who wouldn't mind lighting the match to our funeral pyres, but they were the vocal minority, and we didn't pay much attention to them. There was intolerance everywhere, and we knew better than to think we could eradicate it totally.

But Cryptos? Cryptos were still unusual enough to turn heads. However, their rarity wasn't the problem. "That's not what has me worried, Chase. I think you need to rephrase the question."

He sucked on his lower lip. "Okay, so tell me what the question is, and why their sudden appearance is trouble. Or not."

I frowned. "All right. How about this: The fact that a unicorn is wandering the streets of Seattle is unsettling, not because he's a Crypto, but because unicorns almost always stay in the wild and seldom venture into cities. It's not unnatural for Feddrah-Dahns to be curious about what it's like over here on Earthside, but it *is* unnatural for him to come into the city instead of heading out into the forest. Ergo, you're right. Something's up."

"Interesting." Chase drummed his fingers on the glass display case next to me. "So, why is he standing here in your shop instead of over in Magnolia Park?"

I reached out and smacked his fingers. Gently. "Stop that—not good for the glass." Sliding onto the stool behind the cash register, I leaned my elbows on the counter. "What's up? Beats me. I'll have a talk with Feddrah-Dahns and see what I can find out. Meanwhile, what kind of other reports are you talking about? Standard Bigfoot sightings?"

"No. In fact, some of them are downright frightening. At three in the morning we received a call from a terrified woman who said a satyr was trying to climb into bed with her. He had one hell of a hard-on and was ready to share it. Granted, he left when she screamed and fought him off, but around here, we still frown on rape. If we catch him, he'd better make tracks back to OW unless he wants to spend the next ten years in an Earthside jail."

Oops. Yeah, this could be a problem. Satyrs and other wild Cryptos usually kept to the meadows and forests. What the hell were they doing in the suburbs of Seattle?

"So you didn't catch him?"

"No. We arrived at the woman's house just in time to see him racing through the bushes, but we couldn't keep up. Cryptos are experts at eluding the cops, for some reason."

"Probably because they're good at camouflage. And fast." Most Cryptos were a lot faster than humans. Most of the Fae were, too. Even though I was only half-Fae, I could run rings around Chase's stamina and endurance, but I didn't feel like rubbing it in right now. I took a closer look at the detective. His eyelids drooped, and he looked like he hadn't slept in days. The bags under his eyes would hold a major shopping haul.

"You been sleeping okay?" I asked.

He shook his head. "Nope. Your sister's been keeping me awake at nights and not for all the right reasons. She's taken to chasing her tail in the middle of the night. On the bed. On my pillow. Then she gets in these kneading frenzies that won't quit. I've got the scars to prove it all over my chest. And then, with worrying about satyrs and goblins, who can get any sleep?" He picked up a pen off the counter and rubbed it between his fingers.

"Craving a cigarette?" I asked.

He nodded. "Yeah. Listen, visitors from OW are going to have to learn to play by the rules, or somebody's going to get trigger happy and all hell will break loose." He grimaced. "That damn Freedom's Angels group is stirring up trouble right and left. The more popular you guys get, the angrier they get."

Freedom's Angels were a group of ultra–right-wing hate mongers who took the rhetoric spouted by the Guardian Watchdogs and put it into action, which moved them from the category of *annoying* to *dangerous*. So far, they'd confined themselves to a few minor skirmishes. Mostly, they came out the worse for wear. The Fae were stronger, quicker, and could easily be far more ruthless than the Freedom's Angels were, but that could shift with the right weapon in hand.

I gave him a short nod. "Now that the portal in the Wayfarer is pointed toward Darkynwyrd instead of Y'Elestrial, unauthorized creatures come through the bar several times a week. Menolly had to fight off three more goblins a couple nights ago. They're no match for her, she just feeds them to Tavah, but still, it's an inconvenience. Free lunch, though." Tavah, like my youngest sister, was a vampire—and she was full Fae. Only she was less particular than Menolly about what flavor of blood she drank.

"Well, you can't just shut the portals down," Chase said, pursing his lips.

"No, we can't." Delilah, Menolly, and I had tried to tackle the problem several times, getting us nowhere. But now it was beginning to affect the city.

Seattle—most of Earth, actually—knew about Otherworld and the Fae. We weren't in the closet anymore, but there was so much they *didn't* know. Like the fact that the Subterranean

Realms existed. Like the fact that the ruler of the Sub Realms—a demon lord named Shadow Wing—was out to raze both Earth and Otherworld. And like the terrifying fact that my sisters and I and our friends were the only obstacles standing in his way.

"Here's the thing," I said after a moment. "The Cryptos running loose in the city can't be coming through the Wayfarer portal. Menolly has guards on watch twenty-four/seven."

"Okay, so are there any other portals around?" Chase's gaze wandered back to the unicorn and, for the briefest of seconds, a look of amazement flickered across his face. I smiled softly. Even our jaded detective could be enchanted by creatures from the land of Fae.

"Well, there's the portal out in the woods. The one Grandmother Coyote watches over." I tried to think of other portals nearby.

Chase laughed. "Should I bother to ask you if she'd let them through?"

"Don't be so sure," I warned him. "She's not entirely on our side."

Grandmother Coyote was one of the Hags of Fate, neither good nor evil but straddling the nexus point where the realms of existence balanced out. When things went askew, she and her ilk acted to right the balance. Shadow Wing and his demons had shifted destiny, so she'd called us in to help right it. Could something have altered the path of fate again?

"She might let them pass, if the balance required it." But as I thought about the Hags of Fate, I remembered something the Elfin Queen Asteria had mentioned to us a few months ago. I snapped my fingers. "I know how they're getting in."

Chase tugged nervously on his tie. It was a bright yellow and orange stripe against his navy suit, and complemented the blue in an odd, off sort of way.

"Well, don't keep me in suspense, woman," he said. "If we don't get a handle on this problem, we'll be facing some tough questions from my prick of a boss. The mayor won't be too happy, either. The last thing I need is for Devins to find yet another problem that he can turn into my fault. The mayor's another matter, but still . . ."

I glanced around to see who was in the shop. The unicorn had drawn quite a crowd, and a buzz of laughter and conversation threatened to overwhelm us.

"Over here." I motioned for Chase to follow me into a corner niche where the sound of voices died down to a low murmur. He settled himself on the short mahogany bench between the stacks holding suspense thrillers: Grisham, Crichton, Clancy, and so forth. After making sure nobody was eavesdropping on us, I joined him.

"When Queen Asteria visited us a few months ago after we destroyed Dredge, she mentioned that a number of previously undiscovered portals were being discovered—unguarded portals. And most of them lead to the Pacific Northwest."

Chase blinked. "Delilah didn't tell me that."

"She's a good girl. She keeps secrets. It's something you didn't need to know at the time." I watched his surprise turn into a frown. Oops, I'd just stepped on his toes. I did that a lot with Chase. We had rubbed each other wrong from day one.

"Oh, really? Thank you for your confidence. And pray tell—if you think I need to know—just where do these portals lead?"

Yeah, I'd wounded his ego, all right. "Don't be such a drama queen. There are plenty of things about your job that you don't tell us."

"None of the secrets I keep affect you," he said, squinting. "Oh hell, just drop it. Go on. You said most lead to the PNW?"

"Yes." I took a deep breath and continued. "Apparently a number of them lead to Seattle and the surrounding area. Now, Queen Asteria slapped guards on the portals in her jurisdiction, but there are plenty of portals out in the wild that are being discovered, and *nobody* has control over them. Want to make a bet that Cryptos and other creatures are finding and using them whenever they want?"

"Can't Queen Asteria put a stop to it?"

I shook my head. "As I said, if they're outside the boundaries of Elqaneve and the Elfin lands, there isn't a damned thing she can do. Even with the ones that are within her jurisdiction, well, Queen Asteria hasn't got the manpower to guard all of them. Not now, when she's fully engaged in the war against Lethesanar. You have to understand. War over in Otherworld is to the death, as it is here, but over there the magic involved can cause far greater damage than your tanks and guns. The elder mages can actually warp the makeup of the land. They can change the very structure of the soil and air. It's happened before, down in the Southern Wastes."

A somber expression crossed Chase's face, and his petulance passed. "If you were home—you and your sisters . . ."

"Well, if our father hadn't deserted the Guard and our aunt and cousin hadn't come out as traitors to Queen Lethesanar, we would have been pressed into battle like everybody else in the city. As it is, we'd be tortured and killed. Our entire family is under a death threat if any one of us should enter—or go anywhere near—Y'Elestrial at this time. Until Tanaquar wins, we're homeless . . ." I paused. A thought had crossed my mind several times that I didn't want to examine. I hadn't vocalized it to Menolly or Delilah yet.

"Yes?"

"I haven't mentioned this to my sisters yet, but I think that our father disappeared because he traded sides. His conscience won't allow him to fight for Lethesanar, but he's a warrior and a proud member of the Guard Des'Estar. He can't stand by and hide in fear, nor can he see Lethesanar defile the Court and Crown like she's been doing. I *know* he's in battle somewhere. I can feel it."

"You think he's working for the elves?" Chase reached out and took my hand. I started to pull away, then stopped. He was trying to be kind. I could read it in his eyes.

"Either that or he's directly enlisted in Tanaquar's army. One's about the same as the other, when you look at the end result." I stared at the floor, thinking about Father and the dangers he faced.

"You have to understand, Chase. The three of us are daughters of a member of the Guard Des'Estar. We've been brought up to face danger rather than run away. And our father is the son of a Guard member. We come from a family proud to serve the Court and Crown. Father will stay involved in this war until Y'Elestrial is free from the opium eater's grasp and a queen with honor reigns over Y'Elestrial once again."

Chase mulled over what I'd said. "So what it boils down to on our side is this: Nobody over there is watching any of the new portals?"

I nodded. "That's pretty much the long and short of it. No wonder the Cryptos are getting through, though only the gods know what they want. It *could* be mere curiosity."

"Well, their presence is stamping a big fat red do-not-promote memo on my record, especially when they show up and get themselves wasted." Chase nodded to the door. Sharah and Mallen were on their way over to talk to us. "Here they come. Right before I got your call, I sent Shamas out on another case," he said as he pulled out his notebook and pen. "Somebody reported a troglodyte or something out in Shoreline. I have no idea what that is, but I'm hoping they were wrong. *Really* wrong."

Shamas was my cousin, and he'd come Earthside after being tortured and marked for death back in Y'Elestrial. Actually, he'd managed to hide out in Aladril, the city of Seers, until Menolly and I unwittingly brought him home with us. That had been a shock and a half, though mostly welcome. Since then, he'd moved in with Morio, and we'd inducted him into our makeshift version of the OIA. Shamas took to investigative work like a duck to orange sauce.

"We've got a problem, boss." Sharah swung herself onto the counter. Her legs didn't come anywhere near the ground. She was an elf—niece to the Elfin Queen, actually—and so petite she made supermodels look clunky.

"I don't want to hear about it." Chase flashed her an irritated look.

"Of course you don't," she said soothingly; then her smile disappeared. "But you have to. Here's the deal: The bugbear had this on him." Sharah cautiously retrieved and placed a long stick on the counter. Chase and I both did the jump-for-your-life thing.

"What the hell are you doing with a stick of dynamite?" Chase's shock infiltrated his voice, though he instinctively lowered it. "Be careful, and don't yell. If that stuff's old, anything could trigger it."

I motioned toward the red cylinder. "Get that out of my store *right now*. Things that go boom are *so* not a good thing to have around my magic. They could go boom in a big, bad way. Very big. Mondo bad. And what do you mean, you found it on the bugbear? He was squashed. Wouldn't it have blown up?"

"No, it rolled to the side when he fell, apparently. Before the car could run over it, too. The stick has his scent on it. Trust me, he was carrying it." Mallen, a thin, waiflike elf who was probably more powerful than all of us put together, picked up the stick and headed toward the door. "Sharah, let's go secure this before something happens to it."

I glanced at Chase. What the hell was a bugbear doing running down the streets of Seattle with a stick of dynamite tucked in his pocket? "The goblin! I wonder if he's packing, too?" I jumped up and headed for the back.

"I take it you didn't frisk him when you tied him up?" Chase let out a sigh that told me he'd had more than enough excitement for the day.

"Frisk him? You've got to be kidding. I have no desire to touch anything personal of his. You never know when one of these creatures might be packing spare parts in all the wrong places. I saw a goblin naked once, and it wasn't by choice. Two dicks. Four balls. No waiting."

Chase groaned. "Don't tell me you dated one of those ugly suckers—"

"Bite your tongue before I tell Delilah to! Hell no, I wasn't dating him. He was in a bar, drunk, and he stripped and started chasing the barmaid around the room. I didn't stick around to ask if he came with standard equipment or if he'd been blessed."

"I *really* have to visit your home world sometime," Chase said, following me. He grumbled all the way. "I guess we'd better check. Where is he again?"

"In the room next to my office, around the corner. I tied him up with strapping tape."

"Strapping tape?" He chuckled. "Not quite the same bondage techniques you practice on Trillian and fox-boy, huh?"

Great. Now he was emulating Trillian. Morio was from Japan, and he was the second member of my triad. A youkai-kitsune, or fox demon, he was helping us against the Demonkin and he'd won his way into my heart.

I swung around and held out my hand. "Don't you start picking on Morio like that. It's bad enough when Trillian still does it. And what we do in the bedroom is none of your business, Johnson. And for another thing, I'm no dominatrix. You just keep your mind on Delilah's toy box and out of mine."

He gave me a crooked smile. "Delilah doesn't have a toy box, my dear, and you know it. Except the one containing her fur mice and scratching toys."

"That's your problem, not mine." I repressed a smile, wondering if Delilah's decidedly more sedate nature bothered him. Or maybe he was relieved. I hadn't asked. Besides, Delilah would tell me if they were having problems in the bedroom. We were all a bunch of gossips when it came to our love lives.

As I rounded the bend in the hall that led to my office, I noticed a breeze wafting through the corridor. Delilah's PI suite was upstairs. Surely she wouldn't have left the door open if she'd come in through the back?

I was about to call up the stairs to see if she was in the building when Chase tapped me on the shoulder and pointed. A trail of blood led along the corridor from the back door to the storeroom next to my office. Several yards of used and torn strapping tape littered the floor, and the room looked like it had been hit by a whirlwind. I raced over to my office. Papers and books were everywhere, shredded into a gazillion pieces. My strongbox had been pried open, and all the money was gone.

As I gazed at the damage that would take me hours to clean up, Chase put his hand on my shoulder. "I'm sorry, Camille."

"You aren't half as sorry as that damned goblin and Sawberry Fae are going to be when we catch them," I said. "They're going down. We'll find them, and when we do, I'll feed them to Menolly." When in doubt, shoot first, ask questions later.

CHAPTER 3

A fracas up front interrupted us as I was taking inventory as to what else might be missing from my office. I dashed around the stacks with Chase so close on my heels that he managed to step on the hem of my velvet skirt. The skirt draped down to the floor in back, up to my thighs in front. The clerk had called it an asymmetrical hemline in the store, but in my opinion it was just annoying.

"Get off my skirt, you dolt." I shot a glare over my shoulder, skidding to a halt as I tried to prevent any rips.

Chase bumped into me. "Nice mouth," he muttered but lifted his foot.

I shook out the hem and rounded the corner, straining in order to see what was going on.

The stacks looked clear, though Henry Jeffries was taking the opportunity to root through the Golden Age of Science Fiction section. An SF freak who breathed Asimov and Heinlein, he'd read just about every pulp book that ever made it to the shelves, although he didn't stop there. He'd worked his way through Greg Bear's bibliography and Anne McCaffrey and just about anybody else who could remotely be considered fantasy or SF.

We'd spent numerous afternoons exchanging stories while he tried to flirt with Iris, the Finnish house sprite who lived with my sisters and me, and who helped me out at the store. Apparently, the short time he'd spent talking to Feddrah-Dahns had been enough to satisfy him, and now he was oblivious to whatever the ruckus was, blissfully immersed in an ink-stained heaven.

The shouting echoed from the seating area near the front. Various book groups, as well as the Faerie Watchers Club, met at the Indigo Crescent to discuss their monthly reading choices. And it was in the seating area where I'd ensconced Feddrah-Dahns, sandwiched between two old leather sofas. And now, in front of him, the back of her knees skimming a reupholstered love seat sporting a delicate cabbage rose jacquard, stood Lindsey Cartridge, a friend of mine.

"Please, just let me touch your horn—I just want to touch it once."

She sounded so desperate that I cringed, debating on whether I really wanted to find out what the hell was going on. But there was no going back. This was my shop, and I was responsible for keeping the peace.

I rounded the half wall just in time to see Lindsey make another grab for the unicorn's horn. Freakin' hell, she could get herself gored! Feddrah-Dahns pawed the ground, shaking his head to keep out of her reach. Everybody else had stepped back, worried looks on their faces.

And well they did to worry. Unicorns were dangerous and unpredictable. All this "gentle creature looking for purity" bullshit was just one more way that Earthside history had tried to fluff up a powerful, sensual creature, just like they'd done with my father's people before we returned out in the open. Dancing nature sprites hugging the trees, we weren't. That was more the elves' territory.

A pissed-off unicorn was the last thing I wanted in my shop. He could easily rear up and club Lindsey with his front hooves, or gore her with his horn. And I knew my store insurance wouldn't take kindly to a claim for "assault by unicorn." Not in the least.

I dashed over and insinuated myself between the two, bracing Lindsey by her shoulders. "What the hell do you think you're doing? Don't you have any common sense at all, girl?"

Immediately turning to Feddrah-Dahns, I said, "I'm sorry.

Please, she has no idea of how to behave around a creature of your stature."

He blinked, his molten eyes warming me right through to the cockles. "She seems to be under the mistaken assumption that I can make her get pregnant," he said, speaking in Melosealfôr. "Sounds like she's been listening to fairy tales."

I stared at him. "Wonderful. I had no idea that rumor was floating around."

"Well, I'm fairly certain that's what she asked of me. It's just not physically . . . she'd be terribly hurt." Feddrah-Dahns looked as startled as I felt.

I turned back to Lindsey, lowering my voice. "Did you *really* ask him to help you get pregnant?" If she had, I certainly hoped she'd had something in mind other than the B-grade porno flick that was racing through my mind. And, apparently, Feddrah-Dahns's. Oh yeah, I could even envision the title: *Horn of Plenty*, or some such schlock.

Lindsey lowered her gaze to the floor. Director of the Green Goddess Women's Shelter, she did a lot of outreach for a lot of women who needed self-empowerment and a fresh start in life. She could be a little on the dippy side, but she also had a stubborn streak a mile wide, and she was a staunch advocate for women's rights and social programs.

"Well . . . yes, I did. In a way."

My jaw dropped. "You've got to be kidding. You can't be . . . he's not a Were, you know—"

"What?" She reared back. "You think I meant it *that* way? You have to be joking!"

I breathed a sigh of relief. "Okay, calm down. Now, tell me exactly what you said. English isn't his first language." While Feddrah-Dahns spoke the language perfectly, it didn't mean he had a large vocabulary.

Lindsey blushed. "He really didn't think I wanted . . . oh no!"

I touched her arm and she let out a long sigh. "Okay, okay. I read in a book on mythology somewhere that touching a unicorn's horn will help a barren woman conceive. And I've been trying . . ." She paused, biting her lip as her wide hazel eyes welled up with unshed tears. I could feel her pain seep out, crackling like repressed lightning. "We've been trying for so long . . ."

"Wait a moment." I rested one hand on her shoulder and then

glanced at the crowd. "Everything's fine. Nothing happened. Look folks, I know you're thrilled to meet a unicorn, but I need to close up shop." I leaned over and whispered in Lindsey's ear, "Wait here—and keep your hands to yourself, babe."

As I herded the disappointed throng outside, I caught sight of Sharah and Mallen as they drove away with the remains of the bugbear and the dynamite. Better them than me.

I reassured everybody that I'd do my best to encourage Feddrah-Dahns to return for another visit, then locked the door behind them and leaned against it. Letting out a long sigh, I rested the back of my head on the cool window as I closed my eyes. Sometimes being around my mother's people left me feeling on edge, almost abraded by their emotions. I liked my customers, but their thrill over seeing Feddrah-Dahns had translated to a blast of chattering energy that had battered against my shields.

After a few moments, I shook off the static of emotion and returned to the counter. Chase was propped against it, frowning. As I brushed past him, he caught my arm and in a low voice said, "You going to be long?"

I darted a sideways glance in Lindsey's direction. "Why? You have somewhere urgent you need to be? Look, I just got robbed, a goblin and some demented Sawberry Fae are on a unicorn hunt, and now . . ." I gave him a shake of the head. "Why don't you go see what you can find out in my office while I take care of Lindsey? She really needs to talk to me."

Without another word, Chase disappeared into the back.

Lindsey dabbed at her eyes as I wrapped my arm around her shoulders and led her to the folding card table where I always sat and drank my morning iced latte while leafing through my magazines or whatever current book I was absorbed in. I prefer my caffeine sweet and cold, and my literature in ink and paper, not computer pixels.

As she sat down I joined her, taking her hands in mine. Besides running the shelter, Lindsey had been instrumental in helping my friend Erin Mathews. Erin, owner of the Scarlet Harlot, had recently undergone a major transformation at the hands of my sister Menolly. Even though it was in order to save her life, in a fashion, now Erin was stuck learning how to cope with being a vampire. Lindsey was one of the few who knew that Erin had been turned.

For now, we were spreading it around that Erin was on a long vacation, and Erin helped out by calling friends, purporting to be overseas. Lindsey had taken over as president of the Faerie Watchers Club, and the women's shelter provided a source of temporary help for Erin's store. There were always women staying at the Green Goddess who needed to pick up a few extra bucks to help them get back on their feet. So I owed Lindsey more than just a routine favor.

"Tell me what's wrong." I lowered my masks and turned on the glamour so she wouldn't feel so awkward talking to me. Being half-Fae had its perks, and being able to win friends and influence people were two of the best. I tried to be good and keep myself from abusing it, but it still amazed me at how much power our natural charms held for FBHs.

She swallowed her tears and gave me a weak smile. "Ron and I've been trying to get pregnant for three years, but it looks like for all our trying, it's futile. The odds are that I should have been pregnant at least twenty times over, but nothing. And we can't afford infertility treatments. We were going to adopt, but because of his disability, the agencies aren't interested in giving us a baby." Her voice cracked again.

I sat back, thinking. A lot of people had babies on the brains lately. First our friend Siobhan Morgan, a selkie, had been having trouble getting pregnant. Thanks to Sharah and the OIA medics, we'd discovered the source of her problem—easily fixed—and she and her boyfriend Mitch had just broken the good news to us a week ago. Now here was Lindsey, a human who worked with FBH magic, having problems. Had some god decided to smack a divine moratorium on magical babies lately?

"They actually told you they won't consider you because of his disability? Can't you fight them in court? I thought discrimination was supposed to be a thing of the past, at least for humans." Apparently, I was wrong.

"They didn't come out and say it directly, but I've got a friend in the secretarial pool there, and she snuck a peek at our file. They moved us to the bottom of the list, and the social worker noted on our record that we were a high-risk couple because of Ron's condition and because I work with women who've been battered." Lindsey frowned. "If we had the money, we could take them to court, but even then, it might be years before we won our case."

"Well, that sucks." Lindsey and Ron would make great parents. Ron might be paralyzed from the waist down, but he never let a little thing like his wheelchair get in his way. And Lindsey was a black belt in judo. She could handle any irate attackers without blinking. But this also explained why she was so desperate to get pregnant that she'd chance grabbing a unicorn's horn without permission.

"I hate to burst your bubble, but the old wives' tales are wrong. Rubbing a unicorn's horn won't make you more fertile. It might get you *killed*, but it won't strengthen your baby-making equipment."

She gripped the arms of her chair. "Is there anything you can do, Camille? I wouldn't ask, but since the subject's come up . . ."

Oh man, she had to be kidding. I tried to repress the peal of laughter that threatened to bubble over, but lost. I collapsed back in my chair, my eyes watering.

"Oh, honey, trust me. You do *not* want me messing around with your plumbing!" I wiped my eyes on my sleeve. "First off, I'm not a healer. Second, with the mayhem that creeps in from my bloodline, my magic could make anything happen. Hell, you might end up pregnant from an ogre . . . or worse . . . if my spell backfired."

The melancholy look on her face vanished, and she gave me a sideways grin. "That bad, huh?"

"Yeah, seriously, it could be. Let me think for a moment." It wasn't wise for the Fae to play around with human lives on a magical level, but sometimes we were able to rationalize an exception. "Tell you what. Let me ask around and see what I can find out."

Brightening, Lindsey straightened her shoulders. "Would you really?"

"I can't promise anything," I warned her. "So don't get your hopes up. But I'll ask. Did your doctor tell you exactly what your problem is?" Before letting her get too excited, I'd better find out up front if it was something that no one but the gods could fix.

She chewed on her thumbnail. "No. They can't figure out why I can't get pregnant. Ron's sperm is viable, and I'm ovulating, but . . . it's almost like something doesn't want us to make a baby. We're both brokenhearted. Especially with the mess over adoption."

I nodded. "Okay then. I need to get a move on, but I'll call you as soon as I can. Are you going to see Erin tonight?" Menolly went to see her every other day, but Erin needed to learn how to be around humans—ones who were still alive, that is—without going crazy and attacking them on sight. It could be a little scary for her visitors, but every day Erin was learning a little more how to harness her cravings and her newly developing powers. Sassy Branson was seeing to that. She'd taken Erin on as her personal project.

Lindsey nodded. "Yeah. I'll see you later." With one last, longing glance in Feddrah-Dahns's direction, she took off, the door swinging closed behind her with a firm click.

CHAPTER 4

❧❧❧

I had no idea what my sisters were going to say when I showed up at the house with a unicorn. Feddrah-Dahns was resting in the back of Chase's new SUV. I was convinced Chase had bought the hulking machine in order to fend off some testosterone insecurity, but he wouldn't admit to it. Now though, I was thankful for the monster of a gas hog.

It had taken a lot of cajoling to convince him to let Feddrah-Dahns squeeze into the back. Luckily, OW unicorns were a little smaller than their ES cousins, and with a lot of shoulder-boosting against his beautiful white butt, we'd managed to help him squeeze into the empty back end of the SUV.

"If he shits in there, you're paying for the cleaning." Chase slammed the tailgate shut. "We're both nuts, you know. You for suggesting this, and me for listening to you."

I brushed away his glower. "Give it a rest, Johnson. You're just as enchanted with him as everybody else, and you know it."

Chase snorted. "Yeah, right. Fairy tales and unicorns."

"Maybe not fairy tales, but according to Delilah, you like Faerie *tail* just fine," I said, ducking away when he playfully swatted me. "So, did you find out anything in my office?"

He shook his head. "Nope. Nothing more than we already

know. Let's get this show on the road, woman. Get a move on, or I'm going to toss you over my shoulder, and we'll leave your Lexus right here on the Seattle streets all night long for the downtown boys to plunder. The meter's running, you know."

"You seem to have plenty of time to spare when it comes to playing cat and mouse with Delilah." I smirked, making a mad dash for my car. Chase was my sister's boyfriend, all right, but he still liked to flirt. At least with me, it was harmless, and he knew he wouldn't get anywhere.

Home is a three-story Victorian with a full basement, set on the outskirts of the slightly seedy Belles-Faire district of Seattle. We purchased the house when we first came Earthside thanks to a trust fund set up by Maria D'Artigo, our mother, an orphan who fell in love with our father in Madrid during the height of World War II.

With nothing to tie her Earthside—her foster parents had died in a car crash a few years before—Maria returned to Otherworld with Father. There, she married him and settled in to life on the outskirts of the Court and Crown, but she never fully gave up her ties over here. She also made certain that the three of us had roots in this world via Social Security numbers, a bank account, and birth certificates that fudged our origins. When the portals opened and the government had to face the truth about the Fae, we had them amended, so now they read, "Birthplace: Y'Elestrial, Otherworld," and they listed our father's name and race.

To her dying day our mother was our protector and advocate. And our Father loves us, too. Who can ask for more? But unfortunately, our mixed blood makes life hell at times.

I'm Camille D'Artigo, the oldest, and I'm pledged under the Moon Mother's service. I've been called a lot of things—slut, seductive, passionate, dangerous, warped—but mainly, I'm just a witch who adores my magic, my family, and my lovers. A clotheshorse, yes. And a makeup junkie. And sure, my magic short-circuits—sometimes at a really *bad* time. But life can be exciting when you never know where the lightning will strike.

Delilah, the second-born, is a werecat. She changes into a golden tabby when stressed out by family affairs and on nights when the moon is full. And now, thanks to a recent visit to the

Autumn Lord—we think—she also changes into a black panther when he decides it necessary. He claimed her to be one of his Death Maidens, and she's spirit-bound to reap souls for him during the harvest on Samhain Eve. But that's another story. We tend to pussyfoot around the subject, since there's nothing anybody can do to turn back time.

And then there's Menolly. Back in Otherworld, Menolly was an acrobat—a souped-up spy, you might say—until she was captured by a group of rogue vampires. After torturing her until she begged for death, Dredge, the meanest vampire who ever lived, forced her to drink from his vein. She died, he helped her rise, and then he sent her home to kill our family. I managed to summon aid before she hurt any of us. But our family's never been the same since that night. Menolly's learning to live with being a vampire. Again, not much else she can do, so might as well make the best of it. We seem to be having a lot of those make-the-best-of-it adventures, lately.

My sisters and I work for the OIA, or rather, we did until civil war broke out back home. To avoid the death threats on our head back in Y'Elestrial, we've decided to park it right here, Earthside. Even if we *could* go home, we wouldn't. Because behind all the mayhem lurks a threat that could wipe out both Earth and Otherworld.

Shadow Wing, a greater demon lord from the Subterranean Realms, is after the spirit seals, artifacts that can rip open the portals that join the three realms. If he wins, both Earth and OW bite the dust, razed to the ground by his hordes of minions. If we find them before he does, we'll be able to keep the precarious balance guarded by the Hags of Fate.

Right now, we're two for two. And Shadow Wing is pissed, which makes him infinitely dangerous. And which makes our job infinitely harder.

As I jumped out of my car, I glanced around the yard. Iris had been busy the past few weeks. I'd been so rushed I barely noticed. But now I caught sight of a spurt of daffodils blooming beneath the oak and maple. A profusion of yellow in a sea of green that was more moss than grass.

Rosebushes sported leaf buds where—later—there would be hundreds of rich, red blossoms filling the air with their scent.

Skirting the house, a rainbow of irises and gladiolas nestled, close to blooming. And grape hyacinths snuggled among thick batches of bluebells, primroses, and tulips.

I paused by a large patch of plants. My herb garden. When I'd planted it early on last year, I had no idea of how long we'd be here, so I started a number of seedlings in case our stay was extended. Now, I was glad for that forethought. Belladonna and nettle, thyme and rosemary, spearmint and calendula and lavender all vied for space with the three dozen other plants in the cobblestone-bordered beds.

As I knelt beside the herbs, I could hear them whispering to one another. Just what they were saying, I couldn't quite catch. I'd have to tune in, reach deep into the soil and commune with them to find out. But they were active and aware. Neither of my sisters seemed to master talking to plants, but it was all part of the package once I cast my lot with the Moon Mother. More than once, I'd enjoyed a warm summer afternoon in lengthy communication with some wild bramble. Of course, the plants back in Otherworld were more friendly than the ones here.

Inhaling deeply, as the scent of rich loam and wet cedar filled my lungs, I rose and joined Chase by his SUV. I helped him open the tailgate, and we guided Feddrah-Dahns out of the back. I was relieved to see that the unicorn had refrained from leaving a calling card, beyond a few white silken hairs on the carpeted floor.

Chase just shook his head as he slammed the door shut and followed us up the stairs.

"Easy now, don't take them too quickly," I said as Feddrah-Dahns's hooves clipped a staccato beat on the wood. I was more worried about our porch than his health, to be honest. With those feathered hooves, he could probably punch a hole right through the weaker spots of the planks.

As I opened the door, I almost ran into Iris, who was passing through the hall on her way to the kitchen. She was carrying a tray filled with half-eaten sandwiches, a bowl of stale Cheetos, and two open soda cans. Delilah's doing, no doubt. Iris gave me a tight smile. She hadn't seen the unicorn yet.

"Camille, you have to do something about Delilah. I ask her to pick up after herself, but it just doesn't sink in. You'd think being a werecat she'd be fastidious, but she's rapidly descending into slobhood—" She stopped, staring beyond me. "There's a unicorn on the porch."

"Yeah . . . about that . . . I brought home a houseguest," I said, giving her a guilty grin.

"Where on Earth . . . how . . . oh my goodness! Let me get rid of this tray!" Flustered, Iris scurried off toward the kitchen as I led Feddrah-Dahns into the living room.

I moved the rocking chair so he'd have a clear space in which to stand. "Chase, can you go upstairs and find out if Delilah's home? Menolly should be up soon enough." I glanced at the clock. Six oh five. Another ten minutes, and she'd be awake.

Chase took off for the stairs as Iris came bustling back in. She cautiously approached the unicorn, bowing deeply. She was so petite compared to the horned horse that I hoped nothing would startle him. Iris stood barely over four feet. It would be easy to trample her.

But Feddrah-Dahns gazed down at her, then slowly edged his way down to where he was kneeling on his front legs. He bowed his head to her.

"Priestess" was all he said, but his tone conveyed one hell of a lot. We'd only recently found out that Iris was a priestess of Undutar, the Finnish goddess of mists and fog. She worked with ice magic and snow, and I had a feeling we'd only skimmed the surface of what the Talon-haltija was capable of.

Iris curtsied and reached up to slide her hands over the downy hair of his forehead. He looked like he was enjoying the attention. She whispered something to him, and he whinnied. Backing away, she tapped me on the arm.

"Come help me in the kitchen."

I followed her, wondering what she wanted to tell me. We'd barely entered the kitchen when Iris spun around, her eyes wide.

"Do you know *who* that is?"

I shrugged. "Feddrah-Dahns, a unicorn from the Windwillow Valley. He showed up on the street outside my shop today with a goon squad from OW on his heels. They were intent on bringing him down with a blowgun. Something about him helping a pixie or something."

Iris shook her head with a puzzled air. "Camille, that's not just *any* unicorn standing there in your living room. He's the crown prince."

I stared at her. "Say what?"

"Feddrah-Dahns is the heir to the crown of the Dahns unicorns. You have a crown prince sitting—standing—in your living room."

"Holy Mother Moon." I slid into a chair at the table, unsure of what to think. "How do you know? He didn't say anything of the sort. Are you positive?"

"Didn't you see the etchings on his horn?" Iris leaned against the counter. "Surely you haven't been Earthside long enough to forget all that you learned when you were back home? Hell, *I'm* an Earthside Fae, and even I can recognize him for what he truly is."

"Find out what's keeping Chase, would you?" I hurried back into the living room. At the shop, I hadn't had enough time to focus on Feddrah-Dahns's horn. I'd been too busy keeping Lindsey from hurting herself and keeping the goblin brigade from hurting the unicorn.

As I slowly entered the room, Feddrah-Dahns looked over at me, and in that moment, I saw what I'd so thoroughly missed before. Or maybe he'd cloaked himself from me; it would be easy enough for him to mask his markings. As I watched, a golden glow flickered around his horn, and when I looked closer, I saw that the faint markings etched on the golden spire that were indeed the sign of a king.

I shuddered. Unicorns were rare enough back in OW. Meeting one of their royalty was far from common.

The Court and Crown in our home city, Y'Elestrial, had treated my sisters and me like we didn't exist. We were pariahs, Windwalkers, half-breeds. But now that we were stuck Earthside, facing a bunch of demons and under a death threat, we seemed to be magnets for out-of-the-ordinary royalty. Elfin queens and unicorn kings were making their way to our door like stray cats.

Bringing my attention back to Feddrah-Dahns, I knelt into a deep curtsy. "I'm so sorry, Your Highness. I didn't recognize you until now. A poor excuse, but it's the truth. What may we do for you?"

Feddrah-Dahns let out a long whinny that sounded like a sigh. "It's what I can do for you, young witch. The new portals that have opened are producing mayhem of the worst kind. I told you the goblin and his cohorts stole something from me. It was a gift that I'd sent my assistant to bring to you."

"To *me*? What could you be sending to me? We've never even met."

A wave of dizziness swept over me, and I caught myself on the back of the recliner. *Earth shift.* When major portents streaked across the sky, or when a witch found herself at a crossroads, reality would jostle in a tangible wave. These shifts left me reeling with vertigo. Back in Otherworld, I'd barely noticed them—magic was so embedded within the land. But here, they caught me off guard.

Feddrah-Dahns flared his nostrils, a short burst of steam wafting out. "Shall we wait for your sisters to join us? This involves Shadow Wing."

I rubbed my temples. A twinge was forming behind my eyes, threatening to become a full-blown headache. "I think I need some tea."

He gave a shake of his mane. "As you will, my lady."

"Delilah and Chase will be right down. They got caught up with something on the computer," Iris said, entering the room. With a knowing glance at me, she added, "I set the kettle on for a pot of Richya tea. I thought you might need it."

"You were right." I glanced at the clock. Quarter past six. There was a sudden movement at the archway leading into the living room, and Menolly stood there, in all of her waxen beauty. Pale and petite, with a nimbus of burnished copper braids that floated down to her shoulders, her skin was whiter than any woman's skin should be. But other than that, it would have been hard to tell she was dead, until you glanced at her face. Her story echoed through the haunted eyes with which she viewed the world. Menolly had experienced far too much pain to ever be innocent again.

"Good evening," she said softly, gazing at Feddrah-Dahns. "I see we have company."

Just then, Delilah and Chase clattered down the stairs. Compared to Menolly, Delilah was almost a giant. At six one, blonde and athletic, she towered over both myself and our younger sister.

"Chase said—oh my, he was right." Delilah skidded to a halt in front of the unicorn and sank down on the ottoman. "You're beautiful," she blurted out.

Feddrah-Dahns switched his tail. "Thank you, mistress feline. Now that you're all here, could we get down to business?"

Just a hint of impatience in his voice which, for a unicorn, meant he might as well be throwing a fit.

"Of course." I motioned for Menolly to join me on the sofa. "Feddrah-Dahns is the Crown Prince of the Dahns Unicorns. I met him in front of my shop today when a trio of thugs from OW tried to kill him. Something about pixie theft."

"Ah," Menolly said, nodding. "Pixies are notorious thieves. Almost as bad as goblins."

Feddrah-Dahns let out a loud sound that sounded suspiciously like a snort. "Pixies are nothing like goblins. And not all pixies are scoundrels. This one happens to work for me—he's my assistant. He was carrying something of grave value that I entrusted to him. He came through one of the newly discovered portals, but we didn't realize he was being followed."

"The goblin and his cronies?" I asked. It made sense that they'd been on the pixie's trail rather than it being just some random encounter.

The unicorn whinnied. "Yes. They waited till they were over here to steal it. They tried to kill Mistletoe, but he managed to get away. He contacted me via a Whispering Spell, and I immediately came Earthside to help him. I should never have delegated the task to him in the first place, but if I could foresee the future, we wouldn't be having this discussion."

"Mistletoe? I take it that's the pixie?" Delilah asked, leaning back against Chase's shoulder. She looked ready to throw her arms around the unicorn's neck and plant a big sloppy kiss on his nose. Delilah loved anything that walked on four feet. Well, *almost* anything.

"Yes. He's been with me for two hundred years now and is an excellent assistant. Mistletoe managed to retrieve the object just before I came through the portal. I was on my way to meet him near your shop when the goblin and his group showed up again, only this time, I was in their path. As were you. Meanwhile, Mistletoe seems to be lost. He hasn't tried to contact me since this afternoon."

"Just where is this portal?" I asked, poking Delilah in the arm. "Get a map so we can mark it down." She scrambled up and grabbed our atlas of Seattle off the bookshelf, flipping it open to where we'd marked most of the major magical hangouts or junctures.

Feddrah-Dahns shook his mane. "The portal leads from the

Windwillow Valley directly to a small park near your shop. It's overgrown and looks forgotten. Tiny, really. With a holly tree and a rowan tree on it."

Delilah pored over the map for a moment. "Got it. I'll bet you anything it's this square right here." She showed us a small dot of green on the map that indicated a park. Wentworth Park. And it looked to be two blocks square at the most—short blocks, at that.

"We'll check it out in a little while. We'll need to set somebody to guarding the portal. Someone who won't be noticed." Yeah, like that was going to be easy. Just one more thing on our already overloaded plate. If any FBHs managed to cross through to Otherworld, we'd really be in trouble. The OIA had promised Earth's government that we wouldn't allow any humans over to Otherworld unescorted.

Delilah jotted down a note. "Got it. I think we can probably find a couple of nature devas there who might actually help us out."

"Good thinking. Nobody would notice them anyway." I turned back to Feddrah-Dahns. "Please, continue."

"Mistletoe has never been Earthside. I have no sense that he's dead, so he's probably just lost. But I guarantee that the goblin and Sawberry Fae are still after him. You *must* find him before they do. We cannot allow the gift he carries to fall into their possession."

Delilah glanced back at me and shoved her hands in the pockets of her denim vest. "Well, I *am* a private eye. It shouldn't be that hard to find him. Pixies aren't that common in the city proper, and an OW pixie will stand out like Miss Manners at a food fight." The black crescent tattooed on her forehead shimmered, and a cold breeze suddenly wafted through the room.

I folded my arms as a looming prescience descended in the room. My radar was picking up something big and scary, and it was coming directly toward us. "Just what is it that you brought Earthside? And how do you know about Shadow Wing and our fight against him?"

Feddrah-Dahns gazed into my eyes, and I felt myself falling into those sparkling depths. "I recently had an interesting discussion with Pentangle, the Mother of Magic."

There was our answer as to how he knew about Shadow Wing. Pentangle, one of the Hags of Fate, and Queen Asteria were working together from OW to help as much as they could in our fight against the demons.

A sudden chasm yawned in the pit of my stomach, threatening to suck me in. I really didn't want to hear the answer to my next question, but it needed to be asked. "The goblin and his cronies aren't working alone, are they? You said they took up the chase back in Otherworld?"

"No, they aren't." Feddrah-Dahns scuffed the carpet with one hoof. "They're working for one of Shadow Wing's spies. Apparently the Demonkin have eyes and ears in Otherworld, too. Queen Asteria, Pentangle, and I agreed that you should carry this weapon. After I dispatched Mistletoe with it, Pentangle discovered we were being spied on. The goblin and his thugs are part of a network of spies that thread through both OW and Earthside. They're led by a greater demon here in Seattle. As far as we've been able to find out, he's a general in Shadow Wing's army."

"Shit," Menolly said, standing. She floated up to the ceiling and perched near the chandelier. "I wonder if this has anything to do with the third spirit seal and the Rāksasa that Rozurial told us about." Rozurial was an incubus who had helped us defeat Menolly's sire. He was also one damned handsome dude, though I knew enough not to wade in *that* pond.

"Of course!" I jumped up. "The Persian demon." I whirled back to Feddrah-Dahns. "Are we right?"

"You are." He nodded gravely. "He's very dangerous and tends to leave his enemies alive in order to extort them. Our research shows several other rogue mercenaries have tried to take him out, and not one came close. He's got help, we know that, but his aides tend to disappear after a year or so."

"Then Shadow Wing truly does have his fingers spread throughout both Earth and OW." I frowned. "Highly unsettling. If they're after what you're bringing to us . . . it's not the third spirit seal, is it?"

Feddrah-Dahns shook his head, whinnying softly. "No, but what I am offering you will aid you with your magic against the demons, and they certainly don't want that to happen. While the Fae fight among themselves and ignore the growing threat, the Cryptozoid Alliance has agreed to help you in the greater battle. We stand by Queen Asteria and Pentangle in this decision."

I let out a long sigh. Sometimes, when it seemed we were terribly alone in our fight, a ray of hope broke through. I glanced up at Feddrah-Dahns, gratitude swelling in my heart. "We need all the help we can get," I said.

He leaned down and gently nuzzled my face. "Wipe the moisture from your eyes, Camille. We will do all we can to ensure you are not alone in this. We cannot send an army, but we can send you aid."

"So what is it that Mistletoe is carrying?"

Feddrah-Dahns shook his head, his mane glimmering under the lamplight. "In my family's possession, we've guarded an item from ages past. My father bade me bring it to you, since the need is so great, and the enemy so dangerous. It is my fault that Mistletoe's in danger—I thought he'd be able to handle the task." His voice dropped, and his luxurious long lashes slowly blinked, fluttering in an invisible breeze.

Whatever it was had to be powerful. There was no way the crown prince of the Dahns unicorns would venture Earthside without damned good reason. I waited.

After a long pause, Feddrah-Dahns let out a long sigh. "We're offering you something no human . . . no Fae . . . has ever before been allowed to touch or to see. I'm bringing you the horn of the Black Unicorn."

CHAPTER 5

Delilah, Menolly, and Iris all started to talk at once. I remained silent, crossing to stare out the bay window overlooking the front porch.

Chase joined me. "You okay?" he asked softly.

I nodded. "Yes. I'm just wondering if I have the strength needed for this."

He glanced back at the others. "What are you talking about?"

Leaning against the windowsill, I gave him a sideways look. "First, the fact that we have a demon spy here in Seattle and he's got Fae working for him is bad enough. It means Rozurial was right: The demons are infiltrating and looking for other ways to aid their invasion. But there's also the fact that Rākṣasas are terribly dangerous. They originated in Persia, and they have powerful magic at their disposal."

"Worse than Bad Ass Luke?"

I met his gaze. "Far worse. Trust me, Bad Ass Luke was dangerous, but Rākṣasas . . . Rākṣasas are cunning and brilliant and charming."

"Bad news, then." He glanced back at the others. "And they all know this?"

"Oh yes. We all know how dangerous these demons are. But now . . . we're—*I'm*—offered the horn of the Black Unicorn? Only a spellcaster can wield it. A mage or wizard or . . . witch. I'll have to assume control of it, and I do mean assume control—it's not like driving a car. These artifacts have minds of their own. My sisters won't be able to touch it. And it will be up to me to see that it doesn't fall in the wrong hands." Yet one more responsibility I didn't want to shoulder, but that I'd have to.

"What is this creature? Hell, I figured if you existed, unicorns probably would, too, but . . ."

"A lot of Otherworlders claim that the horn is a myth. They even say the Black Beast himself is a myth, perpetuated by the Dahns unicorns to increase their mystique, since the first Black Unicorn supposedly fathered the Dahns lineage. But my father believed in the legends, and so did my teachers. And apparently," I said, looking over at Feddrah-Dahns, "it turns out legend is based in reality."

"The Black Beast? Is he a demon, then?"

I smiled gently. "No, he's not a demon." Looking out into the growing night, I could feel the spring beckon even through the fog that rose to roll across our front yard. Magic sparkled in the mists. Earthside weather carried elemental forces with it from land to sea to mountaintop. Sometimes I missed our home so much that it hurt, and other times—like now—the realms seemed so connected that I felt like I could close my eyes, and when I opened them, I'd be back in Y'Elestrial.

Chase waited patiently, watching out the window as he stood next to me. I glanced at his face. His eyes were half closed, as if he could sense the magic that permeated the air.

After a moment, I slowly let out the breath I'd been holding. "The Black Beast, or Black Unicorn, is one of the most powerful beings to ever walk the paths of Otherworld. He's a giant, towering over all other unicorns. His horn is crystal, and within it swirl threads of gold and silver. The horn is reputed to wield heavy elemental magic. The magic isn't evil, but shadowed and sparkling with the magic of Darkynwyrd."

"Darkynwyrd?"

"Darkynwyrd, the Wild Forest, filled with oak moss and spiderwebs and bogs and quicksand. The Black Unicorn left the valleys thousands of years ago and retreated to Darkynwyrd, where he and his descendants live deep within the misty woodland."

A smile playing on his lips, Chase winked at me. "Sounds like a fairy tale. How could Feddrah-Dahns get hold of his horn? Wouldn't that kill a unicorn, to lose his horn?"

He actually sounded interested. Too often, I had the feeling Chase asked questions because he had to, not because he really wanted to know the answers.

"Not always, although most unicorns, when they lose their horns, eventually diminish and die. Or they go mad and become so dangerous that the Elemental Lords have to send out assassins to kill them."

I frowned, trying to remember the rest of the story. "The Black Unicorn is an exception. He sheds his horn once every thousand years and grows a new one. There are three of the shed horns that supposedly still exist, but nobody's ever known who has them or where they might be. The horn of the Black Unicorn is worth . . . well, if it were an Earthside artifact, figure in the neighborhood of several million dollars."

Chase whistled. "I see. So this is actually worth a king's ransom. How can its powers help you?"

"I'm not sure, but apparently, I'm going to find out." As the doorbell rang, I excused myself. "I'll get it."

A peek out the peephole sent a warm flush through me. Smoky. Uh-oh. I hadn't seen him in almost three weeks. As I opened the door, the scent of leather and musk filled my nose, sending me reeling as my knees buckled.

"Camille," he said, his voice a low rumble. He reached down and caught me up in his arms before I hit the floor. Embarrassed— I never swooned like that—I squirmed out of his embrace and stepped back, pulse racing.

Smoky was six four, every inch of his lean frame taut and muscled. His ankle-length hair wasn't in its usual braid, but the silver locks flowed around him, a mane that mirrored the pale splendor of his skin. In dragon form, he was a vision in white, almost opalescent. In human form, he was simply beautiful.

I gazed at him, starting at his feet and working my way up. His ankle-length white trench hung open to reveal skintight white jeans that left me trembling. An engraved silver belt cinched his waist, and a pale blue button-down shirt opened to show the V of his neck. As I looked into his face, the only indication of his age was the timeless brilliance of his eyes, pale glaciers from the Northlands, and the faint five o'clock shadow that left his chin slightly rugged.

"What are you doing here?" The heady perfume that swirled around him sucked me under again. He was running pheromones so strong that I could almost taste him on the tip of my tongue. And I wanted to taste more.

"I've come for you," he said.

Oh hell. I owed Smoky a week as his playmate—a bargain that had bought us much-needed help, but so far had brought me nothing but headaches. Caught between wanting to go and knowing that there was a unicorn in our living room who was promising me a king's ransom in help, I shifted from one foot to the other.

"Can we put this off for a week or two?" I asked. If he said no, I'd go. My word was my bond. Dragons and Elemental Lords and Hags of Fate didn't offer absolution on debts, and if I reneged, he'd have the right to carry me off. Or kill me. I had my doubts he'd fry me up for dinner, but I didn't want to take any chances that he'd blame Trillian and crispy-critter my Svartan lover.

Smoky gave me a slow smile, the corner of his lip twitching ever so slightly as he pushed his way into the house. Walking me backward until I bumped into the closet door behind me, he braced himself, hands flat against the wall to either side of my shoulders. Leaning down, he whispered in my ear, "You made a binding oath with me. Trust me, you *will* fulfill it." His eyes flickered. "Are you afraid of me, my Witchling?"

"Afraid of you? Get real. You're a dragon. Of course I'm . . . nervous . . . even if I do think you're hunky-dory." If I tried to deny my fear, he'd see right through me.

"Good. You should be nervous," he said, whispering. The energy crackled through his body, a wave of sparks that flared to catch me in their riptide. I tensed, and he laughed. "Yes, I can see that you are. Don't try to hide your fear, Camille. I care about you, far more than most of your kind. But you should *never, ever* forget *what* I am."

If I'd been nervous before, I was absolutely terrified now. I trusted Smoky as much as I'd ever trust any dragon. And the thought of spending a week doing his bidding still promised to be a romp in the meadow. I'd struck the bargain because we needed his help, but I was beginning to realize that dragon actually *meant* dragon. Not Fae. Not human. Not Supe. But honest-to-gods ancient beast who could crisp me in seconds and swallow me whole if he got angry, and who lived by an entirely different set of rules than I did.

"I . . . it's just . . ." I stuttered, then stopped to collect myself. "Listen, we're in the middle of something important to do with Shadow Wing. I really need to finish talking to Feddrah-Dahns, a unicorn who's offering us help."

Smoky stood back, crossed his arms, and laughed. "Ah . . . well, you luck out then. I'm actually here to talk to you about something else. But don't fret," he said, his voice caressing me. "You don't have to wait for me long."

What? He was here for something else? I smacked his arm. Gently. "You let me think that you were here for me? I sounded like an idiot!"

"It's not your conversation I have a hankering for. And you certainly don't seem averse to the idea," he said with a snicker. "However, today is for another matter. Introduce me to your unicorn friend."

As I turned to flounce away, Smoky reached out and gently grabbed my wrist. He could snap my hand like a toothpick if he wanted, but his restraint was entirely invisible—the chain forged from the authority with which he held me, rather than his strength. "I know you want me. I can make you melt, Camille."

My breath caught somewhere half between my chest and my toes, I swallowed the knot working its way up from my stomach. He was toying with me, and there was nothing I could do to stop it. "I know. Trust me, I know." Whether or not it was time to pay up, I wanted to take him up to my bed right then and there, and fuck him until there was nothing left but embers.

Smoky pulled me close, and his lips grazed mine. His skin was soft and supple, yet demanding even in the lightest of pressure. My body sang with the feel of him pressed against me, his length, hard and rigid and searching. My breasts ached for the touch of his hands.

But he abruptly straightened and let go of my arm.

"As I said, we'll have our time." His voice was once again aloof, but as I met his gaze, I saw the hunger raging behind his cool demeanor.

Shaken, horny as hell, and about to jump out of my skin, I

led him into the living room. Delilah gave him a wave, then slowly lowered her hand as she glanced at me. Menolly blinked. Since Menolly never blinked except when she wanted to make a point, it was obvious that she sensed the tension.

Chase was the only one who seemed oblivious. "Hey, Dragon Dude. How's it going?" He didn't exactly trust Smoky, but he'd gotten a lot more comfortable around Cryptos and Supes since he'd started dating Delilah.

Smoky gave him a brief nod, but his gaze slid past the detective to land on the unicorn. "Camille, introduce me to your new friend."

Hoping to hell that dragons and unicorns got along—it was hard to keep up on all the blood feuds between Cryptos—I cleared my throat. "Feddrah-Dahns, meet Smoky. Smoky, this is His Majesty, Feddrah-Dahns, Crown Prince of the Dahns unicorn herd."

I wasn't sure if the unicorn could recognize Smoky's dragon nature, but Feddrah-Dahns answered that question in short order.

"Was it your mother or your father who was the silver dragon?" he asked.

"He's a white dragon—" I started to say, but Smoky cut me off.

"Very perceptive, Your Majesty," he said, inclining his head. "Few have been able to pinpoint my heritage so well. My mother was a silver dragon, my father a white."

Well, that was news. We'd assumed that Smoky was one hundred percent white dragon. That he had silver dragon blood explained a lot about his magical abilities. It also left open a host of other possibilities, all of which were just a little too scary to think about. Silver dragons were far more powerful than white dragons. Silver dragons had ties to all things who walked the night, including the gods of death.

Menolly slowly lowered herself to the floor. "You're half silver dragon? So that's how you knew how to summon the Autumn Lord."

Smoky blinked at her. "Correct, dear *vampyr*. Unfortunately, I'm all out of prizes today." He grinned, and Menolly actually laughed.

That was one thing I liked about Smoky, he wasn't malicious. At least as far as we were concerned. His jokes and taunts were sprinkled with a dash of whimsy. His rebukes, however, were another thing. Warning. F-5 dragon storm ahead. Ignore at your own peril.

Smoky turned back to Feddrah-Dahns. "Camille tells me you offer help against the demon lord." A statement. Not a question.

Feddrah-Dahns shifted from one side to the other. "Correct. There are many among the Cryptozoid Alliance in Otherworld who fear the impending demonic war. Neither they nor the alliance doubt the veracity of what's happening. The elves keep contact with us, and we keep contact with others in the valleys and forests."

Which brought up the question, just how many other Cryptos were thinking along the same lines? Could we have allies we didn't yet know about?

"What aid are you offering?" Smoky stared at the unicorn, his gaze cool and expectant. I had the uneasy feeling that if Feddrah-Dahns refused to tell him, we'd end up with a battle in the house, after which we'd all be so much burnt toast.

But Feddrah-Dahns answered without further prompting. "The horn of the Black Unicorn. We brought it Earthside, but it was stolen. My emissary recovered it, but now he's missing, and two of the three thieves are still after him."

Smoky glanced at me, then back at the unicorn. "You're actually willing to give Camille the horn of the Black Beast?"

Feddrah-Dahns bobbed his head. "What choice do we have? These girls aren't capable of fighting off a demon lord without help. They may have their allies, but against an army of demons led by Shadow Wing? Under no sense of the imagination can they win without outside help."

"Good point," Smoky said as he sat down, crossing his legs and leaning back. He drummed his fingers on the arm of the chair. "Out of curiosity, to what emissary did you entrust the horn?"

Feddrah-Dahns blinked. "My personal servant. A pixie."

Smoky let out a loud guffaw. "I see. You entrusted a fabled artifact to a pixie. Brilliant."

Uh-oh. That was an insult if ever I heard one. I backed away, noticing that Delilah and Iris were doing the same. Even Chase had the sense to excuse himself into the kitchen, presumably looking for caffeine. Menolly swiftly resumed hovering near the ceiling. She almost looked pleased, and the thought crossed my mind that my vampire sister might make a good addition to the Ultimate Fighting lineup. She enjoyed a good brawl, that was for sure.

Feddrah-Dahns let out an exasperated snort and a whiff of steam and mist rose from his nostrils as he shook his mane. "You presume too much, dragon. Mistletoe happens to be an extremely effective courier. His attackers overcame him with magic."

"Magic? But pixies are immune to most magic. At least, most Fae magic." Apparently Smoky knew his pixie lore. After a moment, he said, "What kind of magic can take down a pixie?"

"Precisely the question," Feddrah-Dahns said. "What kind, indeed? Pixies are the best choice for runners and couriers because they can't be affected by most spells from the Fae, whether Otherworld or Earthside. Which means this wasn't Fae magic at work. And it couldn't be human magic; no human has the power to stop a pixie. But there are darker spells, and magicians . . ." His voice trailed off.

"I wonder if magic of this sort has been detected lately? Pentangle, the Mother of Magic, might know." Menolly glanced over at me. "Perhaps we should ask her."

"I don't want to run to the Hags of Fate every time we have a problem. Look at what happened last time we asked an Elemental Lord for help," I said, nodding at Delilah. "Procuring a demon's finger was child's play compared to what happened to Kitten."

Delilah let out a loud sigh. "Don't remind me," she said, rubbing her forehead. The black crescent tattooed on her brow shimmered, all too alive and vivid.

"Speaking of magic, I've come to take Camille back to my barrow. I have need of her services." Smoky looked at me, then slowly patted his lap.

I swallowed the taste of my lunch again, which suddenly decided to make a long-distance phone call. Some Tums would be nice now. Or Mylanta. Or a good stiff drink. I glanced at Menolly and Delilah, but they merely shrugged.

Returning from the kitchen in time to catch Smoky's comment and gesture, Chase looked about to say something, but Delilah gave him a warning shake of the head, and he closed his mouth.

Swallowing the lump in my throat, I slid onto Smoky's lap. He wrapped one arm around my waist and gave me a delighted smile. As his fingers lightly pressed against my waist, my whole body gave a little shudder, and before I knew what was happening, I threw back my head, gasping as a wave of orgasm hit me. Cripes, he was on fire! And so was I. Hastily gathering my wits, I blushed and hurried to cover my tracks. "What do you want me to do?"

"Do you really want me to answer that in front of your friends and family?" Smoky snorted, and a little puff of steam rose from his nose.

I stared at him. Insert foot in mouth, do not pass go. "I mean, why do you want me to come out to your land? This time. Today . . . that is."

"I don't believe it! Camille's actually blushing!" Delilah grinned like a Cheshire cat.

Menolly laughed, deep and throaty. "She is at that, Kitten. I'd like to be a fly on the wall of that barrow . . ."

"It's not my debt he's calling in," I said, protesting.

"She's right," Smoky said, relenting. "There's something going on out on my land, and I want your opinion. I choose to avoid getting entangled until I know more about what I'm facing."

Chase scowled. "What's going on? We already have a butt load of crap to contend with."

Smoky shifted. I started to get up, but he held tight to my waist, and once again, the heat from his hands burned into me. "It seems I have a visitor. I need you to find out just what she's up to. I believe you met her a couple months ago."

I glanced over at Menolly, who shrugged. "Who is it? And why don't you just ask her what she wants, yourself?"

He let out a slow laugh, almost ominous. "I don't care for the lady. I find her . . . off-putting. And Titania had some dealings with her centuries ago. The two are at odds. But she wants something, and she's made camp out near my barrow. I think she's trying to find Titania, to be honest, but the Fae Queen emeritus is making herself scarce these days."

I frowned. Who the hell was he talking about? But I knew better than to rush him. He'd spill it when he was ready.

"This morning," he added leisurely, "a murder of crows came winging in, with one large raven at the forefront. They landed near Titania's barrow and were pecking around. I fried them for breakfast, save one as a warning to their mistress."

A murder of crows . . . hell's bells.

"I know who you're talking about," I said, prying my way out of his lap. I whirled around to face him. "Morgaine— Morgaine's on your land, isn't she?"

He tapped his forehead. "I knew you'd get it."

Feddrah-Dahns whinnied and stomped his feet. The look in his eye was far from friendly. "You must not let her know about the horn! She's been looking for it long and hard. Morgaine came to the Windwillow Valley not five months past to demand our help. We ran her off."

I slowly turned back to the unicorn. "What on earth does Morgaine want with the horn?" Other than to obtain incredible power, that is.

He nervously pranced in place. "I don't know, but I have a feeling it has to do with the Unseelie Court."

CHAPTER 6

"The Unseelie Court?" I shook my head. "But the supreme courts of Fae were abandoned right before the Great Divide. They only exist in memory now."

Delilah settled on the sofa, cross-legged. "It doesn't make sense."

"No, it doesn't." I turned back to Smoky. "Aeval, the Unseelie Queen, disappeared thousands of years ago. No one knows where she went to or if she's alive or dead. And Titania's pretty much running on empty, as we know."

Titania had been the Seelie Queen before the Great Divide, Aeval the Unseelie Queen. Aeval had been a terrifying spectacle of a woman, as beautiful and cruel and ruthless as Titania had been beautiful and gracious . . . and ruthless.

Smoky let out a perturbed huff. "I have no idea what Morgaine is up to, but I don't want her on my land. However, I thought you might like to find out what she has in mind before I turn her into my lunch." He stood, nearly knocking his head against the chandelier on the ceiling. He brushed past it with an irritated wave of the hand.

"As I said, Titania's in hiding," he added. "After you took that annoying man of hers away, she sank into a drunken stupor and disappeared inside her barrow. I believe she blames me for letting you take Tom. So, if I were you, I wouldn't count on her for help."

Iris headed toward the kitchen. "I'll get us all some tea. I think we can use it."

"Let me help you," Chase said, following her. "I'm about as useless as a blank book when it comes to Fae queens and Supe politics."

Menolly slowly lowered herself to ground level. "Morgaine was always a power-hungry thing. I wonder . . ."

I glanced at her. "Wonder what? Do you think she's trying to resurrect the past, only with herself at the helm? That's a possibility. But if so, why would she be seeking the Merlin? He'd put a stop to her plans immediately if she's looking to create a new Unseelie Court. Morgaine was his greatest pupil, but she's more apt to pull a Darth Vader on him than actually follow in his footsteps."

Delilah grabbed a bowl of Fritos off the table and began to munch. "The problem is, if any of the Fae queens—including any aspiring applicants—are looking to stage a comeback, there must be something going on to spur them into action. Are they looking to gain power to fight the demons? Maybe rally the Earthside Fae against the coming war? Remember, Morgaine *did* show up at the first Supe Community meeting we had. By the way, we've scheduled the next meeting in three weeks to see what progress everybody's made by then."

"Whatever the case, we can't ignore her," Feddrah-Dahns said. "If Morgaine were to gain possession of the horn of the Black Beast, she'd be as formidable as a demon and more unpredictable. She's never respected humanity, even though she's half-human like yourselves."

I glanced at the calendar. We were days away from the equinox. Could there be a connection between Morgaine's appearance and the coming holy day? There were too many questions and not enough answers.

"So what are our priorities? In order?" Menolly asked as Iris entered the room, tea tray in hand. It was almost as big as she was, I thought. We needed to buy a tea caddy for her.

Smoky graciously took the tray from her and set it on the coffee table. She gave him a winsome smile, her golden hair shimmering in the dim light.

"Well, obviously, our top priority is to find the third spirit seal before the Rāksasa does. Second, locate Mistletoe and the horn, and destroy the demon spying for Shadow Wing." I accepted the cup of steaming tea and settled back in the rocking chair, letting the fragrant scent of Richya blossoms waft up to soothe my throbbing head. "And third, we deal with Morgaine and whatever the hell she's up to. I suppose we better find out if she's in league with Shadow Wing first. That's still a possibility."

"Morgaine? Involved with Shadow Wing?" echoed a voice from the hall. The door closed, and Trillian, my Svartan lover and the alpha member of my triad, sauntered into the living room. With skin black as obsidian and silver hair tinged with cerulean that cascaded down to the middle of his back, he was refined and elegant, and his eyes glinted robin's-egg blue, haunting in their magnetism.

Oh, hell. Trillian and Smoky were constantly bickering. The chances for a testosterone match had just jumped sky high.

I started to sweep past dragon-boy when Smoky reached up and pulled me down on his lap again, nuzzling my ear. He was staring directly at Trillian, a hint of challenge baiting that icy cold look of his.

"Not really *necessary*—not now!" I pushed my way out of his embrace.

Trillian glowered. "I thought I smelled the stench of dragon sweat outside. I see I was right. What are you doing here?"

I tapped Trillian on the shoulder. "Pull in the claws."

"I need to speak with you." He was testy, all right. "Alone. Now."

I shrugged and pointed to the parlor. "Fine. I'll meet you in there." Private was good. Privacy might prevent bloodshed.

Trillian strode past me, ignoring Smoky as he crossed in front of him. I flashed a tight smile to Menolly and Delilah. "While I'm filling Trillian in on what's happened, why don't you guys try to figure out where Mistletoe might have gotten himself lost to. If he hasn't used a Whispering Spell to contact Feddrah-Dahns again, he might be worried the goblin can home in on it and use it like radar. And Menolly, can you keep your ears open at work tonight? Maybe you can glean some information about where to find the demon."

Delilah flashed me an impish grin. "And what are you going to be doing?"

"Gee, I dunno. Try to defuse a bomb before it blows?" I shot a scathing look at Smoky. "Got anything to say about that? Or do you just enjoy creating havoc for me?"

He met my bet and raised me twenty. He folded his arms and planted himself in the middle of the room. "I like watching you handle your men. I've seen you handle Morio, remember?"

Once again, I blushed. Smoky had been witness to the first time when Morio and I hit the sheets. Or the grass, rather. We'd been bewitched, and Smoky had a front-row seat for the tryst of the century, though we hadn't known he was there at the time. Hell, under *that* lust spell, I doubt if we would have even cared. I whirled toward the parlor.

"Camille," he said, and I stopped short. His voice had dropped a good octave, and I felt the force behind the command.

"What?" My voice squeaked, and he grinned.

"Good, you're paying attention. Be sure to tell the Svartan that you may be his, but I'm still a dragon, and he'd do best to remember it." He winked, but I could tell he was deadly serious, and I had the distinct feeling I'd been given a warning that might save Trillian's life.

As I entered the parlor, Trillian silently held out his hand, and I walked over to his side. He pulled me into his arms and held me for a moment, nuzzling my neck. My skin began to tingle, as I always did when I was close to him. As magnetic as Smoky was, Trillian was familiar territory, safe and inviting.

"So, he's come to claim you?" He stepped back, his expression aloof, but a grumble in his voice told me just how he felt.

"He didn't come to collect on his debt. Not yet. But he will soon, and you know that I have no choice. The deal was struck, and I always pay my debts."

"This is ridiculous," Trillian said with a growl. "Fox-boy, I can handle. In fact, I've gotten used to him, and he's all right, though don't you dare tell him I said that. But the idea of that dragon mauling you repulses me."

I could tell he was close to exploding. The fact that we'd both recently healed up from some serious wounds—Trillian from an arrow, and me from a vampire's claws—made us both vulnerable to injury. If Trillian got into it with Smoky, I wasn't sure he'd make it through alive.

"Listen to me," I said. "You know that you're my alpha lover, and that's the way I want it. Smoky's a dragon. He could skin you alive with a flick of his talons. But he's also one of our greatest allies. We can't afford to tick him off. And . . ."

I stopped. Did I dare say that I wanted to go? That, as much as I loved Trillian and Morio, I couldn't help but linger over images and daydreams of what delights a dragon might offer? I'd spent more than one night mentally undressing that tall spire of ice in my mind. I was pledged to the Moon Mother, and she ran like silver fire in my blood, sensual and full and ripe. Her followers weren't satisfied with life on the vanilla side.

Trillian circled me, like a thief might orbit the object of his desire. "You want him, don't you? I can smell you—you're aroused. You *really* want the dragon?" He moved in, looping his arm around my waist as he buried his face in my hair. His lips on my flesh were like wine, heady and rich.

I gasped, my lower lip trembling. How could I tell him? And yet, Trillian knew me. We weren't children here. We weren't human—well, not fully—and we weren't married. In our world, there was no promise of *you're my only* to each other. Trillian could handle the truth, but he *wouldn't* put up with bullshit. "I . . . I . . ."

"Tell me," he said, his other hand gently caressing my breast, his fingers tripping lightly over the bustier, setting me ablaze beneath my clothes. My nipples stiffened, and my breath came hard. I'd been through the sexual wringer so much today that I was about ready to scream. He pressed against me. "I saw it in your eyes out there when he grabbed you. You want him, don't you?"

"Yes," I said, both scared and relieved. It had been hard to pretend that I was only going along because of the debt I owed Smoky. "Yes, I want him. He scares me, but he . . . he . . ."

"My beautiful goddess," Trillian said, trailing a circlet of kisses around the back of my neck. "You like to play with fire, don't you? You like the scent of danger on your men."

I shivered. He was right. I liked my men dangerous and dark. Or dangerous and white as the fallen snow. Sweet, light, gentle . . . they had their place, but I lived under the moon. I ran with the Hunt. My passion flowed in jewel tones, not pastels.

"I don't like the idea of him touching you," Trillian continued. "But since you agreed to the pact, and I didn't have the brains to stop it before the deal was sealed, we have no choice. I have no desire to become dragon toast, so when it is time, you will pay your debt, and I won't interfere. But Camille—don't you ever forget *this*."

With that, he spun me around in his arms and kissed me, long and deep and hard, and I fell into the darkened abyss that opened up each time Trillian touched me. His tongue played gently over my lips as I parted them to welcome him in. He tightened his grasp, firmly holding me to him. I let myself flow into the kiss, reveling in the energy that spiraled between us each time we came together. I straddled his leg as he pressed against my hip.

He pulled back suddenly, gasping. "I've never known a woman the way I've known you. When we're together, I feel like I can get inside your soul. When we bound ourselves, we forged a far darker chain than Lishani's circlet."

I felt like I owed him some sort of reassurance. Or perhaps I was trying to reassure myself. "Smoky won't hurt me, and he can never replace you. You know that you've owned my heart ever since that first night at the Collequia. The moment I saw you, I knew we belonged together."

Trillian furrowed his brow. "Camille," he said softly, "don't be sentimental. It doesn't become you. And it's a pale thought compared to the passion we share." And then he laughed and relaxed, dropping onto the love seat and patting the cushion beside him. "So tell me, what does the lizard want of you tonight?"

"You really are incorrigible," I said, curling up beside him as he wrapped his arm around my shoulder. "You can't possibly fear that anything or anyone can sever the bond we forged so many years back. I tried. You tried. If it didn't shatter then, you should know it never will. I've finally accepted that we're bound for life, regardless of other lovers, other friends, other oaths. The only vows I hold stronger than my bond with you is my pledge to the Moon Mother and my commitment to my sisters."

Trillian gazed into my eyes. He reached out to stroke my face. "I would never ask you to break either of those oaths. You know that."

And suddenly, I did. For all his posturing and questionable agendas, my Svartan had a sense of honor and ethics. They just didn't match the rest of the world's. I leaned my head on his shoulder and told him everything that had happened, from meeting Feddrah-Dahns to the concern over Morgaine.

By the time I finished, Trillian had a far different look on his face. Gone was the worry over Smoky, replaced by an ill-defined expression of concern.

"Morgaine is not to be trusted. I warn you, do not underestimate her. She's known in Svartalfheim. She forged some sort of connection with King Vodox, but . . . I'm not entirely sure what happened next, but he banished her from the city. She travels freely through Otherworld. If the unicorn told you that she was seeking the Black Unicorn's horn, then believe him."

I sat up, resting my elbows on my knees. Why did she have to show up now? Back in January, I had worried about her appearance, but in our concern over Dredge, I'd pushed her out of my thoughts. I wondered if I'd made a mistake.

"What's wrong, love?" Trillian stood and stretched, then reached for me. I took his hand, and he pulled me to my feet. "I didn't make you angry, did I?"

I shook my head. Regardless of my disdain for machismo from any male, Trillian seldom angered me. Irritated me? Definitely. Pissed me off? Sometimes. But angered? Rarely.

"No, I've gotten used to your tantrums."

He sputtered, and I held up my hand.

"Give it a rest. You know you throw tantrums. I've learned to accept them as a less-than-endearing part of you. It's just . . . matters are becoming complicated. More players are entering the arena, and I'm scared spitless that eventually we'll overlook a vital clue or part of the puzzle because there are so many factors to keep track of."

He made a tsking sound. "That's a very real fear. Keep alert. That's all we can do. Is that why you're heading out to Smoky's tonight? To talk to Morgaine?"

"Yes, he asked me to speak to her before he got mad enough to crisp her. I don't think he's kidding, so it's better if I comply." I shrugged. "I suppose we should—"

Just then, Delilah slammed open the door. "We've got trouble. Come on, we're going to need everybody's help."

"What's going on?" I rushed over to where she was standing. "Has someone been hurt?"

"Several someones," she said. "There are two trolls loose in one of the parks, and the cops can't contain them. They need us. That goes for you, too, lover boy," she said, motioning to Trillian. "They're not your everyday basic forest trolls, either."

I groaned. Trolls were bad news. Big bad news. They weren't invulnerable by any means, but killing a troll was hard. Subduing one was far harder. Which is why there were so few troll prisoners in Otherworld.

"Mountain trolls?" I asked, hoping for the best. Or second best. Mountain trolls were worse than forest trolls. Cave trolls were worse than mountain trolls. But the worst of all . . .

"Nope," Delilah said, leading us out into the living room. "Dubba-trolls."

As we entered the room, everyone was in an uproar. Iris was holding Maggie, our baby calico gargoyle, keeping her out of the fray as everyone else rushed around, getting ready for battle.

"Dubba-trolls," I whispered, closing my eyes for a brief second. Wonderful. Two-headed trolls with twice the strength and half the brains of forest trolls. And they were always hungry for sweet, fresh meat. Of whatever origin didn't matter, as long as it was alive when they caught it.

"Dubba-trolls," Menolly said, a delighted look in her eyes. "Come on, girls, let's go hunting!"

I shook my head and snorted. "I'm glad *you're* happy. Me, I'd rather tackle something simpler. Like Bad Ass Luke."

Menolly laughed then, hearty and loud in a way she hadn't in years. I glanced at her, grateful that she'd learned to smile again. As we headed out the door, she leaned close and whispered, "Hey, at least it's better than watching your lovers spend the evening sniping at each other."

As much as I hated to admit it, she had a point.

CHAPTER 7

The thing to remember about dubba-trolls is that they're big, stupid, and their hide is pretty much the consistency of magically enhanced leather armor. Bullets bounce off, daggers have to be magical or silver to pierce them, and swords better be serrated, or they don't stand a chance in hell of slicing through that nasty, stinking flesh. But a good hammer or mace, now one of those babies can make a dent, especially on the head. And dubba-trolls are susceptible to fire magic. Ergo, while my magic was bound to the moon and weather, I could call in lightning, which, in its own way, was akin to flame.

We asked Feddrah-Dahns to stay home with Iris and Maggie—the logistics of getting him in and out of Chase's SUV were difficult at best, as we'd already found out—and Smoky, Chase, Trillian, Delilah, Menolly, and I headed out. Chase took his SUV; Delilah took her Jeep. For once, Smoky rode with her and didn't make a scene. Trillian and I jumped in Menolly's Jag.

On the way, we discussed various ideas on how to dispatch the trolls with the least amount of collateral damage.

"I wish to hell I had a couple of Roz's fire bombs," I said.

Rozurial, an incubus, had helped us track and destroy my sister's sire. The man, or minor demon to be precise, was a walking arsenal, complete with everything from a miniature Uzi to silver chains to garlic bombs for disabling vampires, all hiding in the folds of his duster, which he was fond of yanking open like some weapons-crazy flasher. He was a menace to anything alive. Or dead.

"Fuck the fire bombs. I just wish we had *Roz* with us," Menolly said. "But he's caught up with Queen Asteria at the moment. I talked to him via the Whispering Mirror the other night. He told me that he's on some mission for her right now and can't get over Earthside for a week or two."

"What park are these trolls supposed to be in?" Riding shotgun, I stared through the window. It was a Tuesday night, going on eight P.M., and traffic had thinned enough to be called sparse. Seattle did have its nightlife, but the parties and gatherings were found in the clubs rather than out on the streets. New York City we weren't, and I was grateful for that.

"They're near the Salish Ranch Park, somewhere between the cemetery and the arboretum."

The Salish Ranch Park was located on the boundary between the Belles-Faire district and Seattle proper. It buttressed up against the Wedgewood Cemetery. The two were separated by a side street. Menolly made a sharp left off of Aurora Boulevard onto Borneo, which would take us to the park.

"Great, just what we need. Cemeteries aren't exactly the most delightful place to wander around," I said. "I wonder if they're there, scaring up dates. Maybe they have a few ghoul friends hanging around?"

Trillian snorted. "Bad, bad, bad woman." He reached over the seat and traced one finger along my neck. I shuddered.

"Don't start what you can't finish," I warned him.

"Oh, we'll finish it all right . . . but later."

"Get a room," Menolly said, but she grinned at me, the tips of her fangs exposed. I wondered if our play had stirred her up a bit.

"Yeah, well, I wish I knew where Morio was. He was supposed to drop by tonight, and he's never late. I hope he's okay." Together, Morio and I were proving to be a far greater force than I was by myself. My Moon magic could be devastating, or I could lay one hell of a dodo egg with it. But Morio . . . he was teaching me something else, altogether.

He'd been teaching me the death magic he'd learned at his grandfather's knee, and it seemed I had a knack for it. Maybe because it wasn't Fae magic, or maybe I just had a bent for the deadly, but whatever the case, I was proving adept so far. And when we joined forces, we packed quite a punch, although sometimes I wondered how working within the Shadowlands of the astral would affect me on a long-term basis. With what we were facing, though, I pushed those thoughts to the side. If the magic didn't kill me, Shadow Wing's cronies probably would. I'd take death by magic over death by demon any day.

"He probably just got stuck in traffic. Iris will tell him where we are when he arrives at the house." Trillian let out a loud sigh. "At least you *have* magic. About the only thing I can try on them is charm, and you can bet I'm not about to kiss their ugly mugs in order to subdue them."

"You're a lot better in a fistfight than me."

He snorted. "Right. Like my fist—or my sword—is likely to do any more than give them a nasty scratch. And I don't *do* blunt instruments, unfortunately."

"You have a point." I glanced out the window as Menolly turned left onto Fireweed, the street that divided the park from the cemetery.

The fifty-acre park's main attraction was an incredible arboretum. A huge series of glass buildings stretching across at least an acre of land were filled with rare flowers and cacti and delicate ferns, all kept within temperatures designed for them to flourish. Morio and I had strolled through the conservatory more than once, whiling away the evening hours.

My phone rang, and I answered. Delilah was on the other line. "Camille? Shamas just called Chase. The trolls are definitely in the cemetery."

"We're almost there. Give us five minutes," I said, hanging up. "Trolls are in the cemetery. Shamas is there, so at least we've got one other mage on hand."

"If anybody can knock a troll on his butt, it's Shamas," Menolly said. "I'd still like to know how he grew so powerful. He never studied much magic when he was a child, but he might as well sign up for duty as an arsonist by proxy."

As the park came into view on our left, I thanked the gods the trolls hadn't discovered the arboretum yet. I could just imagine them crashing through the glass-plated greenhouses. The resulting destruction would be heart wrenching.

"We've got to stop them before they get anywhere near the conservatory," I said. "Before they cross the divide into the park."

Menolly pulled into one of the parking spaces. "We'll go on foot from here."

We tumbled out of the car and took off at a run. The night was chilly, and I was glad I'd stopped to grab my capelet. Menolly ran on ahead, clad in tight, skinny jeans, high-heeled boots, and a turtleneck. But she wouldn't have noticed the cold even if she ran buck naked through the street at midnight. Trillian wore black pants, a silver crewneck sweater, his scabbard and short sword, and over it all he'd tossed a midcalf duster to act as both heat source and to hide his weapon from any unwelcome authorities who might object.

The cemetery came into view as we crossed the rise leading to the gates. Lit by an updated version of old-fashioned lampposts, the winding dirt paths that led through the maze of tombstones and markers were compacted, with a light cobblestone overlay. The cobblestones were slick, but the dirt acted as grout, keeping them from being too dangerous.

Technically, the Wedgewood Cemetery was open till dusk, but the trolls had bent the wrought-iron gates, and now the twisted metal bars curled to the side, their hinges bent and useless. We cautiously picked our way through, avoiding the metal. It would sting Menolly if she touched it, but Trillian and I were still alive. We could be seriously burnt by cast iron—Trillian even more so than me since he was full-blood Svartan.

We saw Smoky, Delilah, and Chase up ahead, talking to our cousin Shamas and three FBH cops. The cops looked worried, and Chase was arguing with one of the officers.

"You can't shoot them," we heard him say. "The bullets are just going to bounce off. Where the hell are the stun guns I told you to get? With those, we might have a fighting chance."

As we drew near, Shamas turned to us, and his eyes lit up. "Hey, Cuz," he said. Shamas had acclimated to human culture surprisingly well, in both speech and actions. He was dark in hair with violet eyes, like my father and me, and he stood barely five nine. Sturdily built, he had the perfect physique for physical activity, and it never failed to amaze me that he'd favored cerebral pursuits. "Ready to take on the trolls?"

"Dubba-trolls, no less," I muttered.

Chase was talking to a blond officer. He let out an exasperated sigh and jabbed his thumb over his shoulder. "Deitrich, until you can listen to orders, I want you on desk duty. This is the third time this week you've ignored direct orders from a superior officer. You're sidelined. Call for backup, and then get the hell out of here. I want to see you tomorrow morning, first thing. My office. Be there, or I'll kick you out of the FH-CSI and bust you down so far you'll be handing out parking tickets."

The cop shot Chase a look of pure venom, but he muttered a "Yes, sir" and turned to stalk away. Chase watched him go, then turned to the other man. "*You* have any problems with me, Lindt?"

"No, sir!" Officer Lindt shook his head. "I was on my way to get the stun guns like you ordered when Deitrich ordered me to stop. He outranks me."

"Yes, well I outrank him. Never mind. You move your butt back to the cruiser and grab those stun guns. Get back here as soon as you can." Chase waited until the uniformed man raced off to let out a string of oaths. "Damn it, Devins is behind this. He's been on my back the past couple of weeks about the Crypto issue, and he's goading the malcontents."

As Delilah murmured a soft "I know"—when he was on duty, she was careful to maintain a professional stance with him—I scanned the cemetery, looking for the trolls.

"Over there," Shamas said, pointing in a northeasterly direction. "Near the fountain."

And there they were. Two dubba-trolls, four heads, no waiting. I shivered. The damned things were a good eleven feet tall. As I'd told Chase, they were the worst of the troll family, and they loved takeout. Fresh meat on the hoof, no cooking required.

I groaned. "Cripes. You know we're just a platter of appetizers in their eyes. Except, perhaps, for Smoky."

Smoky shook his head. "I'm not about to shift into dragon form here. I've kept my profile carefully guarded for many years, and I want to ensure it stays that way. I'll have to help out the old-fashioned way."

"Too bad. That breath of fire you spout out could be quite handy with these fellows," Delilah said.

"Okay, what's our plan? We can't just rush them and hope for the best." I glanced around the graveyard, unhappily calculating our chances. If we dove in without some sort of strategy, we'd probably come out alive, but chances were somebody was going to get hurt.

Chase narrowed his eyes. "What do you think? Will stun guns do any damage?"

"They might, they're electricity, and that's a lot like fire," I said. "I'll prep a spell to call down the lightning."

Delilah frowned. "I usually use a knife, but I can rush in and do some damage with my fists, I'm betting. I've been working out a lot more lately, and if I can jump on the back of one of those creatures, I can start pounding his skull."

"Uh-huh . . . great," I said, my enthusiasm about as limp as a wet noodle. "Trillian? Smoky? What do you boys have for us?" I still was rooting for Smoky to turn dragon dude and fry them both with one big, fiery breath.

"That I'm a dragon does wonders for my strength in human form. I'll take one of them on," he said. I glanced at him, ever hopeful, but he shook his head. "I told you, woman, I'm not going to change form here. Do you know what that would do to the gravestones and markers? Have *some* respect for the dead."

Trillian actually smiled but quickly coughed to cover it up. "As I said in the car, my sword's not going to do much unless I can skewer one of them in the eye. I'll give it a try, though."

"Great. That ought to do it, all right." I snickered. "Why don't we just escort them over to the arboretum. Shamas, you got anything to help?"

"I was going to give my Fire Spray spell a workout, but you have to let me go in first, or you'll all be caught in the storm." He looked at us expectantly, and we all quickly eased back a step or two, Chase the first to move. He was learning, yes, he was.

"Be our guest," I muttered, wondering just where Shamas had picked up a spell like that. I knew for a fact he hadn't trained with any elemental wizards, and spells like Fire Spray didn't lie around free on street corners.

Shamas marched forward, muttering something under his breath, an anticipatory look on his face. His hair was braided back, a lot like Father's, and a sudden twinge of homesickness hit me. This would be so much more fun if we were back in Otherworld.

"I'm ready to rock," he said, and I got the impression he was actually enjoying himself. The trolls stopped tearing up the tree they were standing next to and stared at him, bewildered looks on their faces. No doubt no one back home was stupid enough to challenge them.

Raising his hands, Shamas looked oddly out of place in his OIA officer's uniform. He called out in a loud voice, *"Shellen, Morastes, Sparlatium . . ."*

There was a loud crackle in the air around him, and a sudden swarm of sparks and darting flames burst from his fingertips, racing toward the dubba-trolls, who suddenly realized they were under attack.

The one on the left—the larger one—gave a loud roar and tried to fight off the fiery volley, while the one on the right stared dumbly at the approaching spark shower. The minute the arrows of flame hit, he roared to life and stumbled forward, followed by his larger friend.

"Holy shit, they're on the move!" Shamas whirled and raced back to us, the dubba-trolls hot in pursuit, all four heads rumbling obscenities in Calouk. If I hadn't been so concerned about being trampled, I would have shot back a few choice expletives. As it was, I whirled, taking off at full speed to the right, Delilah keeping pace beside me. Trillian darted along behind us. Smoky, Chase, and Menolly dodged to the left.

"What now?" Chase shouted from the tombstone he was dodging behind. He reminded me of the mouse Delilah constantly chased. Only she *played* with the creature. She'd given up trying to eat it. The trolls wouldn't accord us any such niceties.

Leaving Smoky and Menolly to guide Chase, I ignored him. Once I was out of the trolls' direct trajectory, I planted my feet on the ground and raised my arms heavenward. "Moon Mother, give me your power, give me your force as I call down the lightning!"

My fingers tingled as a low rumble from the clouds echoed through the graveyard. The Moon Mother was listening. I could feel her energy cloaking me, moving within me, circling me in a cone of power, a tornado of invisible waves that buffeted me so hard I almost broke my stance and stumbled. Hastily, I caught myself and reinforced my position. If I moved suddenly, it could break the spell or send it astray.

And then, I heard *her* laugh. The Moon Mother, her voice

cascading over a waterfall of crystal, filtering down to soothe my fear like mist cushioning a chill night. The sky crackled, and a bolt of energy raced down to my fingertips, lashing me with a thousand shocks. The lightning recoiled in my body, churning as I focused on giving it form, on working it into a giant beach ball o' fun. My teeth started to chatter, and I knew I had to get it out of my system before it overloaded me and sent me into a coma.

"Eat this, boys!" I stretched my hands out toward the nearest dubba-troll. The stupid, shorter one, of course. I always got the stupid ones. He blinked—all four eyes—and was about to scratch his heads when the lightning shot forth from my hands, a round ball of brilliant light, to zing across the space between us. It hit with a loud blast, and his bewilderment turned to anger, then to the realization that he was going down.

I anxiously watched for any signs that my spell might ricochet—which had happened before—but the bolt merely encased him in a neon web of sparks. Within seconds, he keeled over with a tremendous thud, shaking the ground as he fell. His buddy turned and, seeing his fallen comrade, started in my direction.

Right then, a screaming of sirens slashed through the night, and there was a loud bellowing as a police cruiser screeched to a halt and Devins leapt out of it. "Johnson, what the fuck is going on?"

Though I felt sorry for Chase—his boss was a total prick—I had my own problems to worry about. I took off running. Away. The dead troll's buddy was too close for comfort.

As soon as Dubba-Troll the Bigger moved past his companion, Delilah and Trillian raced in. "He's not dead," she called. Trillian brought his sword to bear and stabbed the prone troll, first through one head, then through the other. He aimed for the eyes, the one place vulnerable to regular blades.

"Now he is," he said, avoiding a nasty spurt of eye juice.

"Very nice, but I've got troll number two on my hands!" I dodged out of the way as the bigger troll took a bead on me and changed direction to match mine. But as I tried to shake him, I glanced over my shoulder one too many times. My foot made direct contact with a low, flat tombstone. Pain rippled through my toes as I went sprawling across the marble edifice.

"Hell and double hell!" I tried to sit up, but the wind had been knocked out of me, and I could barely think.

"I've got her covered!" The voice wasn't Chase's. I glanced up. Oh shit! Devins was headed my way, gun drawn.

"Don't!" I tried to yell.

"Bullets won't work on them, sir!" Chase raced after his boss. "Their hide is too tough—"

"Bullshit! I'll show this SOB not to tear up the graveyards in my town!" Devins leapt over an open grave and landed on the other side. As he did so, the troll who was following me stopped, pivoted, and charged toward the chief of police.

"No! Get out of the way!" I forced myself to my feet, screaming. Menolly was flying in our direction, running faster than I'd ever seen anybody run, but she wasn't fast enough. The troll reached Devins before anybody could help him. With one swipe of the wooden club, the dubba-troll sent Devins flying back into the open grave. There was an awful thud as the chief hit the hole at an awkward angle, then slid into it.

Chase skidded to a halt and made a U-turn. Menolly kept up her charge and leapt on the troll's back. She managed to get her arms around one of the dubba-troll's necks, and squeezed. Hard. Very hard. The head went slack, and she let go, falling to the ground as the troll bellowed and swatted at her.

Smoky moved in. He had grabbed the club from the dead troll and was wielding it like an expert. He hoisted it with one hand, even though it was almost as tall as he was, and swung low, clipping the troll across the shins.

The troll bellowed again from its one still-functioning head. Menolly moved in behind it and again leapt, landing high. She reared back, exposing her fangs, and sank them deep into the troll's skull. He roared once more as Smoky took aim again and this time hit him square in the groin.

Watching the troll fold was like watching one of those giant balloons at the Macy's parade deflate. Menolly leapt free, and we all stared as the creature keeled over, groaning. Trillian raced in then, sword raised high, and planted it through the troll's eyes in his still moving head. I limped over to Delilah's side, and she offered me her arm to steady me.

"Thank the gods. It's dead," I said quietly, peering down into the lifeless eyes of the dubba-troll. "They're both dead. Anybody hurt?" My foot still ached where I'd hit it on the tombstone, but it was nothing a foot massage wouldn't heal.

Everybody shook their heads as Chase knelt by the open grave.

"Shine that light over here," he said to Shamas.

Our cousin pointed his flashlight into the hole as Chase lowered himself gingerly to the bottom. "We know the trolls already killed two hobos who were trying to sleep in the park," he said quietly.

Chase reached for Devin's pulse, then glanced up at us and shook his head. "Make that three victims. Devins is dead. His neck's broken."

I leaned on Delilah's arm. Three victims, killed by Cryptos. Joy oh joy. The Freedom's Angels were going to have a field day when they found out.

CHAPTER 8

By the time we got home, I wasn't up to heading out to Smoky's, so he agreed to me coming out the next day to talk to Morgaine and took off walking down the road. Feddrah-Dahns decided to stay the night at our house, though he opted to sleep outdoors. We couldn't go after Mistletoe in the night. For one thing, we still didn't know where to start.

Morio still hadn't shown up by the time we got home, and I ended up leaving three messages on his cell phone. As Trillian and I climbed into the shower together, I couldn't get my mind off worrying about him.

"What's wrong, babe?" Trillian soaped my stomach as I leaned my head back to avoid getting my hair wet. He liked to bathe me, and I was quite happy to let him. Showers—now that was one luxury I'd miss whenever we went home to Otherworld.

"Just worried about Morio," I said. "He never forgets to call."

"Yeah, the little bastard is punctual, all right," Trillian said, leaning down to slip one of my nipples into his mouth. He sucked gently, and I moaned, leaning back against the tile. I was tired, but his touch felt good, and I realized I was up for some destressing.

"How do you spell *relax*?" I whispered, holding his head with my hands.

"I think the answer is f-u-c-k-m-e," he answered, sliding his way up my body. He was hard—ready—and I could see by his eyes he was planning on planting his flag as many times as possible before Smoky got to me.

"Sometimes I think I should have been a sacred harlot," I whispered, my breath ragged. The oath we'd forged acted like a perpetual aphrodisiac, and the longer we were together, it seemed the stronger it got. "Delilah and Menolly . . . their hormones are in check, but mine never seem to stop. I need you, Trillian. I need you to touch me, I need you to fill me up and never stop reminding me that you own me."

As he trailed his tongue along the side of my neck, I pushed him back, then slid down on my knees. The water cascaded down in a waterfall of warmth as I brought my lips to his leg, working my way up his inner thigh, over the taut, jet muscles that convulsed at my touch. Hungry for the taste of him, I sought him out, letting him slowly press his length into my mouth. I gave one long, slow lick along the hardened ridge, from base to tip, and he shuddered.

"You're too passionate to be one of the sacred whores," he said, bracing his hands on my shoulders as he planted his back firmly against the tiled wall. "They perform for men out of duty. You do this out of love . . . love for the act, love for the passion, love for . . ." He didn't finish it, but I could hear the word *us* on his tongue.

I nibbled and teased, pressing my mouth against him as I slowly let his girth part my lips again. He groaned and gently thrust forward as I wrapped my tongue around the head, sucking hard, tasting the droplets that gathered on the tip. They were salty, warm, filled with desire.

After a moment, Trillian pushed me back, panting roughly.

"Stop . . . before I come," he commanded. I stopped, and he lifted me up and pressed me against the tiles. I lifted one leg, balancing it on the rim of the tub, and he dipped slightly, then came up to press against my lower lips, sliding thickly in with ease and familiar comfort. I gasped as his fingers sought my clit, and the next thing I knew, he was teasing me, cajoling me to follow his lead.

"Oh Great Mother, hard. I need you. Hard, Trillian. Give it

to me *hard*." All the sexual tension from Smoky's visit and the stress of the evening had built up in my body, and this was my only release. This was the only way I could ever get outside of my head—escape from my thoughts.

He thrust against me, and we set our pace. With one hand, he grabbed my hair and yanked my head back as he pressed his lips against my neck, sucking deeply. Territorial markers.

"You want me, you've got me," he said, his voice raspy. "Never run away from me again, Camille, or I'll tear the world apart to bring you back. I don't care how many men you fuck, but *never leave me again*. Not for fox-boy, not for the dragon, not for the freaking gods themselves."

I grabbed his shoulders as he plunged so deep and so hard that I was afraid we'd topple over, but a second later, he fingered me again, and I suddenly forgot about the tub, about the water, about everything as I found myself rising, spiraling up and out toward the apex, where a deluge of sensation ricocheted through me. A moment later, I collapsed into his arms, spent, relieved, savoring the release that only sex could offer.

I woke early, long before sunrise, to the sound of chimes echoing from my study across the hall. The Whispering Mirror! I slipped out from beneath Trillian's arm, which was draped over my side, and gave him a satisfied peck on the cheek. He murmured in his sleep, then turned over as I slid into my silk robe and hurried out the door to cross the hall.

Encased in an engraved silver frame, the Whispering Mirror was our interdimensional videophone to Otherworld. Originally, it had been programmed to contact the OIA. Now, with a little rewiring thanks to the elves, it homed in on Queen Asteria's court.

I sat down at the vanity table it was affixed to and removed the black velvet cloth draped over the mirror. The glass sparkled with a vortex of colored mists.

"Maria," I said, activating it. Instead of responding to our voices, it now responded to a code word. We'd chosen our mother's name.

The swirling mist in the glass slowly began to clear, revealing Trenyth, Queen Asteria's advisor and assistant. He looked almost as tired as I felt. He blinked, staring at me with open surprise. I glanced down and realized my robe had slipped open and that I was popping out of my spaghetti-strap nightgown.

I adjusted my breast, giving him a dippy grin. At four in the morning, I just couldn't get upset over offering him a little peep show. "Nothing you haven't seen before, so don't look so shocked. Do you know what time it is here? I've had three hours of sleep. We spent half the night fighting off two dubba-trolls. I'm beat. What do you want?"

"I'm sorry to wake you, but there's been a bit of an emergency over here," he said.

I recognized the urgency in his voice, and all my snarkiness slid away. "What do you need?"

Trenyth, like most elves, managed to keep an impassive expression on his face. He was unreadable unless he chose otherwise. "Is Trillian with you?"

I nodded. "Yes, why?"

"Fetch him. I need to talk to him. Now, if you will." He sat back in his chair, waiting, offering no other explanation.

Worry replacing curiosity, I pushed back the bench and hurried toward my bedroom. What could Queen Asteria want with Trillian? He'd been a runner for her and Tanaquar, but they'd grounded him Earthside for awhile when he was shot by one of the enemy's arrows. Worse than the wound, he'd been outed as a spy, which put him squarely in danger back in Otherworld.

"Trillian, wake up," I said, shaking his shoulder until his eyes flew open. "Trenyth is on the Whispering Mirror, and he wants to talk to you."

Within seconds, Trillian leapt out of bed. He stood there, a naked, gorgeous god, casting a quick glance around the room. I held up his smoking jacket. Actually, it was more of a midcalf robe, one I'd bought for him at Yuletide.

"Here, this what you're looking for?"

"Thanks," he said, as he slid into it and belted it. He hurried across the hall, with me following, and took his place in front of the mirror.

Trenyth straightened his shoulders. "Trillian, I have . . ." He stopped when he saw me. "Camille, this is security business. You'll have to leave the room."

Frowning, I backed away, not wanting to go but well-versed in taking orders. We may not have been the best agents, but it wasn't for lack of trying. I could hear the soft fall of their voices as I closed the door behind me and huddled in the hallway.

"What's going on?" Menolly appeared at the top of the stairs, Delilah right behind her. "I was watching Jerry Springer with Kitten when we thought we heard the Whispering Mirror."

"You did. Trenyth is talking to Trillian. I was asked to leave the room before I could find out what was going on." Still smarting from being told to get out, I glanced back at the door. "My hearing's good, but I can't catch what they're saying."

Menolly winked at me. "Out of the way." She pushed past me and gently pressed her ear to the door. Holding one finger to her lips, she listened.

After a moment, she straightened, her pale complexion even whiter than usual. "In your room," she whispered.

The three of us filed into my room and sprawled on the bed. Delilah pulled the satin comforter around her shoulders, and I joined her beneath the coverlet as Menolly let out a long sigh.

"You'd better prepare yourself. Trillian's being called back to Otherworld. I couldn't catch much else, beyond the fact that the war has shifted, and Queen Asteria needs him for something." She frowned, toying with Belle, the stuffed bear that was sitting on the bottom of my bed. Morio had given Belle to me, and I liked her company.

"What? But he's bound to have a price on his head. What the fuck do they think they're doing in there? What's taking so long?" I jumped out of the bed and yanked off my robe and nightgown, scrambling into a skirt. My hands shook as I fastened the hooks on my bra and slid into a V-neck tank top. "Trillian's just getting over that arrow wound; they can't possibly mean for him to return to duty. Not now. Not yet."

"Listening at the door?" Trillian entered the room and glanced at the three of us. "How much did you hear?"

Menolly shook her head. "Not enough. Only that they want you back in OW pronto."

"What's going on?" I hurried to his side, pressing against him, my hand against the shoulder where the arrow had come close to piercing his heart. "They can't possibly expect you to go back to running messages? You're too well-known. Lethesanar will have all her scouts looking for you."

Trillian shook his head and gently took my hand, kissing each finger lightly before he slipped out of my embrace. "No,

Camille. They haven't asked me to go back to spying. It's another mission. One I can't refuse. Remember, I gave my oath for as long as the war lasts. I can't back out of the deal now."

"But if you're not going back to running messages, why was Trenyth contacting you?" Delilah asked, bouncing to sit on her knees on the bed. Her long, golden shag was caught up in a pair of ponytails, and her kitty-cat pajamas were bright blue, making her look for all the world like Bubbles, of *The Powerpuff Girls*.

"It was the most expedient way of getting hold of me." He looked around, then picked up his neatly folded clothes from the quilt rack that stood near the window. "Now, if you girls will excuse me," he said to Delilah and Menolly, "I need to get dressed. I'll have to leave my Earthside clothes here, Camille. I don't have time to take them home. Will you get me my traveling clothes and kit?"

As I mutely hurried to fetch his tunic, trousers, and cape from the closet, Delilah and Menolly quietly withdrew, closing the door behind them. I watched as Trillian slid into the OW clothes. He took on a decidedly magical air as he did so. Sometimes, he seemed to blend in so well over here on Earthside that I forgot just how rich in Fae blood he was. Svartans were actually an offshoot of the elves, from long, long ago, and the two races normally distrusted each other. But the civil war in Y'Elestrial had brought them together on the same side.

"I don't want you to go," I finally said, debating on whether to stand by like a good Guardsman's daughter and cheer on my lover, or to be honest. "I don't want you to die. We need you here, in the fight against the demons." After a pause, I added, "I need you."

Trillian exhaled sharply. "I know. I know you need me, and I know that the demons are a far greater threat than any war back in OW. But trust me, please. I wouldn't go if it weren't terribly important. And important it is. Camille," he said, placing his hands on my shoulders and staring into my eyes. "Don't try to stop me. Not this time. You'd regret doing so if you knew the reason. And I can't tell you what it is, not yet. All I can say is that you need to let me leave without an argument."

There was something in his words. A warning, a promise . . . all wrapped into one. I gazed at his face, searching for any clue, but the only thing I could see was myself, reflected in his eyes.

"All right," I heard myself saying. "I won't try to keep you.

And I won't ask where you're going. But Trillian, you come back to me. *Alive*. Please?"

He buried his face in my neck, kissing my skin with his warm, honeyed lips. Muffled by my hair, he said, "I'll be back. I promise. But listen to me," he added, searching my face. For once, his arrogance slid away, leaving raw pain—and love. "If something *does* happen to me, then tell that lizard that it's up to *him* to protect you. Morio would die for you, yes, but Smoky can protect you better than he ever could. More . . . more than I can ever hope to. Do you understand?"

Not wanting to even go down that path, I shook my head. "Don't talk like that—don't even joke about it. You're coming back, do you understand? If you don't, I'll come find you, no matter where you are."

"No. Your job is here, guarding the portals, stopping the demons. We are at war, Camille, on several fronts. You're the daughter of a Guardsman. You *will not* shirk your duty." He kissed me lightly on the forehead. "Don't worry about me. I can take care of myself. I'll be back." And then he fastened his lips on mine, and the world ground to a screeching halt as we kissed, long and slow, bathed in fire and frost.

After a moment, he let go and slid his cape over his shoulders. "I'll go via Grandmother Coyote's portal. Trenyth will be waiting for me on the other side. Take care of your sisters. Take care of Iris and Maggie. And most of all, take care of yourself. I need you, Camille. Just as you need me."

Before I could say a word, he turned and slipped out of the room. I hurried to follow him, but he was a dark shadow against the staircase, and before I knew what was happening, he'd opened the door and hurried down the porch steps and vanished into the shadows of the early morning.

I folded my arms over my chest to protect myself from the chill as I gazed toward the eastern sky. The first hints of dawn were vaguely forming, fingers of pale light that penetrated the diminishing veil of night. Not sunrise, not for awhile, but the promise was there. The sky was clear for a change, stars still shimmering in the night. The moon had gone to bed; she was sleeping as she traveled on her journey out of her dark phase. Yet I could feel her pull even now.

The faint chirping of early morning birdsong echoed through the stillness. I turned my attention toward the oak in the yard, beneath which Feddrah-Dahns had settled, sleeping. Even in slumber, he looked regal. As I watched, Delilah and Menolly joined me on the porch. Menolly glanced at the sky, checking her safety zone.

"This is as light as it ever gets in my world," she said offhandedly. "At least, unaided by lanterns or lightbulbs."

I let out a deep sigh. "I wish I could change that for you. I wish I could change a lot of things. Trillian's gone home to OW. He wouldn't tell me why, only that it was of extreme importance. Meaning he'd be dog meat if he refused, considering Tanaquar still holds his contract."

"I wish he could stay," Delilah said. "So much is happening."

"What do you think will happen now that Chase's boss is dead?" I asked.

She shrugged. "I have no idea. I hope he doesn't get fired."

Menolly sat down on the top step and leaned back on her elbows. "You headed out to Smoky's today?"

I nodded. "Later on, though. I have to talk to Morgaine. But first, we'd better check out the leads on that demon." Frustrated, I tripped down the stairs and knelt in the dew-laden grass, plucking at a handful of scant weeds that'd dared to make their home amongst the irises. "There's just too much . . . too much to do, and all of it too scattered to see how the puzzle fits together. Where do you think the third seal is?"

"It could be anywhere, considering the locations of the first two," Delilah said, joining me, still in her pajamas. We weeded together, the dirt wet and loamy against our hands. The pungent smell filtered up with the faint scent of mildew, rich and sour and promising new growth. "If we only had some other clue . . ."

Menolly cleared her throat. "Well, I did find out something at work last night, but I don't know how useful it will be." She joined us but merely watched as we yanked out the beginnings of dandelions and clover. Vampires weren't terribly good with growing things, and she'd never taken an interest in gardening like Delilah and I had.

"What?" I glanced up at her. "Any news is welcome right now." I didn't add that I wanted to hear anything that might keep my mind off Trillian returning to OW, but I could see in her eyes that she understood.

She glanced at the sky again. "I've got about an hour left before I have to be inside," she said. "Okay, here's the deal."

She plopped on the ground beside us, crossing her legs and picking a long spray of grass to play with as she spoke.

"While I tended bar last night, Luke was waiting tables because Chrysandra's on vacation. He stopped by a booth, and when he brought me the order, he told me that the customer had been asking questions about me. I asked Luke what she wanted, and he told me that she'd been asking if he knew where I live, and when I got off duty."

"That doesn't sound good." I tugged at one particularly stubborn thistle root, and it came sliding out of the ground. I tossed it on the pile. "What did he say?"

"Well, of course, he didn't tell her anything, but I did a little bit of snooping. Genehsys was there. You know, the folk singer who occasionally performs at the Wayfarer? Anyway, she's Fae and gifted with the ability to divine magical beings. I asked her to scope out the woman."

"What did she find out?" Delilah stopped to pick up a branch covered in ladybugs. She carried them over to one of the nearby rosebushes and gently shook them onto the leaves. "We've got aphids," she said. "They'll help control the pests."

Menolly raised her eyebrow. "Go, ladybugs. Anyway, Genehsys said that the woman appears to be a djinn."

"Djinn? Shit." Delilah whirled around. "We don't need to tangle with a djinn."

I frowned. "Do djinns and Rāksasas hang around together?"

Menolly shrugged. "I don't know, but you might want to find out. I followed her after she left. I asked Luke to mind the bar. She entered a door next to a Persian rug shop. There are apartments above the shop. Want to bet she lives there?"

"Persian rug shop? Some Rāksasas are Persian." I frowned. "If she *is* working with the demon, he probably knows about us, considering he's been around Seattle for awhile. If not . . . then who is she, and what does she want?"

Just then a whinny interrupted us. Feddrah-Dahns had woken and was standing near enough for me to feel his breath on my shoulder. "You three are awake early," he said. "Are we ready to go in search of Mistletoe?"

Delilah shook her head. "Not quite. Menolly, did you find out anything about pixies running wild before your shift was over?"

She grinned and pulled out a slip of paper. "That's the best part. I was going to leave this for you to find at breakfast. A couple of elves at the bar were griping about a wayward pixie who doesn't belong around the area. He seems to have made himself at home in their garden. I got their address and promised that we'd have a look. They said fine, as long as we convince him to move on."

Elves and pixies were often at odds, more so than the Sidhe and pixies. Nobody really knew why, but the schism had been around since before the Great Divide.

I wiped my hands on the grass and stood. "Then I suppose we should get busy. We've got to check out both the pixie sighting and the djinn. Menolly, you won't be able to help us. You should be getting into your lair shortly."

"Not so fast," came a voice from the top of the porch steps. Iris was standing there, holding Maggie, who yawned sleepily. "What are you all doing out here this time of morning?"

As Delilah hurried up the stairs to explain, I took Maggie and carried her down to the ground. The gargoyle would remain in babyhood for a long, long time yet. I set her down, and she teetered around, trying desperately to balance using her tail. She couldn't fly yet—her wings were far too small still and far too weak—but she had managed to get the hang of walking without always falling over on her nose.

Now she toddled to a patch of dirt that we kept especially for her and gave me a look as if to say, "Are you really going to watch?"

I grinned at her. "Sorry, Maggie. I'll turn around."

"Mooph," came the soft reply as she squatted to piddle and poop.

I turned away, giving her privacy. Maggie was an integral part of our family now. We'd saved her from a demon, a harpy to be precise, and Maggie had become both our pet and our littlest sister. Menolly spent a lot of time with her, helping her learn to crawl and walk, showing infinite patience that she never showed with anybody else except, perhaps, Delilah—her Kitten.

Maggie let out another *mooph* to let me know she was done. I turned back and checked under her tail to make sure nothing untoward had stuck to her wispy, silken fur. She reached up, and I hoisted her back into my arms, bracing her against my hip as she clasped her hands around my arm, resting her head on my shoulder.

As I stroked her downy fur and kissed her gently on the head, Iris clattered down the steps and eyed the weeding we'd done. "Good start. I'll finish it this afternoon. Now come in for breakfast and tell me what's going on."

As we all followed her inside, including Feddrah-Dahns, I took one last look at the boundary lines of our land. The woods beyond led to Grandmother Coyote's forest, where her portal awaited. Thoughts of Trillian raced through my mind. Why had he been called back to OW? Would he be safe? My heart skipped a beat. He'd better be. And speaking of men, where the hell was Morio? He hadn't called yet.

As I turned back to the house, a raven flew overhead, cawing loudly. Startled, I glanced over my shoulder as it landed in the oak. The bird gazed at me, eyes glittering, and I had the distinct feeling it was a message from Morgaine.

Too much, I thought as I turned my back on it and entered the house. It was all too much to deal with. At least until we'd eaten breakfast.

CHAPTER 9

❦

While Menolly kept watch on the clock—she still had a good thirty minutes before she had to be in her nest—Iris fixed breakfast.

The phone rang. Thinking it might be Morio, I grabbed the receiver, but it was Chase's voice on the other end.

"Hey, Camille. Listen, can you put me on speaker?"

"Sure," I said, hoping he wasn't in trouble. After the troll debacle, with Devins so much dead meat, who knew what was going to happen?

"It's Chase," I mouthed as I punched the button and motioned for Delilah, Menolly, and Iris to move closer. Feddrah-Dahns was in the living room, drinking fresh spring water and munching on a bundle of sweetgrass that Iris had somehow managed to get hold of.

"I have news for you—it's good, but it also means I'm not going to be of much use for awhile."

"They didn't fire your ass because the trolls killed your boss, did they?" Menolly asked.

Delilah swatted at her, and Menolly waved her away, grinning.

He snorted. "Leave it to you to think of that first. No, I wasn't fired, though I thought I might be. After all, the FH-CSI is my baby, and we're supposed to take care of things like this before somebody gets hurt. But a lot of people around here didn't like Devins, and I don't think anybody cried over the loss. He forged a lot of enemies in his time."

"Sounds like you took care of the problem, all right," Iris muttered, heading back to her skillet and pancake batter.

Delilah sniffed at her. "Oh hush. Tell us what happened, love."

"Well, the fact is that I've been promoted to Devins's position. *And* I'm still in charge of the FH-CSI. There's so much to sort out here that I'm going to be swamped for weeks." He let out a long sigh. "Which means I won't be much good to you girls, because I'll be working eighteen-hour days just to make sense of the mess in which Devins left his records."

"Congratulations!" Delilah clapped her hands, then frowned. "That means you won't be able to help us track down the demon—"

"Yeah, I know." Chase cleared his throat. We heard the sound of shuffling papers. "I'll do what I can, but for the most part, I'm only good on the information side of things this go-round. I can't afford to mess this up, or it will hurt all of us. I have to make this promotion work in order to keep the FH-CSI in action, not to mention keep my career on track. There's the chance that if I do a good enough job, I might be able to wrangle us more funds."

"What are people saying about the trolls? That little incident can't have gone unnoticed." Delilah glanced over at me.

"With our luck, it made headline news," I said. My guess wasn't far off.

He gave a soft laugh. "Which do you want first? The ridiculous, the sublime, or the frightening?"

Uh-oh. The latter sounded bad. Real bad. "Start us in easy," I said.

"Okay, ridiculous it is. Unfortunately, Camille, you're the recipient of this lovely little piece of news."

"Uh-oh. Why am I always the butt of the joke?" If he was starting with ridiculous, and it involved me, whatever it was couldn't be good for my ego.

Chase laughed and took a deep breath. "Okay, ready?"

"As I'll ever be."

"It seems that one of the local tabloids managed to capture

pictures of the fight on film. I guess they had a police scanner and heard about the ruckus. I saw the early A.M. edition. The shots are pretty clear. Camille, one of them is of you. You were casting a spell. They not only got a good shot of your boobs, but they also captured a swirl of light surrounding you. Looked like something right out of Harry Potter."

That wasn't so bad. "Well, that doesn't sound so horrible. If they had to capture me on film, at least it sounds like they caught a good shot."

"Wait till you hear what the headlines had to say."

Uh-oh. "Spill it."

"The *Seattle Tattler* captioned the picture, 'Alien Seductress Seeks Tryst with Trolls via Fiery Lust Spell.'" He knew enough to wait for my reaction, which wasn't long in coming.

"What the fuck did you say?" I leapt up as Menolly and Delilah snorted. "They said I was out for a roll in the hay with the trolls? Oh gods, I'll never live this one down—not among my customers, and not among the other Fae here in Seattle."

"Let's see . . . apparently, you're supposed to be in league with the grays from outer space. They say here that you're the bait they use to lure in unwitting abductees and that you seduce them, then help with the . . . probing . . . after you drag your victims back to the mother ship." He let out a bark of laughter.

"That sounds more up my alley," Menolly said, cracking a smile.

I cringed. "You can't be serious?" Closing my eyes, I winced as the headache I'd had the day before thundered back, bringing reinforcements. "Not only am I insulted—likening Fae to aliens is just all sorts of wrong—but I can't believe that the *Tattler* believes the public would fall for that."

"John Q. Public believes a lot of things that aren't good for him. Like that the government is honest, that global warming is due to the liberal Faeries dumping woo-woo powder in the scientists' coffee, and that the world was created in seven days." Chase let out a long sigh. "Trust me, even people who know the story's a hatchet job don't care. They eat up anything that hints of scandal. Just like pigs at the trough."

I grumbled, "But I'm half-Fae. We're *real*. The aliens are . . . well . . . we dunno, but they aren't around to answer any questions, now are they?" Pausing, I contemplated what it might take to reduce the *Tattler*'s offices to a pile of rubble. "You think the city would object if I leveled their building by asking Smoky to sit on it?"

Iris let out a chortle. "That'd show them, all right." She flipped another pancake on the stack and carried it over to the table. "Breakfast in ten minutes, girls. Set the table."

Delilah jumped out of her chair and opened the cupboard, taking out three settings of the Old Country Roses china we'd picked out when we first arrived.

"I've got to get underground. Can we hurry this up?" Menolly said in the direction of the phone. "You also mentioned sublime and scary news. What else should we know?"

"Just a minute. I have to put you on hold," Chase said as another voice echoed through the speaker. The line went mute.

"Well, good for him," Iris said. "Promotions are important in the human sphere of things."

"In the OIA, too, which is why we knew we were doomed when they reassigned us over Earthside." Delilah carried the maple syrup, butter, and honey over to the table.

Iris dished up the sausages and bacon while I poured orange juice and tea for the three of us. Menolly didn't eat, of course, and Maggie had been fed before Iris cooked our own breakfast. Now she was curled in her pen, snuggled into a ball as she snoozed gently with little *moophs* and *ummphs* occasionally escaping from her nose. Menolly bent over the playpen to lay a light blanket over her. The house was drafty, and even though she was in a warm place near the stove, we tried to make sure she didn't catch a chill.

Chase came back on the line as we settled at the table. "Okay, quick rundown on the rest. In a turn *nobody* expected, the United Faith Foundation has accepted the Order of Bast as an official church. This appears to be spurring on some of the Earthside Fae to register their own spiritual groups with the UFF. Of course, the fundies are giving them hell over it, but the government's already acknowledged them as a bona fide religion. The UFF is calling for tolerance and acceptance of all faiths."

"Score one for common sense," I said. "At least the Order of Bast will have the law on their side if the zealots take action against them. Okay, bad news next, I guess."

Chase let out a long sigh. "This is really bad, girls. A group of Freedom's Angels are on the run down in Portland. They

OIA had given us a tidy salary, but that was in the past now. Our cover jobs had become a very real necessity, so Iris was pulling a lot of hours as my assistant there.

She grimaced. "I was hoping to get to the spring cleaning today. What do you think about hiring someone to work part-time at the shop? I think Henry might accept minimum wage if you supplement his pay with free books. He usually goes for the used books, anyway."

"Henry Jeffries, you mean?" I hadn't even considered hiring someone from the outside, but it made sense. "I thought you were still avoiding him." Henry suffered a serious case of unrequited love.

"Ever since Bruce and I started dating, Henry's backed off. He's too much of a gentleman to interfere." Her eyes twinkled, a brilliant blue against her peaches-and-cream skin and golden hair. Iris was far older than me or my sisters, but she still looked in her mid-twenties, and she beguiled men in that girl-next-door way. They never seemed to care that she was barely four feet tall. A couple of months ago, she'd met Bruce O'Shea, a leprechaun with his roots in Ireland and a voice that could make any woman melt. Every time Iris invited him over, we begged him to sing to us, and he always gave in with goodwill.

"Is that fair to Henry, though?" Delilah asked. "It seems kind of mean to put him through being near you so much. I mean, he's got a crush on you, and you're dating somebody else."

"Pish. Henry fancies me, yes, but he'll survive. He loves his space stories more than anything, and I think he'd rather be at the shop any day, rather than spend time at home with that shrew of a mother he's got."

At our startled looks, Iris shrugged. "What? Just because I don't want to date him doesn't mean I don't enjoy a good conversation with him. He lives with his mother, yes. She's in her mid-eighties, and she's a mean-tempered bitch."

Delilah gasped, clapping her hand to her mouth. "Iris, that's not nice—she's old—"

"And I'm short. So what? Just because the woman's old doesn't give her the right to treat her son like a slave. He does everything for her, and she never thanks him for it. Henry told me that he can't put her in a nursing home because he doesn't have enough money to keep her there, and she refuses to sell her house. She reminds me of Grandma Buski."

Delilah and I exchanged glances. We'd heard a lot of Iris's stories about her life in Finland, but this was a new name.

"Who?" I asked.

"Grandma Buski. When I was a child and lived in the Northlands, long before I moved back to Finland and was bound to the Kuusis, my best friend took me to meet her grandmother. The Buski sprites weren't Talon-haltija like I am. They were part brownie, part something else—probably kobold or urcadines. I don't remember what, right now, but they were a handsome family. Anyway, Greta took me to see her Grandma Buski, who was a sprite of rare beauty, even in her old age."

Iris paused to take a sip of juice, then continued. "I remember she wore a brilliant crimson and cobalt dirndl dress that showed off every curve. But Grandma Buski was also a spiteful old woman. She was all brownie and had married into the Buskis. Now, you think brownie and you think helpful, cheerful, sometimes annoying but never downright vicious, right?"

Speechless, Delilah and I nodded. Iris was on a roll, and whenever she talked about the "old days," we listened. She was a natural-born storyteller.

"Well, imagine my shock then, when Greta introduced me, and that bitter old hag reached out and pinched my cheeks so hard I burst into tears. She leaned down and, with breath that smelled like tallow and suet, called me a dirt-eater—that was a terrible insult back in those days among the sprites of the Northlands. And then the old hag had the nerve to cast aspersions on my mother's fidelity."

"What did you do?" Delilah asked, her eyes wide. I repressed a smile. Having Iris around was a lot like having our mother alive again.

"Well, I hauled off and slapped her a good one. And I cursed her and told her I hoped a wolf would devour her, but that he'd probably throw her back because she was so old and tough and stringy." Iris giggled, then rolled her eyes.

Delilah giggled. "I'll bet you got in trouble for that."

Iris nodded. "You know it. By the time I got home, word had traveled ahead to my mother and father. My father put me to work in the stables for three weeks after that. And my mother made me fetch my favorite hen over to Grandma Buski as a token of apology. I never told anybody, but on the way over there, I turned Kirka free in the forest and stole a hen from a nearby farm to take in her place. I couldn't bear the thought of giving my sweet hen to such a mean old biddy."

As she finished, Iris held out her teacup. I poured us all refills out of the bone china pot. The fragrant steam from the peppermint rose to soothe my mind.

"Henry's mother is a carbon copy of Grandma Buski," Iris finished. "Only she looks a lot like Whistler's Mother and sounds like Oscar the Grouch. Which is why the poor man never married. He told me that he was engaged once, but Mrs. Jeffries ran his fiancée off. And she's healthy as a horse—doctors expect her to live till she's in her nineties."

"No wonder Henry spends so much time at the store," I said. His life had suddenly come into much sharper focus.

"And there's another reason I won't date him. Not only does he have a mother from hell, he's far too old. I want a family, and he's around sixty-four which is younger than me in actual years, but he's a whole lot farther down the track when you talk about how long he has left. I would never allow my children to be sired by a human, let alone someone as old as he is. They'd never have a chance to get to really know him before he died."

Delilah let out a little burp and pressed her fingers to her lips. She shivered, and I knew she was thinking that she might be facing the same dilemma someday if she stayed with Chase. The same one our father had faced by marrying our mother. I decided to avoid the pitfalls of navigating that land mine of a discussion and turned back to Iris.

"You really don't think Henry would mind working at the Indigo Crescent?"

Iris nodded. "I think he'd be glad to feel useful. He's a brilliant man, if a little geeky, and retirement hasn't agreed with him much."

"Call him today if he doesn't come into the store. Offer him twenty hours a week. Minimum wage plus five used books a week. Next order of business: pixies, demons, and Feddrah-Dahns. What is he doing, by the way?" I peered out the window, trying to catch a glimpse of the unicorn, but he wasn't anywhere in sight.

Iris held up one hand and bustled down the hall. We heard

the sound of the front door opening, then closing. "He's fine," she said as she returned. "He appears to be taking a little nap on the front lawn."

"We need to find that horn," I said. "That's a priority, because if the demons—or even a vamp or wayward Crypto—get hold of it, we're screwed. So I guess we'd better go pixie hunting first."

Delilah nodded, her mouth full of pancakes and honey.

"Then on to the rug shop to check out the djinn who was trying to get the lowdown on Menolly." I scribbled another note on my list. "Meanwhile, we try to figure out where the third spirit seal's hiding. That reminds me: time to try Morio again."

I picked up the phone and punched in his number. It rang seven times before the answering machine flipped on. I left a quick message, then dialed his cell. No answer there, either. A squiggle of fear churned in my stomach.

"I'm worried, guys. Morio should have contacted me last night. He was supposed to stay here, and he never showed up. I still can't get hold of him." I replaced the receiver, but it rang almost immediately. Glancing at the caller ID, I snatched it up. "Morio! Where the hell are you?"

His smooth, silken voice echoed over the line. "I'm all right. I'm sorry I didn't get in touch sooner, but I couldn't pick up a signal for my cell phone out where I was."

"What's going on? Why didn't you come over last night?"

"My car had a flat, and I forgot to put the spare back in last time I cleaned out the back. It took me awhile to catch a ride to the nearest service station where I could call AAA. By the time I got everything sorted out, I was just too tired to even think." He sounded distracted. "Besides, I needed to do some research after I got home. I called, but your answering machine didn't pick up."

Electronics often went on the fritz in our house; we'd already blown our way through a couple of microwaves and three phones in the past year. Something to do with all the erratic power, we thought. But then again, the house was old, and the wiring might not be what it ought to be.

"Research? What's going on?" Something was hanging in his voice, like a thundercloud about to break. "What happened?"

"I was talking to Grandmother Coyote, and she told me about a strange man she saw in her crystal ball. A man who claims to have visions of the future, ranting about the end of the

CHAPTER 10

Hunting pixies wasn't exactly child's play. When I was training with my magical mentors, they'd taught me how to charm a pixie, but that only worked about 50 percent of the time.

Back in OW, pixies were considered pests in the cities and, in fact, a few of the villages had banned them. Lethesanar hadn't gone that far, but they were fair game if they came inside the city limits.

For one thing, most pixies live to annoy. They love causing havoc and mischief; the cliché *pixie-led* wasn't yanked out of thin air. Pixies steal, pixies prod and poke and scatter their various dusts to cause havoc and, in general, are irritating little nuisances. I was surprised that Feddrah-Dahns had entrusted a valuable artifact to one, but then again, there was a first time for everything. Perhaps Mistletoe had gone astray of his nature.

We arrived at 10226 East Parkland Drive on the cusp of nine A.M. We'd brought both our cars in case we needed to run errands afterward. The clouds had parted, allowing a trickle of sun to pass, and everywhere the nubs on the budding trees sparkled where the light refracted through the raindrops that still clung to the branches.

The house was a small cottage type—very New England and

out of place in Seattle—set back off the street. The ever-present rhododendrons had been allowed to grow to tree height, and the creeping moss overshadowed the grass, turning the front yard into a wild place. Here and there, lady ferns clustered together in patches, fronds reaching waist high and taller. The cobbled path to the door was broken in spots, with weeds thrusting through the stones. Another path—this one dirt—branched off to the right, leading around the side of the house to what looked like a weathered picket fence. Rising in back of the house, twin maples towered up over the roof, one on either side of the yard.

I motioned to Delilah. "Come on, let's see if they're home."

We took the porch steps two at a time, and I knocked gently. Elves had fantastic hearing. I wouldn't need to pound on the door.

Sure enough, a moment later a lithe, willowy elf peeked through the screen. Her face lit up when she saw us. "Oh thank gods! You've come for the pixies!" Quickly, she stepped out to meet us and gestured to the yard. "See what they've done? No matter how hard we work, they're turning this place into a jungle."

Delilah and I glanced back at the front yard. From this vantage point, if I looked closely enough, I could see the telltale sparkle of residue pixie dust dappling the leaves and ground. Sure enough, they had an infestation, all right.

I turned back to the woman. "I'm Camille D'Artigo, and this is my sister, Delilah. You told my sister Menolly you have a strange pixie hanging around?"

She nodded, blushing. "I'm sorry, I should have introduced myself. I'm just so excited you're here! My name's Tish. Yes, we do have a new one hanging around, and the creature's causing an uproar. It was bad enough before, but he showed up last night, and now everybody's up in arms. I can't even step into the backyard without getting pixie bombed. My husband's in bed with a headache. He went out to try to dislodge the whole lot of them, and they ganged up on him."

While pixie magic wasn't terribly effective against the Fae, they could cause one hell of a headache if they sprinkled the right dust in your eyes. And with the natural animosity between elves and pixies, I had no doubt that both sides had been up to some nasty tricks.

"Why don't you show us to your backyard?"

As she led us down the porch steps and around the path

leading to the fence, she told us a bit about herself. "I came over Earthside first, two years ago, and my husband followed last year. We're studying human society for the Academy of Anthro-History, back in Elqaneve. I'm a healer, and my husband is a historian. When the Academy offered to send us Earthside to get in some hands-on study time, we agreed to a three-year term. I came over first, since I needed extra time to observe healing techniques here." She made a face.

"Something wrong?" I asked.

Tish nodded. "While their technology is brilliant, it's a sad state of affairs here. Far more die from hunger than back in Otherworld, although more die at home from disease than do here . . . at least in the civilized areas. There's so much potential to ease suffering here, but it's all caught up in warring ideologies and moralities. Tragic, really." She paused, opening the gate. "Right through here. Be careful—the dust is thick today."

As I passed through the gate, I saw what she meant. A layer of pixie dust covered everything, from the tiny lettuce seedlings that were just peeking out of the ground to the marble birdbath to the stone bench in the corner with a gargoyle-shaped crest in the center of the back.

Instinctively, I coughed and covered my nose. Delilah sniffed twice and then sneezed. Loud. With a sudden shimmer of color, she shouted, "Oh crap!" and shifted before I could stop her. It was a lot quicker than her usual transformation. Within seconds, a golden, long-haired tabby cat stared up at me, her eyes wide and confused.

Wonderful. Just what we needed. Tish sucked in a deep breath, covering her mouth with her fingers. "Oh! I'm sorry!"

"Yeah, that usually happens when we're under stress. There must be something in the pixie dust today that forced it," I said, reaching for Delilah. But she was in rare form, and she darted to the left as she saw me coming.

"Come here, Delilah! Now." I gave chase around the yard, jumping for her as she took a flying leap into one of the lilacs. She scrambled up above my reach. I tripped over a tree root, landing *splat* on my face in the damp moss.

"Hell's bells . . ." I pushed myself to a sitting position. My skirt had caught on the root, resulting in a small rip that threatened to spread. I was covered with a layer of pixie dust from head to toe. The shimmering powder glistened on my clothing and face, and I hoped to hell that I was immune to whatever effects it was enchanted to produce.

Trish raced over to my side and helped me up. "I'm sorry. Are you all right?"

I gingerly shook myself out. No broken bones, no bloodied knees or nose. I felt a little woozy from all the magical sparkles I'd been decorated with, but other than that . . . nada.

"I think so. Can you try to coax my sister out of the tree? I'm going to look for Mistletoe."

While Tish made chucking noises at Kitten, I began hunting through the overgrown foliage. Pixies could be hard to spot when they chose, and I had the feeling that Mistletoe was trying to keep well out of sight. The gang of pixies who had already marked their territory here were probably waiting for him to come out in the open so they could attack him and drive him off. Maybe calling him by name would work.

"Mistletoe! I've got a message from Feddrah-Dahns for you." I whistled, hoping to catch his attention. Sure enough, on the third try, there was a rustle from beneath a huckleberry bush, and out flitted a pixie. He was no bigger than a Barbie doll, but pale, almost translucent, flickering with specks of neon light. He flew up to look in my face. I slowly held out my hand, and he lighted on it, warily playing with the bag strapped to his side.

"What do you want?" he asked in Melosealfôr.

"I've come searching for you. Feddrah-Dahns is staying at my house, and he was worried about you. And the horn." I whispered the last. Elves were skilled in speaking Melosealfôr, and no way was I letting Tish find out what Mistletoe was carrying. Or what I *hoped* he was still carrying.

He settled down in my palm, his wings tickling me as he crossed his legs, his face suddenly serious. "I have what you seek, Lady. My Lord entrusted it to me, and I managed to retrieve it. But before I could get to him, the goblin came at me. I flew as fast as I could to hide my tracks and got lost. I fear they might be able to tap into my Whispering Spell and have been loathe to use it again."

I couldn't see anyplace on the pixie where he might be hiding a unicorn horn, at least not one larger than a toothpick. I was about to say as much when Tish wandered over, Delilah in her arms.

"I caught your sister." She blinked as she noticed Mistletoe.

He gave a little hiss when he saw her, but otherwise kept still. "I see you found him. Can you do something about the others? They're getting on my nerves, and pretty soon we're just going to have to move—which of course, they'd love."

"What am I, an exterminator?" I mumbled under my breath, but decided since Tish and her husband had done us a good turn, we owed them one. "Hold on." Turning back to Mistletoe, I leaned in. "Listen, I have to help this elf. Will you sit with my sister if I can get her to change back?"

He blinked, warily staring at Delilah's all-too-interested gaze. She looked like she was eying a giant chew toy. "Don't like cats. Cats eat pixies."

"Cats eat pixies, all right," I said, squinting at my sister. She was squirming as she watched Mistletoe move around in my palm. I leaned over and deposited him on a thick rhododendron branch. "Wait here."

Delilah clambered into my arms as I reached for her, her claws digging into my shoulder through the capelet. I petted her, calming her down, listening as her motor raced along with little huffs and sniffs. After a moment, I could feel the energy shift and quickly deposited her on the ground. More slowly than her first shift of the day, but still almost quicker than the eye could catch and in a cloud of mist and vapor, she returned to her normal form, her bright blue collar becoming her clothes. As she crouched on the ground, I reached down and took her hand, hauling her to her feet.

"Welcome back. Great gods, that looks like it hurts."

"Nope." She coughed, then spat out something that suspiciously looked like a greasy hairball. I grimaced. Couth, she was not. Being part cat meant fending off feline problems, including hairballs, fleas, and using a litter box.

"You okay?" I asked as she hacked out the last of it.

"Yeah. I sure didn't expect *that*. What's going on?" She looked around, saw Mistletoe, and clapped her hands. "Is that him? Did you find him?"

I nodded. "I want you to take him out front, keep him company while I dispatch the pixie problem back here. I promised Tish I'd at least give it a try."

"Hey, I'm not a problem," Mistletoe said in English as Delilah scooped him up and followed Tish to the gate, with the pixie protesting his innocence all the way. As she opened the gate, Tish gasped and jumped back as Morio pushed his way past her. He ignored her as he strode over to my side.

"You're late," I said. "We have a pixie infestation here. I promised the nice elf lady that I'd try to do something about it. What, I'm not sure. Most of my spells aren't meant for dispatching pests."

"I couldn't find my bag this morning and thought I lost it," Morio said, patting the black bag slung over his shoulder. He never went anywhere without it. The bag contained a skull that was his familiar. When he shifted into a fox, if he didn't have his skull nearby, he couldn't shift back. For his full-demon form, it wasn't so important. "Pixies, you say?"

I nodded. "Look at the residue dust they've left around the yard."

Morio's dark eyes gleamed. They shifted to topaz when he shifted into his natural form—his demon self. Lithe and compact, he was tightly muscled but neither tall nor bulky, and his long, sleek ponytail gleamed jet-black under the cool sun. Oh yeah, he was mighty fine. Mighty fine in bed, too. He had a way with his hands that was hard to match, even for Trillian. Both of my lovers managed to complement each other, and I was one hell of a grateful witch.

"I might be able to do something," he said.

Just then, a dart pierced the right side of my neck. On reflex, I slapped the sting and brought my hand away to find a tiny spear plastered to my skin. Giggling from the branches of a nearby maple gave away my attackers' positions. I spun around to find myself facing a row of five pixies, lined up on the branch like birds.

"Okay, knock it off!" Another titter brought another sharp sting to my left cheek. Sure enough, there in the hedgerow, another group of the pests were eyeing us, armed with a bevy of spears and darts. At least they looked uncomfortable; the hedge was holly, and the glossy leaves looked like they were poking into the pixies' backs.

Morio swung around and held out his hand. "Foxfire!"

A thick, green cloud of light spewed out of his hand toward the hedge. At first, the pixies just laughed, but then one shook his head and said something to the dude next to him. I couldn't hear what they were saying, but there was a sudden rush as they tried to vacate the branch before the vaporous cloud engulfed them.

I glanced up at the tops of the trees. The branches swayed in the wind, and I quickly summoned the currents of air to me, gathering the energy deep in my solar plexus, where I let it swirl and churn. Then it was a simple matter of aim, focus, and shoot.

Unfortunately, I'd managed to suck up a little more wind than I wanted to, and the resulting thrust of air not only knocked the pixies every which way but blew me off my feet. I went sailing backward through the yard to land hard with my back against the trunk of the maple. The shock froze me into place—for about thirty seconds.

The second *oops* came when I realized that I had landed off balance. I tried to catch my breath so I could right myself, but it just wasn't going to happen, and I crashed like tall timber, once again falling face-first in a patch of the pixie dust that coated everything.

Cripes, I thought, breathing the rich scent of wet, sour soil and pixie powder. I didn't want to *hurt them*, just shake them up. And I really didn't want to hurt myself. I wasn't a masochist.

As I sputtered, spitting out a blade of grass that had gotten stuck in my teeth, Morio helped me to my feet, a crooked smirk hiding behind his grin.

"You okay?"

For the second time in the past hour, I checked. No broken bones. No bloody knees or nosebleeds. "I'm wet and cold and muddy, but I'm okay." I glanced around, looking for the pixie brigade. "Where the hell are they?"

"I think you scared them. A few were blasted over the fence; the rest vanished. Wherever they went, you can bet we're not going to find them," he said. "Pixies may be annoying, but they aren't stupid."

"Yeah." I felt like grumbling but decided to quell the thought right there. I let out a long breath and looked at Morio. He looked good, though a bit tired. "Give me a kiss, babe."

Morio slid his left arm around my waist and casually drew me in, his lips curving around mine like they might be tasting a fine wine or an aged cheese: gently, with finesse, taking their time to explore every nook and cranny of the new flavor.

I leaned in for more. He was my *second*. My lover, my partner in magic, and also my friend. We stood silent, just lightly touching, as he sniffed my neck and trailed a chain of kisses down my bare chest, stopping where the bustier crested just above my nipples as it thrust my boobs up in a lovely decadence of cleavage.

"Trillian was called back to Otherworld," I whispered as his tongue explored my neck. "I'm afraid for him."

Rather than blow me off with a "He'll be all right," Morio pulled back. "He can't go. He's got a bounty on his head."

"I know," I said, staring past him at the hedgerow. "That's why I'm so frightened for him. There's something brewing. I can feel it, and Trillian's caught up in whatever's going on. Sometimes I wonder if he's been telling me the whole truth. If he isn't playing a bigger part than he lets on."

As I gazed at the unkempt bushes, I couldn't help but think of Father, and where he might be now. He'd deserted the Guard when Lethesanar turned them against her own people. My father was no coward nor a traitor. He was loyal to Court and Crown. But when the Crown abused her power, he'd stepped away and pledged his heart where it belonged—to the throne, not the madwoman who sat on it.

Morio let out a long sigh. "I don't know if this means anything, but a man came to my apartment looking for Trillian not long ago. I don't know why. Maybe he thought we room together or something. He wasn't human, but some kind of Fae. He insisted that he had to talk to Trillian. I wasn't sure who he was, and the man refused to give me his name, so I played dumb. I told Trillian about him the next morning, and he looked as though he'd seen a ghost when I described the man. He wouldn't speak of it after that."

I thought for a moment. "Earthside Fae or OW?"

"I don't know, but he wasn't dressed quite right. My guess is Otherworld."

"Then it could be a spy, come to track him down and kill him. Or someone from Tanaquar's army to give him an update. Whatever the case, Trenyth called in the middle of the night to order him back to OW." I shivered as the cloud cover closed in again, cutting off the sun. "Come, let's take Mistletoe home. So much has happened in the past twenty-four hours."

"And so much is about to happen, I fear." Morio wrapped his

arm around my shoulder and walked me to the gate. "The Degath Squads may have been our focal point the past few months, but there are demons aplenty living in the area who follow Shadow Wing." Degath Squads—or Hell Scouts—were Shadow Wing's vanguard.

"That's true," I said.

Morio sighed. "I'm very much afraid that they're planning something. Menolly should watch the bar carefully. The portal is well-known, and the demons are becoming bolder."

"And there are new portals, ones we know nothing about yet, and they are open targets for the enemy." As we returned to the front yard, I noticed that Tish was sitting on the front steps, talking to Delilah. Mistletoe was sitting on Kitten's other side, pointedly ignoring the elf.

"Don't talk about this in front of Tish or Mistletoe. Not till we get home," I said. "Feddrah-Dahns knows about the Demonkin; that's why he sent me the . . . gift that he did. But we have to watch what we say when we're out in public."

I turned to Tish and, with a beaming smile that I didn't feel, said, "We did what we could. I think we ran them off, but you never can tell when it comes to pixies. We'll take Mistletoe with us."

Delilah stood and dusted the butt of her jeans. "We're good to go, then?"

I nodded. "As ready as we'll ever be. Mistletoe, would you prefer to ride with Delilah or with me?"

The pixie glared at Delilah, then sniffed as he gave me the once-over. "I'll go with you, my Lady. I don't fancy riding with a cat."

Delilah gave a little hiss, laughing when he jumped. "Get a grip. I've never once changed while I was driving. Promise and cross my heart."

Mistletoe let out a choked gulp. "That hiss doesn't lend confidence, you know. Very well, I'll ride with you, but you have to behave. I mean it—one misstep, and His Royal Majesty will run you through. I'm a valuable member of the court!"

Delilah put on a straight face as she scooped him up and deposited him on the passenger seat of her Jeep. "I'm sure you are, M'Lord Mistletoe. I'm sure you are."

Morio followed me in his Subaru. As we headed home, I couldn't help but wonder how things were going to shake out.

Cryptos were everywhere now, far fewer than the human population of course, but they seemed brighter, shinier, louder. They stood out. It looked like the Freedom's Angels had already decided to start their own private war. Now, all we needed was for Shadow Wing's armies to begin their invasion.

CHAPTER 11

By the time we got home, Feddrah-Dahns was munching his way through a patch of tall grass that Iris had set him on. It would save her the trouble of weeding and give him a nice spot of lunch. He told us she'd left for the shop, along with Maggie, so it was just Delilah, Morio, Mistletoe, and me. And the unicorn. Feddrah-Dahns's eyes lit up when he caught sight of the pixie, and Mistletoe flittered over to land on the horned beast's shoulder.

I motioned toward them. "Inside, guys. We have matters to discuss that are better off kept secret." I closed my eyes, feeling for the wards that I kept tight around our land and house. Sure enough, they were still holding. Thanks to Morio, that is. He'd reinforced my work, strengthening my magic where it was weak, shoring it up where it lagged.

Once we were in the living room, I introduced Morio to Feddrah-Dahns. Feddrah-Dahns looked him over carefully, his nostrils flaring. "Demon child, but not unsavory," the unicorn finally said. "You would like the plains of the Windwillow Valley. It's vast and wide, and there are many of your kind there, fox-child."

Morio blinked. "Youkai, in Otherworld?"

"You truly don't believe your kind is limited to this world, do you?" Feddrah-Dahns blinked. "Think—you walk between worlds. Isn't it possible Earth isn't your only domain?"

As he sank into the recliner, Morio leaned back, a pensive expression on his face. "I hadn't really thought of the possibility. My parents won't speak of their history much. My mother learned to be secretive when *her* mother was killed by warriors who considered her fair game. Mother and Grandfather—who was wounded trying to save my grandmother—escaped. Grandfather took her to live with his sister."

I stared at him. He'd never told me about this. "Your mother must have a great fear of humans then."

He shook his head. "No, she blames only the men who killed her mother. But to this day my grandfather hates FBHs. Now, my father has good reason to hate humans, but he and my mother are much alike."

"What happened?" I asked, eager to know more. Morio seldom spoke of his childhood or relatives, and any time he was willing to open up, I was willing to listen.

"Father watched his entire family put to death by a feudal land owner during the middle of the Ashikaga shogunate. Even though two centuries passed before he grew to manhood and married Mother, the fear's still there. My parents taught me to keep my bloodline secret unless I'm called upon by Grandmother Coyote to reveal who I am. They don't blame humans as a whole . . . but . . ."

Hell, what a memory to carry. I reached out and took his hand. "Why Grandmother Coyote? Just what is your connection to her? You've never explained it before."

He glanced at the unicorn and pixie, then at me. "Grandmother Coyote rescued Yoshiro, my father. He was hiding in the woods, and he watched as his parents and siblings were slaughtered. Grandmother Coyote happened to come wandering by. She took my father home with her—she has a portal over in Japan as well as one here—and raised him as her son."

"Your father grew up with Grandmother Coyote?" The thought sent shivers down my back. Delilah was staring at him, mouth open, hand poised over the Fritos package.

"Good gods," she blurted out. "Your father had one of the Hags of Fate for a stepmother? I'm amazed he made it to adulthood alive."

Morio grinned. "It taught him resilience. After a few years, Grandmother Coyote decided to return to North America, and she entrusted his care to Kimiko, the woman who became his godmother. Kimiko's a local nature spirit over in Japan. She rules over the area's devas and flower spirits. She taught Father how to use his powers, and she's the guardian spirit to whom our family pays respect and tribute. But my father owes Grandmother Coyote his life. He would have surely died without her intervention. We honor her requests. Always."

He gave me a little smile, and I suddenly understood a lot more about my demon lover and his sense of loyalty.

I thought about our own grandparents, who had paid scant attention to us because we were half-human. We seldom saw them, and last I heard, they'd died in a freak drowning accident or something. Father didn't exactly cozy up about them, since they'd rejected the love of his life.

"Grandmother Coyote really *is* like a grandmother to you. I imagine she doesn't bake chocolate chip cookies, though."

Morio snorted. "Not likely. And I'd never call her *Grandma*. Trust me on that one."

I made sure Feddrah-Dahns was comfortable, then sat down on the ottoman in front of Morio. He rested his arms around my shoulders, and I leaned back to look into his face as he lightly pressed his lips against mine. Though we were barely touching, the heat between us inflamed me from head to toe.

Trillian's passion was a powder keg, exploding when we came into contact. Morio's was molten lava, running slowly through my veins. His dark eyes were tinged with flecks of golden topaz that took over when he was in full demon form. As always happened when we linked energy, I fell into the deep abyss of magic that beckoned, and the energy between us began to swirl.

"Ahem," Delilah said as she cleared her throat. "When you two decide to join us, maybe we can get on with this talk?"

I grinned. "Sorry, I was just . . ."

"Never mind," she said with a wry grin. "I know what you were thinking. Can we just get on with it?"

I straightened my shoulders. "I suppose so. First things first. Mistletoe, are you okay? Were you hurt when those thieves chased you?"

The pixie shook his head. "No. As I told your sister in the car, I'm fine, M'Lady."

He certainly had better manners than most pixies I'd met. In fact, the majority were rough, crude, loutish types. "Do you still have the horn?" I asked, not wanting to appear too eager. But I couldn't deny it—I desperately wanted to see the thing.

Mistletoe nodded. "Aye, I do. Your Majesty, should I retrieve it now?" He knelt on Feddrah-Dahns's shoulder.

"Yes, my friend, and give it to Camille. She has the strength and fortitude to wield it, even if she doubts herself," the unicorn added, staring into my eyes. We locked gazes, and it was as if he were able to reach deep down into my heart and witness my fears and self-doubt.

Mistletoe whistled a long note, one that sounded like a silver flute. He leapt off of Feddrah-Dahns's back and lightly fluttered to the floor and opened his bag. I watched, curious as to where he was going to produce the horn from. It was then that I noticed a vortex forming inside the bag. He reached into the swirling blend of colors, and when he withdrew his hand, he was holding a velvet box.

"Very clever," I said. "You hid it in an interdimensional portal."

"I wish I'd done the same when my Liege first entrusted it into my care," the pixie said, blushing. His skin was mint-green, and the red tinge to his cheeks lit him up like a Christmas tree. "I made a sore mistake and can only hope to work my way into His Majesty's confidence again."

I blinked. He didn't sound pompous, even though he spoke in archaic syntax. "Have you been Earthside before, Mistletoe?"

He shook his head. "No. I learned to speak English when a mortal man wandered through a portal accidentally. He arrived in the Windwillow Valley well over one hundred Earthside years ago, and His Majesty gave him protection. He was a budding poet, and he stayed for awhile until we were able to return him back to his home. Since then, I've spoken with a few Fae who travel back and forth between the realms."

I blinked. One hundred years ago, a man had slipped through the veils to land in Otherworld and take his place beside the Crown Prince of the Dahns unicorns. "What a shock that must have been for the poor guy."

"Actually," Feddrah-Dahns spoke up, "he was neither shocked

nor terrified. In fact, he was delighted, and it took everything we had to convince him to go home again. I would have let him stay, but Arachnase the Weaver insisted he be returned Earthside. Apparently William Butler had a part to play in destiny here and could not be allowed to stay in Otherworld, or the balance would be thrown out of synch."

"Here," Mistletoe said, handing me the velvet box. "Be cautious when you open it. The horn is powerful and can easily suck you in if you aren't prepared for the blast of energy."

I stared at the box. Resting in my hands, I held one of the rarest artifacts in Otherworld. Treasure hunters had sought the shed horns through the years, some dying in their pursuit of the legendary wealth. A thousand mages would give anything to be in my shoes, and some of them weren't very friendly. In fact, a number of them, if they knew that I possessed such a gift, would gladly blow me to pieces in order to steal it.

Inhaling deeply, I set the case on my lap and slowly opened the lid. A shimmering cloth came into view, woven of spun gold. There was a small fortune in itself, both here and at home in OW. Delilah gasped and leaned in closer to watch. Morio's eyes went wide, and he rested one hand against the small of my back to steady me.

As I quietly unfolded the cloth, my fingers begin to tingle. Then my hand. Then my whole body set up a reverberation that felt like it was going to shake my teeth loose. Shivering, I stared at the horn that rested in the folds of the wrap. The spire was a good eighteen inches long, made of solid, diamond-hard crystal, with threads of gold and black and silver encased within, like rutile needles caught in a quartz crystal ball. It resonated, humming a long, low note, and I hesitantly reached for it, waiting for it to strike out, to char my hand.

"Take it," Feddrah-Dahns said. "It's calling for you."

I closed my eyes and listened. There—on the wind, a faint voice. I couldn't catch the words, they were alien and distant, but the invitation echoed in my heart, in my soul, in the quicksilver glow of the Moon Mother's tattoo on my left shoulder blade where I'd been branded during my rite of passage. The horn wanted me as much as I wanted it.

As my fingers slid around the cool crystal spire, the night of my initiation flooded back full force, and once again, I found myself standing in the grotto where I'd made my oaths and consigned my soul to the Moon Mother for life.

The moon was high and golden and full, pregnant with the promise of magic. I'd trained rigorously for years until now, on my night of Claiming, when my mentors debated whether I should be allowed to take the oath.

"She'll never progress beyond this point," Lyrical said. "Let her leave the city and remain a minor witch."

Lyrical had always been my foil, my nemesis. Her tasks were always set just a little too hard, her demands always a little too impossible. Nothing I could do pleased her, and I'd cried myself to sleep a hundred times, her stinging insults ringing in my ears.

Nigel shook his head. "I think there's more than meets the eye to our Camille." My primary teacher and mentor, he had been just as hard on me as Lyrical, but not nearly so harsh. "It may take time, but she'll travel farther than you or I ever will. She'll fight harder, take on adversaries far greater than we dream of."

He put his hands on my shoulders and stared into my eyes. "Camille, listen to me. You're a leader with an Achilles' heel. You'll always be flawed, but your courage will do much to supplement your lack of ability. Don't be afraid to let the Moon Mother take you over when she calls. Accept her help when she offers it, even if that help comes from unexpected quarters. I cast my vote for allowing you to take the oath."

I remained silent. Lesson number one: *the student must not speak unless directly asked a question*. This was the way it had always been, and the way it would always be.

Tonight, the Coterie of the Moon Mother would either allow me to pledge oath and come into my own, or they'd turn me away in dishonor. There was no middle ground. Students either made it or they didn't.

Those who didn't pass the test usually left Y'Elestrial in disgrace to wander the countryside until they came to a village offering food and lodging in exchange for minor magic, often supplementing the work done by the healers and guardians of the towns.

More often than not, the outcasts led quiet, unassuming lives. Never again were they allowed to enter the temples of the

Moon Mother, though most sang praises to her in private on the nights when she was hanging full and round.

Mees-Mees, the third member of the Coterie, pushed herself out of her chair. "One for, and one against. Rarely do we have ties. Usually an acolyte's abilities speak for themselves. Therefore, you must go before the High Priestess for final adjudication." Mees-Mees wasn't allowed to vote. She was the mediator, forced to permanently reside in limbo with regards to her opinions.

Nigel let out a thin whistle. "Perhaps it's best this way. The High Priestess will be able to see the girl's heart and soul far clearer than you or I, Lyrical. She'll know what the Moon Mother wants."

Lyrical scowled and turned away. "I warn you, we'll be sorry if the half-breed is given the oath. *Half-Fae*, indeed. I'm surprised she's come this far."

I forced myself to keep my mouth shut. I'd blow my chances completely if I tried to defend my honor or my family.

"Derisa is the best choice," Mees-Mees said. "The girl won't feel put upon if rejection is the decree. Nor will there be any call by her father to claim prejudice."

Great. As if I couldn't hear every word they said. But I knew better than to do what I wanted, which was to blurt out, "Excuse me, but I'm right here, people." Maybe I did go off half-cocked at times, but now wasn't going to be one of them.

Mees-Mees wiggled her finger at me. "Follow me."

Without another word, she turned and swiftly strode toward the temple. I followed as fast as I could, but we didn't go in. Instead, we hurried past the gleaming marble walls as we made our way around back to where a small, unobtrusive cottage sat on the outskirts of the forest.

Mees-Mees held up her hand. "Wait here." She entered the cottage, leaving me alone.

I glanced up at the moon. "Don't forsake me," I whispered to the glittering orb. "Don't turn me away. Please." My entire life had been focused on two things: becoming a witch pledged to the Moon Mother, and taking care of my sisters since our mother had died. I was doing all right on the latter task, but wasn't up to snuff on the former. Even if I did manage to pledge in the Moon Mother's service, I seriously doubted I'd ever make priestess.

After a moment, Mees-Mees reappeared. Teribeka followed

behind her. Teribeka was one of the oldest priestesses to the Moon Mother, and one of the strongest. She'd been passed over for the spot of High Priestess, though, and no one ever knew why.

"I hear you are destined to visit the grove," Teribeka said, waving at Mees-Mees, who abruptly departed, returning the way we'd come.

I swallowed. Damn it, if only Lyrical had given in and agreed with Nigel, I'd be taking my oath and then spending the night on my first Hunt.

"Yes," I said, suddenly nervous. So much was riding on to-night.

But to my surprise, the old witch just smiled. "Then we'd best hurry, girl. We can't keep the High Priestess waiting."

The High Priestess of the Moon Mother cared for nothing but to serve the will of the Lady. Her only vows were to the Moon herself, and to the Moon Mother she'd pledged her life and her death. She was the gateway to the goddess.

As Teribeka prepared me for the journey, the stars clustered thickly overhead, raining down showers of sparkling light. I licked my lips, staring up at the ancient orb, feeling the weight of the metal as Teribeka bound an engraved belt around my waist, then fastened my hands with silver chains and cuffs behind my back.

She glanced at the sky. "I feel her pull, too," was all she said, but her words steadied me. I flashed her a wary smile as we started down a woodland path from the cottage. As we crept among the trees, the night air was rife with the sounds of whistling birds and feral cats that padded silent through the foliage, prowling on their hunt.

When we approached the entrance of the Grove, Teribeka stood back. "I can go no farther, child. This is a solitary journey, and you must go forward alone into Derisa's garden."

She paused, then placed a gentle hand on my arm. "Think long and hard before you set foot on this path. If the High Priestess Derisa approves, and you kneel before the Goddess this night, your life will never again belong to you. Your heart and soul will be bound inexorably to the Moon."

I glanced at the orb overhead, listening to the breath of the forest. My breast rose and fell to the woodland's rhythm.

"I don't have a choice," I said. "The Moon Mother called me when I was born. There is no other way." I rattled the chains binding my wrists. "My shackles to her are far heavier and stronger than these will ever be."

Teribeka nodded. "Then think before you speak. Death is less terrifying than the wrath of gods. The High Priestess holds the light of the Lady in her hands, and both she and the Moon Mother reward stupidity with a swift and painful death. The Moon not only watches over the night, but she is the forest incarnate. She is the Light Mother of sparkling magic, and she's the Dark Huntress who leads the pack. She *will* devour you should you stumble."

I forced my feet forward. The branches and decaying leaf detritus clutched at my ankles as if to call out, *Stop, don't go!* but I kicked it away. As I came to the line of trees guarding the entrance to the Grove, I recognized both oak and willow—strength and intuition.

Pushing through the foliage, I paused to rest my forehead against the gnarled bark. The ancient sentinels of the Grove towered so old, so wide that within their crevices they held the bodies of priestesses from ages past, curled in burial repose. Ivory bones gleamed from the voids hollowed in the trunks. Instinct spurring me on, I curtsied at each grave, paying respect to the lineage that had spawned the Moon Mother's order.

Past the sentinels stood an arched trellis, tightly cloaked in wild roses twining up the stone arc. Wisteria draped from the curved ceiling, pregnant and lush. The scent was heady, intoxicating with a hint of decay curling the edges.

The weight of my chains grew stronger with each step. Would I end up permanently scarred? Blistered from the cold fire of the silver? Or was it merely a reminder that I was near the Grove?

The wind fell to a whisper as I entered the Moon Mother's domain.

Hewn of an ancient oak, fashioned by hands long dead, the great throne of the High Priestess was inset with emeralds and peridot, garnets and moonstone. Polished arms wrapped Derisa in their embrace, curving like some great dragon's feet, and iridescent scales of metal covered the back of the seat against which she rested her head. Sprawled in the throne, a booted leg thrown over the arm, the High Priestess of the Moon remained silent until I approached.

And then she stood. Her silhouette cast a tall shadow against the backdrop of moonlight. Clad in a plum and black silken tunic with breeches and boots, she was dressed for the Hunt, and a nimbus of lavender fire surrounded her, her aura crackling with magic. Dark she was, and beautiful, with tumbling black hair that reached her knees and waxen skin so incredibly pale that it mirrored the moonlight. Her eyes sparked with cold fire as she inspected me, her gaze slicing to the bone.

My knees buckled, and I found myself kneeling on the ground, forehead touching the soil at the foot of the throne.

Derisa stepped down and gently prodded me in the side with one booted toe. "Lyrical recommends we cast you out, Nigel that we take your oath. What do you say? If the need arises, are you truly prepared to forsake your family, forsake your life, forsake even your soul?"

Her voice swept past on a gust of wind as her lilting words wove into my heart and took hold, sucking me under. I looked up, terrified. And yet I managed to meet her gaze.

"The Moon Mother called me when I was a child," I whispered. "This is the only path I've ever wanted to walk. I need her—I can't ignore her summons."

Derisa hesitated, then knelt beside me. She reached out and, fingers resting under my chin, lifted my head to look me straight in the eye. My trembling stopped. She alone would decide my fate, she and the Moon Mother. Fear slipped away like a snake shedding its skin, and I inhaled deeply as I gazed into her beautiful face.

After a long, long while she spoke, and this time her words were soft. "Lyrical says you may be lacking in talent. This is true, although perhaps it's simply that your talent goes astray at times. But Nigel speaks the truth as well. Camille Sepharial te Maria, the Moon Mother sees into your heart and soul and finds it clear. You are both true and brave, half-breed or not. Come, child, stand and face me."

I stood.

Derisa leaned close. "The Moon Mother has answered. She will accept you into her service. I ask you once more before you take the oath and there's no turning back: Will you give yourself over to her, to do with as she sees fit?"

I nodded, catching a whiff of lilacs and lemon from her perfume. "Oh yes," I said breathlessly. "I'll swear my life to her. And my death."

"Then I will accept your oath. Listen well, girl, and answer." She motioned for me to stand and, as I did, the silver chains clinked delicately, and a breeze rose up, gusting wildly around us.

"Camille Sepharial te Maria, do you of your own will and volition come to the service of the Moon Mother as one of her witches, pledging yourself to *her*, above everything you hold sacred, including your life and breath?"

My heart began to beat. This was it; I was going to be oath-bound to the Moon Mother, and everything in my life would be set. Nothing would ever again worry me as long as I held the Huntress of the Moon in my heart and soul.

"Yes, oh yes, I swear my oath."

"Camille Sepharial te Maria, do you accept the yoke of the witch, knowing that you chance never seeing the robes of a priestess, that you will never be free to pledge another goddess, that your spirit will forever be bound and belong to no other gods save the Moon Mother as long as you walk the world in this body?"

I could barely breathe. Derisa's voice sounded like it was coming from a million miles away, and I began to soar out of my body, my heart echoing the staccato beat of a thousand drums.

"I do swear by my oath."

Then, the questions came quickly, so quick I could barely think.

Camille Sepharial te Maria, will you live for the Moon Mother . . .

I do swear . . .

Will you heal for the Moon Mother . . .

I do swear . . .

Will you kill for the Moon Mother . . .

I do swear . . .

Will you die for the Moon Mother . . .

"I do swear by my oath." The gusts grew chill and brisk as the High Priestess reached out and pushed away the shoulder of my gown. It fell open, exposing my breast, and she brushed my hair to the right and pressed her palm against my back, on the left shoulder blade.

A bolt of lightning crossed the starlit sky and struck Derisa, burning through her arm, through her palm, into my back. The shock, as cold as Hel's frozen realms, ate into me, and I clamped my teeth shut, repressing a scream as I trembled against the pain. The energy was sentient, moving, a trail of frozen teeth gobbling a thin line of flesh. It filled the raw channel on my shoulder blade with liquid silver as it spiraled into a coiled tattoo of a labyrinth.

I gasped but held steady until the branding was done. Derisa pulled me into her arms, and her lips sought mine. As she kissed me, her tongue flickering against mine in a passionate welcome, the chains binding my hands fell away, and the belt dropped to the ground. With one movement, the High Priestess stripped me bare of my gown, leaving me naked and shivering in the moonlight.

Gasping, I stretched out my arms, feeling the cold light of my Lady as it poured into me, filled my veins, oozed through my body like slow honey. Laughter began to echo through the Grove, and I felt dizzy with power as the Moon Mother seduced me. Derisa pulled me into her arms and kissed me again, leisurely, slowly, her hands drifting over my body.

"Welcome, newest Daughter of the Moon," she whispered.

I caught my breath as it fully hit me: I was forever pledged to the Lady. Her will was my own. "I belong to her . . ." I said, unable to keep the joy out of my voice.

Derisa flashed me a feral smile, her eyes wickedly happy. I said nothing. What could I say? My world had changed forever, and I could only lean my head back to gaze up at the sky, nestled within the embrace of the High Priestess.

And then, a faint noise began to echo within the back of my head. *The Moon Mother was whispering to me.*

And then the whispers became a thunderous tumult—a cacophony of poetry and song. I felt myself teeter on the edge of chaos. *She* was calling me. Into the woods, to run with her. Into the woods, to join the Hunt, to race with the wild pack across the sky. I could see them: hounds and hares, bears and panthers, warriors and hunters long dead, and wild witches who had eons ago given their oath to the Lady of the Night. And at their helm, the Moon Mother herself led the chase, a silhouette of silver fire with bow slung over her shoulder, fierce and howling through the velvet night.

"Come play with us . . . come run with us . . ." the voices beckoned.

With a frantic cry, I looked up at Derisa and saw that she, too, was heeding the call. She reached for my hand, and I

placed it in hers, trusting her, trusting the Moon Mother. As
Derisa's fingers closed around my palm, we were suddenly
aloft, caught up by the Hunt. Caught in the wake of the chase
that crossed the sky every month when the moon was full, we
leapt onto the astral—body and soul—and went spiraling into
the sky, watched over by our giant, brilliant Goddess who gazed
down from the heavens.

Everything blurred except the passion for the chase, the
drive to seek and catch those who belonged to the night. As
reason bled away from my soul, the silver light of moon magic
welled up in my heart, and I let go of my last worry, my last
fear, and gave myself over forever and always to the Moon
Mother.

CHAPTER 12

~⟨≈⟩~

"Camille? Camille?" Delilah's voice jolted through my thoughts. I shook my head, dazed. The unicorn horn was back in its box, which was still on my lap, and Kitten was shaking my shoulders. "Are you all right?"

I blinked, trying to sort out my thoughts. "I guess so. Apparently, I decided to take an unexpected trip down memory lane. How long was I out?"

Morio glanced at his watch. "Six minutes. At first we thought you were communing with the energy of the horn, but when you let out a squeal and put the horn back in the box, I figured that you'd checked out."

A squeal, huh? Delightful. At my most mystical, I was an intimidating and beautiful sight. I knew it was true, so why bother denying it? However, it would seem this hadn't been one of those times.

"I guess my mind decided it needed a vacation." Inhaling deeply, I savored the awareness a lungful of oxygen brought to my thoughts. Breathing did wonders for the brain.

"I think I jumped into something far deeper than a trance. Unless I miss my guess, I stepped out of time, bilocated, and whisked myself back to my initiation night," I said, letting out a delicate cough. "I could swear I just relived the entire evening—but six minutes? Not quite enough time for that."

"The horn didn't harm you, did it?" Feddrah-Dahns's eyes flickered.

"Harm me? No, not at all." I cautiously reached for the crystal again. "I just wasn't prepared for the intensity of its energy. That crystal spire packs quite a wallop. The shock sent me looping back to . . . to another time in my life when another great power took hold of me."

Took hold of me, sank in her teeth, and never let go.

As I reached for the horn, it occurred to me that it might be sentient. I could sense stray thoughts and emotions emanating from the spire, and they sure as hell weren't grounded to anybody else in the room.

I raised my finger to my lips, motioning for everyone to hush as I reached deep with my aura, rooting my energy into the soil and branch and root and twig that lay just outside our door. Though I was no earth witch, I communed just fine with the forests and plants. Their mana would keep me centered.

Once I was prepared, I gently wrapped my hand around the horn and lifted it out of the box again.

This time, when the sweeping range of power swept over me, I was able to keep myself afloat. When I started to flounder in the sea of energy, I forced myself to focus on the horn in my hand, on the chair on which I was sitting, on Feddrah-Dahns and Mistletoe and Delilah and Morio, all of whom watched me anxiously.

And then I heard a distant call, so far away I couldn't even begin to place it. I closed my eyes and let go, following the summons.

I blinked. I was sitting in a meadow filled with apple trees and wild honeysuckle and grass so long it tickled my knees. Inhaling sharply, the taste of plum and jasmine hit my tongue. The horn was in my lap, and a shower of apple blossoms rained gently over my shoulder.

"What the—" I stood. Where the hell was I now? I'd recognized my initiation night, but this . . . I'd never been here before. Never even seen this meadow. I had no idea if I was in Otherworld or Earthside, though I suspected I'd been yanked back to Otherworld, because the woods felt more genteel.

The sound of a tinkling voice rang so faint that I almost missed it, and something tickled my hand next to the horn. I glanced down to see a tiny man standing there, holding onto the side of the spire. He was about six inches tall and reminded me of an oak deva, with deeply tanned skin and rich green clothing. Only he was much smaller than any of the tree devas I'd met over the years.

"Who . . . what . . . you can't be the . . ." I stopped, realizing I had no idea what to say next.

He gazed up at me, a long, luxurious look from behind a tiny fringe of eyelashes. "I'm the guardian of the horn."

The guardian of the horn? Well, I'd thought it might be sentient. This just proved I was at least half right. "What's your name?"

"You will either earn my name, or you will not, depending on what happens. If you earn my name, then you may wield the horn and control its powers." He grinned then, and I saw that he had really sharp teeth. I backtracked really fast.

"Are you a djinn?"

He shrugged, his expression noncommittal. "No. Now, answer me this: am I telling you the truth?"

Great, a jokester. But as I studied his face, I realized he was anything but joking. "I have no idea," I said after a moment. I couldn't read his energy, couldn't really even read his aura. He didn't smell of demon, but he sure wasn't run-of-the-mill Fae.

"Since you don't have a clue as to whether I'm lying, why did you bother to ask? Not too bright, I'd say." He leaned back against the horn and crossed his arms and began to whistle some aimless tune.

I frowned, more at his attitude than what he said. After all, he was right. Asking if he was a djinn had been stupid. If he was one, then he'd probably just lie to me. Djinns weren't inherently evil, but they *were* dangerous, and they delighted in causing havoc. And if he wasn't one, well, that didn't ensure that he was telling the truth.

Glancing around, I asked, "So, where are we? Otherworld?"

The spirit lithely jumped off my hand, onto the box. He sat

down, cross-legged, and leaned back on his hands. "No, not really. And yet, we aren't Earthside, either."

"The astral?"

"No."

He was seriously starting to tick me off. "Listen, bud, I don't have time for guessing games. I don't watch *Jeopardy!*, and I don't play Twenty Questions. So knock it off and tell me what I need to know."

"You don't have much patience, do you?" He jumped off the box and down to the ground. Within seconds, he was cloaked in a puff of green smoke. When the cloud dissipated, he was standing there, seven feet tall and grinning. He held out his hand, and I hesitantly took it, allowing him to help me up. I kept hold of the horn, though. No way was he getting it. Maybe he wasn't a djinn, maybe he really was the guardian of the horn. But either way, I'd be stupid to hand over the artifact to him. It might free him from service, and that could cause one hell of a headache.

"Patience is for those who have the luxury of not being chased by a bunch of demons." I pulled my hand away the moment I was on my feet. The meadow seemed overly bright, and I had trouble seeing very far, even when I shaded my eyes from the brilliant light flooding the lea. The smell of newly mown grass wafted by on the breeze, and the warmth of the sun on my skin made me want to lie right back down and go to sleep. I yawned. "I'm beginning to feel pixie led," I said. "You aren't a pixie, are you?"

"No." He shrugged again. "Don't worry yourself over time. We're outside of it, so this little interlude won't intrude on your schedule. Now, stand here for a moment." He motioned for me to stay where I was, and before I could blink, had receded to the far side of the field.

One minute I stood, holding the horn, wondering what the hell was going on. The next moment, a bolt of lightning came sailing my way, darting like a rocket on steroids. A seriously fry-your-ass-to-a-crispy-critter rocket.

Before I could think about it, I instinctively raised the horn and focused on trying to shield myself, because in the split second I had left, there was no way I could dodge the hundred-million-volt wake-up call barreling my way.

"Dissipate!" As I spoke, a wavering barrier shot up between me and the burst of Electric Death. There was a loud crash, and the concussion knocked me off my feet, back a good two yards to land hard on my butt. But the barrier did its work, and the lightning discharged, harmlessly reaming into the ground.

As I lay there staring at the worms that wriggled to the surface, shocked by the sudden intrusion into their domain, I couldn't help but think that perhaps I'd made a teensy mistake by accepting Feddrah-Dahns's offer of help.

The spirit was instantly at my side. "You seem to have handled that in good fashion. Here, let me help you up."

I ignored his hand and pushed myself to my feet, wavering as a ripple of dizziness ran through me. "What the *fuck* were you trying to do? You could have killed me." Eyeing him warily, I checked myself over to make sure nothing was broken or singed.

"I had to test you. Very few can command the power of the horn, and I'm bound to keep it away from those with whom it won't resonate." His voice was so calm that it only inflamed my outrage.

"And just what would have happened if I'd been one of the majority who can't wield the horn? What then, pray tell?" My shock was wearing off. Not a good thing for my wannabe Ben Franklin dude. He'd better make tracks and fast.

He shrugged again. "You would have died."

I stood, rooted to the spot. My jaw refused to close for a moment. Finally, I shut my mouth as a dragonfly zipped a little too close for comfort. I jammed my finger against his chest. Hard. "*Died?* You would have *really* let me die?" Again, the casual nod as if I'd just asked him if he liked potato salad. "What would have happened to my body since, according to you, we're standing outside of time?"

"Heart attack." Again, the stupid grin.

Oh cripes. Why worry about Smoky accidentally frying me when I had this miscreant to turn me into witch-on-a-stick? Magical creature be damned! I slammed both my hands against his chest, catching him off guard and sending him stumbling back.

"*Who* the fuck do you think you are? This is your idea of a test? Hell's whiskers! *Gee, let's give her a chance—a slim chance—if she can't wield the horn, we'll just toast her right up?* I got news for you, dude. I don't taste that good with butter and jam!"

Riled but good, I clenched my fists and stepped toward him, ready to deck him one. "What the hell is your name, anyway? Since I passed the test and can control the horn, you'd damned well better tell me what it is and what sort of creature you are, or so help me, I'll gouge your goddamn eyes out."

He coughed and straightened his vest. "Get a grip. You aren't hurt. Not if you're acting like this." At my growl, he held up both hands in surrender and jumped back. "Okay, okay! I'm a jindasel."

I blinked. This was a new one. "Say what?"

"A jindasel. We're not very well-known. You were right, in a way. We are similar to the djinn; however, we're created from the spirit of another being—usually one of great power—to be used as guardians. And usually, the object we're set to guard was, at one time, part of our originator's body. Perhaps a preserved hand and arm, or—as in this case—the horn of the Black Unicorn." He caught his breath while I pondered this. "My name is Eriskel."

Unsure of just what to say, I cleared my throat. "A jindasel named Eriskel. How . . . poetical." It struck me that, if he was created from the spirit of the Black Beast . . . "So you're actually siphoned off of the Black Unicorn's spirit? Do you share your creator's thoughts?"

"Not exactly." Eriskel looked intrigued. "No one's really ever asked much about my existence before. It might help to think of me as a minor incarnation of the Black Unicorn. He gave me my own sentience. While I live to serve and obey him, he allows me some independence."

A thought crossed my mind. *The Monkey's Paw . . . The Hand . . .* were they guarded by creatures like this one? Stories horrific and—I had thought—fictional. But now, I wondered. Were these tales based on some knowledge of the jindasel? And the Black Unicorn, was he friend or foe?

"Will you always take this form?"

"Only when you summon me." Eriskel shook his head. "Now that you've learned my name, you can call me forth from the horn. If you abuse the power, I will destroy you. If you give away the horn, I will test the one to whom you offer it. But be aware—this artifact has limitations. It is not infinite, and it must recharge itself under the dark of the moon every month to retain its power. If you use it too often, the horn will forsake you."

"Then you would have destroyed the bugbear and goblin who stole it, wouldn't you?" That would have been quite a shocker for them. Their thievery would have been in vain, if they'd tried to keep the horn for their own use.

"Aye, if their powers were no greater than mine. I'm not invincible, however. Any greater demon—or even some of the lesser ones—would put up a strong fight against me."

I stared at the crystal spire, cool in my palm. "What can I do with this against the demons?"

Here, Eriskel flashed me an enigmatic smile. "Much . . . but exactly *what* is for you to discover. I can't give you all the answers, because I don't know all of them. And some, I'm sworn to protect. Only those truly worthy of the power will find the way to use it. Or those who can torture it out of the horn."

Our eyes met, and I knew when he said that, he meant "torture it out of me." Eriskel was vulnerable against the darker forces we faced. If I lost the horn to the demons, chances are he'd be destroyed in their quest to assume control over it. Which meant I needed to guard it as safely as I could. Another life resting on my shoulders.

I held up the box. "Should I store it in here?"

He shook his head. "Only when you place it under the dark of the moon to recharge. You'll find, beneath the velvet cloth in the box, a special sheath to be worn on a belt. And there is one more thing."

He paused, holding out his hand as if reaching for something. A cloak appeared in his hand, black and velvety soft. It was lustrous against the ethereal sunlight that glimmered everywhere in the meadow. "Wear this cloak, and it will afford you a measure of protection, though don't count on it to save you. Never count on anything or anyone but yourself."

I was surprised to find the cloak was lighter than spider-silk. And yet, when I twirled it around my shoulders and fastened it with the golden star-flower brooch at the neck, I felt warm, almost sheltered. The cloak came to my knees and had four pockets inside, including one that was perfectly shaped for the horn. Side slits for my hands and arms made it much more practical than most capes, and I brought up the hem of the material to caress my cheek. As the soft cloth brushed against my skin, shivers of energy raced up and down my spine. Something very powerful and ancient had provided the velvet for this drape.

Almost afraid to ask, I finally whispered, "Panther fur?" Delilah would have my hide if I came home dressed in catskin.

The jindasel shook his head. "No, far more rare. There have been eight Black Unicorns throughout history."

"Eight? I thought there was only one."

"Only in legend. No, there have been eight, each a descendant of the one prior. Their bones have been preserved in a sacred place, the whereabouts unknown to all but the current king or queen."

With a sudden glimpse of what was coming, I almost didn't want to hear the rest. The thought was overwhelming. "Umm . . . so this velvet is . . ."

"Fur from the hide of the previous Black Unicorn. The bones are bleached and buried, and the skins are used solely for cloaks, each given to one who has earned the right to wield one of the horns. Eight horns in history. Eight cloaks."

Stunned, I could only brush my fingers over the fur. So the Black Unicorns didn't shed their horns like I'd heard. And I was wearing a fortune on my back. I'd have to be careful and never tell anyone what the cloak was made of if I wanted to keep myself alive.

"I'll do my best to keep it safe," I murmured, thinking aloud.

"If you lose it—if someone evil gets hold of it, the cloak will burst into flames. But the horn—each horn is a magical artifact, and each time the Black Beast dies and his horn is shed, his spirit spins off a jindasel before migrating into the next body."

"Whoa. You mean like the phoenix? The Black Unicorn is reborn each time?"

He nodded and folded his arms. "Now do you see why you must not lose the horn? These are sacred artifacts, entrusted to your care. You face demon spawn, and they can overpower me. Unfortunately, you are vastly outnumbered, and if you fail, Shadow Wing will overrun Earth and move into Otherworld. And so the Dahns unicorns approached the Black Beast and petitioned for help. This is the aid he surrendered."

So Feddrah-Dahns hadn't really owned the horn. And he'd probably embellished the truth to keep the real story of the Black Unicorn silent. Just why he needed to do that, I wasn't sure, but he must have a reason. Both awed and humbled by the trust placed in us—in me—I let out a long sigh. Expectations on us kept growing and seemed heavier with each passing day.

I glanced up at Eriskel. "We'll do our best."

"I know you will," he said. With a surprisingly gentle gesture, he reached out to stroke my cheek. "The path isn't all dark, girl. But the shadows are strong, so be careful not to fall along the way."

And then, everything went black, and I found myself floating in a pool of sparkling light.

"Camille? Camille! Snap out of it!" Once again, Delilah's voice penetrated the fog wrapped around my head. I blinked rapidly, forcing my way up through the layers of gauze that had decided to coat my thoughts. After a moment, I was able to open my eyes. Foggily I glanced around at the worried expressions.

"Where were you?" Morio asked. "Your body was here, but your spirit seemed to have taken the five o'clock express. Again." He was kneeling beside me, his hand on my wrist as I held the horn in my hand. "And where did this cloak come from?"

I glanced down. The cloak was wrapped around my shoulders, fully material. It hadn't been a dream or a vision. "That . . . is a long story," I said. "I've communed with the guardian of the horn. I've earned the right to use it."

As I stood, Feddrah-Dahns ambled over to me, his hooves lightly tapping on the hardwood floors. He leaned down and nuzzled the brooch. "It's true then. The bearer of the horn wears the cloak of the Black Unicorn."

I awkwardly stood up, the cloak shifted and moved on my shoulders with a life of its own. "You might have told me I'd be facing a fight for my life."

"What? What are you talking about?" Delilah reached out to touch the cloak and as her fingers grazed it, sparks flew lightly where she touched.

Morio lay a single finger on it and shuddered. "My gods, this cloak is wired."

I motioned for them to back off. "I need some water or juice or something. I'm parched." The faint taste of lightning still lingered in my throat, and I still felt like I'd come within a hairbreadth of turning into LFC—*lightning fried Camille*.

"I'll get you something," Delilah said, dashing into the kitchen.

"You wouldn't have some mead, would you?" Mistletoe yelled as he fluttered up, following her on a blur of wings.

I slowly turned back to Feddrah-Dahns. "You knew, didn't you? That I'd have to face the jindasel?"

He blinked, his long lashes fluttering. "I knew, yes. And I knew you would prevail. Queen Asteria's word satisfies me. She has never dealt false with our kind, and I have utmost trust in her seers."

Her seers? "Then she set you to do this, did she?"

"Let us just say, we came to a mutual agreement on the subject. But it was the Black Beast who made the final decision."

I pursed my lips. "But why me? Why not one of her strongest mages? Why not her, herself?"

Feddrah-Dahns whinnied. "Because your greatest ally is your unpredictability. You and your sisters are half-Fae, half-human. Elves follow established routes, only changing patterns when the need is severe. But you and both lines of your blood—you are wild, feral, unpredictable. A good quality to throw the enemy off guard. And you have roots in both worlds, a strong impetus to protect both worlds. Your failings are also your strongest qualities. Don't even bother trying to plan everything in advance; there are too many variables. Play by the currents of the universe, Camille. Listen to the tides of change."

"In other words, go with the flow," I said softly.

"Yes, go with the flow, and pray it doesn't send you crashing on the rocks," he said.

A knock interrupted us and, still mulling over the advice, I answered the front door. Smoky stood there, leaning against the archway, staring down at me. There was something different about him that I couldn't pinpoint. He was far more intense and focused than I'd ever seen. And I could smell him: desire and lust and greed and passion all swirled into one, all rolling right toward me like one big boulder.

"You're late," he said. "Come now. And be prepared to spend the night." With that, he turned toward the living room and, over his shoulder, added, "You have fifteen minutes, and then I take you with me, willing or not."

CHAPTER 13

"You can't just barge in here and order me around like that. I was headed out to your place in a little while, so cool your jets, dragon-boy!" Without thinking, I reached out and grabbed Smoky's arm, yanking him around to face me as we headed into the living room. I'd been rubbed a little too raw in the past twenty-four hours and was feeling a tad touchy.

He stared at my fingers on his arm for the barest of moments, then ran his gaze up to catch mine. He did *not* look amused, and I had the feeling that I was two seconds away from a massively nasty retaliation for being so presumptuous.

Slowly let go of the dragon and back away . . . Take a deep breath, hands off, sheepish expression on face . . . Maybe he won't eat you for lunch.

Or maybe he will, and you'll like it, a suggestive voice tickled in the back of my thoughts.

And then indignation flared, and I found myself wallowing in a mixture of irritation and self-pity. "Listen, in the past twenty-four hours, I've fought off a bugbear, a goblin, and a Sawberry Fae. I've helped kill two dubba-trolls, corralled a bunch of errant pixies, and found a missing one." I ticked each item off on my fingers, swallowing my fear as he waited for me to continue.

"What else? Oh yes, then there's the matter of the lightning bolt I managed to dodge. It could have fried the city, it was so amped up, but no—it was aimed straight at *me*. If I'd failed the test, not only would I have missed out on being the new owner of this snazzy Black Unicorn horn, but I'd be fried to a cinder in astral-land, and my body would have had a heart attack."

"Anything else?" he said, sliding into a smirk.

Annoyed now, rather than afraid—Smoky's moods were as unpredictable as my own, it seemed—I rested my hands on my hips. "Yeah, now that you mention it. If you want to huff and puff and blow the house in, then you can damn well go ahead and do it. But I'm not going to move one minute faster than I already am. I'm hungry. I'm stressed. And right now I wish I could turn into a tabby cat like Delilah and go curl up for a nice nap!"

Morio and Feddrah-Dahns stared at me like I'd just grown a second head. Perhaps I'd been a little too vocal? Venting was one thing. But lashing out wasn't my usual pattern. And Smoky wasn't responsible for anything that had happened.

He gave me a speculative look. "I know a sure cure for stress. We'll give it a try later." And then he swept past me over to the Morris chair, where he leaned on the arm and addressed Feddrah-Dahns. "Hello, again. So, you found your pixie?"

Feddrah-Dahns whinnied and shook his flowing mane. "Yes, thanks to Lady Camille and her sister."

"What? What did I do?" Delilah asked as she returned from the kitchen with a tray filled with soda cans and sandwiches. Mistletoe followed behind, eyeing the tiny goblet of cola she'd poured for him with suspicion. It was actually a thimble, which meant it was as big as a saucepan to him.

"I don't know about this," he said, squinting. "I've never tasted Earthside food. Are you sure you aren't trying to jinx me with this? It's bubbling."

"It's carbonated, not enchanted," I said, breaking in. "Honestly, Kitten, why didn't you just offer him a glass of mead or wine?"

"Because I didn't think of it," Delilah said, glancing at Smoky. "Hey. Didn't hear you come in. You want something to eat, too?"

He rubbed his temples and shook his head. "No, thank you. Every time I show up here, at least two of you are bickering. What on earth do you do when company goes home? Get into a knock-down, drag-out chick fight?"

Delilah and I simultaneously turned to him and said, "Hey, watch it!" And then she promptly broke into peals of laughter, while I eyed the sandwiches on the tray, my stomach rumbling.

"Stereo, even," he moaned. "Camille, *please*, get your things. I need you to come talk to that woman on my land. She's driving me batty, and if you don't come find out what she wants, I swear, I'm going to charbroil her and then sit on what's left until she's squashed like a bug. She knows what I am, and she's constantly harping at me, asking if I know where Titania is—"

Feddrah-Dahns shuddered. "Don't let her fool you. She may be a nuisance, but she can be a dangerous enemy, if you're talking about Morgaine. We don't trust her in the valley. That's why we ran her out."

"Trillian told me King Vodox exiled her from Svartalfheim, too," I said, glancing at Morio, who had a bemused look on his face. He just leaned back, put his hands behind his head, and waited. I eased my way back over to Smoky's side and placed a light hand on his shoulder.

"Let me eat lunch. Then I have to make a phone call. After that, I'll come with you. Meanwhile, Delilah, why don't you and Morio check out that rug shop this afternoon? See what you can find out."

"Sounds good to me," Delilah said, her mouth full. She handed me a sandwich, and as I reached for it, Smoky snaked his arm around my waist and pulled me into his lap.

"You got a thing for me sitting on your lap, huh?" I asked.

He grinned. "It's conducive to my thoughts. Eat fast," he said. "Delilah, be a good girl and get your sister some nightclothes. Since you're obviously wrapped up in something important, I've decided to choose my days and nights with you as I see fit. Consider tonight the first. I'll let you know when it all adds up to a week."

I stared at him. Oh yes, this was all just so peachy keen I thought I might toss my cookies. Couldn't even just one thing work out without something throwing a monkey wrench in the works?

"*You'll* let me know when I've spent a week's worth of time with you? Oh no, that will never do. Trillian won't stand for it—" I stopped as Delilah stuffed a ham sandwich in my hand. I automatically brought it to my mouth and began to chew.

"Trillian has nothing to say about the matter," Smoky said,

his pale eyes turning glacial. "I neither like nor dislike your boyfriend, but know this: He will *not* interfere. Our contract is between *us*, not between him and me. Trillian better get that fact through his head before he wears out my patience." Taking a deep breath, he added, "Contrary to what you've speculated in the past, I am fully capable of killing and eating anyone who gets in my way."

A shaft of ice stabbed through my heart. Beneath that suave, persuasive exterior, there lurked the heart of a dragon, not the heart of a man. And dragons played by their own rules, at their own pace. I kept forgetting it, and it was a mistake that could turn out to be fatal. If not for me, then for Trillian.

"Hicc!" The sudden belch roared through the sudden silence, breaking the tension. I whirled to see Mistletoe land on one of the console tables. His belch had acted like a sudden puncture to a balloon, sending him flying across the room.

"Mistletoe!" Feddrah-Dahns shifted nervously, trying to navigate through the furniture over to the pixie's side.

Delilah beat him to it, kneeling down beside the table. "Are you okay? Mistletoe? Are you hurt?"

The pixie staggered to his feet. "Blimey, that was one hell of a ride," he muttered. "What kind of poison is in that drink you gave me?"

I pulled myself free of Smoky's embrace and hurried over to help. "I guess pixies and soda pop don't mix. How's your stomach? Are you bloated? You have a lot of gas?"

Delilah gave me a disgusted look. "Why'd you ask him that?"

"If he's got gas, this could happen again. He's like a bottle rocket." I snorted. "Congratulations. Only you could find a way to launch a pixie into orbit, Delilah. We'd better put him someplace safe where he won't break his neck." I glanced around. "Trouble is, we don't have a padded cell, pixie-size. Carbonation is a powerful tool. I'm amazed that FBHs don't find some way to turn it into a weapon."

Truth was, I didn't even like soda. As much as I liked sweets, I found the taste too cloying. I could handle all manner of sugars in my coffee, but for cool drinks, I preferred wine or water.

Mistletoe glared at Delilah. "Leave it to the cat to give me something to make my tum sick." He rubbed his belly. "I feel a bit under the weather. My insides feel distended." And sure enough, I could hear the gurgling.

I glanced around. "I know! Delilah, cover the sides of Maggie's playpen with pillows, and put Mistletoe in there until the bubbles wear themselves out."

With the pixie complaining every step of the way, Delilah took him into the kitchen. Meanwhile, I turned back to Smoky. "I'll make that call, and we'll be off," I said weakly. He wasn't going to be in a good mood much longer, and I wanted out of here before his patience vanished in a puff of smoke.

"Right," he said, looking put out.

I hurried into the kitchen, where Delilah was making up a padded cell for the pixie. "Cripes, this is just the most convoluted couple of days we've had in a long time." I pulled out my notepad and punched in the number I'd looked up for the Mountain Aspen Retreat.

"Who are you calling?" Delilah asked.

"That mental institution—the one Morio talked about. There's a man there who knows about the third spirit seal. Trouble is, he's an inmate and won't—hold on," I said as a voice came on the other end of the line.

"Mountain Aspen Retreat, how may I direct your call?"

I thought fast. "I'm a relative of one of your clients, and I want to come visit him. Who do I talk to about scheduling a visit?"

"One moment," she said, putting me on hold.

Delilah narrowed her eyes. "Give me his name, and I'll run him through Chase's computer before Morio and I head out to check out that shop."

I motioned for her to hand me a steno pad and scribbled Ben's name on it, and the name of the Mountain Aspen Retreat. As I handed it back to her, a different receptionist came back on the line.

"Front desk. Ms. Marshall speaking. May I help you?"

"Yes, I'd like to make an appointment to come see my . . . cousin. He's a patient at Mountain Aspen." Cousin was good; I could hide my glamour if I tried. Buy a simple dress for the occasion. Yeah, right, I thought. If nothing else, I could charm the receptionist to let me through.

"His name, please?"

"Ben. Benjamin Welter." I thought for a moment, then added,

"I know he's not very responsive, but I thought I'd like to just come sit with him for awhile."

A brief pause. "I see here that it's been seven weeks since his last visitor. Are your aunt and uncle still on their world cruise?" A hint of disapproval in her voice. Ms. Marshall probably cared more about the patients than their own families. I decided to capitalize on it.

"I have no idea. I've been away at school, and this is the first time I've been home in over two years. I had no idea that my cousin was having problems until now. My name's Camille, by the way."

"When were you thinking of coming out, Ms. Welter?"

I didn't correct her. Let her think that I was related on the father's side—it didn't make any difference to me. "Would tomorrow be too soon? Around three P.M.?"

The sound of tapping keys and then she said, "I've got you scheduled and on the visitor list. Thank you, Camille. We encourage families to visit as often as possible. Even when the patient is as unresponsive as Benjamin, it seems to help them. You know, just having people here who care."

As I hung up, I felt like a first-class rat. But then again, Benjamin didn't *want* human companionship. Whether I was actually his cousin or just the stranger I really was, it probably wouldn't matter to him. And maybe, just maybe, there was something I could do to help. I pushed back the chair and stood.

Delilah glanced over at me. She'd managed to fashion a padded pen of sorts for Mistletoe, who looked miserable, stretched out on the mattress pad. He groaned and rubbed his belly.

"I've got to go. Smoky's about ready to blow. I'd better go find out what Morgaine's up to out there." I took a deep breath. "Everything should be okay but . . . just in case . . ."

"Do you want me to come with you?" she asked immediately. "You can break the deal. We'll find some other way to pay him back for his help." She hugged me, the black crescent tattoo beating a staccato pulse on her forehead.

I stared at the mark. A tremendous burden had been thrust upon her when she suggested we seek help from the Autumn Lord, and she seldom complained. Though she was bound to the Elemental Lord as one of his Death Maidens, Delilah took it in stride with as much grace as she could muster.

The Autumn Lord hadn't offered her a choice. Smoky had given me the option. Spend a week with him, and he'd help us contact the Autumn Lord. One week of pleasure, compared with a lifetime of fearful bonds to an Elemental prince? I had no right to complain.

I cleared my throat. "Everything will be fine. I'm looking forward to it, actually." And I was. For the most part. Yes, I was afraid, and yes, Smoky was likely to wreak havoc with my life. But who *hadn't* dumped a bucket of chaos into our lives in the past six months? Might as well be in the form of a tall, cool drink of water.

"I'll be home tomorrow," I told her. "We can discuss what you and Morio found, and what I've discovered about Morgaine."

She gave me a tentative smile and then pulled me in for another hug. As my head rested under her chin—at six one, she was a good six inches taller than me—I closed my eyes. It almost felt like Mother was holding me again, tight in an embrace that was forever safe and welcoming. Delilah reluctantly let go, and I stepped back.

"Have fun." She winked. "Smoky likes you. He won't hurt you. And if he does . . . we'll get him."

Laughing at the thought, I made my way out of the kitchen and into the living room. Morio was handing Smoky a satchel.

"I see you've been pawing through my goodies again," I said, sticking my tongue out at him.

"I like pawing your goodies," Morio said, arching his eyebrows. He planted a long, slow kiss on my lips. So different than Trillian. Bewitching instead of demanding. Trillian overwhelmed and conquered, whereas Morio encouraged his conquests to hand over the keys to the kingdom without so much as a twinge of regret. Trillian was alpha, Morio stood outside of the whole testosterone match and calmly bided his time.

I lingered in his arms, and he playfully pinched my butt. "You better get a move on," he said, then leaned close to my ear. "I'll be out there tonight, watching, to make sure you're okay." Without another word, he pulled away and gestured to me with a flourish. "She's all yours, Smoky. Treat her with care."

Smoky let out a long breath. "I never intended anything else," he said and turned toward the door.

I ran over to Feddrah-Dahns. "Stay for a day or so; you'll want to hear about Morgaine, I'm sure."

"Just don't let her get hold of that horn," he said. "You must not allow the horn to fall into the wrong hands."

Like Morgaine could withstand a million-amp lightning bolt any better than me, I thought, but left the thought unsaid. "Right." And then, without further ado, we were off.

"Did you want to take my car?" I started to say, but Smoky motioned for me to come closer.

He wrapped his arm around my shoulder. "Now you'll find out how I travel." Cryptic, but enough to warn me that I'd better prepare for something out of the ordinary.

I steeled myself as a swirl of magic spun up, a vortex with us as its focal point. *Dragon magic.* While I'd felt it moving within Smoky's aura before, the power had never gone raging through me like it was now.

One moment I was standing on the front lawn with his arm around me. The next moment the sky opened, and stars whirled above us as the world shifted. A chill a million degrees colder than the grave stabbed into my body, like someone had thrust a dagger made of ice between my shoulder blades. This was ancient magic, old and cunning and whirling us about like we were two leaves in the wind as we fell into the void. A crashing of thunder, and then mist rose around me, and I heard the persistent lapping of waves against a beach.

Oh cripes, I knew where we were.

We were swimming, but not like any fish or whale or porpoise I'd ever met. No, Smoky had shifted us between the veils, and we were zipping along through the icy currents of the Ionyc Sea.

The astral, etheric, and spirit realms were all vague and nebulous to physical life. An astral or etheric entity could pass through a corporeal form, and while the person might feel the sensation of intense cold, or sense someone there, the two realms wouldn't clash for space.

But out in the astral, the three realms of intangible force were joined by several other dimensions, and together they all comprised the Ionyc Lands. The energy that connected them also managed to keep them separate, for they were forever shifting and moving. That same energy also allowed passage from one land to another. This energy swirled around the Ionyc Lands in canals, like the waters of Venice.

The Ionyc Sea was a vast, churning ocean of currents that prevented the different realms of force from colliding. Collision was a bad idea. Collision of the differing Ionyc Lands could set off a chain reaction capable of neutralizing life as we knew it.

Essentially, the Ionyc Sea was a demarcation zone: open to all, dangerous to all, and eternal. Very few creatures, especially those of flesh and blood, traveled along the channeled canals that ferried the seas' volatile waves.

Creatures of the northern lands—those whose life force came from ice and snow and wind and vapor—could conceivably find a way through. Mythic ice serpents routinely crossed the Ionyc Sea. And, apparently, so did some dragons.

Whether it was his silver or white dragon heritage that allowed him to forge through the energy currents, I didn't know. And now was not the time to ask. I had no intention of distracting Smoky. Who knew how hard it was for him to keep up the protection that kept the currents from zapping our bodies to dust? Better to keep my mouth shut until we were safe and back on solid ground.

Smoky's arm felt suspiciously like a large wing as it draped around my shoulder, and I could see that we were encased within some form of barrier. Spherical in nature, it surrounded us like an invisible bubble.

How long we journeyed through the sea, I couldn't tell. Time ceased to exist here. A second might feel as long as a year, and a year might wing by in the guise of a week. After awhile I began to grow tired. I leaned my head against his shoulder and let the rocking motion of the currents lull me to sleep.

"Camille? Wake up. We're here."

At first, I didn't recognize the voice. It wasn't Trillian. Nor was it Morio. That much I knew. Wondering why I felt so stiff—I usually slept deep and well—I forced myself to open my eyes. The glint of late afternoon sunlight blinded me, but there was no heat behind it, and as I pushed myself up, I shaded my eyes with my hand. Where the hell was I?

The ground felt springy beneath me, and I looked down. I was on an air mattress, a blue one partially covered with a crisp white sheet. Huh? And then I remembered.

"Smoky? Smoky? Where are you?" When I swung my head

to the left, a wave of dizziness rushed over me and, moaning, I fell back on the mattress. The world was spinning like I was tied to one gigantic wheel of fortune.

"I'm right here." His voice was soft and coming from behind me. I leaned my head back and saw that he was squatting, frozen in place, watching me. "You'll be okay. You'll feel much better in about ten minutes, as soon as you sit up and drink this." He held out a mug filled with something that was bubbling. A cloud of steam drifted up from it, and the fragrance smelled like spring meadows and wildflowers.

"What happened? What's that? Why am I lying on an air mattress in the middle of . . ." I slowly—very slowly—glanced around. Forest. Woodland. My guess was that we were near Smoky's barrow. "In the middle of the woods?"

He set the mug down and scooted in behind me, slowly helping to prop me up so that I was leaning back against his chest. Despite my dizziness, I decided this wasn't half-bad. I sank against his tightly muscled shoulders and felt his hardened body shoring me up. *Change that.* Not bad *at all.*

Smoky reached for the tea with his left hand, while he kept his right arm cinched snugly around my waist. He brought the tea to my lips, and I reached up to steady the cup. "First, drink. Then questions."

I tasted the brew. Honey, that much I could tell. And lemon. Rose hips and peppermint, and something else I couldn't identify.

"Good," I whispered, taking the mug and cupping it in my hands. I hadn't noticed at first, but now I realized I felt frozen to the core, as if I'd walked into an ice cave and fallen asleep for a long, long time.

As I drank, strength began to seep back into my muscles, and the dizziness started to subside. A few minutes later, I drained the mug and handed it back to him. Smoky tossed it to one side but kept me tight against him, nuzzling my ear.

"Tell me, now that I don't feel ready to keel over," I said.

"When humans and Fae traverse the Ionyc Sea, even though they may be encased inside of a barrier, they still can't fight the tides of energy. It sucks the warmth from your body and drains energy, then cycles around. If we rode long enough, you would have woken up while we were still in the sea, full of vigor and strength. And the pattern would have continued: drain, then recharge. But we had only a short distance to travel, so you didn't get the chance for the seas to refresh you."

He planted a delicate kiss on my earlobe, then another on my neck. I shivered, and this time, it wasn't from the chill. Here was a creature as ancient as almost anyone or anything I'd met. And yet, he wanted me. The thought was overwhelming, but I'd had too many bizarre things happen over the past year to brush it aside as whimsy.

Whether it was something in the tea or something left over from my ride through the Ionyc Sea, I felt a stirring within me, a quiver of desire that quickly became a flame, shooting from my breast to belly as it unfurled like tendrils on a maidenhair fern. I caught my breath, and he felt it.

"You want me, don't you? You want me as much as I want you. From the first time I saw you, I knew that I had to have you. That I *would* have you." His voice was deeper now, more demanding. "I'm flush with wanting you. I'm coming into rutting season, and *you* are my chosen mate."

The time had come. I knew it in my heart. There was no turning back, and now that we were down to the count, my fear slid away like water on duck down. Smoky and I had an appointment to keep, made that first moment I gazed into the dragon's liquid crystal eyes when he stood before me, majestic, wings spread, ready to take me down if I made the slightest mistake.

I twisted around, pushing deeper into his embrace, and leaned into the kiss. "I want you," I heard myself say. "Take me into your world, and teach me what it means to love a dragon."

CHAPTER 14

Smoky gathered me up in his arms and rose as if he might be holding a kitten. I pressed against him, wondering what would happen next. I'd been with a lot of men and yet never one so alien. Morio was a fox demon, and it had taken me awhile to get used to his shape-shifting during sex, but he was more human than Smoky, even when he didn't look it. And in some ways, Morio was more human than Trillian.

Though I doubted that my dragon lover would shift form in the bedroom—or at least I prayed he wouldn't—a little niggle of fear still squirmed inside me. *Better push it aside, girl,* I told myself. *No need to even go there.*

"Camille," he whispered again, pressing a kiss to my forehead as he strode toward the barrow. I'd never seen the inside of Smoky's home before. Nobody had that I knew of. Curiosity made me want to jump down and nose around, to see what kind of home he kept. But stronger than my curiosity was the feel of the arms that held me, the hands that cushioned my legs and back, the musky fragrance of arousal that lightly drifted off of his skin to mingle with the scents of spring moss and damp woodland.

As we neared the barrow mound, still blackened with scorch

marks from his dragon fire, a door opened, and he stooped his head to enter. At six four, Smoky was too tall for the archway. As we crossed the threshold, a crackle of energy shot through me, and I jerked, looking around nervously. Lines of pale blue lightning framed the arch.

"What the . . ."

"Just a portal." Smoky gently deposited me on the floor. "Guaranteed to keep intruders out . . . and guests within." He gave me a long look that said more than his words ever could.

Was it a warning? My senses had shifted to high alert as we entered the barrow. There was ancient magic here, with its beginnings lost in the mists of time. It wove itself around us, a cloak of stars and shadows.

I turned back to look at the door. I could still see the trees and the clearing, but the pale sunlight of spring lingered outside, not crossing the doorstep. As I approached the arch, Smoky cleared his throat, and the door slammed shut by itself.

"Don't try to leave the barrow without my help. You aren't strong enough to negate my wards and bindings. You could hurt yourself."

"So I'm trapped here?" I glanced up at him. Once again, I realized that I really didn't know him very well, for all the time we'd spent together.

He silently swung around behind me, wrapping his arms around my waist, leaning down to trail kisses along my shoulder. Damn, his lips were soft. "It would seem that's about the size of it."

The real question was what about the size of *him*? A brief thought that I'd bitten off more than I could chew ran through my mind as he pressed hard against my back. It dawned on me that Smoky could do whatever he decided he wanted to with me. Nobody around here had the power to break through that barrier covering his door.

As my eyes adjusted to the dim glow—about the same level as a reading lamp on an autumn evening—I realized that the barrow mound was cavernous, far bigger than it looked from the outside. Eye-catchers provided the light, the glowing orbs hovering near the ceiling.

We were standing in a human-size living room, complete with leather sofa and chair, old heavy walnut tables, and a bookshelf. But instead of a back wall, the tiled floor ended at the edge of a chasm, where I could see a staircase leading down into the deep cavern, the bottom of which was filled with coiling mists.

There would be plenty of room down there for Smoky to change shape in and easily maneuver around, and the sound of splashing water signaled an underground stream flowed somewhere in the rocky ravine. And if I wasn't mistaken, there might be a waterfall down there, too.

I backed away from the edge, looking for any signs of a kitchen or bedroom, but only saw two doors, one to either side of the living room.

"So this is your home," I said, more to break the silence than anything else. What else do you say when a dragon has coerced you into his lair and effectively trapped you until he's ready to let you go?

"I'll give you the tour," Smoky said, then let out a low laugh that echoed through the chamber. "But first . . ." And his eyes shimmered, diamond dust falling in them like snow in a snow globe.

"First . . ." I repeated, shivering. An updraft from the cavern swept past, and the temperature plummeted.

"First . . ." He took a step toward me, never letting me out of his sight. I stepped away, barely able to breathe.

"Camille, come." He held out his hand, and I swallowed my fear. The compulsion to obey was stronger than any fear or doubt, and I slowly walked toward him. When I reached his side, he leaned down to stare in my eyes.

"All mine," he said softly, then silently led me toward the door on the right. It opened as we approached.

The room reminded me of some ancient king's chamber, with a four-poster bed carved from marble and a step stool leading up to thick mattresses piled high with silver and blue bedclothes. A dresser, dark walnut, and a matching armoire graced one wall, and a rocking chair sat near an alcove that was sheltered from view with a full-length trifold screen of Japanese design.

The walls were covered by tapestries, scenes of dragons winging on the sky, attacking villages, woven from silver and gold threads.

Propped in the corner, a shield caught my eye. Polished to a high sheen, the front of it was formed of lapis lazuli and reminded me of a coat of arms. Yet the aura surrounding it told me it had seen use in battle. It felt older than Smoky, older than even Queen Asteria.

Engraved on the center, a dragon glanced over his shoulder, nine silver stars shooting out of his mouth into the sky. Over the dragon, in silver relief, a pair of foils matched blades, and beneath the dragon, a trail of nine silver snowflakes fell from the sky. The shield was edged with a wide border of silver, and two perpendicular lines of silver engraving wove in a knotwork to the left side of the dragon.

I slowly approached the shield and reached out, not touching. The years rolled off of it, ten millennia and more. For over ten thousand years this shield had stood watch. All this unfolded in my thoughts as I stared at the armor.

Smoky rested his chin on the top of my head as he leaned over my shoulder. "This is my family crest, my family shield."

Swallowing abruptly, I realized that he was inviting me into his life—a rare honor from a dragon. "It's seen battle, hasn't it?" I kept my voice low, hesitant. I didn't want to press too far, ask too much.

"Yes," he said softly. "My father carried it, and his father before him. And someday I may, too, carry it into battle. I am the ninth son of a ninth son of a ninth son. I carry the family history in my blood, in my memory. In my very bones, marrow, and hide."

I wasn't sure what this meant—numbers were magical, but I had no idea exactly how dragons divined them—but the significance was rife in his words. Smoky wasn't just any everyday dragon. "What battles did your father fight? And why would a dragon need a shield?"

"My father saw several battles," he said, easing beyond me to caress the lapis of the shield. "But none were as catastrophic as the one my grandfather fought in. As to why we need a shield . . . There are times my family has stood beside humans on the field. Tight quarters require us to shift out of our natural form, hence the shield. The leather that covers the metal beneath the stone was taken from the body of the first of my lineage. The lapis was mined from the walls of the first dreyerie built by my ancestors."

"Dreyerie?"

"Lair . . . nest."

I stood perfectly still, staring at the shield. There was so much about Smoky that I would probably never know. He would outlive me and my sisters, and many generations to follow. I was barely a blip in his life.

"What war did your grandfather fight in?"

He closed his eyes and, as if he were reciting a poem, said, "My grandfather fought alongside the Lord of Ice and the men of the north against the fire giants, who were led by Loki and his great wolf child. The frost drove the fire giants back to the depths, out of the Northlands. Then the northern shamans covered the world with a sheet of ice to keep them at bay. By the time the ice age had vanished, the giants had forgotten the battle and were off creating havoc elsewhere."

"This was before the Great Divide?" I asked, already knowing the answer.

"Long before. We had little keep with—or knowledge of— the Fae back then. The Northlands are a harsh realm, and only your Snow Queen and her Court were able to take refuge there."

Bleakly, I thought that Smoky might yet see a battle to match his grandfather's. If Shadow Wing broke through, we'd be facing the war of all wars. Smoky must have sensed my mood, because he spun me around to face him.

"Enough talk of war and battle and death. Kiss me, Camille."

Shivering, I raised myself on tiptoe and draped my arms around his neck. He caught me up by my waist, lifting me so that we were eye level, and I wrapped my legs around his waist.

As I gazed into his face, the tides of time rolled past. His features were frozen forever young, and his skin was as smooth as my own, but his eyes . . . They were the eyes of a god, the eyes of one almost immortal, the eyes of a dragon. He searched my face, and I leaned in, stomach burning. I wanted him more than I'd ever wanted anyone or anything.

Cold fire sparked between us as he softly bit my lip, worrying it with his perfect teeth. As his tongue gently sought entrance, I opened my mouth ever so slightly, just enough for him to pry his way in. His arms held me fast, so close I could barely tell where he left off and I began.

Shaking in earnest now, I could only close my eyes as the storm bore down, a wave of passion so dark that I didn't even know it existed. Lost in his kiss, I went spiraling under, caught by the riptide, swallowed by the glacial floes that lingered in his aura. He spun me around, his lips never leaving mine, in a dance so old that the Moon Mother herself had witnessed its birth.

As if in a dream, broken images wove together as I let myself flow into our meeting. His lips sought refuge on my neck, my shoulders, across my face, down my breast, and my bustier went flying. Perhaps he'd unlaced it, perhaps I merely wished it off, but my breasts were free, and he lifted his thumb and forefinger to gently caress my nipple, cupping my breast in his palm, squeezing just hard enough to shoot a line of flames to rage between my thighs. And then I was standing again, and his shirt was off, his milky-white skin shimmering in the dim light of the bedchamber.

I pressed my lips to his chest, kissed his heart, let my lips follow down the line leading to the center of that perfect V hidden beneath his jeans.

Head back, he gasped, a kaleidoscope spinning in his dragon's eyes. He lifted me to my feet, gently, and with one hand unzipped my skirt. I fumbled with the snaps on his jeans. As they popped open, I forced myself to breathe.

"Take them off," he said, and his word was my command. I slowly eased the white denim down over his hips, and there, found myself facing his desire, incredibly silken and smooth and . . .

"Great gods, you have the biggest . . ." I bit my tongue, not wanting to break the mood, but he laughed and snatched me up, tossing me on the bed. With another laugh, throaty and wild, he pounced, landing beside me on his hands and knees. He stretched out on his side and slid one hand over my breasts. His feral smile made me catch my breath as I caught a glimpse of him in dragon form, mounting a silver dragon. Their bellows ripped through the sky like thunder. Startled, I tried to pull away, but he held me fast.

"Going somewhere, my Witchling?" he whispered, and in a flash he was straddling me, on hands and knees, staring down.

"I . . . I . . ." I couldn't speak, for over his shoulder rose the ghostly image of wings and smoke.

"Ssshhh . . . don't speak," he said, pressing one finger against my lips. "Not a word. Don't move. Let me explore you."

Frozen, I couldn't move, yet every nerve in my body blazed. He leaned down, letting his tongue do the talking, and traced one nipple, tugging at it with his lips, the barest tips of his teeth biting. And then I felt a light finger gliding down my stomach, tripping over the skin, setting off minor explosions with every touch. With a quick brush of his hand, Smoky parted my legs and slid his fingers between my thighs.

I shifted, trying not to focus on where he was headed, yet unable to tear my attention away. A whisper of another touch startled me and, surprised, I glanced to the side. A lock of his silver hair, free and hanging loose to his ankles, had risen like a snake and was caressing my shoulder. To my left, another tendril of silver strands coiled around my nipple, tickling me gently. As other locks wound themselves around my ankles and wrists, pulling my arms and legs wide and holding them taut, he slid his fingers inside me, beckoning me, playing gently against nerves in my body I hadn't known existed.

"Do you like this?" he whispered. "Do you like it when I touch you? Answer me."

"Yes." I gasped, barely able to speak. I felt like I'd been holding my breath for hours. Pent-up, I was poised near the brink, but Smoky wouldn't allow me fall into the chasm. He pulled back each time right before I neared release. Frustrated and terribly aroused, I tried to clench my thighs together, tried to stem the tide of moisture that his touch had coaxed from deep within me.

"Trying to keep me out?" Smoky asked, leaning between my legs, his hands resting on my bent knees. His hair still held me prisoner. He was primed, ready, and by the musky fragrance that cloaked his body, I could smell just how much he wanted me. "Too late to turn back, Camille."

"No, no . . . I don't want you to stop . . . I just . . . please . . ." I shivered, praying he wouldn't stop.

"What? Say it." He leaned down to kiss my lips. "Ask me, and I'll give you everything."

A moan slid out of my throat. I needed him in me; I ached for the feel of his body pressed into mine. A hunger rose up, so fierce it threatened to overwhelm me. "Inside, please. I need you. I need you—*fuck me*."

"No."

"What?" I looked at him. After all this, was he just going to tease me, to toy with me? Dragons could be cruel, that I knew, but surely he wouldn't leave me hurting, aching. "Don't you want me?" Tears welled up in my eyes, and I struggled against the manacles of silver hair.

"Oh, I want you, Camille, make no mistake about that. And I always get what I want." He smiled then, so softly it frightened me. The smile of killers, of kings, of dark knights who rode in and lured away the princess from her prince. "But no, I will not fuck you. I leave that to Trillian. However, I *will* make love to you."

The cloud of tears threatened to spill over as I quivered, needing him so desperately I wanted to scream. I let out a choked cry.

"Don't you understand by now?" He slowly began to lower himself into me, and I let out a whimper as his flesh met mine, stretching me wide and deep. "I thought surely you would have guessed. I'm in love with you, Camille. And I choose you to be my mate."

He plunged then, driving himself deep, dragging me out of myself, onto the astral with him. As our bodies found their rhythm, our spirits coiled together, darting, dancing, sparkling with his every thrust, with my every reply.

And with one long, guttural cry, I understood what it meant to ride the dragon.

CHAPTER 15

The room was very still as Smoky rested beside me. I stared at the ceiling, not knowing what to say.

"What are you thinking, love?" Smoky traced a finger down the side of my cheek, then bopped my nose. His eyes were luminous, glowing, and his words felt intimate in a way they never had before. Not just sexy-intimate, but heart-intimate.

I cleared my throat. What was I thinking? Good question. For one thing, I was starting to remember through my afterglow-hazed brain that he'd said something . . . something that . . . oh hell. *I'm in love with you, Camille. And I choose you to be my mate.* What was I supposed to do with *that*? Maybe if I ignored it, he'd forget he said it. Maybe it was just something he'd blurted out in the throes of passion. Didn't all men temporarily fall in love with the women they were fucking? Sex with Smoky had taken me beyond words, to a place I'd never been before. Hell, I could barely remember anything either one of us had said, let alone make sense of what was going on.

I pushed myself up, leaning back on my hands. My clothes were scattered around the room, along with Smoky's jeans and shirt. I stared down at my body, which was glowing with a rosy hue I seldom saw on my pale skin. Slowly, feeling almost shy, I turned toward him. Hands behind his head, he was whistling an aimless tune. His body was so long and lean and hard that he might be a sculpture. A sudden thought struck me, and I let out a giggle.

"What?" he asked, lazily squinting at me through half-closed eyes.

"I was just thinking, the *David* has nothing on you." It occurred to me that I'd be wise never to mention to Trillian just how well-endowed Smoky was, or I'd set off a testosterone war that wouldn't quit until one of them was dead. Size wasn't everything, but Smoky had both size and experience, and that would piss Trillian off to no end. But I wasn't complaining. That was for sure.

Smoky chuckled. "I'll take that as a compliment." He shifted, turning toward me, and ran a light hand over my thigh. My body responded, and I realized I was still hungry for him. As if he could read my thoughts, he reached for my hand. I hesitantly let him lead my fingers to his penis. With pent breath, I traced one finger down him, closing my eyes as the silky shaft responded to the touch of my hand. Within seconds, he was ready again and, with a low growl, grabbed me by my waist and lifted me astride his hips. As he stoked my fires back to life, I sank onto his hardened length.

We rose and fell in rhythm, matching pace, matching strides. He reached up to stroke my breast with one hand as his hair coiled around my wrists and braced my back to hold me steady and give me balance and strength.

Once again, I slid into the slipstream of his passion as we rode the storm.

"We'd better get dressed. You have an appointment with the Crow Lady," Smoky said, leisurely rolling out of bed. He might as well be smoking a cigarette, he looked so relaxed. A gilt mirror on the wall captured my reflection, and I blinked—talk about looking relaxed. I was oozing with that after-sex glow that infuses every good tryst.

As I leaned over to pick up my skirt and panties, Smoky reached out and gave me a sharp smack on the butt. I whirled, on pure reflex, my hand whistling through the air before the thought occurred to me it might not be such a good idea. But Smoky was quicker than me, and before I could graze his cheek, he wrapped his hand around my wrist and held me firm.

"Camille . . ." A warning. I could hear it in his voice.

If it had been Trillian or Morio, I would have gone right ahead and dove headfirst into the fray. But then again, neither Trillian nor Morio would smack my butt, not unless I wanted them to. They knew better.

I gazed into Smoky's face. Time to backpedal. Fast. The old standard about gorillas worked for dragons, too. *Where do you let an eight-hundred-pound gorilla go? Anywhere he wants. What do you do if a two-ton dragon spanks you? Say, "Thank you very much."*

But being me, I couldn't just let it drop. "Why the hell did you slap my ass? That sure wasn't a love pat. Do you get off on spanking? Because I don't. Well . . . at least not usually." I tensed, waiting, but he just laughed.

"Just a reminder for you to behave yourself. For now, you're my consort, and you will behave as such. Don't forget it. Now get dressed, and I'll fix you something to eat. There are . . . amenities . . . behind the screen," he added, pulling on a long white robe that I'd seen him wear around the land.

Cripes. I opened my mouth, then closed it again. Best to leave it alone. Maybe I'd just wait till I got home to remind him that it wasn't considered good manners to smack your consort on the butt that hard unless you were both into playing yes-sir, no-sir. Come to think of it, he probably was into it. Yep, once out that portal, I could say anything I wanted, but until then . . . he might not let me leave if I ticked him off.

He cleared his throat and whispered, "Braid." At that moment, his hair divided into three sections, and they began to plait themselves into the long braid I was used to seeing him wear.

"Man, that hair of yours can do just about everything, can't it?" I said without thinking.

He leisurely shrugged. "It's expedient. When we have more time, you can brush it for me."

I felt suddenly shy for some reason. "I'd like that."

"Let's just say my hair is a very vital part of me. Neither I nor it allow others to touch it. With the rare exception, that is," he said, a slow smile spreading across his face. Before he finished speaking, the strands had finished braiding themselves and hung straight, firmly woven. Smoky left the room, closing the door behind him.

As I watched him go, it occurred to me that while the reality had lived up to and overshadowed the fantasy part of *Life With Dragon-Dude*, I hadn't considered our interaction beyond the bedroom. Vaguely disconcerted, I picked up my clothes and tossed them on the bed.

I peeked behind the screen. There was a marble tub, but no sign of any running water. A toilet had been built over an odorless hole in the ground. The seat was spotless, ornately carved in polished oak. A bowl and matching pitcher sat on a vanity table. The pitcher was filled with rose-scented water, and soft, fresh towels were folded beside it, along with glycerin soap.

At least he was a good host. Since I could find no practical method of filling the tub, I took a sponge bath with a washcloth and soap.

When I emerged from the alcove, I found the bag containing my other clothing sitting on the bed. I shook out a long velvet gown, low-cut and black as the night sky, and slid into fresh panties, a Victoria's Secret bra with the firmest support I could find, and the dress. I fastened the buckles on my ankle boots before peeking out of the bedroom.

Smoky was in the living room, waiting for me. His eyes slid over me, and he let out a slow breath. "Camille . . ." He swept me into his arms and met my lips in a delicate kiss. "You take my breath away," he whispered. "Is it any wonder I can't get you out of my thoughts?"

I swallowed the lump growing in my throat. Obsession was a scary thing. But it could also be a heady elixir, and Smoky's charm was a powerful spell. I felt like I was standing on a razor's edge, a web spun by three men, all of whom I loved—in one way or another—and I wanted each and every one of them in my life. Just neatly organized, not standing around beating their chests like some manic episode of *Tarzan Gone Wild*.

He tucked my hand in his and brought it to his lips, kissing each finger in turn. "Dinner is served," he said, extending his arm.

The lump in my throat began to melt as my reluctance began to slide. Would it be so terribly bad to be the consort of a dragon? *Backtrack real fast,* I thought. Playmate was one thing. Consort held far too many implications. I was a soldier's daughter, not some lady of the manor. Feeling distinctly out of place, I rested my hand on his elbow. He folded his other hand over mine, then escorted me through the door opposite.

The kitchen was as large as the bedroom. A woodstove, polished to a high sheen, crackled with warmth. An old-fashioned icebox stood in the corner.

I stared at the icebox. "You have electricity out here in the barrow?"

"Does it look like I do?" He shook his head, grinning. "Think, girl. I'm white and silver dragon. I may breathe fire, but my magic's based in ice, wind, and snow."

Duh. Chalk one up for playing the airhead, I thought. And I couldn't even claim *blonde* as an excuse. As I looked around, I noticed a table against one wall. Carved from a solid block of marble, with two matching chairs, it was set for two. I wandered over to it.

"Old-world china, place mats, Waterford crystal . . . you don't stint, do you?" I held up one of the goblets and very gently ran my finger around the edge. It rang, loud and clear. "I suppose you've had a long time to collect all of this. How old are you, Smoky? How long have you lived out here?"

"I hope you like steak," he said, ignoring my questions. "I happened to be passing by a cattle ranch yesterday, and there was this plump heifer standing there . . ."

Blinking, I abruptly put down the goblet. "Yes, I like steak. You eating with me, or did you gobble yours down raw?" Somehow, I didn't think a twelve-ounce sirloin was enough to stave off a dragon's appetite. Even with baked potato and all the trimmings. Maybe with cheesecake on the side, I mused.

He snorted. "I'm offering you an elegant dinner here. Work with me, girl." As I stared at him expectantly, he let out a long sigh. "You're exasperating. I think that's why I love you. To answer your question, yes, yesterday I ate most of the heifer. *After* I butchered off meat for the steaks and for barbecued ribs."

"Barbecue? You like barbecue?" I took my place at the table, letting him slide my chair out for me. I wasn't *trying* to be difficult. To be honest, I just wanted to get outside and talk to Morgaine. I was starting to feel claustrophobic. Underground was not my favorite place to be.

"Of course. I especially like hickory smoke flavor." He

dished up our dinners. A good thick steak, some fried potatoes. I had the feeling he didn't eat many vegetables. I could manage without the carrots and peas. I was just grateful he hadn't left the beef on the hoof.

All through dinner, he talked and I listened, feeling like I was in some surreal dream. The Cleavers with a warped twist. Except I didn't vacuum in pearls, and Smoky blew Ward out of the water.

"Saint George has been having a bad spell," he said. "Estelle had to sedate him twice last week. I wonder what makes a human snap like that. She said that, as far as she knows, he was like that from birth. Always off chasing windmills. And dragons." He touched his lips with his napkin. "Would you like some wine?"

"Thank you, yes." As he filled my glass, I examined the label. It was old and rare, probably worth thousands, and he was pouring it into our goblets like it was water. I cleared my throat, trying to keep my thoughts on the conversation. "Georgio is luckier than most in his condition. Which reminds me. Tomorrow I have an appointment to see Ben Welter. At three P.M. I can't be late."

"I'll make sure you get home in plenty of time," he said. "You need to leave at daybreak in order to talk to Delilah, I assume?" A faint glower washed over his face.

I nodded. "Yes. Smoky, may I ask you something?"

"Of course. I might not answer, but you can *always* ask."

I slid my knife through the steak. It was fork-tender and cut like butter. Taking a deep breath, I said, "What will you do if Shadow Wing breaks through?"

He shrugged. "Probably retreat to the Northlands for awhile. Why? Are you worried I'd leave you? Don't be. You'd go with me, of course, and your sisters. I'll take Iris, and Delilah's man, and I'll even take the fox, if you like. I might consider rescuing Trillian, but that depends on how he behaves—"

Cutting him off at the pass, I shook my head. "You know very well that we couldn't go. My sisters and I are the only defense between Earth and the demons. We made a pact. We're in this for the long haul. I was hoping you'd stay and fight on our side."

He blinked, staring at me silently. Finally, he said, "We'll discuss the situation later, should it become necessary. Now, finish your meal, love, and then I want you to go talk to that blasted sorceress. I have errands to do this evening. When you've found out what you need to, come straight back to the barrow. Wait for me outside if I'm not home yet. Whatever you do, don't go wandering off the path without me."

I slowly finished the last bite of my steak and wiped my lips, not sure what I felt. Smoky was an incredible lover, and I considered him a good friend, but his continual use of the word *love* was beginning to scare me a little. When we'd first met, he'd threatened to carry me off, saying no one could stop him. Had that been a precursor of things to come?

Since we'd come Earthside, I'd noticed that my sisters and I had a tendency to forget that Cryptos and other Fae played by very different rules. Life over here had dulled our senses. At home, the various races were always aware of each other's divergent natures. Here, we'd let that awareness slide. A dangerous—and potentially deadly—mistake.

Smoky was just being true to his nature. No sane person would ever contradict him if they knew what he was. He took it for granted that when he said "Jump," people would jump. Without question. And what a dragon wanted, a dragon always managed to get. And he was dragon, all right, down to the core.

"Whatever you say." I pushed back my chair. "If you'll tell me where I can find Morgaine?"

"When you leave the barrow, follow the path another quarter mile, and then turn to your left by the giant cedar. You'll be able to find her. Trust me."

Before I left, I stashed the Black Unicorn horn in the slash pocket of my new cloak, in case I should need it. Though I had no idea *how* I'd use it. Yet. But it had saved me from the Eriskel's lightning, so I figured it probably had plenty of other tricks I might find useful against Morgaine's powers.

Smoky walked me to the door, where he waved his hand and said something under his breath that I couldn't catch. The portal opened. A charm, I thought, to negate the wards. I noticed he'd whispered it low enough so that I couldn't hear the words.

As I moved to go through, he lifted my hand and kissed it again. "Camille—one more warning. Don't even think about going home tonight. If there's an emergency, I will take you. But otherwise, best not to entertain the thought. Do you understand?"

As I met his gaze, our compact hit me full force. I'd given him a week of my life. This was the first night. I owed him obedience.

"I understand," I said, wondering just what the hell I'd gotten myself into with this little adventure.

The woodland around Smoky's barrow was rife with his wards and bindings. Tall sentinels soared into the sky, fir and cedar, maple and birch. They were flush with new growth, the coniferous trees bearing pale green needles that would darken over the summer. Leaf buds lined the branches of the bare maple and birch limbs, preparing to open into a riot of burgeoning green.

As I set out on the path, dusk spread its inky fingers over the sky. I shivered. Living in the city—even on acreage like we did—dulled the senses, too. Out here the land was still wild, and it didn't welcome intruders. I folded my arms across my chest as I walked, more to comfort my nerves rather than ward off the evening chill of the air. The cloak kept me plenty warm.

A noise to my left startled me, and I darted a glance to the side. An elk stood there, a bull, regal in silhouette. As I passed him, he dipped his head, and I saw that he had only one antler. Shedding season, I thought. I inclined my head in return. We recognized each other; he knew I was not fully human, and I knew he was a woodland watcher.

As the dusk spread quickly through the land, the trees began to glow, a faint glimmer surrounding them. Most of their auras were green, indicating healthy growth. Here and there I caught a glimpse of a red aura—the sign of a dying tree. And more rarely, a golden corona. Those trees were home to tree devas, and as fully sentient and aware of the world as I was.

The stars began to appear in the growing darkness, and it seemed to me that I could hear music: a rhythmic drumming, a lute or zither, and a flute. *What the* . . . as I rounded a bend in the path where the huckleberry and fern overshrouded the ground, I came to a giant cedar. This had to be the tree Smoky told me about. I turned onto an even narrower trail to the left, and as I did, I could feel her. Morgaine was near. The scent of bonfires, the sound of crows calling, the sense of Moon magic was thick around me. I quickened my pace and hurried down the path.

The track opened into a sheltered meadow, surrounded by a ring of oak and rowan. The trees around the clearing were thick with crows and ravens. A holly stood in the center, and the ground was thick with patches of spongy moss.

And in the center of the clearing, I saw Morgaine. She and Mordred and Arturo were there, all three of them, sitting around a bonfire. Two large tents had been raised off to one side, along with what looked like a yurt, only with vinyl tarps stretched over the frame rather than skins or leather.

I entered the grove and slowly approached the fire. Morgaine stood. She was petite, shorter even than Menolly, and she still made me catch my breath, although I wasn't as starstruck as I had been on our last meeting.

Morgaine was wearing a long black dress, similar to mine, and she wore a silver crescent moon around her neck and a silver tiara that reflected the glow from the fire. Arturo, a stately man with grizzled hair and an otherworldly air, quickly rose and bowed. Mordred, her nephew, remained sitting. He stared at me, an insolent smirk on his face.

I gave Morgaine a quick curtsy, not quite sure how to open the conversation. But the sorceress took care of that for me.

"The dragon sent you, didn't he? He doesn't like me much, I think." Her voice lilted over the words. Oh yes, she was half-Fae as well, and her blood ran thick with darker, older magic than my own. And then it clicked. Morgaine's powers strengthened under the dark of the moon, while mine rose to their zenith during the full. She ran crone energy through her veins.

Arturo motioned for me to sit on the log between them. I opted for the end of the long trunk, instead. Easier to get away, if I needed to escape. As I settled down, Mordred squinted at me, then pulled a tin mug off of a makeshift table and filled it with something brewing over the fire. He handed me the cup. I accepted it out of courtesy, but I sure as hell wasn't planning on drinking anything they gave me.

"We just want to know what you're doing here. This is his land, and he's . . . curious." I pretended to take a sip, then set the cup down on the ground next to my feet.

"*We?* So you are the creature's mistress, are you? I thought I smelled the scent of dragon on you. You'd better be careful, child. Do you have any idea what you're doing, cavorting with dragons?" Morgaine slid closer to me.

I automatically scooted away. Though I didn't sense any evil or anything remotely akin to the Demonkin, she gave me the willies. Maybe it was the sheer magnitude of her power, or perhaps I still had a bad case of fangirl-itis . . . but whatever the reason, she made me terribly nervous.

I cleared my throat. "Who I cavort with is my own business. But tell me, what are you doing here?"

She paused, then glanced at Arturo. He shrugged. Mordred mumbled something under his breath, but she ignored him. "There's no harm in telling you. You and your sisters can't stop me, even if you wanted to. And somehow, I doubt you'll try. We're looking for a cave—"

"For the Merlin?"

"Hush. Mind your manners around your elders, or didn't those teachers in *Otherworld* teach you anything?"

Her abrupt command shut me up, but I wondered what the hell was going on. Last we'd met, she'd been seeking to find and awaken her mentor. Had her plans changed?

She sniffed. "There's a cave out here somewhere. It contains a far greater ally than that stuffy old lecher. I must find that cavern."

"But why? And what sort of ally are you hoping to find there, if not the Merlin?"

Who the hell was she looking for? And then the thought that my sisters and I had already discussed came creeping back, eating at the edge of my consciousness. What if Morgaine was seeking a way to contact the demons? What if this "ally" she was talking about turned out to be Shadow Wing? Or someone from his army?

She tapped her nose. "Enough said. All will be answered in good time. There was a time when the Fae of this world ruled supreme. We held the world safe in our arms from outsiders and invaders. That day will come again. I give you my word on that."

What a load of crock! The Fae had fought among themselves for as long as I could remember—at least it was that way in Otherworld, and I doubted if it had been much different here.

"Of all the closemouthed, pigheaded, stubborn . . ." Frustrated, I jumped up, knocking over the mug as I did so. "Give it up, Morgaine. What's your purpose? Who are you looking for and why? We know you're up to something. Are you out to join forces with Shadow Wing?"

She rose slowly, with deliberate focus. My heart leapt into my throat. Never anger a sorceress who could make mincemeat out of you. I felt for the unicorn horn, my hand sliding into the inner pocket where I'd stashed it.

"You little fool. Shadow Wing? Pah! I have no love for Demonkin. But I refuse to stand by and watch you and your sisters hand over this world to the demon lord because you're so inept. You want to know what I'm doing? *Fine.* I'll tell you. I plan on raising the Seelie and Unseelie Courts again, and the Queens of Fae *will* unite to stop the demon threat. You can join me, or you can stand against me. Which do you choose?"

My jaw must have dropped a mile. Feddrah-Dahns was right.

"But . . . you mean to set yourself up as the Unseelie Queen?" The thought of Morgaine wielding the title of Queen of Darkness was terrifying. With her at the helm, the Earthside Fae could easily send civilization back to bow and arrow.

She stared at me for a moment, then began to laugh. "You are so earnest and so easily misled. I know you've been keeping company with the Dahns Prince. Whatever you find to talk about, I can't imagine. But no, to answer your question. I'm not after the Dark Crown. I will rule the Seelie Court and raise it to heights that Titania could only dream of, even in her heyday. I first came seeking her, hoping to gain her aid, but rumor has it she's a drunken sot who's lost most of her powers as well as most of her wits. So I'll do this on my own."

I glanced at Arturo and Mordred. Neither looked happy under my scrutiny, but their expressions backed up her words.

Slowly crossing to the holly tree, I fingered one of the sharp leaves. "So, if you are determined to take the crown of the Seelie Court, then who do you expect to take the crown of Unseelie?"

Morgaine gave me a feral little smile that reminded me all too much of Grandmother Coyote's steel teeth. "Who else? The Queen who held it last. Aeval is rumored to be trapped in a cavern near here, frozen in time. Since the Fae Courts must be balanced here on Earth, why not offer her the freedom to return to what she does best?"

Aeval had been one of the queens of Fae before the Great Divide, as ruthless and terrifying as any modern dictator. She made Lethesanar look like a pouting schoolgirl. I shuddered.

"You seek to return the Mother of the Dark to the dark throne? Are you mad? She's—"

Morgaine let out a short bark of laughter. The fire seemed to spark and grow higher, and Mordred grunted. "She's everything the Unseelie Queen needs to be. There must be a balance, Camille. You cannot have light without dark, clarity without shadow."

She circled around me, her eyes glittering. "Look at your own queen. Lethesanar's reign has festered, and there is no Queen of Light to balance out her actions. Now that the pendulum has swung too far, her sister seeks to take the throne. If Tanaquar wins, if she destroys her sister, you can be certain the same thing will happen in a thousand years unless they find some way of uniting their powers. Take one side away, and you upset the universe. That's when the Hags of Fate step in and rearrange matters, and they make all of us—all the Fae—look like bumbling infants."

"But how can they rule jointly? They're at odds. That's why the Courts of Fae were disbanded here when the Great Divide happened." I shook my head. "There cannot be joint custody over one land—"

"So you think, but you are so ignorant. You know nothing of that time, of the battles that raged," Morgaine said. "Think about it. All of nature hangs in balance. Winter, summer, spring, and fall. Even in the lands of extremes, there's a balance when you take the long view. The heat of the deserts—the chill of the ice caps. Earth is in peril, the balance has been disrupted. Mankind has meddled with it, the Fae have forsaken it. The demons are pounding at the gates. Without returning the great Courts, this world has no chance of survival. The Queen of Darkness and the Queen of Light keep the balance in check."

I blinked. Could she be right? Was the only answer to solving the crises facing this world to return the Light and the Dark to their thrones? It made sense, in a terrifying way.

She was at my side then, in a blur of movement. Taking my wrist, she pulled me down to kneel beside her on the ground, where she clawed up a handful of soil and thrust it in my face. The sour tang of moist earth filled my lungs.

"Breathe deep. This is the world that gave birth to your mother. This is the world that gave birth to the Fae before the Great Divide. Moon Mother watches over us. Mother Earth gives us life. The world is in danger—from within and from without. We know that Shadow Wing threatens to bathe this world in a wall of flame and fire."

"But what can you do about it? What hope can raising the Courts again possibly offer?"

Dropping the soil back on the ground, she grasped me by the shoulders. "You know you can't fight the demons on your own. You need allies. You need more than the Elfin Queen and a dragon to fight off the coming apocalypse."

A tight knot worked its way into my stomach. She was right. We needed allies. Hell, we needed an army. I pulled away from her and stood.

As if she could read my mind, she said, "Aeval and I will raise our armies. We will reunite the Fae of this world. While we may also fight against each other, for a foe like Shadow Wing we will unite. And then we will reclaim our rightful places in this world. Humans hunger for our kiss, for our magic. You've seen the way they opened their arms to you and your kin. It's because they miss their own magical heritage. They were done a terrible disservice during the Great Divide, and the separation of worlds not only destroyed the balance of the world, but it shredded the human race's connection to its *own* magical nature."

Her voice drifted off. I held my breath as a nasty look crossed her face—an *I'm gonna kick you in the balls* look. "But . . . I need something you carry. Give it to me. Give me the horn."

Startled, I stumbled back. Mordred moved then, rushed toward me at lightning speed. I matched his pace. He might be part Fae, but my bet was he'd never lived among his otherworldly kin. My blood was at the top of my veins, his was buried in history.

"Don't even think about it," I said, dancing away. I slid my hand in my pocket again and wrapped it around the horn. "Don't even try it. The horn was a gift for *me*, and only I can use it. And if I do, it will shatter you." A bluff, of course, but conceivably true. It sounded good, at least.

As I backed my way toward the trail, I wondered if I'd be able to make it to the barrow before they caught me. There were three of them, although Arturo didn't look nearly so keen on catching me as did Morgaine and her nephew.

I was debating on whether to turn and run or to try to face them down when a blinding flash startled the hell out of me. Could it be Smoky?

"Leave her be. This is *my* territory and you are trespassing on it."

I swung around. There, standing tall and regal and crowned in a swath of energy far stronger than before, stood Titania. And she didn't look happy.

CHAPTER 16

"Titania!" Morgaine's voice echoed through the clearing.

The element of surprise was clearly in the Fae Queen's court. Titania gave Morgaine a warning look as I raced over to her side.

"Am I ever glad to see you." Maybe she'd overlook me stealing away her lover just this once. After all, it wasn't like I'd taken Tom Lane for myself. I glanced up at the tall, gossamer beauty, and she gave me a sly smile. Good sign? Bad sign? Not sure, I opted to hope it was good.

Titania stepped in front of me, and as she did so, she whispered, "Your scaly boyfriend asked me to keep watch over you."

Scaly boyfriend? I did the wisest thing I could think of. I kept my mouth shut.

Morgaine gave Titania the once-over. "So, last I heard, you were so deep in your cups that you might as well roll over in the gutter and die. What happened? Run out of wine?"

Hokay, that was enough for me. I backed away. Titania might be a shadow of her former self, but she could still mop up the floor with me and wring me out to dry afterward. If Morgaine provoked her enough . . .

Titania straightened her shoulders. She no longer reeked of booze, and her powers crackled around her, a nimbus of sparks. Oh yeah, apparently her stint in magical rehab had done wonders. Her dress, a gossamer see-through gown, seemed to float from her shoulders, and her long, golden hair shimmered under the bonfire light.

"Upstart. I know what you're doing. Don't you even *dare dream* that you could replace me. If the Courts of Fae rise again, I will be riding the crest, not you. I could squash you like a beetle with one hand." She moved forward, gliding as if she were skimming the grass with her feet.

Morgaine caught her breath, and I saw her step back, fear washing across her face. Yeah, mighty sorceress she might be, and half-Fae, but she was a baby compared to Titania's age and full power.

"You . . . you have hidden out for so long and now you expect to step in and reclaim a throne you willingly vacated years back? The Merlin told me you were fickle, when he taught me so long ago—"

"Fickle? We're *all* fickle, you snot-nosed brat." Titania squared her shoulders and raised a finger, pointing it at the sorceress. "You, me, her—" She swung around to nod to me. "Anyone with Fae blood will turn their backs on someone they love, sometime. It's in our blood, it's in our nature. Don't you know that the Merlin was *my* lover long before you were born? He was an old fool who cared too much for his reputation and too little for what he could offer to the world. If you seek his help to raise the Seelie and Unseelie Courts, you'll understand what it truly means to be betrayed."

Morgaine opened her mouth, then quietly closed it. She dropped to one of the fallen logs and clasped her hands together. "I know. That's why I stopped hunting for him. But we have to do something. I cannot allow this world—and all that I love about it—to fall into the hands of the demons. And that girl is no match for a demon lord." Again, a nod to me.

I was beginning to feel invisible, the proverbial fly on the wall. I started to speak, but Mordred, who had inched his way over to my side, shook his head.

"Don't get involved. It isn't safe." He had a dark scowl on his face, and I wondered what he thought of the whole matter.

But I didn't ask. I wanted to hear everything I could that Titania and Morgaine were saying.

Titania gave Morgaine a dangerous smile, showing her teeth just enough to remind me of a snarling dog. "Don't dismiss the girl and her sisters so lightly. And remember this: They are under my protection and the protection of the dragon who lives on my land."

I blinked. Obviously, Smoky and Titania were having some sort of dispute over property boundaries. I idly wondered if he'd ever slept with her, but decided not to go there. At least not right now.

"Morgaine, we have much to discuss." She turned back to me. "Camille, return to Smoky's for now. Do not stray from the path; there are dangerous traps and creatures that wander this land. We will be in touch with you soon. You are not out of this yet."

"But the horn—she has—" Morgaine jumped to her feet.

"Enough!" Titania's voice shook the clearing, and Morgaine cringed. "Leave it be for now."

I chose that moment to make my exit, stage left. I gave a short bow to the Fae Queen emeritus and the sorceress. As soon as I was away from the clearing, I started to jog along the path, wanting to put distance between me and the sparring women. What the hell were they up to? Titania looked far stronger than the last time I'd met her. I would have bet my pay that she couldn't have returned from the sodden state she'd been in, but I'd been wrong.

As I rounded the bend, a noise startled me. I glanced over my shoulder to check if Mordred had followed me, but there was no one there. Just then, a beautiful red fox raced onto the path and blocked my way. I dropped to my knees.

"Morio! I'm so glad to see you." I recognized the particular glint in his eye. Within seconds, he'd changed back into human form and retrieved his bag from beneath a huckleberry bush.

"Camille, I was worried about you. I saw everything. I've been prowling the land all day. Smoky and Titania have the place loaded with magical traps, but I'm good at spotting most of them." He helped me to my feet and slid his arms around my waist, pressing a quick kiss to my lips. "I thought I was going to have to jump in there and help you get away from that witch."

"You mean *bitch*, don't you? I don't think I like Morgaine," I said, frowning. "Grandmother Coyote was right. She's power hungry."

"She may be, but she's right about one thing: We need all the help we can get to fight Shadow Wing." He drew me to the side of the path. "This area is safe. I checked."

As we settled down on the lush patch of grass, Morio held out his arm and I leaned into it, realizing how comforting it was to be on familiar turf again. Morio and Trillian were safe. I knew them, we had our routine and rhythm down. But everything out here felt dangerous. Smoky included.

"I'm scared," I said. "I just want it to be tomorrow so that I can go home."

"It will be soon, just hang on a little longer," he murmured.

I leaned forward and propped my elbows on my knees. "So, what did you and Delilah find out about the rug shop?"

"Demon scent there, all right. I went in, just in case they recognized Delilah. The owner wasn't there, but his assistant was. A woman named Jassamin. I think she's the one who was asking after Menolly."

"What's she like? Do you think she's a djinn like we thought?" Djinns were tricky to pinpoint, but there were ways to flush them out. And Morio was well-versed in identifying magical beings.

"She's beautiful, she's sensuous, and yes, she's a djinn." He grinned at me as I slapped him on the arm.

"Beautiful and sensuous, huh?" An odd little flutter inside warned me that I was tripping close to playing the jealousy card. I had no idea where the feeling had sprung up from. It had never bothered me before if my lovers had their own private flings. But something was shifting, and it had started when we came Earthside.

He snorted. "I knew that would get your attention. Don't worry, I have no intentions of getting involved with a djinn. I don't like them, for one thing. For another, anybody hanging around a greater demon has to be bad news. I think she's young, in terms of her abilities. The underlying wards on the shop were very strong, but the ones that I could tell she had erected were weak and easily overcome."

"Did you say greater demon?" My blood turned to ice.

He nodded.

"But djinn technically aren't demons, they aren't even

considered to be minor demons like imps and incubi. So where do you think the scent of greater demon is coming from? I can't believe one just wandered through the shop."

Morio shook his head. "I don't think so, either. Honestly? I think it's the owner. The scent went beyond the areas they allow customers in. I snuck into the office while the girl was off checking on a nonexistent order I'd put in, and sure enough, the room was rife with it. The stench is stuck in my nostrils and driving me nuts."

My breath quickened. "Want to make a bet we've found out where the Rāksasa lives?"

He nodded. "Again, that seems logical. Whoever he is—and it's a he, that much I could tell—well, he's big and he's bad and he's dangerous. We're going to have our hands full with this mess."

"What mess?" Smoky suddenly appeared from around the bend. He gave Morio a long, studied look, then slowly turned back to me.

I jumped to my feet, suddenly feeling guilty for talking to my lover. "We're discussing the demon. Probably a Rāksasa, from what we know. And a nasty one, at that."

Morio smoothly rose to his feet and gave Smoky a casual nod. "We've also got a djinn on our hands who might be in cahoots with him."

With a slow blink, Smoky let out a little huff, and I saw the faint trace of smoke wisp out of his nostrils. Disconcerting, to say the least.

"Not only that," I hurried to say, "but I found out that Morgaine is planning on resurrecting the Seelie and Unseelie Courts, and she's nominated herself for the title of Seelie Queen. Titania is over there right now, stone cold sober, and ticked off like you wouldn't believe."

"Wonderful," Smoky said, looking like he couldn't care less. "As long as they keep the battle off of *my* lands, it doesn't matter to me what they do. Meanwhile, Morio, I assume you came out here to tell Camille about the demon?" *And nothing else* was heavily implied in his voice.

Morio shrugged, ignoring the hint. "Yes, and to make sure she's all right. You're a dragon, yes. You could hand roll us on your thighs and smoke us like Cuban cigars, true. But that won't stop Camille's friends and family from making sure that she's okay. We like you enough, don't get us wrong, but she's our . . . she's *my* mistress, and her sisters are worried about her."

Smoky considered his words, then turned back to the trail. "Come then. We can talk better inside, where there are no prying ears to listen, nor eyes to take note of our actions."

Morio gave me a surprised look, and I shrugged. Who knew the whys and wherefores of Dragonkin? I fell in behind Smoky and, with Morio at my heels, we headed back to the barrow.

The warmth of the barrow—even as cavernous as it was—felt welcoming after the chill of the spring night. Morio gazed around, politely refraining from asking any questions. But I noticed he was paying careful attention to the layout of the place. Casing the joint, I would have said if I didn't know him better.

Smoky ignored him and crossed to a hand-carved bar that sat in the living room area, where he poured three snifters of brandy. He motioned for us to sit.

"Come, we'll discuss your demon problem. You say a Rākṣasa? I've never had a run-in with one, but some of my Asiatic cousins have. They can be extremely dangerous, and they're very good at . . ." He paused. "Morio, would you do me a favor?"

Morio stared at him. "What do you want?"

Smoky motioned toward the kitchen. "Will you bring me a bottle of Perrier? It's in the icebox."

Confused—Smoky seemed such a gracious host, and it seemed odd for him to ask a guest to run an errand—I stood. "I can get it for you."

"Camille, sit." He spoke quietly, but one look in his eyes told me that I'd be treading deep water if I didn't obey. I sat.

"Sure," Morio said, still frowning. He rose and went into the kitchen. As soon as he was gone, Smoky whispered something in a low voice—again, I couldn't make out what he was saying—and pointed toward the kitchen. A faint shimmer of blue fire wreathed the door.

"Now we'll wait," he said, glancing at me. I opened my mouth to ask what he was doing, but he shook his head. "In a moment."

Morio came bopping back through the door then, his

attention on the bottle in his hand. He walked through the fire without blinking. At least, he did for three steps. Then he turned and stared at the door behind him.

"Checking to make sure I'm really who I say I am?" He tossed Smoky the green bottle of water, and Smoky caught it with one hand. "Can't say that I blame you. Not with a Rākṣasa in the picture."

"What does that have to do with anything?" I asked, feeling both insulted and yet strangely protected by Smoky's actions.

"Smoky obviously knows his demonology. Rākṣasas are masters of illusion," Morio said. "He was just making certain I'm not the demon taking the shape of someone you know and trust."

I blinked. "I hadn't thought of that."

"Well, you should," Smoky said. "You and your sisters have to start thinking the way your enemy thinks—cunning and devious and without compunction. The demons certainly won't cut you any slack for sloppy thinking. Know this, Camille: They are *ruthless*. Demonkin make dragons look like choirboys. They enjoy pain, they enjoy torture, and they suckle death like a baby suckles its mother's teat."

He paced the room. "I don't like you being involved in this. The Elemental Lords caused this entire situation when they gave away the spirit seals, and they refuse to take responsibility for cleaning up the mess. I have no truck with any of them, save for the Harvestmen and the Queen of Snow and Ice." He paused. "I'd say dump the entire problem in their laps."

"You really think that's feasible? That they'd even blink? Most of the Elemental Lords don't give a crap about humanity—"

Smoky held up his hand as I started to protest. "I know, I know. You can't . . . or rather you *won't* walk away. As misguided as I think you are, I admire you for it." He turned back to Morio. "Tell me, you say you smelled a demon. Did you, by any chance, catch wind of the fragrances of orange and jasmine? And, perhaps, sugar vanilla?"

Morio frowned, squinting. After a moment he nodded. "Now that you mention it, yes, I do remember those scents. They were everywhere in the shop. An odd combination, like a perfume that was on the verge of crystallizing. Too sweet," he said. "It was too sweet. It cloyed on the tongue, smelling like it was on the edge of decay."

"Then rest assured, you have a Rāksasa on your hands." Smoky opened the drawer on the end table nearest him and pulled out a pipe, tamping it full with herb from a leather pouch. He leaned back and motioned to me. "Camille, light my pipe, if you will."

With a glance at Morio—I never did things like that at home—I shook my head. "You know smoke of just about any kind bothers both Delilah and me." But I crossed to Smoky's chair and knelt by his side. "No smoking inside while I'm here. I have to insist. *Please*," I added.

"This is a side of you I've never seen," Morio said, an odd look on his face, like he might actually find the idea of me playing the submissive girlfriend appealing.

"Don't get any ideas," I muttered, flashing him a snarky grin.

"Oh, I always have ideas when I'm around you," he quipped back.

Smoky cleared his throat and put away his pipe. "Not a problem."

"Why did you say we definitely have a Rāksasa on hand?" Morio leaned back in his chair, sipping his brandy.

Smoky shrugged. "Those scents, or rather, the combination, is their natural fragrance. Here, Earthside, it can easily pass as a perfume, so most people wouldn't pay it a second thought. The only reason I know is because when I heard you might be facing one, I called in a few favors and gathered what information I could."

He said it as calmly as he might have been giving us the weather report, but both Morio and I turned to stare at him. I threw myself into his lap and wrapped my arms around his neck.

"You meant to help us all along! You were just stringing me along." I planted a kiss on his lips and pulled back, suddenly finding myself staring intently into his eyes.

A long lock of his hair unbraided itself and reached around to encircle my waist as he gently returned my kiss. "You like to think so, don't you? I was just curious, perhaps?" But his kiss had told me everything I needed to know.

Suddenly aware that Morio was watching us, I started to get off of Smoky's lap, but Morio held up his hand. "Don't get up on my account," he said. "I can see you . . . have come to an understanding."

Smoky met Morio's gaze, and his lip curved up to just the slightest degree. "Don't forget, I witnessed your first tryst with Camille here in my woods." He let out a low huff. "I know perfectly well that you and Trillian love this woman, and you know perfectly well that I intend to do my best to steal her away. But that may take some time, and in the meanwhile . . . I'll be on my best behavior."

Once again feeling like the Invisible Girl, I pushed my way out of his lap and parked my hands on my hips.

"Excuse me, but in case you haven't noticed, I happen to be in the room. And believe it or not, I can hear every word the two of you are saying. I wasn't so quick to point this out to Morgaine and Titania, because they're both off their rockers and might just take a notion to blast me into smithereens. However, since I doubt either of you has the balls to chance it, you'd better listen up! You will *stop* referring to me as anybody's property, you will *acknowledge* my presence, and you—are you laughing? You'd better be listening to me!"

Smoky and Morio broke out in full-blown howls that echoed through the chamber.

"I'm serious! I don't find this funny in the least—"

"The woman has a point," Smoky said, ignoring me and speaking to Morio.

Morio shrugged. "I suppose so, but it's more fun to watch her get all apoplectic. She can fly into a fury, I warn you."

"I'm all too aware of that, but her delights make up for the tantrums." Smoky reached out and ran his finger down the outside of my thigh. I could feel his energy through the dress, a series of miniature lightning bolts sending off warning signals through my body that a welcome intruder was near.

"Knock it off, both of you—"

Smoky's laughter died away as he leapt to his feet, swept me into his arms, and turned to Morio. "Since she refuses to be owned by *one* man, what do you say about showing me some of her favorite tricks?"

Sputtering, I tried to squirm out of his embrace. "We need to talk about the Rāksasa. You have to tell us what you know."

"After." Smoky held me fast.

"Who the hell do you—" But then I stopped. A dragon, that's who he thought he was. And he was right. And I *had* promised him a week on his terms. I stopped fighting.

"Fine, you want to have a play date with both of us, I'm down with that. But Morio has to agree, and you have to promise not to hurt him."

Smoky shrugged. "I never intended on harming the fox. It's your Svartan lover I'd like to teach some respect."

Morio looked at Smoky, then at me. "All right," he said slowly. "I'll join you. But know this, dragon. I'm part of her triad, and that triad includes Trillian. I owe my allegiance to Camille, first, and then to Trillian, not you."

And with that sobering thought, Smoky carried me into the bedroom with Morio following.

CHAPTER 17

~≈≈~

As Smoky swept me into the bedroom, I began to rethink the idea. The whole situation seemed rife for misunderstanding and somebody getting hurt. Which would be bad. Very bad.

I glanced up at Smoky. Maybe he was trying to please me, to compromise a little so that he could come into my world and be with me? *Right . . . get a grip,* I told myself. Dragons didn't like to share. So why the hell was he accommodating Morio? There had to be an ulterior motive lurking under that reptilian heart that I fancied so much.

And if I was totally honest with myself, I knew I could handle a lot, but *both* a youkai and a dragon? At the same time? Was I that good—or at least, that resilient? A sudden flock of butterflies took up residence in my stomach, and they weren't the good kind.

Smoky set me on the bed and stood back. He glanced at my face, then at Morio, who had paused by the doorway. No one said anything for a long moment, then Smoky sat down next to me and began to undress me. I let him slide my dress down to my waist, and then he leaned down and began to kiss the length of my neck.

Morio slipped in behind me and gently ran his hand up my

arm as he moved my hair aside, pressing his lips to the center of my back.

I shivered at the touch of their lips. Maybe not such a bad idea after all. Oh, this was going to be good. Terrifying, but good.

"See, you won't miss Trillian at all," Smoky said, breathing heavily as he ran his cheek against mine.

Bingo! I knew it. I pushed away from both of them. "I know what you're up to, and you can just stop it right now!"

"What?"

"I'm quite delighted to be in your bed, and I wouldn't have any qualms about spending the night with both you and Morio, however . . ." I looked over at my youkai lover. "Morio is *part* of my relationship with Trillian. They complement each other, they've accepted one another. They are *my* men. And you're trying to cut Trillian out by inviting Morio to play with us."

That was it; that was what felt wrong. This was Smoky's way of sliding in between Trillian and me.

The look on Smoky's face told me I'd been right. I tensed. Was he going to blow up because I'd figured him out? Retaliate, perhaps?

Morio smoothly stood and put himself between the dragon and me.

Smoky gave him an icy stare. "Move. Now."

"Not until I know you aren't going to hurt her." Morio stood his ground.

Smoky looked like he wanted to send him flying but, after a quick look at me, he let out a long breath and relaxed. "Then it looks like Camille will be the only one sharing my bed," he said, his voice cool. "You shouldn't try to cross the land in the dark. I know you're a talented shifter, but there are energies stirring in the wild with which I do not recommend tangling. You may sleep on the sofa. Don't interrupt us."

Morio looked back at me. I nodded. "It's okay. Everything will be fine."

He was at my side in an instant. "Enjoy your night. I have no doubt that Smoky will ensure you are both *safe* and satisfied." As usual, he remained calm and collected. Thank the gods for small favors. Trillian would have been duking it out with Smoky by now.

As Morio closed the door behind him, I felt a little jump in my heart and realized how much I loved the youkai. Trillian was my oath mate, bound to me for the rest of our lives even when we wanted to smack each other silly. Morio had won his way into my heart through a quieter—but no less potent—way. When the time came, I'd tell him how I felt. I suspected he already knew.

Smoky watched the door shut and then turned to me. "Camille, I want you to listen to me. Don't answer. Not yet. I know you love them. I know you refuse to choose between them and that each one brings something to your life the other can't. But, Camille . . . I'm offering you the whole package, in one person. One man."

"One *dragon*," I said, shivering. "Please, can we talk about this later? If you force me to choose, I guarantee you won't like my response. And neither will I, because I don't think you'd take it very well."

But as I gazed into his frost-shaded eyes, a flicker of uncertainty made me wonder. "Smoky, I don't even pretend to understand why you've chosen me to be your mate. You're . . . a dragon. I can't give you children, I'll die long before you. Look at everything you've seen and experienced."

"Your father loved your mother," he said simply.

I swallowed. That was true, but this seemed so . . . so different. "All I know is that you're incredible. When you touch me, I forget where I am. I forget what's going on out there with the demons and the war, and everything that's horrible." I pointed toward the door.

"And that's a bad thing?" he asked, looking confused.

"No!" How could I explain so that he'd understand? Or maybe he did, and just didn't want to acknowledge it. "Smoky, I feel safe around you in a way I've never felt before, even if I don't particularly feel safe *from* you. Don't make me choose. Don't try to break my oath to Trillian, because I don't want to walk away from you. And I will, if it comes to that."

"Then let me make you forget your worries. For now." He leaned down and kissed me, and all words were forgotten as my dragon took me to bed and made love to me again, and again, and again.

When I woke at first light, Smoky was sitting in a chair in the corner. He was staring at me so intently that I thought something might be wrong. But when I asked, he just shook his head.

"Just watching you sleep," he said.

I climbed out of the tangled bedcovers and stretched. Smoky held out his arms, and I walked over and slid onto his lap. I thought he was going to suggest another romp between the sheets and tried to think of an excuse. He'd worn me out the night before, and I felt like I'd be walking bowlegged for days. As much as I enjoyed sex, I didn't think I had it in me for another go this morning. But instead of motioning to the bed, he just pointed to my bag.

"Pack. While you dress, I'll make breakfast." And then he was out the door, shutting it softly behind him.

By the time I washed up and dressed, Smoky had fried up eggs and sausage and more potatoes. Morio was setting the table, and he glanced at me. I gave him a wan smile. If this had been one day with Smoky, I couldn't imagine what a solid week would be like. I'd probably forget my name by that point. After we ate and returned to the living room, Morio wandered over to the edge of the cavern.

"Where does the cave lead to?" he asked, staring down into the ravine.

Smoky shrugged. "To a series of underground tunnels. There's an exit that I can fly out from in my natural form. And if I should choose to alter the vibration of the portals, I can enter other realms from there."

"All of your exits and entrances are protected, aren't they?" A sudden image of demons storming Smoky's lair assaulted me.

He gave me a look that asked if I'd gotten up on the blonde side of the bed. "Don't worry yourself about it. And don't even think about trying to strengthen them for me. I've *seen* the results of your magic," he added with a smirk.

"Hey, I'll have you know I'm pretty formidable when it comes to death magic," I said, shaking my head. "Listen, you were going to tell us what you knew about the Rāksasas, by the way."

Smoky nodded. "Last night, while you slept, I transcribed what I learned so you can show your sisters. Let me get my notes for you." He bounded away into the bedroom.

Morio leaned forward and whispered, "He plugged directly into the Energizer Bunny?"

I thought of the throbbing ache between my legs. He'd managed to introduce me to muscles that I didn't know existed.

"Well, he does keep going and going and going. Nice in some respects but . . ."

Morio snorted. "Finally found somebody who can outride you? Maybe I should have stuck around last night, just to witness the miracle."

I swatted him lightly on the arm. "Yeah, right, you should talk. Between you and Trillian, it's a wonder I ever get any sleep."

He winked at me, then leaned over to plant a quick kiss on my cheek. He backed away then, just an inch or so, and held my gaze, searching my face. "You aren't going to leave us for him, are you?" he asked.

And once again, I was pulled back into my reality.

"No," I said. "Trust me, I have no plans on deserting either of you for Smoky. But it's been like a bizarre dream. He's incredible, but his life feels so . . . outside of my reality."

"Maybe that's what he's meant to be for you. A retreat—a safe haven perhaps—for you when you need to get away from who you are and from what's going on." Morio slid back into his chair as Smoky returned to the room, a sheaf of papers in his hand.

As Smoky handed the papers to me, I thought about what Morio had said. Was the dragon my safety net, where I could come when I needed to feel isolated and insular? Could I play Persephone, spend part of my time in Smoky's world, the rest out where I was needed—fighting demons and saving worlds? And would Smoky be content with that?

"Thank you," I said as I leafed through the neatly printed notes. "You're a sweetheart, even if you won't admit it." He looked pleased as I leaned over to plant a peck on his cheek. "You really are," I whispered. "I would have come to you even if we didn't have a contract between us."

Smoky relented then and pulled me to him for a long, slow kiss, then let go with a huff, but this time he didn't sound put out.

I glanced at the papers. His handwriting was precise, and he used blue ink on a frost-white notepad. I decided to wait until I got home to read it, so I could talk everything over with Menolly and Delilah.

"We'd better be going," I said, standing. "Morio, did you drive out here?"

Morio arched an eyebrow. "No, I flew. Of course I drove. My car is near Georgio's house." He turned to Smoky. "With your leave?"

Smoky slipped into his white trench, and I found myself entranced by his beauty again. The man was just too gorgeous to be real. He wrapped his arm around my shoulder and hoisted my overnight bag with his other hand. "I'll walk you to the house. I should ask Estelle how Georgio's doing today."

As we wended our way through the woodland, I felt like I could breathe again. The barrow had been too confined, but out here it felt perfectly natural for Smoky to have his arm around me. I leaned my head against his shoulder.

"I'm sorry we have to split up the week," I said.

"No you're not," he countered. "But that's all right. It just means you'll be bound to me longer than you thought—what with all the days in between. I'm not going to insist you come out tonight. I know you'll be busy with the demon business."

"Thanks." And there was far more at stake than just the *demon business*, I thought.

Titania was scary-powerful again, and Morgaine was no slouch, herself. What if Titania encouraged Morgaine to take over the Unseelie crown, and they raised the courts that way? What if Morgaine decided to try to kill Titania? That alone would marshal the Fae from both OW and Earthside into action. But not the kind of action we needed.

I stared at the path. The leaf debris from last autumn had worked its way into the mulch of soil and undergrowth, and the trail was wet but not sink-to-your-boot-tops muddy. As we stepped over rock and branch, I tried to tune into the land to see if I could find out what Titania and Morgaine were up to.

For a few moments, all I could sense were the usual comings and goings of the forest, the scurrying of creatures, the wind whistling through the branches, the sun trying to break through a heavy cloud cover. And then, slowly, my attention narrowed. I could feel the signature of a huckleberry deva as we passed by a stand of the shrubs. And over there, a group of nature sprites working on a fir who was ailing.

Then I felt it—a stirring, almost like a vortex.

"There's a disturbance in the force, Luke," I muttered.

Smoky frowned. "What does that mean?"

"No kidding," Morio said. "Even I can feel it. Something big is on the horizon."

As I sorted through the energies whirling in the maelstrom, I began to sort out two distinct presences. One, a swirl of leaf and branch, of stone and wood and autumn colors and summer scents . . . the other a cacophony of mist and shadow, of starlight and crystals and deep caverns, but the energies weren't in conflict.

"It's almost as if . . . oh gods. Oh Great Moon Mother, what the hell are they up to now?" I jerked out of my trance and opened my eyes before they could sense me. The sudden jolt almost sent me sprawling across a root that caught my toe as I stepped forward.

"Who?" Smoky's tone demanded an immediate answer as he caught my elbow, keeping me from falling.

"Titania and Morgaine. They're working together. I dunno what they're up to, but whatever it is, you can bet it's going to cause major havoc. Last night they were almost at each other's throats. What happened between then and now?" I tried to zero in on the exact nature of the energy, but nobody was giving away any secrets.

Morio joined me, taking my hands in his. Even with his added boost of power, we couldn't pinpoint the nature of the spell they were casting together.

"Okay, *that* makes me nervous." I glanced over my shoulder at the forest behind us but could see nothing out of the ordinary.

"Don't let it bother you," Smoky said as we entered the clearing near the house that had once belonged to Tom Lane. The place now housed a broken, fragile soul name Georgio Profeta. Or Saint George, as he thought of himself. Saint George was forever trying to slay the dragon. Namely, Smoky. Georgio's plastic chain mail and foam sword couldn't do much damage, but in his eyes, they were the finest armor, fit for a royal knight.

Morio's SUV was parked off to one side, and as he unlocked the doors, I said good-bye to Smoky.

"Call me if you need me," he said, softly nuzzling my face. "For anything."

"Thank you," I whispered back. "Thank you for offering me a glimpse of your life, of your love."

He shook his head. "Don't thank me for that until you accept my invitation."

With a short laugh, I turned toward the car. "Think about it. I cannot bear dragon babies, and you'll want to father children someday, being the ninth son of a ninth son of a ninth son. And you know perfectly well—"

"Yes, yes, I know," he said. "You love Trillian. You love Morio. But Camille, I *know* you love me, too. For now go and do what you must. You'll return. And I'll be waiting." He winked at me then, waving as we drove off, heading back to the city. Heading back to the reality of my life.

CHAPTER 18

~⋙⋘~

Morio and I didn't speak much on the way. There wasn't much to say, really, and I wanted to save speculation for when we could talk to Delilah and Menolly so we didn't have to cover old territory.

As we pulled into the driveway, a thought occurred to me. "You didn't tell me the rest of what happened at the rug shop."

"Not much. I tried to poke around, but that djinn was watching my every movement once she figured out that I wasn't really in the market for a carpet. There was no reason for me to hang out, so I left. But I'll bet they have security cameras and now have my picture plastered on their back wall as a 'to-watch' individual."

He opened my door for me, and I slipped out, taking a long breath. It was good to be home. As I stared up at our house, I felt like I'd spent the past eighteen hours in a dream. I grabbed my overnight bag and dashed up the stairs, throwing the door wide as I burst into the house.

"I'm home!" I called, but my words were lost in an uproar.

Iris and Delilah were in the living room, Delilah frantically punching buttons on her cell phone.

"Camille! Thank heavens you're here. I've been trying to

call you for the past half hour. We have an emergency." She slapped her phone closed and jammed it in the pocket of her jeans. They were ripped, as usual, and her shirt was a tank top with a pretty white Persian on it. Cat, that is. Not demon.

"What's wrong?" I pulled out my cell and groaned. "Great. Looks like being in Smoky's barrow fried my battery or something."

Morio checked his. "Mine, too. Okay, note: Leave all cell phones outside the barrow. Also laptop computers, BlackBerries, and anything else that might get fried."

"No time for that." Iris was pulling on a sweater. "We've got problems. Come on, we'll tell you on the way to the car."

It suddenly occurred to me that she wasn't at the store. "Excuse me, but what the hell is going on? You aren't at the Indigo Crescent, so who is? And where's Maggie? Where are we going?"

Delilah pushed me out the door while Iris shoved Morio along. "We don't have any time to waste. Chase needs us. *Now.*"

"Chase? Why?" I hurried down the stairs, the rest of them following. "Is he hurt?"

"No, but he might be if we don't get downtown," Iris said. She pointed toward my car. "You're the designated driver, since we can all fit in your car."

"Get in," I said, pulling out my keys. "And for heaven's sake, answer my questions."

As I clicked my seat belt into place, they piled into the car. Morio rode in back with Iris while Delilah rode shotgun with me. I started the ignition. "Where are we going, and why?"

"Downtown. Pioneer Square." Delilah bit her lip. I thought she was going to cry, she looked so worried. "We need to get there ASAP."

"Maggie's in Menolly's lair. She'll be fine until we get back. I know you hate to leave her there, but you're going to need my help." Iris fiddled with something in her pocket.

"Chase is fighting a band of goblins who broke through a newly opened portal. They're terrorizing Pioneer Square. People are being hurt, one woman's already reported being robbed and assaulted. These suckers mean business." There was a catch in Delilah's voice. "I'm worried that Chase and his men won't be able to fend them off—goblins have magic. Humans don't."

"Goblins . . . *goblins*? Why the hell didn't you say so sooner?" I slammed on the gas, and my Lexus jumped into high gear as we sailed down the street. "Damn it, I wish Smoky was here."

"He can sense if you're thinking about him, remember? He said so a couple months ago," Iris said. "At least until you've completed your contract. Focus on him; maybe he'll sense your need."

I glanced back at Iris before returning my attention to the road. "You're a genius. Hold on." I swerved off to the shoulder and jumped out. "Delilah, you drive while I try to get through to him. Otherwise we could end up in a ditch." We changed places, and she took the wheel while I leaned back in the shotgun seat and let my mind drift back to the dragon and his dreyerie.

Forming a mental image in my mind wasn't hard. Once again, I found myself swept back into his bed, with him—naked and ready—leaning over me.

Whoa! Slow down. I tried to focus on his face, on our need for his help, on my own desire to see him again away from his land. There was a tiny click, which might mean I'd gotten through—or maybe not. I couldn't tell. Whatever the case, I shook myself out of the trance and glanced over at Delilah.

"There. We'll see if he answers."

"So, did you have fun out there?" Iris asked, an impish grin slipping across her face.

I tried to glare at her but ended up with a stupid grin on my face instead. "Oh yeah."

"Details!" Delilah said. "Take my mind off worrying about Chase."

"Hmm," I said. "You want details? He's as controlling as I thought, but . . . it's pretty damned easy to obey him. Under those clothes lurks the body of a god. After I managed to keep from swallowing my tongue, I found out that he's one of the three best lovers I've ever had."

I glanced over my shoulder at Morio. "And you know who the other two are, so don't get yourself in an uproar. Hmmm . . . Smoky's hair does pretty kinky things all on its own, which I really have to admit was pretty damned hot. And . . . he says he's in love with me and wants me to be his 'mate.' Just what that entails, I dunno, since I can't bear his children."

Iris let out a strangled *gack* as Delilah swerved into the other lane before she regained control of my car. Morio was the only one who remained calm, but then, he knew the story already.

"In love with you? I can see that, but he wants you to be his mate? He talking about marrying you?" Delilah held the car steady, but her voice shook.

"I don't know if the word *marriage* enters into it, and I didn't ask," I said, a little irritated. "I was hoping you guys— and maybe Menolly—might have some advice. Not seeing him again isn't that much of an option, I think."

Thank the gods neither Delilah nor Iris pulled out the "What about Trillian and Morio" card. It wasn't like I hadn't already turned the whole mess over and over in my mind. In fact, I was thinking about Trillian, Morio, and Smoky far too much for my own comfort.

Iris cleared her throat. "I suppose the question is, do you want to be his mate? I'm guessing he doesn't want to share."

"You're guessing right," I muttered. "And no, I don't want to be his mate—not *now*, not *here*. But when I'm with him, I feel myself waver. If I didn't know better, I'd swear that he's able to charm me. I mean, the guy is gorgeous, he cares about me, he'd be good to me, but I'm not cut out to be consort to a dragon. I'd feel like I was having to watch every word I said, every day. *Don't make him mad, he's a dragon, he might toast me . . .* that sort of thing."

Morio spoke up then. "So you feel safe with Trillian and me, but not with Smoky?"

I thought about his question, staring out the window at the strip mall we were passing as we approached the Belles-Faire district. Once there, another eight minutes, given good traffic, and we'd be downtown in Pioneer Square.

"In a way. I feel safe with him, but not in the same way," I said. Damn it, I hated to admit I was afraid of someone I'd slept with. But then, perhaps *afraid* wasn't exactly the right word.

After a moment, I realized what made me so uncomfortable. "It's not that I'm really afraid he'll hurt me, but I feel like I have to be someone other than myself around him. I feel like I'm a pet, in some ways."

"I can see that," Delilah said.

"I mean, look at how accommodating Trillian was when Morio came into my life." Everybody snorted, but I waved them silent. "I mean it. At first, yeah, he was an ass about it, but look at us now. With Smoky, well, I just don't think he plays well with others. And I know perfectly well that if I agreed to what he wants, I'd be locked up out in that barrow. He'd try to keep me safe from the world. I can't afford to play the delicate maiden. Not with Shadow Wing around."

I turned around to look at Morio.

He gave me a quiet smile. "I thought as much."

We passed a bookstore at that moment, where a throng of people crowded around the doors. Right, I thought. The newest Shala Morrison book had just come out—the female answer to Harry Potter. By rights, Iris should be down at the Indigo Crescent, selling copies.

"Hey, Iris, you didn't answer me, what about the shop? Why aren't you there?"

She leaned forward, peering between the front seats. "I hired Henry yesterday. He's handling the rush today and seems glad for the work. I don't think he needs the money, but . . . like we talked about before—his mother."

Good, somebody was down there. "And Feddrah-Dahns and Mistletoe? Where are they? I'm surprised they didn't want to come with us."

"We sent them down to Birchwater Pond," Delilah said. "Feddrah-Dahns was getting claustrophobic." She pulled into a Bartell's Drugs and jumped out of the car, hurrying around to my side. "Here, you drive. I like my Jeep better. Besides, I want to call Chase and tell him we're almost there."

"No. Morio, would you take the wheel? I want to see if I can figure out a way to use this horn against the goblins." I pulled the Black Unicorn horn out of my pocket as Morio played musical seats with Delilah. As he took the wheel, she popped out her cell phone and punched a button.

"Yeah, we're on our way . . . No . . . Well, great gods, be careful—what? . . . No, those are poisonous, stay away from them! We'll be there in under ten . . . Yeah, me, too, sweetie." She flipped the phone shut. "Damn it, the goblins have blowguns and tetsa darts. Chase said most of the civilians are off the street, but there are officers there, and those darts can lodge in places their vests may not cover."

I could tell she was worried about Chase. He was all too

human for these sorts of interactions, and all too vulnerable. Tetsa darts were toxic, needle-sharp winged missiles dipped in a mixture of haja frog venom and the toxic soup made from the liver of the pogolilly bird. Both frog and bird were incredibly beautiful. And incredibly deadly.

As I fingered the horn, it set up a vibration, almost as if it were singing to me. At first I thought it might be Eriskel, trying to communicate, but after a moment, I realized the voice was delicate, ethereal . . . floating on the breeze. Female? I closed my eyes and leaned back against the seat, sinking farther into the swirl of energy that beckoned me in.

There was a hush, then a tug, and I found myself standing in a room, black with stars studding the ceiling. Or were those really stars? The room was framed by four mirrors covering the walls, like a funhouse. Only I couldn't see my own reflection in the glass.

In the first mirror, a woman who looked like a dryad, draped in a gown of leaf green, held a wand carved out of oak. Her skin was as brown as the earth, her eyes and hair the color of fresh corn. The moment she saw me, she curtsied, dropping to one knee.

As I turned to the second mirror, a winged warrior landed on an aerie overlooking a ravine, high up on a barren mountain. Lightning flashed through the air behind him. Pale and tall, with flaxen hair, he was dressed in soft leather, and his eyes were round like an owl's. He carried a sword, long and glittering sharp. Catching sight of me, he nodded graciously and came to attention.

A noise from the third mirror caught my attention. A woman in a dress formed of glowing magma turned, her eyes so brilliant their flash nearly blinded me. Her hair, a trail of hardened pillow lava, flowed down her shoulders, and a wreath of vines shrouded her forehead. She leaned forward to stare at me for a moment before she, like the dryad, curtsied and stayed down, kneeling.

If it followed suit, the fourth mirror should contain a water Elemental. And sure enough, when I looked, a merman rose out of the depths. Coiling hair the color of kelp trailed down his azure skin, and his eyes were onyx black. He was either in the ocean or a lake so vast that I could see no horizon of land in the distance behind him. He leapt out of the water like a dolphin, splashing back in, only to break through the surface again. Raising a bronze trident, he saluted me.

"Who are you? What is this place?" I could almost understand the flow of thoughts and feelings coming toward me. They were waiting for me to give them some sort of command.

"You discovered the heart of the horn," Eriskel said, sounding pleased as he suddenly appeared beside me.

I jumped.

"Are you all right?" he asked.

"Pardon me if I'm a little wary," I said. "After all, you sent a megawatt lighting bolt my way. I understand this place on a primal level, and I can feel a connection forging between my third chakra and this room, but I'm not quite clear about how to make contact. Any hints without trying to fry me again?"

Eriskel grinned, and it was then I noticed the incredibly gorgeous white gold and diamond hoops hanging from his ears. I started to salivate. Apparently, he observed my distraction and the source of it. "You want the earrings?" he asked, rolling his eyes.

"Yeah, if you don't." I blushed then; I didn't normally hit up people for their jewelry, but something about them . . .

He shook his head. "For the love of . . . oh here, I can just make another pair for you. I have some powers similar to those of a djinn, you know, even though I'm *only* a jindasel." Within seconds, he held out an identical pair. They were a good three inches in diameter, just my style. I couldn't help it. I let out a delighted squeak. He stared at me. "Are we done with fashion week now? Can I get on to answering your question?"

"Please, yes." I slipped the hoops into my ears. They'd be there when I came out of trance. "So . . ."

"So." Eriskel circled me, eyeing me closely. "You've managed to find the heart of the horn. That's just one more sign you are meant to wield this artifact."

"What does that mean? The heart of the horn?"

He gave me a long look. "The heart is where its essential power resides. When you countered the lightning blast, you instinctively called up a shield of protection from the Master of Winds."

"You mean, he fueled my ability to protect myself?"

"Yes. By the way, the other Elementals are to be addressed as the Mistress of Flames, the Lord of the Depths, and the Lady of Land when you speak to them directly. They can sense your needs, and if you call, someone will answer, but the request has to be within their capabilities. If you were to try, for example, to deliberately focus Moon magic through the horn, it will not work."

"The horn of the four elements." I stared at the mirrors.

"Exactly."

"But I charge it under the dark of the moon, right?"

Eriskel nodded. "Yes. The dark of the moon is a powerful time for magic connected to the earthly elements. You should introduce yourself now that you've managed to find your way here. It will seal your bonding to the horn. You will never be forced to use it—and it will not help your Moon magic—but the power should prove especially handy when facing creatures of flame and fire."

"Like the demons," I whispered. The Master of Winds had erected the shield against lightning, so it stood to reason that the Mistress of Flames would help protect me against creatures of fire.

"Like the demons," he said. "Do you see now what this horn can do for you? Don't use it foolishly. The Elementals must be allowed to recharge. They do not have unlimited powers and must rest after major spellwork. Stand on your own two feet when you can, but the horn may save your life when you most need it." And then, like so much mist and smoke, he was gone.

I turned back to the east. Running on instinct, I knelt and bowed. "Master of Winds, I am Camille, priestess of the Moon."

"Welcome, Camille. I will serve you to my own death." He pressed his palms together and bowed.

Turning to the south, I again knelt and then the west, and then the north, until all four Elementals had pledged their service to me. As I stood, an inner voice pushed me on.

"I will never abuse the horn's powers. I will never abuse your powers. My oath, under the moon and stars and sun." And there was a ringing of chimes, a thunderous crash, and something was burning my hand.

I jerked and opened my eyes. The crystal of the horn was red-hot, and it had left an imprint on my hand. As quickly as it burned me, it cooled again. I hefted the heavy spire and stared at it. So much power and so many forces. If the horn had this much power, what must the Black Unicorn be like? Someday, perhaps we'd meet. Someday, perhaps I could thank him for his gift. For now, though, I wrapped the horn up in the cloth and tucked it away safely in its special sheath looped on the belt of my skirt.

The sheath was idiot-proof—both easy to access but hard to open accidentally. I'd left the cloak home. It was far too unwieldy to battle goblins in. But I'd remembered to bring my silver dagger, and its sheath hung on the opposite side to the horn.

As I let out a long sigh, Iris leaned forward. "Nice jewelry."

I laughed. "Yeah, real nice, huh? Compliments of the guardian of the horn. By the by, I won't be using the horn during this battle. We can mop up the goblins on our own. But come the next showdown with demons, well . . . it should make life a little easier."

Morio eased past a line of hastily parked cars on the steep grade of James Street. As we approached First Avenue, I caught sight of a police officer crouched behind a police cruiser, gun drawn. Morio slid into a parking spot, and we leapt out of the car. I immediately began grounding in to the energy of the clouds, searching for any lightning that might be in the area.

There—just over the horizon. A thundercloud.

As I beckoned it to move closer, Iris pulled out the Aqualine crystal Menolly and I'd brought back for her from Aladril. She had fastened it on the end of a silver rod. Whatever she planned on doing with it would probably produce one hell of a show.

Delilah immediately looked around, searching for Chase. A few seconds later, he ducked around the corner, out of Pioneer Park, and raced toward us. A bloody cut traced a jagged line from his temple down the side of his face.

"You're hurt!" Delilah rushed forward, grabbing him by the shoulders as she examined the wound. "Are you okay?"

"Never mind *me*. The goblins are in the park, and I've got two men down, and a third that I can't get to. He's wounded, but he's in their midst. What the hell can kill these things? We've tried bullets, and it seems to knock them back, but they just keep coming." He turned as one of his officers hurried up.

"Sir, should I order the men to fall back? We're being whipped. Maybe we should call in the SWAT team?"

"Forget it—they won't do much better," I said, stepping forward. "Your weapons just don't work very well on most Fae or Crypto creatures. If you nuked them, yeah, or went kamikaze, maybe, but goblins are tough buggers, and that skin of theirs passes for a form of natural armor. Get your men out of danger, and let us take care of it."

The officer turned to Chase. Chase glanced at me, then at the rest of us and nodded slowly. "They're right. Tell the men to fall back. Any more bullets go spewing around the area, and some bystander is going to get hit. No matter how hard we try, there's going to be some joker who sneaks beyond the barricades. Just because they're stupid doesn't mean they should die."

Morio let out a low growl. He was starting to change; he could do a lot more damage in his youkai form. Chase stared, eyes wide, as Morio began to grow, his body morphing into a mixture of fur and flesh, claws and tail, hands and feet. His eyes took on a yellow shine, and a primal, feral yip erupted from his throat. Close to eight feet tall, he was a merger of human and Canidae features, forming a terrifying blend of the two.

"Jeezus . . . remind me never to get on his bad side," Chase said as Delilah pushed him behind her. She unsheathed her silver dagger—a match to my own. Our father had given them to us, and they were almost as long as a short sword and twice as sharp.

I moved to the front, Morio flanking my right, Iris on my left.

"I'll set up a barrier of frost," she said. "I can hold off the darts long enough for us to get too close for them to use blowguns. Just don't waste any time."

The lightning was within reach now, and though I was tempted to use the horn to strengthen it, I remembered Eriskel's warning. Never abuse. What if a demon popped out after we'd cleaned up the goblins? Not knowing how many jolts I could get out of the horn, I erred on the side of caution.

Inhaling deeply, I sucked a breath of the supercharged air into my lungs and held it as the lightning went coursing through my arms, legs, from the tip of my head to the soles of my feet. Then, ready to play French fry the goblins, I straightened my shoulders and marched toward the corner.

Beside me, Iris murmured a low chant. As the first goblins came into view, a clear barrier rose between us, their darts bouncing off to the side. They looked confused as we rushed toward them. And then we were within striking range. The battle was on.

CHAPTER 19

~∞~

The goblins were thick in the park, a small, roughly triangular space wedged on the corner where First Avenue, James Street, and Yesler Way intersected. There must have been fifteen of them. Squat, brutish-looking creatures with inky green skin and shoulder-length hair that hung in matted knots, they had solidly muscled potbellies and a bowlegged swagger. Their needlelike teeth glistened as they eyed the fallen men. Goblins weren't above eating their enemies. My stomach dove for cover before I lost my breakfast.

Iris's barrier was still holding, but I could sense it weaken as their shaman focused some sort of shield-breaking energy our way. I picked up the pace and charged ahead, the others following. When we were within striking range, I let loose with the bolt of energy, and it shot out of my hands in a fork of silver lightning. The barrier went down as two of the goblins screamed, hit full-on by the blast.

I held my breath, but no sign of magical backlash. Score one for our team.

Morio and Delilah raced in to engage the brutes in combat, while Iris held out her wand, murmuring another soft chant. I turned to find myself facing one of the beasts as he bore down on me. He was a good eight inches shorter than me, but he wielded a nasty-looking dagger, and I had no desire to be on the receiving end of his love bite. As I whipped out my own blade—he was too close to chance another magical attack—he lunged at me.

The bricks under our feet were slippery, and as I leapt to the side, my heel slid, and I found myself on my butt as the goblin laughed and raised his blade. As he plunged his dagger down, I rolled to the left, and the metal bit into the wet sidewalk. I came to my feet with a war cry and lunged for him. We both went down, this time with me on top. As he scrambled for his dagger, I thrust my blade into his chest and fell on it, pushing as hard as I could.

The silver sparked as he screamed—goblins and silver do not mix well. He thrashed as a bloody pool welled up and out of the wound. There was no time to think, only act. I jumped off him, pushing myself to my feet. As I turned, I saw we'd been mistaken about the number we were facing. Another group of at least twelve goblins raced across the street to help their shrieking comrades. Where the hell had they come from?

Iris had frozen two in place—some sort of frosty freeze spell—and as I watched she whipped out what looked like a serrated icicle and slashed their throats, knocking them over when she was done.

Delilah and Chase were scuffling with a group of three goblins; it looked like they'd dropped at least two more. Morio had changed into full demonic form. He had a goblin clenched in his teeth and was shaking him by the throat. That left eight alive, with five on the loose. And the twelve that were incoming.

I whirled as a sound near my back alerted me. Two goblins on the hunt. I had to get clear. One goblin, I could take on in a physical fight. Two would be pressing my luck. I raced across the bricks parallel to the low iron fence that encircled the totem pole and the trees in the little park, my opponents following. They were fast, but I was faster, and when I'd put enough distance between us, I spun around, calling down the lightning.

As it crackled out my fingertips, a shrill scream—it sounded like Delilah—distracted me, and the spell sputtered and flew wild, splitting one of the giant trees. Oh shit! The London plane tree shuddered as its forked trunk split in two and, heaving a great sigh, half the tree cleaved off and thundered to the ground, right atop the iron pergola that had only a few years back been restored. I winced. Hell, that wasn't supposed to happen.

I darted a glance over Delilah's way to see her nursing her left arm before a hoarse laugh brought me back to the fight. The two goblins had paused, but now they were advancing again. I tried one more stab, this time focusing on the Mordente spell that Morio had taught me. I didn't like to use death magic without him by my side because it was tricky, but my adrenaline and anger fueled the power.

"Mordente, mordente, mordente . . ." I focused solely on the two goblins as they approached, feeling a dark shadow rise within me. The shadow of crows, of beetles and spiders and bats. It began to trickle down my arms, into my fingers, like thin rivers of ice and steel.

The energy knocked on my heart, and as always, a shiver of doubt made me fear opening myself to it, but the look on the goblins' faces was enough to shake me out of hesitation. I lowered my resistance and let the wave of shadow flow through my heart, through my soul, through every cell in my body.

"Mordente, mordente, mordente . . ."

And it swept through, a roiling cloud bank—gray and heavy and looming—as it rolled out of my hands to surround the approaching goblins. Only they and I could see the clouds, and their eyes went wide as the fog began to seep into their bodies, into their lungs, squeezing the air out of their lungs, shutting down organs, draining the life from their souls.

The cloud quickly dissipated. I wasn't strong enough to take both of them fully to the end using the spell. The pair dropped to the ground, moaning. They'd be hurting from the inside out. As I watched them struggle, it occurred to me that the Moon Mother hadn't cast me out since I'd begun practicing death magic. No, the Lady of the Moon had her own dark side, and when the Moon went silent, the bats and undead and spiders came out to play.

Forcing myself out of my dark reverie, I hurried over to dispatch the goblins. A quick thrust of my silver short sword, and they were history.

I turned in time to see Iris running from a goblin at full tilt, but before I could take off to help her, Morio came swooping in from behind and body-slammed the creature high into the air and out into the road.

Delilah and Chase had managed to take down their three and

were facing another queue. I was starting to think that we'd be damned lucky to get through this without anybody getting seriously hurt. We needed something that worked better than what we were doing now.

As I prepared to take on the next group of miscreants headed my way, the sound of a whistling freight train rumbled through the area, and the next thing I knew, Smoky appeared, fresh out of the Ionyc Sea no doubt. With one look at the chaos around him, his lips curled into a delicate smile as he took aim toward the three coming my way. They barked out something I couldn't catch and prepared to engage him in battle. And that was all she wrote.

Smoky held out his hands, and his nails grew into talons. And then he became a blur of movement, faster than I could keep up with. He darted around the goblins, who were screaming now, and swiped once, twice, thrice. Within seconds, the goblins were lying dead, surrounded by a thick pool of blood, and he'd moved on to another group, his deep laughter rumbling through the park.

The smell from all the bloodshed was thick and cloying, and I was having trouble focusing. I had no idea how long we'd been here, but it was beginning to feel like forever. But there was no time to rest, no time to stop. Yet another goblin came at me, and it was back into the fray.

I'd expended so much energy on the death magic spell that I didn't have much left in reserve. I was down to my short sword. Once again, I blessed my father's foresight in giving us the silver daggers. They'd been magically enchanted, and although they weren't terribly powerful, they were enough to take on creatures with extra-thick hides. Menolly had one, too, but now that she was *vampyr*, she couldn't touch it.

The goblin and I circled each other. He looked more cautious than his fallen comrades, and I doubted that he'd let himself fall into any traps. Too bad for me. I was starting to tire, and tired opponents often ended up dead.

He parried, and I darted to the side. As I did so, I caught a glimpse of one of the storefronts across the street. It was the entrance to Underground Seattle. The city had burned in 1888, and reconstruction had lifted the city over thirty feet in some areas. In 1907, the Underground portion closed for good due to bubonic plague. But there was an entire portion of the old Seattle still accessible, still open to the public.

Several more goblins emerged from the entrance. Cripes! I darted out of the way of the goblin's dagger and screamed as loud as I could, waving my hands toward the opposite side of the street.

"They're coming through the Underground Tour entrance! There must be a portal down there!" What the hell were we going to do? We needed somebody to go down in there and wrest control of the portal to keep the goblins and whatever else was waiting on the other side from pouring through.

"Hey, Boobs! How about you surrender, and I let you live? For awhile." The goblin was speaking in Calouk, and if he'd meant to make me mad, he succeeded.

Angry and tired and fed up, I decided to hell with it. If it fried me a little, so what? I raised my arms and called out for the lightning, feeling the charge back up in me like an approaching storm as it swept through my body. Maybe I'd short-circuit myself, but by damned, I'd had enough of these riffraff. Rather than aim the storm directly at the one goblin, I focused it on the entrance to the Underground Tour and let loose a bolt that ripped through the air to explode the stone around the door.

The building shook, and for a moment I thought I'd just caused one hell of a tremor. The structure held. The door and the bricks around it, however, did not, and a cascade of rubble broke off and rained down on the emerging goblins, crushing them as they tried to escape. The doorway quickly filled up with chunks of stone and brick and twisted wood, and the goblins who were still alive and fighting stopped to stare at me.

My opponent slowly began to inch away, his face a mask of fear. The energy from the lightning bolt had left me furious, caught in the wake of the storm that had boiled out of my hands, and I marched toward him, dagger up and ready. He blubbered something and turned to run, but I was hot on his heels, and he went down without a fight.

The rest of the goblins in the square were scrambling, looking for an exit, and the others easily picked them off in the confusion. Meanwhile, I saw Iris race over to the building and press her hands against the sidewalk in front of it and murmur something. A barrier began to form around the base of the Pioneer Building. It looked like ice, but ice would melt, even in the chill. I hurried over to her.

"What are you doing?"

"Preventing further damage. The barrier won't hold for long, so Chase—call out the city crews to check the status of this building. Meanwhile, we have to prevent any more goblins from coming through the portal down there. We need guards, and we need them now." Iris motioned to Delilah. "What about the Puma Pride? Can they help?"

"I'm on it. I'll get some of the Supes down here—ones who are good in a fight. We can post them on guard duty over the portal until we contact Queen Asteria." She flipped open her cell phone and punched in Zachary's number. Within less than a minute, she had secured his promise to send five of their strongest members down to help until we could secure permanent guards.

"Until they arrive, I'll keep order. I can get through the rubble without a problem," Smoky said, coming up behind me and wrapping an arm around my waist. He leaned down to give me a quick kiss.

"Thank you." I took a deep breath and looked around us. Pioneer Square was littered with goblin bodies. We all looked like refugees from a bloodbath, except for Smoky, whose familiar white trench and jeans were spotless, as usual. Someday I had to ask him how he managed that. I was smudged head to toe with goblin blood, and—I suspected—some of my own. At least two policemen were wounded or dead. Chase was checking on them now.

"Go, please; keep them from breaking through until we can set up permanent guards." I pressed his hand to my cheek, and it felt cool and soothing and strong.

He nodded and within seconds vanished from sight, riding the Ionyc currents. I wasn't worried. Smoky would be okay. If something happened down in the Underground, he could just hop back into the slipstream.

Exhausted, feeling like I could drink a gallon of water—the lightning had left me parched—I wearily dropped to sit on the curb. Delilah joined me and took my hand.

"This is too much. We can't fight them all," she said.

"I know. We need help." I was silent for a moment. "Maybe Morgaine's right. If the Courts of Fae are restored, then we can hit them up for aid." I quickly filled her in on what I'd found out on my jaunt out to Smoky's place.

Delilah thought for a long moment, then shook her head. "They won't want to take orders from half-breeds, Camille. I can't see how it will be any different than when we were children in Y'Elestrial. We'll be the outsiders forever, no matter where we are. They'll try to take control of our operations, and they won't know what they're doing. The Queens of Fae care far more for their own prestige than they ever will about humans. How long before you think they'll try to forge a truce with the demons? At least, the Queen of Dark?"

"It won't happen," I said stubbornly. "Earth is the first stop for Shadow Wing, and both Morgaine—and now Titania—know it. They can't betray us without betraying themselves."

But Delilah's uncertainty had set up questions in my own mind. How much could we really trust Titania? And Morgaine? Grandmother Coyote had already warned us that Morgaine's thirst for power was one of her weaknesses. What if Shadow Wing promised her dominion over the Earthside Fae? Would she take the bait, betray both her mother and father races?

Iris wandered over to join us. She looked tired, and her spotless white robe was spattered with flecks of blood. The Talon-haltija had more courage than a good share of full-size Fae I'd met. I gave her a grateful smile.

"We couldn't have done it without you. Thank you." I stared at the street. Without our friends, we'd have been dead long before this. And if it took Smoky to help us put an end to a small group of goblins, then what the hell were we going to do when Shadow Wing sent in more than a few demons at a time?

Delilah shoved herself to her feet and reached for my hand. I gave it to her, allowing her to pull me up. "Okay, let's go find out what happened to Chase's men," she said.

I wanted nothing more than to go home and drop into bed and sleep for a week, but I followed her over to where Chase was supervising as two of the fallen officers were loaded into ambulances. The coroner was there for the third.

"One's hanging on by a thread," he said before we could ask. "I don't know if he'll even make it to the hospital. I thought he was already dead, but he's still clinging to life. The other is seriously wounded, but he should survive and possibly recover fully if everything goes all right. But his vitals are all messed up, and we're not sure what's going on with that."

"The poison!" Delilah shivered. "Chase, chances are both men were poisoned. Get an OIA medic over to the hospital now, and tell them to check for tetsa poison. Your blood tests won't pick it up, but our healers will know what to look for. Tetsa can be applied to blades as well as the darts."

"And while you're at it, have them check that wound of yours for poison." I pointed to the laceration on the side of his face. It had stopped bleeding, but his face was covered with blood. Heads and hands always bled more. Though the wound looked nasty, it wasn't life-threatening, unless it became septic. "I'm afraid you're going to end up with a scar from that one."

He shrugged. "Had to happen sometime, in my line of work."

"It'll just make you all the more rugged," Delilah said, clinging to his arm.

"Oh yeah . . . as long as you like it, babe," he said. "What about you? Any of you hurt?"

Delilah held out her left arm. The jacket she wore had been sliced, and as I helped her slide out of it, she winced. The goblin's blade had gone through the material of both jacket and shirt, gashing into her arm. The blade had missed any major arteries, but she was going to be damned sore for awhile.

"You'd better get that checked out. We have some immunity to certain poisons, but that doesn't mean you won't be affected. Ah hell, we'd all better go in and have Sharah take a good look at us naked. I'm so numb I can't tell where I was hit and where I wasn't." I wearily headed back toward the car.

Morio wrapped his arm around my waist, and I leaned on his shoulder. "Do you need help? I can carry you," he said. "I'm not too tired."

"Liar." I grinned at him. "You look just as beat as the rest of us. I'm not ready for a walker yet." I glanced back at the bodies. "Who's going to clean up that mess?"

"I called a couple units in. All the bodies will be taken to the FH-CSI morgue. At least we don't have to worry about them rising like vampires." Chase shook his head. "Speaking of, we haven't heard hide nor hair of the rogue vamps that got away a few months ago. I don't like it."

"Don't borrow trouble," Delilah said. "Face what's in front of us first. We'll deal with them when and if they become a problem." But she flashed me a worried look, and I returned it. A rash of killings a couple months back had left several rogue vampires running through the town and, try as they might, Menolly and Wade—the vampire who ran Vampires Anonymous—hadn't been able to track them down.

We passed a truck containing the Channel 11 News team. Great. They'd manage to get a good shot of the goblin bodies before they were all cleaned up. No matter how hard we tried, it seemed the media were able to get in every place we wanted to keep them out of. It wasn't that I didn't appreciate freedom of speech, but responsible journalists seemed a rare breed, and we'd graced the pages of far too many tabloids and exploitation-TV shows over the past year.

I heard Chase swear under his breath.

Iris cleared her throat. "I know you'd like to see things like this stay under wraps, and I understand. But once those first portals were opened, both humans and Fae threw their fates together again. News will travel, and like it or not, the bad side of the Fae will have to be acknowledged, just as the rotten apples of the human world are exposed. Goblins killed a policeman, and they were killed in return. How is that any different than a shoot-out with a gangbanger hyped up on crack who gets mowed down by the cops?"

"I'm just worried this will give the groups like Freedom's Angels more license to go out and commit hate crimes. The only good Fae is a dead one, in their eyes. They're fanatics and bigots—a dangerous combination." Chase paused, leaning against the building next to us. James Street was on a fairly steep grade, like many of Seattle's streets, and I could tell he was out of breath.

As he and Iris continued their debate, I began to notice an odd feeling. It was almost as if someone was watching us. I turned around. On the opposite side of the street was an open-air parking garage. Without thinking, I crossed the street and stood at the entrance, searching the lot for whoever was spying on us.

And there I saw him. *Them.* Two men and a woman, standing by a red BMW. The woman was exquisite, a vision of flowing long hair, black as the night, with olive skin and almond-shaped eyes as green as liquid emeralds. She was wearing a lemon chiffon gown.

One of the men was tall and lean; he looked almost Fae, with pale blond hair smoothed back in a short shag. His face was craggy and gaunt, but his eyes burned with a strange fire, and I realized I couldn't place their color.

When I looked at the second man, my heart skipped a beat, and it wasn't because he was oh-so riveting. Power emanated off him in waves, and I instinctively looked around for a place to hide. This man was trouble with a capital *T*.

And yet . . . I couldn't look away. Tall and stocky, he was bald, and his eyes were so dark that I could dive in and never find the bottom. Dressed in a suit that looked expensive and yet old-world, he turned to face me, and a slow smile spread across his face.

The woman said something to him, pressing his arm with her hand, then stood back as he began to walk toward me, the other two following at a distance.

My heart pounding with the alarms that raged through the back of my mind, I tried to move but could only stand frozen. As he slowly approached, the urge to run began to disappear, and I couldn't take my eyes off his face. He glanced around at the rest of the parking lot. Midday, it was full, and people were hurrying by, to and from their cars. They seemed to take no notice of us.

He stopped about three feet from me and casually shook out a cigarette and lit up. The scent of tobacco and cloves made me cough, but below it was another fragrance that set me on edge.

"The name's Karvanak. I know who you are, of course, but why don't you introduce yourself anyway?" An accent filtered through his words. I tried to place it, but the fragrance of his cologne was interfering with my ability to focus.

And then I knew who he was. The bald man smelled of orange and jasmine and sweet vanilla, slightly rancid. I was facing the Rāksasa.

CHAPTER 20

Cripes and double cripes.

I tried to shake myself free of the lethargy that had come over me, managing to stumble back a few steps. Was he planning to kill me right here, in broad daylight with at least a dozen witnesses?

"Don't get your panties in a wad," he said. "I'm not going to gut you here. Not *yet*," he added, curling his lip into an unpleasant smile.

"Stay where you are," I warned him, fingering the horn in my pocket. No way in hell did I have the strength to fight a demon right now—especially a greater demon—so if it came to blows, I'd have to rely heavily on my new little buddy. "What do you want?"

"I can think of several things," he said, running his eyes over me lightly. "I doubt you'd like any of them, but then again, I don't give a fuck what you want, so that wouldn't matter, would it?"

I forced myself to remain calm, taking slow, deep breaths. I couldn't allow him to throw me off my equilibrium, or he'd have the advantage. Hell, he had the advantage as it was.

I had to alert Delilah and the others without putting them in danger.

"Just tell me what you want." I forced myself to stare into his eyes, shielding as best as I could. Rāksasas were masters of illusion and charm. If I could remember that, maybe I could resist his traps.

He took a long drag on the cigarette and blew the smoke directly in my face. I coughed, my lungs burning. With a short bark of laughter, he motioned toward the others, and they began to move in our direction.

What now? I could break and run, but demons were like wild animals. If I acted like prey, I'd become his quarry. Just then, I felt someone standing at my back. I glanced over my shoulder to see Morio. He pressed one hand against my lower back, and I could feel his energy seeping into mine, calming me and giving me an anchor.

At that moment, the woman and other man joined us. Karvanak didn't even glance at them.

"Meet Jassamin and Vanzir, my associates." The demon's attention was focused on me, but his eyes flickered toward Morio, and he looked mildly disconcerted. "You have something we want, Ms. D'Artigo. A gem . . . a very beautiful gem. Or if you don't have it, you know where it is. The sooner you cooperate with us, the better off you'll be. I'm prepared to make it worth your while, should you choose to play it smart and change sides. I guarantee you'll be much happier if we aren't at odds."

"Change sides? Team up with the likes of you? How stupid do you think we are?" I jerked as Morio prodded me in the back with one finger. Calm . . . I had to remain calm. I took a long, shuddering breath and let it out slowly.

"Talk it over with your family. *And friends.* We can accomplish this smoothly—in a win-win situation—if you accept our offer. Or we can do it the hard way, if you ignore us. The choice is yours." He glanced across the street, where Chase, Delilah, and Iris were watching us, eyes wide. "You have more than yourself to think about, Ms. D'Artigo. Best to remember that. We'll be in touch."

Without another word, he turned and—followed by the djinn—sauntered back toward his car. Vanzir paused, staring at me with an intensity that made me feel like I was looking into a dizzying void.

"Don't underestimate him," he said softly. "He's serious. You can't win. He'll tear you to shreds."

"Who the hell are you? And why are you on his side?" He traveled with the demon so he couldn't be any good, but I had an odd feeling about the man.

Vanzir looked like he wanted to say more, but then he suddenly broke off eye contact and turned abruptly, sprinting back to Karvanak's side.

Morio grabbed my wrist, and we took off across the street. "We need to get out of here and go have our wounds examined."

I was silent as we crossed the street and climbed in the car. I started the engine. The Rāksasa had just threatened every friend we had. When Dredge, Menolly's sire, had arrived in town and targeted our friends a few months ago, I'd been terrified. *Collateral damage* was such an ugly term. But now I realized that we needed our allies—every one of them.

The demons wouldn't spare anyone when they invaded, regardless of how much distance we put between our friends and us. Even if we did as they asked and helped them, the creatures were born liars and would have no compunction offing us as soon as they had what they wanted.

"That was her, the djinn," Delilah said. "And . . . was that . . ."

"Yeah, that was the Rāksasa. His name is Karvanak. And his buddy's name is Vanzir. I'm not sure what kind of demon Vanzir is, but there's something weird going on there. Karvanak is trying to blackmail us by threatening our friends if we don't give him what he wants."

"What does he want?" Chase asked.

I sighed. "He seems to think we have—or know the whereabouts of—the third spirit seal. And he wants it. He offered to make it worth our while if we turn sides and join him. Of course, that translates to, *I'll kill you later instead of now.* We're going to have to be very careful. He's strong. Very strong. I can sense it, and he scares the crap out of me. This is one fight we can't win straight out—he'll eat us alive."

"I hate to interrupt," Chase said, "but I'm feeling woozy all of a sudden."

Delilah felt his forehead. "He's starting a fever. Let's head for the FH-CSI offices. We can't do anything about Karvanak right now, so let's focus on what we can take care of."

I fell silent and drove, but my mind was racing a million

miles an hour. We needed to talk strategy. We needed to bring somebody else in to help us. We needed . . . so many things, and we weren't likely to get any of them.

The Faerie-Human Crime Scene Investigations offices were in a building specially built just for the purpose of dealing with Otherworlders. Damaged in the rogue vampire onslaught a couple of months ago, the broken doors had been fixed, and the magical security system had been reinforced, changed just enough to prevent the same disruption from happening again. No doubt somebody would come along in the future who could beat it, but as with hackers, each time it was defeated, we'd rebuild it stronger and more secure.

The morgue was in the basement, three stories down, while the medical facilities were on the first floor. We burst through the doors, and I waved hello to Yugi. The Swedish empath had recently been promoted to lieutenant, and he ran the ship when Chase and Tylanda weren't around, Tylanda being a full-blooded Fae and Chase's ex-assistant. She'd returned to Otherworld as ordered by the OIA, but we hoped to fill her spot soon.

Sharah drew samples of all of our blood. If we had any cut on us that had been touched by the tetsa poison, it would show as she added the reagent. The toxin entered the bloodstream quickly.

She shook out several grains of a blue powder into a small vial and added a quarter cup of water, swirling it until it dissolved. Then she lined up the blood samples and, using an eyedropper, squirted three drops of the bluish liquid on each sample. Morio's blood just sat there, as did mine. Delilah's sizzled a little, and Chase's let out a loud hiss as it bubbled up.

"Chase, Delilah, you show signs of tetsa in your blood. You'll both have to take the antidote."

Chase jumped. "What? Are we going to die? What about my men?"

"Calm down, Chief," she said, digging through a cupboard. "I've tested your men already and administered the antidote. Both are alive, but I'm not hopeful about Trent—he fell to the poison awfully fast. But Mallen is taking care of them, and if he can't pull them through, nobody can. You, on the other hand, are still walking, and that's good news," she said absently. After a moment she turned, a tall vial in her hand. The liquid inside was brown and frothy.

Delilah wrinkled her nose. "Ugh. I know what's coming."

"Do we have to drink that?" Chase asked, swallowing and looking a little green. "That looks vile—oh God, it smells vile, too!"

Sharah had popped open the bottle, and a pungent odor filled the room, like acrid vinegar mixed with sulfur. "Quit being a baby. Yes, you have to drink it. Lucky for you, I have to dilute it first." She poured two tablespoons into a glass, two into a second glass, then added tap water, stirring it until it stopped fizzing. Handing them each a glass, she added, "Bottoms up. Now."

Delilah took a deep breath and chugged hers down, wincing as the flavor hit her tongue. Chase was a little slower, but finally held his nose and swallowed the drink, gagging a little as he did so. But the glasses were empty, and Sharah looked pleased with herself.

"You should live, but I want the both of you to stay for observation for the next few hours. Camille, you and Morio can go." She waved us away.

"But Camille needs me—" Delilah started to say.

I cut her off. "Hush. You stay here, make sure the antidote took. My cell is out, and so is Morio's, so you won't be able to contact us until we get home—"

"Take mine," Iris said, handing me her cell phone. "Are you heading home first?"

I nodded. "I can't very well drive up to the Mountain Aspen Retreat covered in blood and all bruised up. I need to change clothes and put on some makeup and try to make myself look a little less beat up. I suppose I can always claim a recent accident."

"I'll ride with you, then, and make sure Maggie's all right. I'll give Henry a call, too, and see how he's doing at the shop." She bustled toward the door. "What are you waiting for? Let's get a move on."

I kissed Delilah on the cheek and patted Chase's shoulder. "Be careful. I'll have Iris's cell phone. Call me if anything happens."

As we headed out the door, I turned to Morio. "If one more thing goes wrong today, I swear, I'm going to scream so loud that I break the windows."

He laughed. "Don't make that a promise, okay? It's barely noon."

I grimaced. Barely noon! And all I could think about was: What was going to go wrong next?

The Mountain Aspen Retreat was south of the city, a little ways past Normandy Park, sitting on twenty-five tree-lined acres. We drove south on Marine View Drive, and it took us two wrong turns and stopping by a small convenience store for directions to find the place.

As I turned onto 206th Street, the houses thinned. We were in an area that, while developed, still had some leeway when it came to strip malls and so forth. After a couple blocks, I took another right, then hung a left onto a maple-shaded lane—or it would be maple-shaded once the leaves opened out in full force. The area reminded me a little of the road leading to our house, only it looked like there was more upkeep here; these were *grounds*, rather than a lawn.

"How should I approach him, do you think? Will he rat me out, I wonder?" Just because Benjamin was nonresponsive didn't mean he couldn't talk and respond, as Morio had found out in fox form.

"I'm not sure," Morio said. "You might actually get a response by mentioning the demons. He's terrified of his dreams, and both you and I know he has reason to be. Some FBHs are prescient, and it seems he has that ability."

"Are you sure he's all human? I'm not saying full-blooded humans don't have psychic powers or can't wield magic, not at all. But on the whole, it's a rare soul who's discovered his or her abilities—and an even rarer one who's managed to develop them." We passed a sign indicating a left turn up ahead to the Mountain Aspen Retreat. I flicked on the turn signal.

As we came to the graveled drive, I made a slow left turn, and we began to wend our way along the gradually inclining road. To either side were vast lawns—as I said, *grounds*— dotted with maple, oak, and the occasional willow tree. The resort, which we could see in the distance, was on a small butte that overlooked the strip of beach running along Puget Sound. Across the harbor was Vashon Island.

"You know," I said, "it seems that more often than not, FBHs like to ascribe their powers to other beings. The devil made me do it . . . God is talking to me . . . I hear voices . . . rather than acknowledging their own power or responsibility."

"It's easier," Morio said. "It's easier to blame somebody else, or to give up responsibility just in case something happens, and you're not up to shouldering what you did. Being the bad guy is easy if you don't get caught, or if you can claim it was somebody else's fault."

"There's the resort. Looks like everybody's out getting their exercise." As we approached the large building—or rather, group of buildings—I noticed a number of what had to be patients slowly making their way through some of the well-tended gardens. Some walked with nurses who were wearing crisp pink uniforms; others walked in pairs, talking—or not—as they took in the brisk afternoon air. Everybody except the nurses and attendants wore street clothes, but I noticed right away that everyone who seemed to be a patient sported a neon-red bracelet.

"Want to bet those bracelets have sensors that alert the guards if anybody leaves the grounds?"

Morio glanced over at a trio of patients who were examining the budding crocuses beneath a willow tree. "You're probably right. There's the parking lot."

I eased into the lot that ran parallel to the main building and turned off the ignition. "Ready to go? Do you think I can pass?"

I'd changed into one of the most conservative outfits I had: a black rayon skirt that skimmed my knees and a peacock-colored silk tank top with a plum-colored velvet jacket. My four-inch black patent leather pumps worked just fine with the outfit, and I'd rummaged in the closet until I found a snakeskin purse in burgundy. Altogether, when I masked my glamour, I looked like a slightly surreal human woman.

Morio, posing as my fiancé, had changed into gray slacks and a cobalt V-neck sweater and loafers. Just your average yuppie couple out to visit one of the wacked-out relatives, Your Honor. No harm. No foul.

We slowly got out of the car and looked around. I closed my eyes, trying to get a feel for the place. There was a lot of chaotic energy around. Some of it seemed to hinge on the edge of shadow magic, but when I examined it more closely, the madness that really *did* exist here swam to the surface. But beneath the true mental illness, I could sense actual magic and a reaching out—searching for something. There were psychics here, and natural-born witches who had no clue to their own powers, and whose families had deemed them unsuitable for everyday life.

"There's so many conflicting energies snarled up together that I don't know if it can ever be sorted out." I opened my eyes and put on sunglasses. My eyes were one of the most telling features of my father's Fae blood. Cloak them, mask my glamour, and I might just make it through posing as Benjamin's cousin.

"At least they don't stone people anymore for being touched. Or throw them in a madhouse and leave them to fight and kill one another." Morio looked me over. "I never thought I'd see the day when you'd be voguing it up."

"Oh please," I said, catching my hair back into as tidy a bun as I could. Stray strands kept trying to escape. Curly hair does not for smooth shininess make. "I'm a little over the top for *Vogue* . . . but I think this will work. Passable?" I slipped my bag over my arm and posed, hand on hips.

His eyes crinkled at the corners, and I could see the smile behind them. "You always look beautiful, no matter what you're wearing. Even in that getup. But you sure look . . . unnatural . . . without your breasts popping out." And with that, he held out his arm. "Shall we? And if anybody asks, we're getting married in June—that's the standard wedding month."

"June, huh? In Y'Elestrial weddings are often during winter, when the city slows down and the Yuletide holidays near." I gave him a veiled smile. "My mother and father were married at Midwinter. She had never seen a Fae wedding, of course, and she wanted a white gown, like an Earthside bride would wear. That's not traditional over in Y'Elestrial, of course. But Father commissioned the seamstress to make her one out of snow white spider-silk and spun gold."

"Your father loved your mother very much, didn't he?" Morio asked as we strolled toward the building.

"That he did. He loved her enough to take on the Court and Crown and petition to gain her citizenship rights. He loved her enough to stay with her after she refused to drink the nectar of life, and he loved her enough to live through her death. I still have her dress, you know," I said quietly.

"Her wedding dress?"

"Yes, tucked away in the back of my closet. I'm glad I brought it with me, considering all our things were either hurried into storage or confiscated by Lethesanar. I'd hate to lose it. It wouldn't fit me—I'm too curvy—but I've always imagined we might be able to alter it for Delilah. I know she'll get married someday. It's in her nature."

"And what about you?" Morio stopped then, turning to me. "Are you ever going to marry? Trillian . . . or anyone?"

I wondered if there was an "or me" behind his question but wasn't going to put him on the spot by asking. Instead, I inhaled deeply and let out a long sigh. "Marriage? How can I even think of it? If this were Y'Elestrial, or *anywhere* in Otherworld, I'd marry the both of you the minute you asked. We could legally form a triad there. But with the demons . . . The truth is, I don't know if I believe in the future now. I don't know if I believe we can win against Shadow Wing."

And there it was, my inner fear revealed. A part of me whispered that we were all doomed. That we were headed down the path to hell, and there was a fiery demon lord on the other end waiting for us. That didn't mean I'd give up, but I was rapidly losing hope that we could forever stem the demonic tides washing up against the shores of our worlds.

Raising my head, I stared at him. "My duty comes first. Father raised me to honor my commitments and to accept my responsibilities, even when I'd rather run like hell the other way. The battle matters most."

Morio said nothing but looped his arm through mine as we approached the entrance to the Mountain Aspen Retreat. We were almost to the door when an attendant opened it for us, flourishing his arm as he motioned us in.

The entrance reminded me of a grand foyer to some luxurious hotel. With faux marble floors polished to a high shine and an antique gold and green color combination, it was hard to believe we were walking into what was, essentially, an institution.

I leaned over to whisper in Morio's ear. "They have to have some high-end fees to pay for this layout."

He gave me an imperceptible nod. "From what I could tell on my visit last time, most of the patients come from extremely well-off families. This is old money territory, and the families who drop their problem children off pay well to keep it quiet.

This is a good place to deposit a wayward child or aunt who's developed a reputation for being a social embarrassment."

"I think I prefer Otherworld," I said. "Although Court and Crown life has its own bigotries and social pressures."

Scowling, he shook his head. "White bread—white bread without flavor keeping the status quo. That's pretty much what this place is all about. I've no doubt they have qualified professionals on staff, but I also have the feeling they strive for conformity over happiness."

I looked around. There were several sitting areas, some of which had patients watching television or doing needlework. Some were just staring into space. A curving staircase, when I peeked up at the grand ceiling, led to a second floor, which looked like it held more of the professional offices.

From where we stood, it wasn't clear where the patients were housed, but logic would argue that the residence halls were in the back where the guests wouldn't immediately see them. That way if someone got out of hand, it wouldn't disrupt visitors or the placid, serene facade with which they'd plastered the entire institution.

The check-in area had a blush-colored marble countertop and the sign-in book was manned by a silver pen on a chain. The only disparity that reminded me we weren't registering at the Hilton was the bulletproof glass that encased the front desk. As we approached, the pink-clad receptionist jumped up and met us at the counter with a brilliant smile.

"I'm Nurse Richards. May I help you?"

"I'm here to see Benjamin Welter. My name is Camille . . . Welter, and this is my fiancé, Morio Kuroyama." I assumed a harried air that said, "I'm important, don't bother me with questions, just put me through right away."

As I was expecting, she said graciously, "May I see some identification?"

I cleared my throat and glanced around. Nobody else was paying attention. I pulled off my sunglasses and lowered my masks, allowing my glamour to shine through full-force.

Leaning in, I said, "You *really* don't need to see my identification. *You know* I'm who I say I am. And *you know* that I'm safe and won't hurt anybody here. *Don't you?*"

Either Nurse Richards didn't think for herself much, or she

wasn't the brightest bulb in the socket, because her smile faded for just a second, then returned twice as wide. "Of course, Ms. Welter. You're safe and you won't hurt anybody. Nice to meet you and your fiancé. Congratulations on your engagement. If you'll sign in and then follow me, I'll take you to see Benjamin."

I winked at her, and she giggled. As I signed in and handed the pen to Morio, I thought about how easy some people were to charm. Those with the strongest resistance weren't the most suspicious, actually, even though it seemed logical they would be. No, I'd found that the most difficult people to charm were the cold, aloof types who registered high in intelligence.

After signing the guest book, she called to one of her assistants to watch the front desk, then led us down the hall, where she turned left. "He lives in our long-term-care residence hall. This way, please."

We left the building through a back security door manned by two burly looking guards, albeit with pleasant smiles and the ever-present pink uniforms. She led us across a covered courtyard where wrought-iron benches provided a place to sit and soak up the sun or fresh air, even on a drizzly day. I steered clear of them. Though they had wooden slats for seats, one slip, and I could end up with a nasty burn.

The brickwork was laid out in patterns, several of which I recognized as Celtic knotwork, and here and there, a square of flowers brightened the otherwise terra-cotta color scheme. Daffodils and crocuses were on the menu now, along with primroses and pansies that had been recently planted in the freshly tilled soil. Across the courtyard stood a five-story building, and connected by another sheltered overpass, a two-story residence hall.

"Benjamin has been such a good patient," Nurse Richards said. "He's never any bother, except when you try to talk directly to him. A word of warning, if you haven't seen your cousin for awhile. If you say something to the wall, or to an inanimate object, such as, 'It's time for Benjamin to eat dinner,' he'll pay attention and follow you to the dining hall. But if you look at him directly and say it to his face, he's likely to go into a screaming fit. So try to never talk directly to him while you're here. He doesn't mind if people sit near him, but don't touch him."

I nodded, filing away the information. We had no shortage of mentally unstable beings in Otherworld. Thank the gods, our shamans could treat some of the mild to moderate cases through soul mending and other techniques, but the truly lost causes were usually allowed to wander without restraint as long as they didn't hurt anybody.

In a number of villages, they were watched over by everybody, fed when they were hungry, given shelter in barns and outbuildings when the weather grew cold. If they became a danger to themselves, they were kept under watch. If they became a danger to others, they were destroyed.

"There he is—he's taking some air today," the nurse said, pointing to a man sitting on the grass, staring at the sky. He was alone, although I noticed a couple attendants policing the grounds nearby. Benjamin seemed to be perfectly content.

As we walked up to the blue-jeaned young man, Nurse Richards started talking loud enough for him to hear. "My oh my, isn't it nice that Benjamin's cousin has come to visit him? She might want to sit down over there near the oak tree—there's a little bench there—and just enjoy the fresh air." She gave me a meaningful nod, and I headed toward the bench, gritting my teeth. I'd have to make certain no exposed skin hit the armrests or the rivets that decorated the wooden slats.

As I gingerly sat down, I gave Benjamin a quick glance, then looked away. He was watching me, a curious light in his eyes. When he saw Morio, he looked confused, then gawked at him. The nurse excused herself. She stopped by one of the attendants, pointed toward us, then headed back to the main building. The attendant kept an eye our way but didn't come any closer.

After a moment, Benjamin spoke so softly that if I'd been human, I wouldn't have heard him at all. "Mr. Fox looks different today. I guess this is Mr. Fox's girlfriend?"

Morio started. "Benjamin knows who I am?"

"Of course," Benjamin said. "I can always spot shape-shifters when they're disguised as human. But I can't figure out why she's posing as my cousin, or who she is. She's not a shifter, but she's not a regular woman, either."

I flickered a quick look at Morio, who gave me a quiet nod. "My name is Camille, and I need to speak to Benjamin about the cave and the amethyst gem he told Mr. Fox about. A lot of people's lives ride on this. Benjamin could make a big difference in helping us save the world—"

The word had barely escaped my mouth when Benjamin looked at me full-on. He blinked twice, then whispered, "Don't look at me, or the guards will know something's up. You're one of the Fae, aren't you? And you're fighting against the demons that I see in my visions?"

I stared at a patch of long grass growing near him. The breeze picked up, rippling the stems like a wave of green. I realized that Benjamin was hiding here more than anything else. But from what? The demons? "You're partially right. I'm half-Fae, and I'm from Otherworld. And yes, we're fighting demons. We need your help, Benjamin. Will you talk to us?"

He cleared his throat, then leaned back and stared at the sky again. After a moment, he said. "All right, but you have to promise you'll get me out of here."

"We'll do our best," I said, not knowing just how we'd keep that promise—at least on a long-term basis. Obviously, Benjamin wasn't as broken or fragile as Morio had first thought.

"I guess that will have to do," Benjamin said. "All right, I'll help you. What exactly do you need to know?"

"Tell us everything about the cave and the gem. From the beginning, and don't leave anything out." I let out a long, slow breath. Finally, we had found the break we were looking for. Maybe we had a chance after all.

CHAPTER 21

~≈≺≻≈~

Benjamin lay back on the grass, hands under his head. I studied a patch of rhododendrons that were blossoming out into huge, fuchsia flower heads. Morio stretched out and put his head in my lap, as if we were just spending a quiet afternoon, sitting near my "cousin."

"A year ago," Benjamin softly said, "I was out near Mount Rainier. I was on a day hike by myself. I traveled up past Goat Creek—something was urging me to go that way, so I did. I left the trail and headed in toward Misery Rock when I saw the cave."

My ears pricked up, and I darted a quick glance in his direction, then went back to stroking Morio's forehead and focusing on the flowers. "You said you found this cave out past Goat Creek?" That was near Smoky's place—a few miles into the wilderness beyond the house and barrow.

"Yes," he murmured. "I stumbled onto it. There was nothing marking it on the map. The opening was covered with moss and vines, and I pulled them aside and went in. It felt . . . something felt weird. Like I'd just stepped into a different dimension or world. I can't explain it, but maybe you can understand."

Oh, I understood all right. A portal—it had to be a portal.

Which meant he'd either traveled into Otherworld, or perhaps a different realm.

"Go on," I whispered.

"The cave was filled with crystals in all shades of green and purple and blue and red. Some were as big as me, jutting out of the ground and down from the ceiling. I was starting to get afraid. I know we don't have caves like that here in Washington State. I thought about leaving, but . . . it was too beautiful. I had to continue."

I closed my eyes. Curiosity killed a lot of cats, especially the two-legged kind. "You were lucky, Benjamin. To get out of there alive. What did you find?"

He pulled a long blade of grass and began playing with it, tying it in knots and running the edge along his finger till a drop of blood glistened as it oozed out of his thumb. "There was a sword there—in the center of the cave. And I saw a woman trapped inside a giant stalagmite of quartz. I tapped on the crystal, but she didn't seem to hear me. So I picked up the sword . . ." Faltering, he tossed away the stem and pulled another. His words were shaky, and he looked like he felt queasy.

"Are you okay?" Morio asked, his eyes still closed.

Ben cleared his throat. "I don't know. Every time I speak—or even think—about the sword, it makes me sweat."

"What did it look like? And was it stuck in a stone?" I prayed we didn't have some weird cross rip in space leading us into Avalon, but then again—what would Avalon be doing *here*? And Arthur had been a man, not a woman.

"The sword . . . the sword . . ." Benjamin sounded like he wanted to cry. His eyes were flashing a dangerous color, and I softly raised my gaze, checking to see if the attendants had noticed us. But we were in luck. They were focused on another group of patients who had gotten into a bit of a scuffle over what looked like a game of bocce. I wanted to hurry him, but I had the feeling that any sort of pushing would backfire and send him spiraling into a fit. Or silence.

After a moment, he let out a small sob. "The sword was resting on a crystal platform—like a small table. It's silver, with an amethyst in the hilt—a big one. I picked it up and felt something trying to pry open my mind—it was like a mass of feelers peeling open my skull—"

The spirit seal. The amethyst had to be the spirit seal.

He jumped up then. "I need to walk. You walk a few steps behind me, and look at the scenery."

We obeyed, trailing hand in hand together behind Benjamin, who nervously fidgeted his way down the path. As we crossed from a stand of oaks to a stand of willows, the attendants shot us a look. I waved my hand, smiling wide. They nodded and went back to untangling the argument between the lawn bowling fanatics.

After a couple of minutes, Ben leaned against one of the trees, and I parked myself at a nearby picnic table. Morio dropped to the grass next to me.

"You'll think I'm crazy," Benjamin said. "Or maybe not. Or maybe I really *am* nuts and should stay locked up here forever. I picked up the sword, and it felt like . . . like I could understand everything there was to know, if I tried hard enough. It was as if my mind opened up and started soaking in knowledge and images. But then the floor started to move, and I realized that I was in the middle of a cave during an earthquake. I dropped the sword and ran. It took me a while to find my way out."

He hung his head, scuffing the ground. "By the time I got to my car, I couldn't remember how to drive. I was too confused. Everything seemed so different, and I couldn't figure out if I'd dreamed the whole episode or if it had been real. I tried to call my mother, but my cell phone didn't work."

"Were you okay?" I wondered what would happen if we took our cell phones home to OW. Would they fry going through the portal? Menolly and I'd left ours home when we went back to Aladril.

"Not really. I started walking down the highway, and a state patrol officer picked me up and took me to the hospital. He thought I was stoned. The hospital said I was in shock. I went to sleep after they gave me five different sedatives. That was the first night I dreamed about the demons."

The look that swept over his face transformed him. In a matter of seconds, he went from troubled young man to terrified victim looking for an escape route. What the hell had happened? Had the spirit seal triggered off the dreams? And what about the expansion of consciousness?

As I kept him in my peripheral gaze, I began to notice a faint shimmer in his aura. I usually didn't notice people's auras—not unless I was trying. But there was something more to Benjamin's energy. Something that sparkled and moved in a way that—holy hell.

I repressed the desire to clap my hand to my mouth and forced myself to keep on topic. "What about the dreams?"

"They come several times each week. Images, mainly, of demons—huge demons with horns, others are bloated and squat. Still others look like we do—like humans—but I know they're not. And they drive a wall of death and destruction before them, tearing up the land, crumbling cities in their wake. They destroy the planet, and us with it. The government responds by setting off nuclear weapons. The world goes up in flames."

Tears were flowing down his cheeks now. "I'm so tired. I can't think anymore. I just dream, and when I try to stay awake so I won't, they pump me full of drugs to make me sleep. Help me. Help get me out of here? I thought I could hide here, but I can't, and now I can't get them to release me. My family's keeping me locked up."

His voice was so plaintive that it made me want to cry. I stared helplessly at Morio. What could we do? His family would pitch a fit if they knew we took him out. But what if he were to *run away*—to just vanish? Would his family care? They might sue the institution, but they didn't want him back in this shape, that much was obvious.

"We'll do our best, Benjamin," I said. "I promise you—we'll try. Thank you for talking to us."

"You aren't human. You're angels . . . guardian angels. I don't care what anybody says about the Fae. You're sent from the hand of God." Benjamin shook himself as if he was waking up. "You'd better leave now, or they'll get suspicious. My family never stays more than fifteen minutes."

We stood up and motioned to the attendants, who came over to escort us back to the main building. They led Benjamin off to his room. As I glanced over my shoulder, I could see him—head down and shuffling—as he allowed himself to be led away. There had to be a way to help him.

After a quick and charming reinforcement to Nurse Richards

that my visit had been good for Benjamin and that she probably shouldn't mention it to his parents, should they come by, we left with an invitation to come back as soon as we could.

On the way home, we ran over and over his story. The sword—the cave—the dreams . . . My thoughts kept running back to the conversation between Morgaine and Titania about Aeval. Could the Unseelie Queen be the woman Benjamin had seen trapped in the crystal?

As we drove north back to Seattle, and finally hit the Belles-Faire district, I swerved off the road when we passed by the Tucker's Chicken stand. Tucker made the best fried chicken I'd ever tasted. I loaded a twenty-four-piece bucket, some coleslaw, a chocolate cream pie, and a box of biscuits into the back. Then I hit the drive-through Starbucks for an iced quad shot caramel venti mocha. Morio stared at the drink, which was sporting a rounded cap of whipped cream, and shook his head.

"How can you eat so much? You never gain any weight." He ordered a tall coffee with cream and sugar.

"I'm no stick figure, that's for sure. But our metabolisms run faster than the average human's since we're half-Fae. We have to eat a lot." I sucked on the straw and smiled as the soothing iced flavor of caramelized sugar and slightly bitter coffee raced down my throat. "Yum. Love it."

I switched lanes, frowning. Rush hour traffic had started, and we were caught right smack in the center of the Belles-Faire end-of-the-day jam. I needed to get in the left lane before too long, or we'd miss our turn.

"I assume you're eating dinner with us?" I asked, guiding the car cautiously between a Hummer and what had once been a VW van but now just looked like a pathetic survivor from the sixties love generation. It must have had at least ten coats of paint on it, with patches flaking off here and there to give it that psychedelic edge, and it was emitting enough exhaust to choke a horse.

"Of course. I'll eat dinner at your place and stay the night," he said.

As he spoke, Iris's cell phone jangled. Morio retrieved it from my purse and flipped it open. "Yeah? What? Okay, we're on our way. We're in rush hour traffic, so we'll be there in about twenty minutes if things keep moving like they are." He closed the phone and slid it back in my purse.

"More trouble?" All we needed was another batch of creatures come through the portals. I didn't know if I could take another goblin fight—or troll fight—or *anything* fight. At least not until tomorrow.

"Maybe. I don't know. Iris went out to take Feddrah-Dahns his dinner, and he's gone. The pixie is missing, too. Neither one said anything about leaving, and there appears to be some blood on the grass near where the unicorn had settled down. Iris thinks it's unicorn blood," Morio said softly.

I groaned. "No. The Crown Prince of the Dahns unicorns absolutely *cannot* have gotten hurt at our house. It just *can't* happen. I don't want his father coming out here to rip us a new one for putting his son in danger."

"Maybe he just cut himself on some baling wire or an old nail and went to look for help?" Morio was trying to be helpful, but I knew—because in my life, the worst-case scenario always seemed to be on the menu—that the answer had to be worse than that. There was no way we could get off so easy. The Hags of Fate seemed determined to make us sweat every inch of this journey.

"Something's wrong; you can bet on it. Did she mention whether the wards were broken or not?"

Morio shook his head. "No, she didn't say anything about the wards."

I pushed the pedal to the floor as we came to the junction leading to our house. I was about to turn into our driveway when a siren from behind me whirred to life. "Freakin' A, just what we need now."

I slowly coasted over to the shoulder of the road, unmasking my glamour as I did so. By the gods, there was a limit to how much one person could take, and I'd reached mine twenty seconds ago. I rolled down my window and looked up into the face of the officer who had pulled me over, prepared to charm the pants off him and fuck him under the table, just so long as he didn't give me a ticket.

"Hey gorgeous, you realize you're dangling so much sex appeal in my face that your sister just might have reason to scratch your eyes out. I'm only human, for God's sake." Chase was standing there, leaning in my window, a hungry grin plastered across his face.

Unsure whether to hit him or kiss him, I just shook my head and lowered my glamour. "Come on, you idiot. Get your butt up to the house. We need to report a missing unicorn and pixie."

As Chase laughed again and sauntered back to his car, I glanced at Morio. "Not a word, buster. Not a single word."

CHAPTER 22

Our driveway was long and winding, leading through a stand of alder and fir. As I drove past the boundaries signifying our land, I could feel the wards shrieking. They'd been broken. Somebody had been here, unwelcome and probably up to no good.

I put the car in park and left it running, jumping out to check on the warding circles that stood sentinel over the entrance to the drive. I slowly approached the boundary line, which was marked by two tree trunks, one on either side of the graveled road, both surrounded by a circle of quartz spikes.

Some great force had broken through. This couldn't have been just the goblin and Sawberry Fae. They wouldn't have the power for it, even if one of them happened to be a shaman. No, the faint scent of demon lingered in the air.

Running back to the car, I hopped in. "Wards were broken. The demons were here. By the faint odor, it's been a while. I'm praying they didn't come after Iris called us."

Morio's face darkened, and his eyes began to shine. "They may still be here. We'd better get ready, just in case."

"Oh gods, Chase. Hold on." Once again, I jumped out, hurrying back to Chase's undercover Ford Taurus. I pounded on the window, and he rolled it down.

"What? What's wrong? I noticed you looking at the stumps back there. What's up?"

"Demons have been on the land. They might still be here. You need to be careful. When we get to the house, stay in your car and lock the doors until we make certain they aren't hiding inside."

"Demons? Delilah and Maggie! Hurry up!" He rolled up his window as I raced back to the driver's seat and leapt inside. It was going to be hard getting him to stay in his car, now that he was worried about my sister. I slammed on the gas and took the rest of the drive at a shaky fifty miles an hour—as fast as I dared, given the bumpy curves in the road.

As the house came into view, I turned off the ignition, looking around. There was no sign of any disturbance or destruction that I could see. Everything looked as peaceful as it usually did. But if Iris had found the unicorn missing, then there was a good chance that the demons had nabbed Feddrah-Dahns and the pixie. But why wouldn't they take on the house, too?

I cautiously stepped out of the car, pausing to listen. Chase leapt out of his Taurus, and I whirled around. "Get your ass back in that car and lock the door. I can't afford to be worrying about saving your butt if the demons are inside. Face it, Chase, right now you'd be a liability in there. Fighting goblins is one matter. Demons are a whole different ball of wax."

He scowled but obeyed. Morio and I slipped up to the window that looked into the kitchen, and he boosted me up as I peeked inside. There, Iris and Delilah were poring over a map at the kitchen table. Maggie was in her playpen, and all looked well with the world. Frowning, I motioned for Morio to let me down.

"Looks okay," I whispered. "I'm going around back. You stay here."

I slipped around the back and quietly edged up the steps leading to the back porch. As I opened the door, it creaked, and within seconds, Iris was poking her head out.

"Camille? What are you doing sneaking in this way?" She looked perplexed.

I frowned. "Is everything okay in there? Nothing amiss?"

"Everything's fine, except for Feddrah-Dahns and Mistletoe being missing. What on earth has gotten into you, girl? You're as pale as Menolly." Iris started to bustle me inside, but I paused.

"I'll come through the front door. You lock the back door and the porch before you go back in the kitchen. I'll tell you why in a moment." I clattered down the steps and ran around front. Morio was waiting there. "I need you to cast a Dispel Illusion spell on them, just to make sure they aren't the Rāksasa and his crony in disguise. Can you do it from out here?"

Morio frowned. "That would be difficult. Let's go in, and I'll have one prepped. If they are demons . . ."

"Then we're about to get our butts whipped. Ready?" I inhaled deeply and gathered energy from the air, from the sky, to form a barrier. Then I pulled out the unicorn horn. "Mistress of Flames," I murmured and instantly felt her stir within the crystal spire. "Be ready to strengthen my barrier." And to my surprise, I heard a faint voice whisper, "I am ready, Lady Camille."

"Let's go," I said, heading through the front door.

Morio was right on my heels, and the moment we barged into the kitchen, he held up his hands. "Be seen!" A flash strobed the room, and Delilah and Iris both yelled and covered their faces. As the flickering light died away, they peered out from behind their hands.

"What the fuck are you doing?" Iris almost never swore, and to hear her use the F-bomb was a surprise, although a welcome one, given she hadn't shifted form into a demon of any sort.

"It's you. It's really you," I said, dropping into a chair with relief. "We have to check the house. Now."

"What are you talking about?" Delilah said, squinting. Her eyes always took longer to adjust, considering that she was part cat.

"Demons," I said hoarsely, not putting away the horn. "Demons broke through the wards—they've been on the land. We thought the Rāksasa might be here—that you might be . . ."

"One of his illusions," Iris said softly. "I understand now. I never thought to check the wards when I was out looking for Feddrah-Dahns. I was so worried. Damn it, how could I have been so *stupid*?"

"Me, too," Delilah said. "All I could think about was where the pair had gotten themselves to. And then I wondered if they'd been chased off by wild dogs or something."

"Far worse than wild dogs," I said. "Did you smell demon energy down by Birchwater Pond?"

Delilah shrugged, looking ashamed. "I didn't even try."

"Morio and I'll head down there. You go out and get Chase, help him bring in dinner. He's probably peeing his pants, worrying about you. Iris, come with us and show us where you found the blood."

While Delilah and Chase searched the house, Iris led Morio and me down to Birchwater Pond. The path through the forest seemed darker than usual, but the birds were singing, and we saw a squirrel darting up a tree. A good sign. If demons were still prowling the woods, the animals would have been silent.

On the way, Iris told me what happened. "Feddrah-Dahns and Mistletoe were down by the pond. Feddrah-Dahns gets a little claustrophobic around buildings. When they didn't return for lunch, I began to worry. Delilah came home—by the way, she and Chase are no worse for the wear, considering they were poisoned—and she and I went down to fetch them."

"Good deal. I meant to ask Chase how he was feeling, but things are spiraling out of control, and I'm not exactly on top of my game at the moment."

I was tired. Bone-weary. I wanted nothing more than to hit the bed and sleep for a week, but I had a feeling it would be a long time before I'd have a chance for that luxury.

We turned the bend in the path and came out near the pond. Surrounded by a ring of cedars and firs, Birchwater Pond was in a clearing in the center of the wood. The pond was on our land and had become our home away from home—reminding us, on a much smaller scale, of Lake Y'Leveshan back in Y'Elestrial. Huckleberries and fern crowded the banks, and on one side, a grassy knoll where we held picnics. We'd started holding our rituals down here, and when I needed to talk in private to the Moon Mother, I'd meander down the path under her light and sit on the edge of the dark water that glistened in the oval-shaped crater.

Iris glanced up at me. She said nothing but reached out and took my hand in hers, squeezing gently. I gave her a soft smile, wondering how we'd ever gotten along without her. She was as much family as any of our aunts, and more so than most.

"Here," she said, stopping beneath a maple that towered over the clearing. I gazed up at the branches that were rife with leaf buds. Nothing unusual there. But below the boughs, near the trunk, the moss that covered the ground had been indented as if a heavy creature had been lying here. A horse . . . or a unicorn. I cautiously crept toward the patch, Morio right behind me.

As we stared at the ground, I began to see the dark patches that indicated blood. I inhaled a long breath, holding the scents deep in my lungs. The scent of wild meadows, fresh and laden with shaga flowers, overwhelmed me. Feddrah-Dahns, the Crown Prince . . . his musky smell was infused with reminders of our home world. And pixie dust. The tingle of pixie magic mingled with the scent of the unicorn. And then, a top note: the metallic smell of blood soaked into the mix. As I dug deeper into the energy of the fragrances, there it was—faint but present. Orange and jasmine and sugar vanilla, cloying and overripe.

"Karvanak was here," I said, straightening up. "The Rāksasa was here. I don't know about the djinn, or whatever the other demon is that assists him."

"Oh, no. No, no." Iris paled, sinking to the ground to examine the blood. "Do you think . . ."

"That he killed Feddrah-Dahns? I don't know, but I don't see signs of a struggle. And Feddrah-Dahns can fight, believe me. *That* I've witnessed." I stared out over the pond, trying to will what happened to unfold in a vision for us. But I didn't have the gift of hindsight—the ability to *see* what had already taken place.

"Perhaps Feddrah-Dahns and Mistletoe escaped," Morio said. "As you pointed out, there aren't any signs of a struggle, and we know the unicorn wouldn't willingly walk away with the demons."

Iris stood up, grasping something in her palm. "I found something," she said, holding out her hand. Resting on her creamy skin was a small piece of cloth. White in nature, it had been ripped from a gown or tunic.

I slowly picked it up and closed my eyes. This cloth was familiar, both in texture and energy. It was heavy with magic, steeped in power. I began to smile. "I know where they went. Or at least, I'm pretty sure."

"Where?" Morio leaned over, staring at the cloth.

"Smoky's land. This is from Smoky's robe that he wears. I'll bet you anything that somehow, Feddrah-Dahns contacted Smoky for help. Whether he fought the demons or just swept

Feddrah-Dahns and Mistletoe away before they could be hurt any further, I don't know. But this is from Smoky's robe. I know the energy of my lovers."

Iris let out a long breath. "Why hasn't he called, then?"

"Because Smoky doesn't have a phone. Because Smoky takes his own time in doing what he will. Let's go back to the house. If I don't eat, I'm going to be sick. After that, I'll go out to Smoky's and find out what happened."

Morio wrapped his arm around my waist as we turned and headed back to the house. "We'll have to reestablish the wards and strengthen them. We need stronger charms and spells. The demons broke through without a problem."

"Yeah, they did. We need so many things. And time to gather them is a luxury we no longer possess." I stared at the approaching dusk as it spread long fingers across the sky. The stars would be out soon, and the air was growing damp and chill. The clouds would be coming in soon. Rain was on the way.

Back at the house, Delilah and Chase were waiting anxiously. They'd checked through all the rooms, and everything was clear, but I don't think any of us felt very safe.

Delilah had unpacked the food. I slid into a chair, leaning back to close my eyes. Morio stood behind me, rubbing my temples.

"Thank you," I whispered. Every jolt, bump, scrape, and jangled nerve of this hellish past few days had worked its way into my muscles, and I could barely keep my eyes open. Even the fun parts—especially with Smoky—had produced an overload of stress.

"You look beat," Delilah said.

I nodded and opened my eyes just a slit to look at her. "You aren't vying for spring chicken of the year, yourself. You still look a little green."

"It's the tetsa poison. It tints the skin for a day or two, even after the antidote takes effect." She leaned forward and propped her head in her hands. "I cannot believe that things have gotten this crazy. By the way, Zach and four of his buddies are down in the underground tunnels now. Smoky found the portal, and when he dropped by here, he told us that it leads directly into Guilyoton."

"Cripes." I took the ice-cold bottle of water that Morio handed to me and chugged half of it down. Guilyoton was the goblin forest—and city—that lurked in the shadowed lower lands near Darkynwyrd. The goblins of Guilyoton were far more independent than their weaker cousins who were helping Lethesanar.

"Wait. Smoky was *here*?" That would make sense. "Did he say he was going to stop by and say hi to Feddrah-Dahns on the way out?"

Iris nodded. "Yes, he did. And . . . I see. He probably took Feddrah-Dahns home with him after he left the house."

"What? He's the one who took Feddrah-Dahns? He didn't hurt him, did he?" Delilah looked confused.

"No. In fact, he probably saved Feddrah-Dahns's life. What else did Smoky say when he was here?"

"He might drop by tonight. Apparently, he cast some sort of barrier across the entrance to the portal in Underground Seattle, but he doesn't think it will last once the goblins get their shamans to work on breaking it down."

She jumped up to help Morio dish out dinner. They piled everything in the center of the table while Iris fed Maggie her cream and sage drink.

I dug into the food as soon as plates were on the table. My stomach was kicking up a tantrum, and I chowed down, wishing I'd remembered to buy drinks and fruit salad. Delilah ate like she was starved, too. In fact, it was obvious there wouldn't be any leftovers tomorrow.

As the last rays of the sun disappeared, I pushed back my plate and jumped up. "Chase, you and Morio go in the living room—*now*."

Chase glanced at the clock. "Time for her to wake up, huh? You know, eventually we're going to see the entrance to her lair. It's got to be in the kitchen somewhere. Don't you trust us by now?"

I shook my head. "It's not *you* we're worried about." When he gave me a blank look, I added softly, "Think, Chase. Say one of the demons happens to capture you. Or one of the Elwing Blood Clan. Maybe somebody still kicking around after the battle with Dredge. Somebody who might be after Menolly. How long do you think you'd last under torture—"

Chase blanched, shuddering.

"Yeah, it sounds bad, but it could happen, and you know it."

"You could be more tactful—" Delilah started to say, but I cut her off.

"I'm over sugarcoating anything within our little group here. We can't afford to ignore the possibilities anymore. As I was saying, how long do you think Chase would last before he told them where the entrance to her lair is?"

I turned to him. "You may think you know it's in the kitchen, but there are the hall and the back rooms. You really don't know as much as you believe you do, and trust me, that's a *good* thing."

As I ran out of words, I realized everybody was staring at me. "What? We're in a fight, not only for our own lives, but for two worlds. And look at who we are! Morgaine was spot on when she told me we needed more allies. We may not be able to trust her, but at least she was honest about it. And we have to be blunt with ourselves, too. When mortals are dreaming of demons tearing apart the world, and when Rāksasas are living in the open right here in the city—the problem's a whole lot bigger than we feared."

Realizing that I was on a rant, I dropped into my chair again. "Sorry, sorry . . . I'm just . . . Chase and Morio—living room, please. We'll finish dinner in a few minutes." As the two men filed out, I leaned my head against the table.

Delilah stood behind me and wrapped her arms around my shoulders. "I know you're worried. We all are. And you're right. We have to be honest with ourselves, or we'll make mistakes. But you're tired. You can't let this mess drain away your hope—"

"Let what drain away her hope?" Menolly pushed open the bookshelf that hid the entrance to her lair and slipped out, carefully shutting it tight again. "I thought those two oafs would never leave. I've been standing in there for five minutes."

She blew kisses to Delilah and me and paused to press light fingers on Iris's shoulders. Menolly wasn't a huggy person. Most vampires weren't very good with showing physical emotion.

While Iris summoned the men back to the table, Menolly poured herself a goblet of lamb's blood. We kept spare blood on hand for her from an organic ranch outside of Seattle. They saved it for me when they butchered their livestock, and we had a freezer full. It wasn't all that tasty, and Menolly often complained, but it worked in a pinch. Morio was working on a spell that would change the taste to some of the foods she missed from when she was alive, and so far it looked promising.

When we were all gathered around the table again, Chase said, "Can you fill Menolly in on the goblin and demon mess after I leave? I want to hear what you found out at the institution today. Then I have to get back to work. I'm probably not going to see my bed until well past two or three tomorrow morning."

"No problem," I said. "To cut to the quick, we know where to look for the third spirit seal. It's not going to be easy, though."

Morio and I filled them in on everything Benjamin had told us. After we finished, Delilah jumped up, drumstick in one hand, biscuit in the other, and started to pace.

"You think that the woman in the crystal might really be Aeval, the Unseelie Queen? What's going to happen when somebody uses that sword? Do you think she'll wake up? And was she the one who put it there in the first place?"

I shrugged, biting into another chicken thigh. Starved, I wished now that I'd bought a bigger bucket. Iris retrieved a cold ham from the refrigerator, and a fruit salad, and set them on the table. I flashed her a grateful smile.

"You read my mind," I said, slicing off a thick piece of ham. I turned back to Delilah. "As to your questions, I have no idea. We're going to find out, that I guarantee you. Because no way in hell am I allowing anybody else to get to that spirit seal first. But there's something else. Something I sensed while we were out at the retreat. I haven't even told Morio my suspicions yet, and I'll bet anything that Benjamin has no idea."

"No idea about what?" Morio dished out the fruit salad and slid a bowl across the table to me.

I gave him a grin. "I think Benjamin Welter is part Fae."

CHAPTER 23

Of course, that broke the conversation wide open.

"How do you figure?" Iris asked.

I shook my head. "I'm not sure, but I tell you, I was picking up on some very strange flares in his aura. His energy field was all over the place, and some of the spikes I recognized as Fae energy."

"I don't get it," Chase said. "Can you give me the twenty-cent version?"

"Hold on," I said, digging into my fruit salad. "Damn, I'm hungry." My head hurt so bad, it was about to pound me into the ground.

"Eat. I'll put on the kettle for tea and fetch dessert." Iris put the kettle to flame and broke out the chocolate pie I'd bought, dividing it into thick, creamy slices.

I patted my lips with my napkin. "Okay, maybe if you think of it this way it will help. Imagine that Benjamin is a star—like the sun. I can see the corona around him. Now, imagine there are several types of suns. Say human suns, Fae suns, demon suns, and each one has a halo that's a different pattern, depending on what race they are."

"I'm with you so far," Chase said.

"Okay, I looked at Benjamin, who should be a human sun, for example, with a plaid pattern. What I saw was an aura with a little bit of—oh, call it a polka-dot pattern—mixed into the plaid. And since polka dots belong to the Fae suns, it means that he has Fae energy in him."

Menolly snickered. "Polka dots? What, are mine, blood colored?"

I stuck my tongue out at her and turned back to Chase. "*Of course*, that's just an example, but do you get the drift? I can tell Benjamin's not FBH. He has some Fae in him because his aura has some Fae energy mixed into it."

Chase nodded slowly. "I get it. If you were looking at his DNA under a microscope, it would be a different pattern than mine. And his energy signature is a different pattern than mine. Okay, so you say he doesn't know he's part Fae?"

"I doubt it. The blood is probably recessive. Somewhere along the line, there was an intermarriage or liaison with one of the Fae. Long enough ago to fade the powers down so much they almost died out. But something sparked them off, and it's my bet that entering the cave triggered everything. The energy there probably awakened the Fae blood in his veins, and he had no idea what happened."

I suddenly felt very bad for Benjamin. He was locked up for something he couldn't help, he wasn't a danger to others, and yet he'd been tossed to the side in order to keep his precious family from being embarrassed.

Delilah stared at her plate. "How can we help him? You said he wants to escape?"

"Yeah, but I have no idea what to do once we manage to get him out of there. Where can we take him? We certainly can't take care of him, and we don't dare bring his family down on us." I frowned at the table.

"What about Smoky? He takes care of Georgio. Could this Benjamin live out there with them?" Menolly sipped at her blood wine. She was staring at the chicken with open lust, and I realized that she must be craving what she'd had to leave behind.

"I don't think Smoky would go for that," I said as Chase's cell phone rang.

"I'll be right back," Chase said, stepping into the hall to take the call.

"Even if Smoky agreed, Benjamin's family would eventually track him down. They have money. Even though they tucked him away in a nice quiet padded cell, they'd use every means they had to trace him. I know people like that. No, if Ben's to get out of there, he's going to have to go somewhere they can't follow him."

Morio caught my attention and stared at me. "We know of one place they can't trace him."

"You're talking about Otherworld?" I put down my fork, suddenly full. The thought of turning Benjamin loose in OW was frightening. He'd end up dead in no time. There was no way in hell that he was prepared to take on an entirely new world. He couldn't even cope with the one he was already part of.

"I think—" I stopped as Chase returned, a strained look on his face. "What happened? More Cryptos run amok?"

He shook his head. "No, I don't think so. Though it's hard to tell for sure. I just got a call that the rug shop—the one you were checking out because of the demons? It's burned down, along with the building next to it. The cops think it's arson. Know anybody who might be out firebombing a demon's hangout?"

Delilah slowly pushed her chair back. "You don't think it was one of *us*, do you? Chase, how could you? We'd never endanger innocent lives that way!"

Chase sputtered and held up his hand. "Did I say I thought you guys did it? The fire marshal is down there, talking to *Mr. Karvanak*. He apparently passes himself off as a pretty tame human. What crosses my mind is this: If this demon is as tricky as you say he is, won't he mention that you guys don't like him? He knows you aren't going to go blabbing about Shadow Wing's attempts to take over Earth, so he's safe from you outing him."

Holy hell. The thought that he might use FBHs to interfere with us hadn't even occurred to me. "We all have excuses. I was out at the Mountain Aspen Retreat with Morio, and they can vouch for that—"

"No they can't," Morio said. "You charmed the nurse and told her not to mention our visit so that Benjamin's parents can't ask any uncomfortable questions."

"No, I told her not to mention it to *Benjamin's parents*. Let's see . . . Delilah and Menolly's asses are covered. Iris, too." I squinted, staring at the table. The chicken caught my eye. My stomach rumbled.

"So we can prove your whereabouts. Good. What about the unicorn and the pixie?" Chase was jotting down notes as fast as he could. "Could they have done it?"

That quieted us all down. Feddrah-Dahns was still missing, and we had no idea where he was, or even if he was okay. I was about to say something when the doorbell rang. I excused myself and went to see who it was.

Smoky was standing there. I gazed up at him, and before I realized what I was doing, I was pressed against his chest as he wrapped himself around me. His lips lingered on mine, his tongue toying with them just enough to get me going. The stress from the day made me tremble, and he ran his thumb down my back, pressing my spine taut.

"You see, your body knows where you need to be," he whispered.

With a shiver, I finally let go, trying to catch my breath from between my thighs, where it had spiraled. "We have a problem. Several problems." I motioned him in.

"One of them, I think I can ease your mind on," he said, following me into the kitchen. "Feddrah-Dahns is out on my land, along with the pixie. The unicorn has been hurt, but he'll survive."

Everybody started talking at once, but Smoky gazed around the room, then held up one hand. "Enough."

I waited until everyone quieted down. "Who wounded him? Demons?"

Smoky nodded. "That's what he said. The Rāksasa managed to get in a few swipes before Feddrah-Dahns and the pixie got away. Apparently unicorns can outdistance demons. He shook the Rāksasa just as I was headed down the trail to speak with him. I hastened him and his pixie away immediately but didn't have enough time to stop and tell Iris."

"And you say Mistletoe is okay?"

Smoky blinked. "What? I don't have any mistletoe out there that I know of. Moss, yes. Lichen, definitely. Mistletoe? None."

Delilah let out a long sigh. "Not *mistletoe* the plant. Mistletoe, the pixie."

"Ah, I see." Smoky lifted one eyebrow with a quirky grin. "Yes, Mistletoe is fine. Feddrah-Dahns got raked on the side. He has some nasty wounds, but I had a batch of powders and ointments that Titania left with me some time back, and I used those to patch him up. Seems to have stanched the bleeding and slowed down the pain. There's something odd, by the way."

Not another out-of-place puzzle piece. "What?"

Smoky stared at the food on the table. "The dream chaser demon that walks with him?"

"Dream chaser?" I frowned. "I've never heard of them."

"Vanzir, his name is. Dream chasers feed on human energy during sleep—from inside a person's dreams. Anyway, Vanzir apparently stumbled between the Rāksasa and Feddrah-Dahns right during a critical swing. Missed getting hurt but foiled the demon's last attempt to kill the unicorn. Apparently his stumble gave Feddrah-Dahns enough time to get away."

I motioned for Delilah to help Iris clear the table. "Somebody just burned down the rug shop that belongs to the demons. You can vouch for Feddrah-Dahns being on your land all afternoon, right?"

Smoky snagged a piece of chicken before Delilah whisked it away. "Yes. He's been out there for several hours. We need to talk about that portal downtown. I hopped through to take a look where it went."

"That's what Delilah said. You're positive it leads into Guilyoton?"

He nodded, biting into the drumstick. I watched as he fastidiously cleaned the bone in under a minute flat, but without ever seeming to chew or drop anything on his bleachy clean trench. The trench covered his usual gray turtleneck and butt-hugging white jeans, doing wonders to beckon my thoughts away from where they should be lingering. Smoky caught my eye and gave me a sly wink and pursed his lips in an air kiss. I weakly slid into my chair.

After he finished eating, he tossed the bone into the garbage and turned a chair around, straddling it and leaning his elbows on the back. "I'm all too aware of the goblin lands over in Otherworld. The creatures are still numerous in the Northlands, and in some of the higher mountain peaks here Earthside. They breed like vermin and taste just about as bad. I had a suspicion that the portal might lead there, and when I jumped through, saw that I was right. The bogs and swamps reek of goblin, and the land feels tainted by their magic."

"That would be Guilyoton, all right." Forcing my attention to return to the matter at hand, I retrieved a notepad and pen.

"Okay, what do we have going here? We have the Crypto problem, which is getting worse. I'm sure the goblin portal isn't the only one working overtime."

"The demons are our biggest concern at this point. Especially since they're well aware of who we are and where we live. And they think we have the spirit seal or know where it is." Delilah pulled out her laptop and fired it up.

"We do know. *Now.* Another problem—Morgaine and Titania. They're searching for the same cave Benjamin found. I know it in my gut. Which means if they find it before we do, they'll have the spirit seal." I jotted down another note. "Also, I have the unicorn horn, and both Morgaine and the demons would *love* to have that little goody."

"Don't forget, the demon's shop burned down. Who do you think they're going to blame?" Menolly leaned in. "Even if we have proof we weren't there, they're going to find a way to blame us."

"And Benjamin. We can't forget him," Morio added. "If we discovered that he knows about the spirit seal, my guess is the demons will figure it out before long. What if they tailed us out there? They'll tear him apart to get the information about the cave."

"Shit," Menolly said. "The demons are the crux. If we can get the spirit seal first and deliver it to Queen Asteria, then they won't have a reason to bother Benjamin. But they'll still be after us, so we have to take them out. The djinn, too. If she's mixed up with them, you know whose side she's on."

"I wish Trillian and Roz were here," I said. "With Zach and his men guarding the portal, we're down on manpower. And Karvanak is going to be a difficult kill. Hell—I forgot! Smoky gave us information on the Rākṣasa, and with all that's gone on today, we haven't had a chance to look it over." Rushing into the living room, I found my bag where I'd dropped it. Yanking the papers out of the side pocket, I hurried back into the kitchen and sat down.

Smoky reached for them. I handed them over. "Since you're here, maybe you can fill us in on what we need to know."

He pursed his lips. "They're masters of illusion. After tonight, you're going to have to make sure that when you've been separated for any amount of time that you aren't talking to an impersonator. In other words, Dispel Illusion spells would come in very handy at this time. Who besides Morio has them? I can set up a barrier that will force illusions to be shed, but I can't cast a spell on a person, per se."

Iris cleared her throat. "I can dispel illusion, especially when a nonhuman creature tries to pass as human."

"Don't look at me," Chase said. "I can't even twitch my nose."

Delilah snorted. "Yeah, but you've got other saving graces." She gave him a delicious grin, and I let out a soft laugh. Demons or not, it was good to see her happy.

"Well, none of my spells are good for clear sight, so that pretty much leaves Iris, Morio, and to some degree, Smoky. Iris and Morio, we need to make sure we only split into two groups, and that one of you is with one, the other with the second." I stared at the paper. "I guess our first task is set. Find the cave and retrieve the spirit seal. I'm exhausted—we all look tired—but we've run on less sleep before. Let's head out there now. Menolly can come with us that way."

Morio spoke up. "Want to bet some Freedom's Angel member found out the demons aren't human and burned the shop? He wouldn't have to know they were demon, maybe thought they were a Supe."

Chase tapped the table with his pen. "You have a good point there, Morio. I've decided that I'm coming with you tonight, then I'll pull a double shift at work. I've got a cot there I can catch a few hours of sleep on. I'm running two departments now." He sighed and stuffed his notebook into his pocket and stretched, yawning.

"Okay, baby," Delilah said, wrapping her arms around him and giving him a long kiss. "But be careful. I don't want anything to happen to you, and we're facing some pretty potent enemies."

The phone rang again. I snagged up the receiver, hoping it was just a telemarketer for once. But no such luck. It was Nurse Richards.

"Ms. Welter? I'm afraid I have some bad news, and since Benjamin's parents aren't in the country and didn't leave contact information, I thought I would call you." She sounded frantic.

Hell. What now? "What's wrong? Is Benjamin all right?"

"That's the problem. We don't know. He seems to have . . . disappeared."

I stared at the phone. "Disappeared? What the hell do you mean? Where did he go?" Even as the words escaped my mouth, I realized how stupid they sounded.

"We have no idea. We're searching the grounds for a third time. Tonight, two men and a woman showed up, asking about him. They weren't family, they said as much, and they insisted on speaking to him. I called the doctor, and he denied their request. They left, but they were in a foul mood when we turned them away."

The demons and the djinn. Had to be! Or . . . Morgaine, Mordred, and Arturo.

"You did right," I said. "They were probably media folk, looking for ways to expose our family problems. So what happened to Benjamin?"

She cleared her throat, and I could hear the wheels turning. She was probably terrified the Welters would sue.

"When we went to give Benjamin his nightly medication, he wasn't in his room. We scoured the residence hall, and we've been searching the grounds, but no luck. Right now, we're hoping he just found a quiet place to sleep in one of the empty rooms. But I wanted to tell you. You asked me to call if anything unusual happened."

Thank gods for Fae glamour. I thanked her and said we'd be out as soon as possible, then hung up. "We have to find that cave. Benjamin is missing, and I think the demons were there, looking for him."

"Crap," Menolly said. "Come on. Iris, you stay here with Maggie. Lock the doors and go hide in my lair. You know the secret exit, in case anything should happen."

Iris nodded, pale and looking worried out of her mind. She hurried to gather up Maggie as we readied ourselves. I tucked my silver dagger and sheath onto my belt, then made sure the unicorn horn was firmly in the inner pocket of the cloak Eriskel had given me. In a nod to speed, I switched from stilettos to granny boots with thick heels.

Delilah, in thick jeans and a V-neck sweater, shrugged into a leather jacket and fastened her silver short sword to her leg holster. Menolly slid a blue denim jacket over her black turtleneck and traded her heels for a pair of Doc Martens Eye Zip Boots. As soon as Morio made sure he had his bag with his skull familiar, we headed out the front door.

"Morio, let's take your SUV. It will hold all of us," I said, but a noise interrupted me, and I whirled around, sucking in energy as I prepared to blast whoever it was to kingdom come.

"Hold your fire," a familiar voice rang out.

I slowly lowered my hands. As we clattered down the porch steps, Trenyth and Grandmother Coyote stepped out of the shadows. Neither looked like they were the bearers of good news.

CHAPTER 24

—⁂—

"Trenyth! Grandmother Coyote?" I skidded to a halt on the bottom step, and Delilah tripped against me. We both went tumbling to the mud-soaked ground below. I winced as the sharp tip of the unicorn horn jabbed me in the hip. While I wasn't worried about it breaking—it could probably withstand being run over by a truck—I *was* concerned about accidentally setting off its powers. I still didn't know how the damned thing worked, for the most part.

"Youch! Watch where you're going!" Delilah said, rubbing her butt. She pushed herself off the ground and helped me up.

Menolly was standing behind us. I expected her to be snickering, but her expression was dead serious as she stared at our visitors with a veiled gaze. Morio and Smoky swung in behind us.

"The fact that both of you are here at the same time doesn't give me any fuzzy feelings," I said, gingerly rubbing the sore spot on my hip. "What's up?"

"We have to talk," Grandmother Coyote said, her steel teeth gleaming in the dim light. We were a few days past the new moon, and I could still feel the energy from the Dark Mother rumbling in the air.

"Do you want to go inside?" I asked, gesturing to the house.

She shook her head. "No. We have no time for niceties. You must make haste. The scales will tip tonight. Tomorrow is the equinox, and the balance *must* shift. What has long been set askew can be righted this night. The powers that once reigned will rise again. *You* must be present to bear witness, and you must do what you can to help the shift occur."

Riddles. It was always riddles with Grandmother Coyote. I didn't even bother to ask what she was talking about. I knew better. We'd find out the hard way. We always did.

I turned to Trenyth. "And what bad news are you bringing to the table? It's got to be bad in order for Queen Asteria to send you through the portal after she said she didn't want to risk your neck."

He sucked in a deep breath. "It *is* bad news. I hate to be the one to tell you this, but there's been a slipup. It's about Trillian . . ."

I began to breathe hard. "No . . . no . . ."

"Camille, listen to me—"

"Don't you *dare* . . ." A rush of energy raced through my body. My heart was beating so loud I could barely hear myself think. I began to shake.

"Trillian's—"

"No! He can't be dead!" I bit my lip, and blood poured into my mouth. This couldn't be happening—it was too much. It was all too much.

Delilah jumped behind me, shoring me up. Smoky was down the steps instantly, and I leaned against him.

Trenyth rushed to say, "He's not dead. His soul statue its unbroken." He shook his head, and my lungs gave a jump start, and I let out a ragged breath. "At least, he's not dead . . . yet."

I let out a strangled cough, and Smoky held me tighter. "What the fuck do you mean? Not dead *yet*? Was he wounded? Hurt? Just tell me what's wrong!"

Trenyth sighed. "We think he was captured by a goblin contingent. Another informant saw the battle go down."

And then my world went black.

As I regained consciousness, I was aware of someone leaning over me. I blinked, willing my vision to clear. What had happened? Why was I lying on the cold ground?

Grandmother Coyote's gleaming teeth came into focus as she smiled down at me, her hand caressing my cheek. Her fingers were rough, and her eyes bored deep into my soul, calling me back from wherever it was my mind had fled. I gasped and sat up as a jolt passed through her hand, into my face. Like rough whiskey, it shocked me awake.

"Come, girl, get up. You don't have time to mourn. You must shoulder the burden and move on for the night. Ask your questions. You can cry later," she said.

I shook the fog out of my head and looked around. Smoky was sitting beside me. My head had been in his lap. Morio and Menolly were kneeling on my left, Delilah and Chase on my right. They helped me up, and Smoky slid his arm around my waist while Morio took my hand.

"Are you okay?" Delilah asked.

"How can I be okay?" I asked, staring at her. "You know what the goblins do to their prisoners. Capture is as good as a death sentence."

She turned away, but I couldn't stop talking.

"Trillian and I belong to each other—through life and through death. When he reentered my life, I was terrified, because I knew that I'd never be able to send him away again, that I'd never leave him again. No matter how many other lovers we take, no matter how many miles stretch between us, we are bound forever." I closed my eyes. "Tell me what happened."

Grandmother Coyote interrupted me. "There isn't time."

"Then *make* time!" I turned on her, feeling as frozen as the northern wastes. "Trillian is my *oath lover*. I *will* know what happened to him and why he was sent on another mission even though he was already pegged as a spy. The world can shatter like glass for all I care right now. *But I will know!*"

She stared at me, and for a moment I thought she was going to strike me down, but then she motioned to Trenyth. "Hurry. We don't have time to waste."

Trenyth tugged at the collar of his robe. "Trillian was the only one Queen Asteria could trust for this mission, and you'll understand why when I tell you."

"We'd better." My hand moved toward the silver dagger at my side.

He flashed me a cold look. "Your *father* was due in Elqaneve a few days ago. He was going to join our intelligence operations."

"Father! What do you know about our father? We haven't heard from him since he ran from the Guard." I tensed. Delilah and Menolly did the same.

"Your father sent word he was coming. We needed him. He has secret information about the armies of the Court and Crown. But along the way, he vanished."

"Shit. Not good. Not good at all. Any idea what happened to him?" Menolly kicked a rock out of the way as Delilah glumly dropped into a squat. I watched her carefully for a moment, but she didn't transform.

"We found out through an informant—you know Rozurial— that your father's soul statue is still intact. But we need the information he was carrying. We have to find out where he's disappeared, and why. Trillian was the only one we could trust in this matter. He knows your father. He knows the whole story."

"Oh Great Mother," I said, leaning against Smoky as he helped keep me onto my feet. "Then the goblins—"

"Once they realize he's a spy, they'll torture and kill him, unless he can escape." Trenyth's voice dropped. "I'm so sorry. We still don't know what happened. There were no reports of goblin activity in the area we sent Trillian into. We have no idea how they showed up there so fast."

"The portals." Menolly snapped her fingers. "That's how! They're using the rogue portals. And want to make a bet that a few must have escaped back to Guilyoton with information about us after today's fight?"

"Fight? What are you talking about?" Trenyth looked confused.

We filled him in on the battle that morning.

"Oh crap, and don't forget the goblin and Sawberry Fae!" Delilah jumped up and dusted off the butt of her jeans. "Want to make a bet they not only fed what they know to the demons but to their compatriots at home? Goblins are sneaky little bastards, and they never stick to their word."

"If that's so, they've probably been spying on us since before they ever came to the shop after Feddrah-Dahns," I said, as numb as if I'd been pumped full of Novocain. "Want to bet

Karvanak has been watching us for awhile? If he's been in Seattle since before Bad Ass Luke came through, then maybe he's been keeping tabs on us all along. Who knows how much the demons know? Or Queen Lethesanar?"

My concerns about Trillian and my father took on entirely new and unwelcome dimensions. "You don't suppose Lethesanar might actually be in cahoots with the demons?" The thought was bone-chilling. If so, then she was turning traitor on two entire worlds.

Trenyth frowned. "I doubt it, but I'll be certain to discuss it with Queen Asteria. There's not much else I can tell you."

"What now?" I said, still feeling faint. Inside, I just kept repeating, *He's not dead yet . . . he's not dead yet . . . hold on to that glimmer of hope.* "We have to rescue Trillian. I know he's trained for this situation, but goblins are merciless, and they'll tear him apart before he willingly gives them information."

"There's nothing you can do," Trenyth said softly. "We'll do everything we can, but there's only so much . . ." He reached out to rest a hand on my shoulder. Smoky reached out and pushed Trenyth's hand away. Trenyth hung his head. "You don't know how much I regret having to bear this news to you, Camille. I know what Trillian means to you."

"Yeah, right," I said softly. "Is there anything else?"

He shook his head.

"Then maybe you'd better go and talk to Queen Asteria about all of this." I turned away before he could speak again.

"Child, don't punish the messenger." Grandmother Coyote's voice echoed in the still night, and I whirled around, ready to argue, but she shook her head, and I fell silent. "He could have kept silent. He didn't have to come here."

I inhaled a deep, shuddering breath. "You're right. Trenyth, thank you for telling me yourself. I guess we'd better get moving. If there's nothing more you have to say?"

They turned in silence and walked away. As I watched them go, my heart dropped like a lodestone, heavy and dragging me down. I walked toward Morio's SUV. Everyone followed me, and their unspoken questions weighed on me like a suffocating rock.

I glanced at them. "There's nothing you can do to make it better, so don't even try. Trillian's doomed, and our father's missing. This is the nature of war. Unless they allow us to return to Otherworld, to undertake the rescue ourselves, then what the

fuck is there for anybody to say? And even if we could go, there
would be a thousand places to search."

Morio unlocked the car. As the others clambered in, leaving
the front seats empty, Smoky and Morio flanked my sides. I
stared mutely at Morio. The molten topaz of his eyes melted my
heart, and I felt a sob jog in my chest. Morio slid his arms
around my waist. Smoky came up behind me and draped his
arms around my shoulders. His hair rose up to stroke my arms,
my forehead, along the length of my leg.

"Camille, you must do something," Smoky said. "Trillian . . .
there is a chance to save him. This is not some dragon trick
meant to bind your will."

"What can I do? How can I find him?" My voice was faint as
I vied for control of my emotions. I wanted to cry, to weep, to
fall apart and let them pick up the pieces. But as always, I
forced myself to stand rock-solid.

When Mother had died, I'd been the glue to hold together
the family. And never once had I let them down, even though I
was screaming inside.

When the other children had taunted Delilah into
transforming, I'd been the one to beat the crap out of them in
order to rescue her, and got myself beaten up in return. But I
hadn't cried. I didn't dare show my own vulnerability, because
they might pick on her even worse.

And when Menolly had come home, blood-crazed and
ripped to shreds, I'd held my wits together long enough to fetch
help. And then I'd cushioned the pain for my father and Delilah,
keeping my own fears and horrors at bay because that was what
I was expected to do. I was the rock. I was the anchor.

And now, Trillian was as good as dead, and our father was
missing in action. And we had a mission to accomplish. Once
more, I was called on to push aside my feelings. To let go of my
own needs in order to tend the greater good. Maybe that's why
I never wanted children. I'd already given everything I had to
give.

"I will tell you what you can do," Smoky said. "Perform a
binding ritual with Morio and with me. Accept us as your
husbands. Then can we protect you like we need to—and then
we can unleash all our powers to help you find Trillian." His
look was so intense that it frightened me.

I searched his face, searched Morio's expression, looking

for something to verify that Smoky was telling the truth. Morio nodded, his lips pressed together.

"Are you serious? Marry the two of you? For one thing, this world has rules about that—or at least, this country—"

"Fuck the rules and regulations. We aren't talking about legal documents here," Morio said. "And we aren't talking a simple wedding ceremony or valiant words. No, I know what Smoky's talking about. He's talking about performing the Soul Symbiont ritual."

I shook my head. "What the hell is that? I've never heard of it. Is it an Earthside custom?"

Smoky let out a little huff. "Not exactly. It's a ritual that's kept secret within several of the Supe lineages." He shot a warning glance at Morio. "Don't even ask how I came to know of it; you won't get an answer."

Morio glanced at the car, waving as Delilah stuck her head out. "We'll be right there." He turned back to me. "The ritual binds souls in a magical union. That union brings with it certain powers. For one thing, soul-bound members can *always* track down the other members of the union. Now, while Trillian won't technically be bound to us, the fact that you and he are yoked so strongly via magical rites, well—that might be just what we need. You can draw on our power. With the three of us searching for him magically, we might be able to find him."

I stared at them. "You mean, if we do this, we can track him down?"

"There are no guarantees, but I'm willing to take the chance." Morio lifted my chin. "Camille, you know that the elves won't risk finding Trillian. In fact, they might think he's a liability now that he's been captured. They might even request that Tanaquar send in one of the triads of Jakaris, like they tried with your cousin Shamas. Trillian doesn't have the raw power Shamas does. He couldn't grab hold of the assassins' magic. They'd kill him."

Jakaris was a Svartan god of vice, but for the duration of the war, King Vodox had ordered the triads—each a group of three monks who were skilled magical assassins—to work with Tanaquar and Queen Asteria. If they took a bead on Trillian, he'd be stone cold dead.

"Holy hell. And both of you . . . you'd do this for me? You'd forge a soul bond with me to help me rescue Trillian?" I stared at them, unable to believe the gift they offered.

Morio nodded. So did Smoky.

"How long does the union last?" In my heart, I knew the answer, but I wanted to hear it from their lips.

Smoky cleared his throat. "For life . . . and beyond. And it means that we won't ever be able to part for too long. If you go home to Otherworld for more than a few months, Morio and I would have to follow. If one of us dies, our body will find its way home to the others for funeral rites. We don't offer this in friendship, but as lovers. You *will* be our wife."

I turned back to the car. Should I accept? It was the only way . . . and yet, it would change so much in my life. And then, I thought of Trillian and made up my mind. Whatever it took, I'd find him.

"Let's get moving. We have work to do." As we headed toward Morio's SUV, I added softly, "I love both of you. I hope you know just how much. And I love Trillian. If we rescue him, I'll expect you to bring him into our marriage. I'll be honored to be wife to both of you. But remember, I'm already Trillian's wife, even if we've never mentioned marriage. Are you both willing to share me with him?" I looked at Smoky. Moment of truth here.

Morio opened the passenger door and stood aside, waiting for me to get in. "I know, and I have no problem with the idea. Provided . . ."

"Provided *what*?" I asked.

"Provided Trillian's still sane and on our side," Smoky finished. "I acquiesce." He climbed in the back next to Menolly.

Morio shut the door, and I fastened my seat belt, thinking about the future. Delilah reached through the front seats to rest a hand on my shoulder, and I absently patted it.

I bleakly stared out the window. With such odds facing us, it seemed insane to make any lasting commitments, to form any long-term attachments. And yet, they were already formed. Without benefit of ceremony or certificate, I was bound to Morio and Smoky, as I was to Trillian. Why not make it official? Why not give ourselves an edge that might prove handy later on?

Letting out a long sigh, I looked over my shoulder at Smoky.

He gave me a little wink—just a tiny one, but it said everything I needed to hear. *I'm here. I'll help you. I love you. You're mine, but I've decided I'm willing to share you with the ones you love.*

"Let's get this show on the road," I said, as Morio pulled out of the drive and we headed out toward Smoky's land.

CHAPTER 25

~⚜~

Morio cast an illusion spell over the car and cranked up the speed. We arrived in record time. As we eased into the driveway leading to Tom Lane's house, or rather, Georgio's house, I sensed a looming presence overshadowing the land.

"What the fuck is that?" I said, jumping out of the car the moment we pulled to a stop. I glanced around, looking to find the magical party-hearty scene going on. A tremendous pressure felt like it was suffocating me: deep magic, ancient magic, Fae magic, Sidhe magic. Oh hell. Titania and Morgaine.

"The demons?" Delilah asked, as she emerged from the SUV next.

I shook my head. "I don't think they've found their way here yet. No, I'm sensing heavy Fae magic. Moon magic, too—and Morgaine is a Daughter of the Moon like I am."

Everybody poured out of the car then, and Smoky's nose twitched. He growled, low in his throat, and I quickly looked around to see if he was transforming, but he stood there, tall and cool against the night sky.

"Titania and Morgaine are searching for the cave," he said. "I can feel them opening rifts, searching out the hidden niches of magic in the land. They'll find it, and we need to be there when they do."

I closed my eyes, buoyed up by the stiff breeze that had started to blow. The winds were shaking the trees, bending branch and limb, moaning softly as they swept in from the west. "It's coming from the west, from the shining shores."

"From Avalon?" Menolly asked.

Listening, I tried to pinpoint the origin of the currents of air that swept past us. They were rife with ocean salt and seaweed and the call of the gulls, and the sparkling phosphorescence that glittered in the water on warm nights when the tides were full. Fae magic, those shimmering lights were, trapped in the realm of the sea creatures.

As I followed the trail of kelp, it led me right back to myself. I was standing in the inner sanctum of the Black Unicorn's room, staring at the Lord of the Depths. He swam toward me, his long hair glistening with faerie light, his eyes round and brilliant in their darkness. As the merman rose out of the water, I saw that he was accompanied by a pod of dolphins.

I curtsied, and he quickly inclined his head in a deep bow. "Lady Camille, what is your wish?"

"Does this magic originate from Avalon? Is the isle still lost in the mists, or has it returned?" I waited, counting the seconds as he closed his eyes and plunged his hands into the water. When I'd counted to twenty, he looked up again, gazing at me through the mirror.

"No, this magic is not Avalon in nature. The sacred isle has drifted so far in the mists that no one—not even I—can find it. This is the magic of the Moon Mother's waves, of the crashing ocean currents, of the great goddesses of the sea and ocean. This is Grandmother Water's magic, and she sings on the wind tonight, for she is being summoned."

That was all he could tell me. I thanked him and withdrew, easing out of my trance as easily as I might shake out of a sudden nap.

"Not Avalon. They aren't trying to reawaken Arthur, that's for sure." I closed my eyes and caught the thread of magic again. It called to me, summoned me, beckoned me on, and I couldn't help myself—I had to follow. "Come on! It's deep in the forest, near where Benjamin told us he found the cave. Let's go."

I started off, but Smoky held out his hand. "Stop. There are traps aplenty. Let me go first," he said, taking the lead. "I can negate them."

Sanity prevailed, and I stood back, letting him move to the front. Morio and I were next, followed by Menolly, Delilah, and Chase.

We set off into the night, under the sliver of moonlight that peered down from behind a thin veil of clouds. I could feel her up there, watching with her frost-borne eyes. The Crone Mother had thrown off her black veils and was now peeking out into the heavens, the barest of Maidens once again. She would grow full and lush and ripe over the next two weeks, dripping with passion and lust and eggs ripe for the quickening, and then she would bid us race into her skies with the Hunt, scouring the land for those ready to join the parade of hunters and prey.

The forest was a variation of grays and blacks, with auras flaring brightly in the monochromatic night. Smoky swiftly navigated through brush and tree, around bends in the path that would have sent me careening into the undergrowth. During the Hunt I could see clearly, but other nights, though my sight was better than most FBHs, I still had to slow down when in strange territory.

I paused as Smoky held up one hand. Waiting as he trod on ahead, the others stood behind me. There was a muffled *whoomf* and the sound of a small explosion rocked the immediate area, but there was no sign of smoke nor fire, and Smoky looked unharmed. He glanced down at me as he turned back to us, and I could feel him reach out to embrace me, to pull me into his energy field and hold me secure.

The path led on, past the turnoff to where Morgaine had made camp. A fire flickered in the distance, no doubt next to their caravan. Smoky motioned for us to stop once more as he raced down the path. After a moment, the flames disappeared, and the darkness pulled in around us again. I shivered unaccountably. I wasn't cold, but the Fae energy—Grandmother Water's magic— was growing stronger by the minute, and I could barely think, it was so thick.

Looking back at Morio, I whispered, "Can you feel it, too?"

He nodded. "Oh yes, though I think not so strong as you. But it's calling to me, too, and I'm having a hard time ignoring it."

Delilah leaned forward. "This is a wild land here. Smoky has kept it that way on purpose, but I wonder if he hasn't let it get out of hand."

"Let what get out of hand?" Smoky asked, reappearing as quickly as he'd vanished.

She stammered. "The . . . the land. It's wild and primal—"

"And that is the nature of *wilderness*," he said, giving her a cool smile. "Girl, do you realize how old these forests are? Your forests in Otherworld were born during the Great Divide. The forests here were born in the distant memories of the planet. They are entities with their own worlds. The woodlands have no need for humans, because humans have become a blight on the face of the world. Dragons, too, and all things that walk the paths of the forests. We all trample and devour and destroy. It's in our nature; we can't help it. But that doesn't mean the forests accept it and look the other way."

"In OW, we've found other ways to interact with the trees," I interjected. "There are primeval forests there, to be sure, that don't care for the touch of the two-legged creatures, but none are quite so intimidating as the ancient groves here."

"None except Darkynwyrd and her shadowy cousins," Menolly said, joining the conversation. "It doesn't matter where you go. There will be forests and wild places with welcome mats out, and then there will be the kind this woodland hearkens from—the kind that prefers to be left alone."

"Enough talk," Smoky said. "Their caravan is there, but Morgaine is not. Arturo and that impatient beast she calls Mordred are there. Mordred stinks of soot and fire. He's likely your arsonist."

Mordred? That made sense. It would seem that Morgaine was already starting her campaign against the demons on her own.

We took off again, following Smoky as he took an abrupt right turn and began to hike up a road with a steep incline. I could hear Chase puffing away behind us. The three of us girls and Morio had far more stamina than he did. And then the puffing stopped.

Concerned, I turned to look. Menolly's eyes gleamed in the night, and I could see that she'd hoisted Chase on her back. He looked scared spitless but was hanging on for dear life as she gave him a piggyback ride to the top. Delilah glanced at him, but when he scowled, she turned away, careful to keep a straight face.

Smoky stopped so suddenly that I plowed into his back. He

reached behind with one hand and grabbed my wrist, dragging me to the front with him.

"Look," he said, turning me so I was facing west. There, against the hillside, a brilliant light filtered out from a cleft in the rock. The light, a cerulean blue with sparkles dancing in it, shone like a soft mist in the night.

"The cave," I whispered.

"The cave," Smoky said.

We slipped down the path leading across the meadow that buttressed the cave entrance. I didn't ask Smoky if he'd seen the cavern before. I knew this was as new to him as it was to us. As we stole across the lea in single file under the silver crescent of moon, I could feel the pull of the cavern even stronger. The energy was dizzy with the lifeblood of the Moon Mother and swirled with the currents of Grandmother Water.

The magic dipped and swayed, spiraling like a labyrinthine dance, leading us on. Will-o'-the-wisps dappled the meadow, the dangerous Fae of wild moors and heather-clad hills singing siren songs. I fell back to Menolly's side. Chase was behind her, and I glanced into his eyes, worried. Orbs of light, entities without form, will-o'-the-wisps—or corpse candles as they were commonly called—beckoned to humans like sirens in the night. Usually to their death.

Chase's eyes were glazed, and his nostrils flared. I tapped Menolly on the shoulder, not wanting to speak lest our words be captured by the wind and carried on ahead. She stopped, watching as I motioned to the detective, then to the corpse candles. Understanding dawned in her eyes, and she dropped back by his side, taking him firmly by the wrist to lead him on.

Satisfied that he wouldn't go wandering off to his death, I slipped silently through the knee-high grass to Smoky's side again. Morio joined us, as Delilah fell back beside Menolly and Chase.

I looked up at the moon. Her newborn crescent glittered like the blade of a scythe, and a cold wash of fear and lust ran through my blood. She was my Lady, my Huntress, my goddess.

"Will you live for her? Will you die for her? Will you kiss her lips on your wedding day, and accept her kiss on your brow at the edge of your grave?"

Nigel's voice echoed in the back of my mind. He'd tried to dissuade me from joining the Coterie of the Moon Mother, as he did every acolyte. To court the Moon when you weren't summoned invited insanity at best, a chill and dire death at worst. But she'd been with me since I first held my hands up to her as a child, desperate to touch her, to hear her words in my heart, to answer the call that echoed through my soul.

"Come. We can waste no time." Smoky's voice startled me out of my reverie. I realized I'd been standing in the middle of the field, lost in her passion. As the scent of soil and damp moss hit my nostrils, I shook my head to clear my thoughts and jogged along behind him.

We were almost to the cave when I heard the first call, deep within my heart. *"Camille, we need you. Come to us, girl. You are as much a part of this as we are."*

"What? Who?" I stopped short, looking around.

"Who are you talking to?" Delilah asked, staring at me, a worried expression on her face.

"I don't know. I heard a command to go to the cave. The magic has been calling me since we first arrived on the land, and it's grown stronger with every passing step." I bit my lip. "I need to go. I need to go into the cave."

"We all need to go into the cave," Menolly said, still holding Chase firmly by the wrist. He was off in la-la land, that much was obvious, and I had my doubts he'd be any use at all to us until the charm of the meadow was broken or until we got him far enough away from the meadow to negate it. We should have left him home.

"What do we do with him? If we leave him out here, he'll be mush by the time we get back. If we take him with us, one of us will have to keep a watch on him." I stared at Chase, trying to decide what our best course of action was.

"I'll watch him and make sure nothing happens. Come on, let's get moving," Delilah said. "I'm stronger than Chase, so I can protect him."

"There's no help for it, then." I motioned toward the entrance. "All right, I'm going in first, since I'm the one being called. I don't smell Demonkin here, so whatever's going down is separate from them. I hope."

Smoky and Morio nodded and took their places at my side, then Chase and Delilah. Menolly swung around, skulking through the shadows so that she couldn't be seen. She'd be our invisible guard. Better than invisible, since she was silent and left only her scent in her wake.

I stared at the cave, now just a few yards ahead, and readied the horn, keeping it in the folds of my gown. Finally, I ran toward the entrance, Smoky and Morio on my heels. As my feet touched the first fingers of light emanating from the cave, the icy shaft of the Moon Mother's power impaled me, shattering into my heart with the echo of a thousand chimes.

I broke through the entrance and stumbled into the cave.

Morgaine and Titania stood beside a forest of crystals, guarding a woman trapped inside a huge stalagmite. Their grins feral and Fae, they beckoned to me.

Titania stepped forward, holding a short sword that contained a faceted amethyst that shimmered under the shifting lights of the cave. *The spirit seal.* Just as Benjamin had said.

"We've been waiting for you, Camille," she said. "You will help us free Aeval. You have no choice."

"What if I say no?" I stared at the two of them. Where before they'd been at odds, it was now clear they were working together, and that Titania had regained much of her former power.

Morgaine stepped forward. "Camille, you are the crux on which the equinox turns this night. You alone can help us raise the Unseelie Queen. We will bring her back to life and right the balance that so long ago was thrown off when the worlds were divided."

"The scales will tip tonight. Tomorrow is the equinox, and the balance must shift. What has long been set askew can be righted this night. The powers that once reigned will rise again. You must be present to bear witness, and you must do what you can to help the shift occur."

Grandmother Coyote's words echoed in my ears, drumming like a timpanist gone mad. And then I understood. She had ordered me to help Titania and Morgaine. The Courts of Fae were destined to rise again, and I was the one on whose shoulders the final decision rode.

If I didn't help, the balance would be thrown further out of whack. If I did help, who knew what I'd be setting in motion? And there was no time to weigh decisions. The demons were on their way from one direction. Benjamin was on his way from another. Feddrah-Dahns and Mistletoe were coming from yet another—from Georgio's house where they'd been hiding. And they were going to converge here, in this cave, before the night was half-past.

All of these images collided in my mind as I looked back at the others, who stood watching, saying nothing.

Smoky had a dangerous look on his face, Menolly one of disbelief. Morio just gave me one small nod. Delilah stood beside Chase, her hand on his arm. They were near enough the entrance that they could run if need be.

I turned back to Titania and Morgaine. "What do you want me to do?"

CHAPTER 26

Titania motioned for me to move beside her. She looked at the others. "You will not interfere. Do you understand?"

Smoky raised his hand. "A moment. Morio, cast your spell."

I caught his drift. "Do it. I'm certain they're okay, but . . ."

Morgaine began to bristle, but Titania relaxed. "Be our guest, Master Fox."

Morio nodded, stood back, and held out his hands. After a moment, he chanted something in Japanese, and a bright light filled the cave. There was a shimmer around all of us. As I watched, a series of rotating images flashed where Delilah was standing, alternating between her, her golden tabby shape, and her black panther form. Smoky, on the other hand, was swathed in a mist that mirrored the image of his milky dragon self. Chase—now, Chase was interesting. There was a glow to his aura that told me he was who he was and yet, there was more. Faint—a promise of things to come.

Neither Morgaine nor Titania shifted form, nor did the figure encased within the crystal change shape.

Relaxing, Morio shook his head. "They're not illusions created by the Rāksasa. They're the real thing."

"I guess we'd better get on with it," I said, looking around the cave. The chamber went back a long ways, covered with quartz spikes jutting out from the glossy black rock. A crystalline sheet that resembled glacial ice covered the floor, reflecting a light that seemed to emanate from the very core of the walls.

A dais, also formed of crystal, rose in front of the stalagmite holding Aeval prisoner, and on that dais was a chalice blown from volcanic glass, and in the chalice a steaming brew, the mist overflowing the rim to slowly creep out into the air.

Titania motioned me forward. I gave the others one last look. "I have to do this. Grandmother Coyote foretold it. I have no choice. Destiny is too strong." Even as I spoke, the energy of the chamber forcibly pushed me forward.

I quit resisting and joined Titania and Morgaine.

Titania motioned for me to flank her on the left. She stood in the center, Morgaine on her right. The Fae Queen emeritus held out her hand and instinctively, I placed my own hand, palm up, in hers. She gazed into my eyes, and the years rolled backward, the millennia sliding away as her power began to coalesce around her. A cloak of swirling magic, a nimbus of immortality. She straightened her shoulders. Morgaine gasped as Titania lowered all her masks, and her beauty and brilliance filled the cavern with an audible sigh.

I could only gaze up at her, filled with pride. Here was the noble Titania of legend and lore, here was the Fae Queen who terrorized and seduced mortals by the score. Here was the Lady who our own queen should be emulating. Titania knew how to be a true queen. She had only forgotten herself for a time, steeped in unhappiness and liquor. But now she was back.

She lifted the short sword with the spirit seal fastened in its hilt and brought it down on my palm, slicing through the flesh. My blood spilled into my hand and overflowed, drizzling to the floor.

"Join us," Titania said, pointing to the chalice. I raised my hand over the goblet and tipped it palm down, watching as the blood trickled into the liquid. The mist rising from the brew hissed and popped and billowed up with a violet flame.

Morgaine reached for my hand, and I let her take it. She raised it to her lips and kissed the wound, and the flesh began to heal, mending together as if an invisible seamstress were stitching it taut.

Titania turned to the dais. "Only the union of the blood of the Fae and the magic of the Moon Mother, bound together in a free agent, can free Aeval from her crystalline grave and restore her to the world of the living. I cannot strike the blow to shatter the spike since I am Aeval's opposite. Nor can Morgaine, since she aspires to the Court."

She paused, staring down into my eyes. "But *you*, Camille, you have both Fae blood and you are a Daughter of the Moon. And you do not covet our crowns. You shall free Aeval. Drink the elixir and then strike the crystal with the sword. Break the spell cast upon the Queen of Unseelie by those who divided the worlds and disbanded the Courts so long ago."

Her words reverberated in the chamber. *Break the spell cast upon the Queen of Unseelie by those who divided the worlds and disbanded the Courts so long ago.* So Aeval had been trapped since the Great Divide, and I'd be undoing a spell of immense power cast by . . . by . . . who? I cast an anxious look at Titania.

"Whose spell is it?"

She reached out and cupped my chin in her hands. "Four of the Elemental Lords joined together to forge the spell, even as they cast the spell on me to drain away most of my powers. I've managed to break free of their trap, but I cannot undo what was done to Aeval."

"And you think I can . . ."

"Now that you possess the horn of the Black Unicorn, you have the strength to wake her. We know what powers the horn possesses. The Elementals within the horn can strengthen your magic enough to overcome the power of those who bewitched the Courts and brought them to their knees."

Brought the Courts to their knees? I hadn't heard this part of history. "Are you saying that the Great Divide was actually a *battle*?"

Titania gazed at me. "Child, don't you *know*? The Great Divide was the greatest battle the Fae have ever waged among themselves. Those who feared the demons fought to divide the worlds in a way that unbalanced the entire sphere of existence, and things have been getting more and more skewed since then. Oh, for awhile it worked to keep the Demonkin at bay, but the system is breaking down; more portals are opening on their own. The seals long to be reunited to set the world at balance again."

Morgaine spoke up. "The plan was flawed from the beginning. The victors turned their backs on their heritage as they left for Otherworld. *After* they decimated the Courts of Seelie and Unseelie. So much has been lost in obscurity, but those of us who led the Courts in battle remember all too well what destruction the war brought about."

"Then, by doing this, I'm betraying my family, my home world—" Frozen with indecision, I felt like a fulcrum, caught between two worlds who balanced on my shoulders. Tonight was the equinox. Grandmother Coyote was one of the Hags of Fate. She told me that it was my destiny to help rebuild the Courts of Fae, Earthside. But what ramifications would that have back in OW? And wouldn't that just lead to more warfare?

Morgaine impatiently grabbed me by the arm and yanked me around to face her. "Your family got its start right here on Earth. You are indeed a daughter of Fae, but do you know who your ancestors were? Do you know *where* your father's roots lie?"

I shook my head, scared now. Something big was coming— I could feel it. Morgaine looked up at Menolly and Delilah. They were alert, ready for action.

"This involves the *two of you*, as well. Listen carefully. I wasn't going to reveal this, because some things are best left in the past. But if you need to feel like you aren't betraying your *family*, then perhaps you'd best know. Just where do you think your family tree leads back to? Well?"

"I don't know. Father said a lot of the records were lost eons ago." My teeth were chattering now, and I could barely catch my breath. Her fingers dug into my flesh, bruising my arm as she shook me lightly.

"Camille, look at me. What do you see? *Look at me.*"

And I looked. Deep into Morgaine's violet eyes, into her waiflike face, at her raven-blue hair. *And I saw.* I saw what she was trying to tell us.

"Great Mother . . . you . . . you . . ."

"I'm one of your *ancestors*, you foolish child. You are from the same line that spawned me. We're from the original family who formed the worship of the Moon Mother long before the Great Divide. All three of you carry the same blood that I do in your own veins. Your father and I are cousins, of a sort. I may be only half-Fae, but my work with the Merlin extended my life by far longer than any mortal can ever hope to see. I will live as long as any of the full-blooded Fae. Your father was born after the worlds divided, but *his* grandfather and my father shared a common bond. I dug into the past when I first saw you a few months ago. Your blood sang to mine."

I abruptly sank down on the floor. A glance told me Menolly and Delilah were struck speechless. "We're family?" My great-grandfather had died long, long before I was born, in a battle against some nameless beast in the forest. Nor had my father met him.

The Great Divide had plowed forward, ripping the worlds apart, uprooting families, destroying records, tearing asunder clans and long-established communities. But we'd always believed it had been a necessary juggernaut, something that all Fae had agreed upon to prevent the demons from tearing through the world. Now a dark cloud settled over every stitch of history we'd ever been taught.

"You might as well call me cousin. Stand up and quit your cowardice. You know what you have to do—so do it!" Her eyes narrowing, Morgaine roughly hauled me to my feet and pushed me toward the dais.

"You have a lousy way of showing your love," I grumbled, but at least she'd managed to shake me out of my fear. Even if I forever ruined my reputation in Otherworld, I knew I had to do this. Knowing what I did now—that the Great Divide had been forced on the Courts—at this point, I trusted Grandmother Coyote far more than I trusted anybody back home.

The crystals jutting from ceiling and floor began to hum as I accepted the glass that Morgaine handed me. The brew swirled within, dark and deep and rich with a dozen different herbs that I could smell. The mixture bubbled softly, and I could smell my blood in it, mingling with the lifeblood from Titania's and Morgaine's veins. A glance at Menolly told me she was holding up just fine, even though she had to be smelling the spilled blood.

I inhaled deeply, then raised the chalice to my lips, hoping that whatever was in there wouldn't kill me. A swallow, and the taste of bittersweet mead ran down my throat. Honey and musky yeast, and rich apple. Blood and mugwort and cannabis. And . . . the faintest taste of mushrooms in the background.

As the liqueur rolled down my throat, an icy fire began to churn in my stomach, radiating out—javelins of pain and plea-sure racing through my veins to lick at my toes, to flutter in my heart, to spread throughout my body like a butterfly unfurling its wings for the first time.

I looked up to see a web radiating between Titania, Morgaine, and me. It was forged of thousands of droplets of energy, and I realized we'd created our own version of the Ionyc Sea right here, to bridge the gap between our separate powers. I could feel them: Titania, relieved that she was recovering her essential self. She was angry at Morgaine, but she would work with her for the greater good. Morgaine was greedy, hungry to increase her strength, but her purpose was clear, and there was no love of Demonkin in her soul. She might be power hungry, but she wasn't going to hand us over to the enemy.

"Look at that. Can you see it?" Chase's whisper cut through the silence, and all three of us turned to stare at him, a warning to keep silent. Chase's eyes widened, and he backed up a step, but Smoky put his hand on the detective's shoulder to steady him.

I gazed into Smoky's eyes, and his lip twitched. He said nothing, but he pursed his lips and blew me an irreverent kiss. A halo of energy surrounded him. Mist rose from the hem of his trench coat, and within that mist I could see the swirls of dragon energy coiling, twisting, waiting for me.

As my gaze lightly passed from Smoky to Morio, to my sisters, I could see each in turn, the powers inherent within their souls cloaking their physical form. I loved them all, I realized. In differing ways, but even Chase, who showed a small pinkish halo of energy that told me he had some sort of power, even if he didn't know it yet. Human, yes, but still—he was an unrealized canvas.

"Are you ready?" Titania asked.

I turned back to the Fae Queen emeritus. "Let me prepare the horn."

She nodded.

I felt in my pocket for the horn of the Black Unicorn, and as I touched it, a sudden flare of fear and pain crashed through me. Feddrah-Dahns! I whirled to the others. "Feddrah-Dahns is out there, and he's in trouble. Go help him, now! I must stay here, but go find him. The demons are on the land."

Smoky took the lead, his long trench flowing in his wake, followed by Menolly and Delilah. Morio gave me a torn glance, then turned to Chase. "You stay here. With demons and will-o'-the-wisps out there in the dark, you don't stand a chance."

"He's right, Chase." I said. "Park it and get ready in case somebody barges into the cave."

Chase let out a deep sigh but merely gave me a quick nod as he watched the rest of them race out the door. He pulled out his nunchakus and crouched, facing the entrance to the cave.

I grasped the horn. We were almost out of time. No more time to ponder, to worry, to doubt. As my hand clasped the crystal spire, I thrust my essence inside the horn, seeking the chamber of mirrors. One second, two . . . and I was standing in the center, all four Elementals waiting for me. Eriskel was standing there, watching carefully.

"I need all four of you to shore my powers up. Strengthen my energy," I said. "I'm about to break an incredibly strong and ancient spell cast by Elemental Lords. I need the power to break through the wards and guards."

They bowed, without a word, and I felt their energy begin to stream through me. Kind of like being plugged into four different outlets at once.

I leapt out of the horn, back to my body, and to my surprise, the web of energy connecting me to Morgaine and Titania was now thick with colored beads. Earth mana, water energy, the power of air, the swords of fire—and all the energy was flowing directly into me.

Without a word, Titania handed me the sword. I stared at the spirit seal. The amethyst was set in a pendant that was affixed to the hilt, and the lights within the gem danced, sparking like a broken power line. The seal was alive, it knew I was here, and it was ready for use. For just a second, I was tempted to reach out, to tap into the seal and forge it to my own will, to make it my own. Then reason prevailed, and I turned my attention to the crystal spike within which Aeval had rested for so many thousands of years.

I raised the sword and focused on the crystalline grave. One swing, and it connected. "Wake!"

A loud hum filled the air, and I pulled back and swung again. "Break!" Again, silver and steel kissed crystal, and the chamber began to reverberate with harmonics as a loud ringing rippled through the cave.

"Third time's the charm!" I brought the sword across the crystal again.

There was a pause, a moment muffled in silence, and then

the crystal began to shatter, shards of quartz shooting out like ammo from an AK-47. I stared as a vein spread like a spiderweb through the huge spike, and then there was one loud, thundering crack, and the rest of the crystal exploded.

As a howling wind rose to shake the cavern, I dropped the sword and fell to my knees. Titania and Morgaine went flying back as the explosion rebounded on us. The shock waves cascaded through my body like a series of punches. I raised my head, my ribs aching like a son of a bitch.

A swirl began to form around Aeval, a vortex of breath and life and magic. The fingers of mist touched her lips, parting them, and slid into her mouth. Her body convulsed as she sucked the mist into her lungs, swallowing it like some primal elixir. And then, Aeval's eyes fluttered—the color of snow and frost—and she opened them wide. Clad in a gown the color of the indigo night sky, she stepped out of the remains of the crystal like a ballerina dancing on toe point.

Tall she was, and dangerously beautiful. Her lips quirked in the faintest of grins as she surveyed her surroundings. Her gaze fell on Titania, and she let out a low trill of laughter.

"Well, and so I am free. And so are you. I take it we did not win the war?" She looked at me. "And who are you? Fae and yet . . ." She sniffed. "Half-breed. And not any sort of Fae that I've ever met."

Titania was on her feet in seconds, followed by Morgaine. "Aeval, there's no time to waste. We must reawaken the Courts. The balance is at stake."

Morgaine looked uncomfortable. "And what of me? I was willing to—"

"Hush . . ." Aeval brushed her hand over her lips as she looked at Morgaine, and Morgaine fell silent.

I glanced at my cousin. She hadn't shut up because Aeval asked her to. No, Aeval had cast a subtle spell, one that could instantly silence Morgaine. As I watched the Unseelie Queen, I began to realize that her powers hadn't been muted at all, merely frozen in time. And she was a very deadly woman. I backed up as her gaze turned to me.

"You gave me back my life. I owe you a favor, half-breed. You'd do well to keep it for later. It might just save your life someday."

My stomach churned. If I'd had a bottle of Tums, I would

have upended it right there. Aeval was scary-freaky, all right, and I filed her warning away under Get Out of Jail Free cards.

Titania quickly moved to put herself between the two of us. "We have much to talk about, my sister. And I include the sorceress Morgaine in that. She may not be full Fae, but she began the quest to raise the Courts, and I would not have you kill her. In the time you've been sleeping and I've been languishing, she's kept our memories alive."

Aeval considered Titania's words and nodded. "Very well. Let's go. I want out of this damned cave."

Titania turned to me. She pointed to the sword, her eyes warning me to keep silent. "You may have that—and what is affixed to it. Do as you will with both. We will be in touch soon." And with that, she put her arm around Morgaine's shoulders, and all three of them faded into a thick mist that swallowed them up.

I stared at the broken crystal, at the sword, and then over at Chase, who was crouching behind a rock. He jumped up and hurried over to my side.

"Are you okay? Camille? Do you need help?" He offered me his hand, and I slowly stood, testing to see if anything was amiss. The powers of the horn were beginning to fade; it would need recharging after that jaunt. And the dark of the moon would not come for nearly a month. The magic that had flowed into my hands as I struck the crystal had left me crisped through. Running the energy of four Elementals, as well as those from a Fae Queen and a powerful sorceress through my body had left me charred, every nerve raw and stinging.

I was about to answer when a noise at the entrance of the cavern startled both of us. As I struggled to raise what power I could, a figure burst into the cave. Chase jumped in front of me, his nunchakus raised, but then lowered them as the man moved into the light.

Benjamin Welter stood there, a wild look in his eyes. "Help me," he pleaded. "The demons are after me. And they're after the gem!

CHAPTER 27

"Benjamin!" I pushed around Chase, running over to Benjamin's side. The poor man had a wild look in his eyes, like the hounds of hell were chasing him. In a way, they were. Only much worse; demons made hellhounds look like a bunch of yapping poodles. "Get over there. Chase, help him find a hiding place."

If the demons were coming, I had to protect the seal. I grabbed up the sword, studying the welds that fixed the seal to the metal. Something clicked in the back of my mind, and I summoned up the last of my energy and brushed my hand across the seal.

"Release!"

The pendant came loose and fell into my hand. I stared at the spirit seal, wondering what the hell to do with it. If the others didn't come back, there was no way Chase and I could fend off the demons. I glanced around the cave. No good; they'd tear the place apart looking for it.

With no other choice, I slipped the seal down my bra, resting it between my breasts where it hummed lightly. They'd have to take me down to get their hands on it. I might not be able to muster up any more spells at this point—my energy was drained in a way it had never been before—but I had a sword, and I'd fight to the end.

"Do you think Titania will come back to help?" Chase asked, a catch of hope in his voice.

I wanted to tell him yes, to set his mind at ease, but in my heart I knew this was our fight. The Fae Queens weren't going to ride cavalry to our need. I shook my head. "Don't count on it. We have to hope the others return in time. Meanwhile, get behind me. I can take more damage than you can—"

"No. I won't be pushed aside time and again just because I'm human—" he started to say, but I turned on him.

"Listen: What good is it if they just cut right through you to get to me? If I go down, I go. But I can fight long enough to buy us all some extra time. Get it? We *both* have a better chance of surviving if I'm in front."

Without waiting for an answer, I whirled back to face the door. There was the sound of scuffling outside, and then Feddrah-Dahns and Mistletoe raced in. They took one look around, then hurried to our side.

"Are they coming?"

"Yes. The demons are in front of your sisters and friends. We tried to lead them away from the cave, but they seemed to sense that something happened. Whatever you were doing in here sent a ripple throughout the astral realms that must have been felt back in Otherworld." Feddrah-Dahns scuffed the floor with one hoof and whinnied.

"Hell, that means we've got to keep them occupied till Delilah and the rest get here. Warning—I don't have any magic left. I'm thoroughly drained. If I tried to summon down a bolt from the Moon Mother, I couldn't hold on to it, and I'd be fried to a crisp, along with anybody standing near." I inhaled deeply, holding the breath in my lungs to recharge me. The adrenaline was rushing through my body at least, keeping me on my feet.

"Noted. Mistletoe, take your place with the constable. Help him if you can." Feddrah-Dahns glanced at me, and I shot him a grateful smile.

As we waited, a bevy of thoughts raced through my mind. The fights were getting harder, the white and black hats more difficult to differentiate. We were all becoming slaves to the sword, but the only other option was so horrifying that we had no choice. Bloody warriors, bloody swords, bloody days.

No wonder spending my nights out at Smoky's seemed like a dream vacation to me—secure within a dream of mist and smoke that actually existed, that promised a sanctuary.

The image of Trillian loomed large in my mind, but I couldn't even muster up a single tear. I was all cried out. He was off facing goblins; I was here facing demons. Perhaps he had the better chance to live. Was he worried about me? Probably, but Trillian would face his fear and do what he needed to. And so would I. I wouldn't let him down. I'd make both him and my father proud.

As I straightened my shoulders, another movement at the door alerted me. The scent of jasmine and oranges and sugar vanilla wafted in on the breeze. They were here.

Karvanak strode into the room, followed by Vanzir and Jassamin. I swallowed the lump of fear that rose in my throat. They looked human, but that was mere illusion. They were ruthless killers, hungry for the seal, and it was my duty to keep them from getting it.

I held out my sword. "Come no further. You are not welcome here. Get your butt out of here, and we'll let you live."

Karvanak snorted. He began to shed his human form like a snake shed skin, and I found myself staring at a naked man's body with a tiger's head. His eyes narrowed, and he bared his teeth, pulling back his lips to snarl at me.

"We gave you enough time," Jassamin said. The djinn swung in beside her master. "You chose to ignore us."

Vanzir appeared on the other side. "Give us the seal now, and we'll make it easy." There was something in his voice—a hesitation, a pause, that made me give him a long look. He caught my gaze and held it, like in the parking lot, and I felt he was trying to tell me something, but I was too tired to understand.

"You know I can't give it to you; I can't let you have it. Shadow Wing must not be allowed to break the seals." I held my ground, trying to buy us some time. Show fear, and it would be over before I could breathe.

The Rāksasa let out a growl and motioned to Jassamin. She nodded and moved forward. She was wearing a skintight PVC catsuit and thigh-high boots, and I swore that if she died and I managed to live, I was stealing her outfit. She threw back her head and laughed.

"Djinn against Moon Witch. Fitting, but you look bedraggled to me. Tired, sweetie?" And with that, she let loose and sent a blast of wind at me.

I braced myself, trying to throw up what shields I could. The bolt of air hit me head-on, but instead of breaking every bone in my body and sending me flying, seconds before it touched my skin, the gust parted and flowed around me on both sides.

What the . . . ?

"I am here. We will do what we can to protect you, though we can't give you the energy to cast spells."

The Master of Winds! The Elementals were trying to help me. Jassamin jerked back, staring at me quizzically. I took advantage of her confusion and leapt toward her, slashing out with the sword. The silver nicked her skin, and she let out a howl as the blade sizzled against her. Apparently djinns did not like silver. At least, not this one.

"Bitch," she said with a hiss, and backhanded me across the face. That blow struck, and I went flying back to land beside Feddrah-Dahns.

The unicorn began incanting something in a language I didn't recognize, as Chase grabbed my hand and pulled me to my feet. I had barely managed to stand when Jassamin was on us again, this time a razor-sharp scimitar in her hand. She swung wildly, barely missing me, but the blade made contact, landing on Feddrah-Dahns's shoulder before the unicorn could get out of the way. He let out a loud whinny as blood spurted to stain his milk-white coat. Mistletoe screamed, showering the ground with pixie dust.

A haze began to rise between the demons and us. I frantically glanced around the cave, searching for something more than the sword to use as a weapon.

Jassamin burst through the mist, her eyes watering. She was sans scimitar, but she was still aiming for me. I stumbled, trying to get out of the way, but there was nowhere to go from where I was standing. Instead of attacking, Jassamin grabbed my wrist and yanked me toward her. Her strength was immense; there was no way I could pull away.

"No!" I tried to focus the Moon Mother through me, but it was like trying to coax water out of an empty tap. I just couldn't muster the energy to summon the lightning. Not even a spark.

"Good, very good," Karvanak said as Jassamin pushed me into his arms. He gave me an insolent grin. "First the seal . . ."

"Please don't . . . Think of what you're doing. Do you really want to destroy two worlds? No one in their right mind can see the—" The feel of his fist smashing into my jaw shut me up, and I moaned, tasting blood in my mouth.

He laughed, then, and thrust his hand down my top, fumbling in my bra. A light glimmered in his eye that I didn't like as he felt for the seal. I froze, praying that some miracle would happen, but his fingers found it between my breasts, and he wrapped his hand around the gem.

"If we had more time," he whispered, pulling me close, "I'd eat you up, I would. In so many ways, ending at the table. But I'm on a schedule . . ."

I heard Chase shouting and turned my head to see him grappling with Jassamin. "Chase, no! Leave her alone. She'll kill you!"

Karvanak barked again, a laugh so crude that it made me sick to my stomach. "You really believe we'd leave you alive? Stupid girl. You had your chance to live, and you declined. When Shadow Wing overruns this world, when we take control and enslave the herds of human sheep, then maybe your soul will look out from the dungeons of hell, knowing that you had a very *special part* in making our victory complete."

I struggled against him. He was going to kill me anyway. I'd rather go out in battle. "You can kill me. You can kill my friends. But there are others who will fight you to the end. There are still six spirit seals left. You can't hope to find them all."

Karvanak shrugged. "Let them come. Let them come in droves. Jassamin, Vanzir, kill these fools. I'm off to present our gift to Lord Shadow Wing." He polished the seal on his chest and looked at it, a glint in his eye.

"Oh, and Vanzir," Karvanak said, turning to the other demon, "this is your last chance. Fuck up again, and I'll send you over to Razor's. And you *know* what he'll do to you."

With that, he tossed me toward the dream chaser and turned toward the door. He'd barely gone two steps when a burst of noise came from the cave entrance. "Shit." Within seconds, Karvanak had shifted, and now he looked for all the world like Chase's identical twin. He raced toward the entrance.

"They're in there, the demons, and they're killing Camille!" His voice was the same timbre as Chase's as he disappeared out the mouth of the cave.

Before I could scramble to my feet, Smoky burst into the room, followed by Delilah and Menolly. Morio was hot on their heels.

"That wasn't Chase, that was Karvanak, under an illusion." I swayed but managed to remain standing. "He has the seal! Stop him!"

Smoky immediately headed back out the door, followed by Menolly, Feddrah-Dahns, and Mistletoe. Morio raced over to my side as Delilah caught sight of Chase.

"Chase!" She raced across the crystalline floor of the chamber. I turned to see Chase covered in blood and Jassamin reaching down to lick his face. Before Delilah could reach them, before I could reach them, Vanzir leapt forward, his saber out and gleaming. But instead of aiming for us or for Chase, he slid it neatly through Jassamin's back. As it impaled her, she screamed and fell forward.

I stared at him, wondering what the fuck was going on, as Morio sent three shooting stars directly into the demon's side. Vanzir groaned, but instead of returning the attack, he once again turned to Jassamin and brought his saber down, smack on the top of her head. This time, she roared and tried to stand, tried to face him. But it was too late, a stream of energy poured from the top of her head as her body folded and dissolved. Within seconds, there was no sign she'd ever been there, except for Chase's wounds.

Delilah skidded to a halt beside Chase. Morio and I moved in on Vanzir. What was going on? He hadn't made a move against us.

He dropped his sword and put up his hands, not moving, not speaking.

"What is this? Some sort of trick? What's going on?" Was he buying time for his master by offering his life? Or was . . . ? No . . . the thought was impossible.

But Vanzir hung his head and said the words I never thought I'd hear a demon say. "I submit. I surrender. Please don't kill me."

Morio and I looked at each other, unsure of what to say. After all, demons fought to the death, always. *Didn't they?*

"Why? Why do you want to surrender to us?" Gingerly, I kicked his saber aside.

He raised his head, his eyes clear and his expression firm. "I cannot follow Shadow Wing. I cannot let him invade this world. It's a mistake—a grave mistake. I want to change sides. I want to help you stop him."

"But you're a demon—"

"I'm a dream chaser. I can be of invaluable assistance to you. There's much that I know about your enemy's plans . . . as well as the names and addresses of other spies living in the area." And then he smiled.

By the time Smoky, Menolly, and Feddrah-Dahns returned, empty-handed, we'd tied and gagged Vanzir as best we could. Whether that would do the trick, I didn't know, but it was all we could come up with on short notice. Benjamin had come out from where he'd hidden behind a crystal. Delilah had Chase sitting up. She'd torn his shirt and her own to use as makeshift bandages.

"We lost the seal." I walked over to Smoky, and he pulled me close and kissed my forehead.

"You're exhausted and hurt," he murmured softly.

Feddrah-Dahns spoke up. "All of you are wounded and sorely tired. You need rest and food and medical attention." As he spoke, the cave began to shake.

"Quake—get out, now!" Smoky spun and, carrying me, raced out of the cavern. When we reached a few yards from the entrance, he gently placed me on the ground. "I'll make sure the others are out," he said and ran back toward the cave.

The ground folded in waves like an ocean gone mad as it rippled under my hands and knees. I crouched on all fours, trying to ride it out. Menolly emerged next, carrying Chase, and Delilah was right behind her. Morio came next, holding the sword and leading Benjamin and the unicorn and pixie. Lastly, Smoky came running out, our prisoner tossed over his shoulder.

As the ground bucked harder, I prayed that the houses in the area would hold fast and that the mountain wouldn't blow. Rainier was a time bomb. If she blew, it wouldn't matter if we were Fae or human or youkai, we'd all be toast. Well, maybe Smoky would escape.

"The light! It's fading!" Delilah pointed toward the cave. I jerked around. The light from the cave opening was flickering and, as we watched, it vanished.

"The cave returned to the mists." I glanced around the

meadow. The horde of will-o'-the-wisps seemed to have left for other haunts. "For good or ill, we've set in motion a new chapter in history tonight."

"I don't understand. I don't understand any of this." Benjamin was sitting a little ways to the side, rocking back and forth, holding his arms tightly around himself. Menolly sighed and walked over to him, softly touching his shoulder.

"What next?" Morio said. "What do we do now?"

What indeed? The seal was in the hands of the demons. We had a turncoat dream chaser on our hands, who seemed determined to join us. Trillian was missing. And we were tired. All so very tired.

"I suppose . . . for now, we go home." There wasn't much else to say.

CHAPTER 28

The next morning—the equinox—dawned cold and chill, and yet there was something in the air that felt different. As I opened my eyes, my first glance showed Smoky to my right side. He was lying there watching me with the hint of a smile crinkling his lip.

I groaned. Every muscle in my body felt on fire. An arm draped around my waist from behind me, and I realized Morio was in bed with us, too. I tried to coax an explanation from my fog-soaked brain, but all I could remember was coming home, weary and defeated, and then it was all one big blur.

"Good morning," Morio said, leaning over my shoulder. He tossed Smoky a look that said they'd already had "the discussion" and that I didn't need to play liaison.

"How are you feeling this morning? Any better?" Smoky propped himself up against the headboard and patted his lap. I squirmed up to lay my head on the soft Egyptian cotton sheets, and he smoothed my hair away from my face as Morio ran his hand gently over my back, lightly massaging my aching muscles.

I winced. "I'm sore as hell, and I feel two quarts low on joy juice. Seriously, I depleted all my reserves last night. And for what? The demons won."

"The demons may have won this battle, but they haven't won the war," Smoky said. "Always remember: No one is unilaterally successful. We can't let this stop us if we're to prevent them from getting any more of the seals. But we'll have to be very careful from now on. Shadow Wing will be able to make use of the power in that gem, even if it's not full strength."

"Stop *us*?" I glanced at his face. "You aren't headed toward the Northlands?"

He shrugged, smiling gently. "It seems, since I'm to marry you, my plans are subject to change."

I forced myself to sit up. Sweet mother, every part of me hurt. "I feel like I'm bruised from head to toe." I bent my knees up and propped my elbows on them, leaning my chin on my hands. "What are we going to tell Queen Asteria? She's counting on us."

"We'll figure that out when we talk to her," Morio said. "But last night does answer one question."

"And what's that?" I blinked, jonesing for some caffeine so bad I had the shakes. "I need coffee. *Now.*"

He snorted. "You always need caffeine. The question I'm referring to is why you seem to take to death magic so easily when your own innate Moon magic fritzes out a lot."

Smoky began rubbing my shoulders, and I melted under his hands. The night was starting to come back—after the fight, returning home—and then I blushed as images flooded my mind. Smoky and Morio in my bed, leading me out of the pain, out of the sorrow over our failure, helping me to forget the battle. Smoky bracing me up as Morio thrust deep inside of me, Smoky's hair once again coiling around my wrists . . . *oh yeah* . . . No wonder I was so sore in places no punch nor flying bolt of magic had touched. This was going to be one hell of a rocket ride, all right.

"So tell us," Smoky said. "I'd like to know, too."

Morio slid down to the bottom of the bed and began rubbing my feet. If I'd been Delilah, I'd be purring like an outboard motor.

"It's because of your heritage," he said. "Morgaine is one of your ancestors. Morgaine works with heavy magic—not unlike Aeval—and her connection with the Moon Mother is through the shadowed side. She said you both come from the original family who founded the Coterie of the Moon Mother. Camille, you must have inherited some of the same magical ability that Morgaine did. You think you work best under the full moon, but my guess is the dark of the moon will sing in your blood, too, with all of the shadows that walk beneath it."

It made sense, I had to admit. Perhaps my link to the Moon Mother went beyond the half-Fae, half-human aspects. Perhaps I had focused on the wrong phase of the moon when I'd studied with the Coterie.

A knock on the door interrupted my thoughts. "Camille?" Delilah's voice.

"Come in."

She peeked around the door, giving me a faint grin when she saw us curled up together. "We have visitors. Several of them. I think you'd all better come down before we end up with a magical brawl on our hands."

Oops, that didn't sound good.

"Right there," I said, climbing over Smoky. He traced a finger down my thigh as I slid over his lap, and I felt a tug from my nipples down to the tips of my toes. I caught my breath.

"Later," he mouthed as Morio reached across to place his hand on my leg next to Smoky's. Oh yeah, they'd had "the talk."

Delilah withdrew as Smoky and Morio threw back the covers and climbed out of bed. We dressed quickly. Feeling unaccountably shy, I avoided their gazes—or any other portion of their anatomy—and then we all clattered down the stairs. Actually, Morio and Smoky clattered. I inched my way down, aching with every step, until Smoky noticed.

He marched back up the steps and tossed me over his shoulder without further ado. I started to protest but then, sensing that this would get me downstairs with the least amount of pain, gave in without a fight.

As we hit the hallway, he put me down. I smoothed my dress, and we walked into the living room.

Iris was serving tea all around to our guests. Our guests being Queen Asteria, Rozurial, Titania, and Morgaine. The four of them were spread out on the sofa and love seat. There was no sign of Arturo or Mordred.

"Cripes. We've got enough firepower sitting in our living room to decimate the state." I looked around for someplace to sit.

Smoky dropped into the recliner, and I sat on his lap. Morio squatted by the side of the chair. Delilah was sitting on the ottoman, looking weary and tired. Chase was nowhere in sight. Menolly had gone to bed, of course. I looked around for Maggie, but Iris caught my eye and shook her head.

As she handed me tea and a scone, she whispered, "Best remain silent on some things . . ."

I nodded and bit into the scone. After a moment, Queen Asteria rose. "Delilah has been telling us what happened to the seal. You could not hold it?"

I swallowed hastily and slurped my tea, wanting nothing more than a huge vat of caffeine in which to bathe my senses. "Two humans and one half-Fae cannot take down two demons and a djinn. Not unless one of us is a superhero. And none of us are that."

She nodded. "Of course. Forgive me. I'm just heartsick about this. I know you all did your best. Even you, young beast," she said, looking at Smoky.

"Please, have you any news of Trillian?" Impulsively, I shoved my cup into Smoky's hand and found myself kneeling at the Elfin Queen's feet. "Anything? At all?"

The furrow in her brow deepened, and she shook her head. "Would that I could say yes, my child, but no. No, there is no news. His soul statue is still whole, as is that of your father's, but nothing has been seen nor heard from them. I'm afraid it's only a matter of time—"

"Don't say that!" I jumped up. "What are you doing to find him?"

She sighed. "War is rough, girl, and there are many losses in every skirmish. We cannot spare men to search for one missing man . . . or even two. We need the information they carry, so I've sent out rescue teams, but don't get your hopes up. There's little else I can do."

So Smoky was right. The elves weren't going to help, beyond the most superficial of efforts.

"Well, I'm going to do something. I'm binding myself to Smoky and Morio in the Soul Symbiont ritual. Since no one else will go looking for Trillian, we'll do it our own way. I'm bound to Trillian, and though the oath between us is from a different ritual, it should hold true for our purposes."

Delilah gasped and stared at me. "You're what?"

"Don't try to stop me," I warned her, shaking my head. "I'm going through with it. We've faced too many losses already. I refuse to lose Trillian."

She pressed her lips together and murmured a faint assent.

"There's no guarantee that will work—" Queen Asteria started to say, but Titania cleared her throat.

"Let her try. She's loyal to her men. Can you say that of most of our kind? We have other matters to discuss, such as the demons possessing the spirit seal, this Vanzir you spoke of, and the return of the Fae Courts."

Queen Asteria frowned. "As to the spirit seal, there's nothing we can do now but go in search of the fourth. And this time, we must find it first and hold on to it. As to this Vanzir, I know little except that Demonkin are treacherous, and I wouldn't be quick to place trust in one, no matter how changed he says he is."

"That's why we're not," Iris said. "There is a ritual I learned from the shamans of the Northlands to bind demons into servitude. None but the most powerful can resist it. Vanzir has agreed to go through with it and bind himself to the girls and me. Menolly and I had a little talk with him last night. We'll take care of this on the night of the waxing moon. If he breaks the oath, he'll die a horrendously painful death on the spot."

"Speaking of which, where is he?" I asked, looking around. We couldn't just let him walk around free.

"Remember the holding pen at the Wayfarer, where we were going to put that rogue vampire?" Delilah grinned.

I frowned, then nodded. Apparently, the OIA had outfitted the Wayfarer with a pen that could hold minor demons. "Yeah. So he's there?"

"Locked in, tight as a drum. Can't use magic, can't summon anybody or anything. He'll be fine for now." Iris handed me a cookie. "Eat. You're starving."

She was right. I scarfed down the cookie. "Well, with that out of the way . . ." I turned to Titania and Morgaine. "You're both in one piece, I see. What happened after you left?"

Queen Asteria let out a huff. "What happened is madness. You must have been daft to do as they asked you to last night." She was clearly Not Happy.

"Grandmother Coyote decreed it. Not even the royalty of

Fae nor elves may go up against the Hags of Fate," Titania said, staring at her. "We have been long distanced from each other, but you are still the prim, stuffy woman you always were. Don't you understand? Times have changed, the world has changed, and we will adapt with it."

"You think I don't see the necessity for change? Why else would I be working with King Vodox, or pledge Elqaneve's lot in with that of Svartalfheim?" Queen Asteria started to stand, and I had a sudden vision of the elderly elf starting a brawl. She'd whip butt if she did.

I jumped up. "Please, no more fighting! I can't stand this anymore. I've had it up to *here* with fights and bloodshed and war and battle. Just tell us what happened, and if somebody doesn't like it, well, tough shit! Do you understand? All of you! *My sisters and I* are the ones standing on the front lines in this battle, and we're doing the best we can."

Suddenly aware that I'd been screaming in the face of a thousands-year-old Elfin Queen, and an equally ancient Fae Queen, I took a little step back. From behind me, I heard Smoky snort, and then he broke out in laughter.

"That's my Witchling," he said. "You tell them, girl."

I whirled. "And you, quit stirring the pot, you overgrown lizard. No matter how good you are in bed, or how good . . . you smell . . . or . . . oh, just shut up!" Everybody was gaping at me. I cleared my throat and sat down on his lap again. "I've been under a lot of stress lately," I said weakly.

"So it seems," Titania said, but she was smiling. "To make a long and complex negotiation short, the Courts of Fae have risen again, thanks to your help. Only there are three Courts now, rather than two."

"Three?" I blinked. Delilah and Iris looked equally confused.

"Three," Morgaine said. "Things can never be as they were, that we know and accept. So from now on, rather than a morning and evening court, rather than a summer and winter court, we have established the Court of the Three Queens. Titania will rule over the Court of the Mother—the Seelie Court of the Day, with all its brilliance."

"Aeval will resume her throne as Unseelie Queen, the Court of the Crone, the Crown of Night," Titania said. "And Morgaine, though not our equal, will rule over the Court of Twilight, the bridge between the Seelie and Unseelie realms, as the Maiden of Dusk. She will be the emissary between the mortal world and the world of Fae."

"There is another matter," Queen Asteria said. "This Benjamin—I am taking him with me. I've set my scholars to researching the ancient texts. Benjamin, as well as your Tom Lane, both have parts to play in the future battles against the demons. If you find other humans bearing the spirit seals, or who've been affected by them—humans who are not Supernaturals of any sort—then bring them to me. More, I cannot tell you at this time."

"My Tom . . . my sweet Tam Lin," Titania sighed, looking sad and nostalgic. "But better he's gone from me now. I have too much to think about, with the reemergence of my Court."

Queen Asteria sighed. "And so, yes, there are three Earthside Courts of Fae. And whether it be for good or ill, we'll have to see. But if Grandmother Coyote wills it, there's not much we can do."

She stood, and for the first time since we'd known her, she looked old. "Since I am responsible for Trillian's disappearance, I leave Rozurial in your service, to aid you as much as he can." She headed for the door, Titania and Morgaine in her wake.

At the door, she turned back to look at me. "Feddrah-Dahns will be returning with me. He was hurt sorely, but he will live. He asked me to give you this for your friend. The one looking to have a child." She handed me a small pouch in which rested assorted herbs and stones.

"What's this? For Lindsey?" I took it and tucked it away in my purse.

"A charm to help her. He said it should work within three months' time."

I choked up then. The unicorn had gotten under my skin, and I fretted that we'd lose touch. He'd been a gentle reminder of the grace and beauty of my home world. As if she could sense my sorrow, Queen Asteria patted my hand.

"Feddrah-Dahns sends you his love and bids to meet you again. He places his trust in you that you will use his gift wisely. As do we all."

I looked into her ancient eyes. They were filled with love and compassion. "I'll do my best to be worthy of his gift . . . and his friendship," I whispered, tearing up.

"He knows how hard you're trying here. As do we all." And with that, she swept out the door, the two Fae Queens behind her.

CHAPTER 29

Two nights later, when Chase could make it and when we'd recovered from the worst of the beatings we'd received, we gathered at Birchwater Pond. The moon was nearing a crescent, and she sang to me through my veins, promising me that I was making the right choice.

Morio was there, in his full kimono, dressed in red and gold, sword displayed at his side. Smoky wore his long white trench over a gold and blue vest, a pale blue button-down shirt, and a pair of white, tight jeans. Both had their hair unbound, and the pale sliver of the Moon Mother embraced them in her silvery light. She was not yet at waxing, but close.

Delilah and Menolly stood beside me. Delilah was wearing her golden gown she'd worn at Solstice, and Menolly, her black. I was dressed in silver. The silver of the Moon Mother, the silver of Smoky's dragon heritage, the silver of Morio's sword, the silver of Trillian's hair.

Delilah and Menolly had wanted me to wear Mother's wedding dress, but it didn't feel right, even if it had fit me. Mother bound herself to one man. I could never follow her path in love. It just wasn't my way.

Chase and Zachary stood to one side, Rozurial, to the other. Chase held Maggie. Iris was standing on a dais near the pond, and she held a chain forged of silver and a crystal wand that I'd never seen before.

"Are you sure about this? This is a bond deeper than marriage, you know," Delilah said. "You go through with this ritual, and you belong to those two forever—bound through all of time with their souls."

I gazed at the two men who were waiting for me. Two men who loved me. Smoky wanted me all to himself, but he was willing to give up that dream, to bind himself to me and one of my lovers, so that we could search out a man to whom I'd long ago pledged my heart. Morio was offering to bind himself to me out of love and loyalty. And he, too, cared about Trillian. I could sense the concern emanating from him.

And I . . . I loved both of them so much that I couldn't even explain it. For me, love had swelled to include three men, all different and yet, I was meant to be with all of them. Each provided a part of the whole that I needed.

Forever? I whispered. *So it would seem,* came the answer.

"I already belong to you. You're my sisters. *My family.* And that family expanded to include Iris, and Maggie, too. And now, my family grows again. And who better to choose for my husbands than a fox demon and a dragon? Can't ask for much more protection than that."

"But forever? To be bound *forever*?" Delilah seemed torn.

"Better that than always wondering if I could have saved Trillian." I glanced down the path. "We have to find him. He's like a mirror of myself. My heart says we will, but I can't do it on my own. And maybe . . . maybe if I find Trillian, I can find Father, too."

Delilah started to protest again, but Menolly shook her head. "We all make choices, Kitten. We all decide on one path over another. You can't stand at the fork in the road forever." She looked meaningfully over to where Chase and Zachary stood in an uneasy truce. "Sometimes, when your playmates won't play together, you have to choose."

"Come, it's time," I said, putting an end to any potential squabbles. "Be happy for me. How many people find even one person to love in this world? Or our home world, either? I'm blessed. I've found three men who hold the keys to my heart. Now, Delilah, I want you to promise that you aren't going to change into a pussycat during my wedding. Well, *weddings*."

When we were in front of the altar, Iris cast the runes once more, and once more, they blessed the union. She began the ceremony. As her words drifted into the night, I looked up at my dragon lover—soon to be husband. And then over at my youkai-kitsune—soon to be husband. They looked sure of themselves, sure of the ritual, sure of this step we were taking. And who knew where it would lead? When we found him, Trillian would be brought into the marriage. He'd give me hell, but he'd come around. I was sure of it. There was too much between us for him to turn away.

"Camille, do you accept the binding oath from Smoky and Morio, each to become your soul mate, each to eternally link himself to you? And you to them until the end of time?"

I realized they'd already assented their vows. My heart pounding, I opened my mouth and said, "I do."

"Then join hands." Iris held up the enchanted silver chain.

I held out my left hand. Smoky placed his left hand atop of mine. Morio placed his left hand beneath mine. Iris wound the chain around our wrists and began a low incantation.

She sang in some ancient language, but the intent was clear. As her words hit the air, the chain reverberated and began to fade. I watched as it sank into Smoky's hand, then through mine, then through Morio's, the atoms of the chain changing and transforming to forge an unbreakable bond in our auras, in our souls. Another moment, and it would be too late to ever reverse the spell.

I glanced at them quickly, wondering if they would change their minds, but Smoky leaned down and kissed my lips, and Morio leaned in and kissed my cheek, and the chain disappeared. An incredible sense of peace swept over me as our paths merged. Another moment, and we'd be fully bound for the rest of time. No matter where we went, no matter what we did, we'd always come back together. And with the grace of the Moon Mother, we'd find Trillian.

"It is done," Iris whispered.

I looked down at our hands as our fingers entwined. Though the chain was nowhere in sight, it was everywhere we were. I was married to my dragon lover and my fox demon. We were soul mates in the eyes of the universe, in the eyes of the gods. And nothing anyone—demon or otherwise—could ever do would sever the bond.

GLOSSARY

Calouk: The rough, common dialect used by a number of Otherworld inhabitants.

Court and Crown: The *Crown* refers to the queen of Y'Elestrial. The *Court* refers to the nobility and military personnel that surround the queen. *Court and Crown* together refer to the entire government of Y'Elestrial.

Crypto: One of the Cryptozoid races. Cryptos include creatures out of legend that are not technically of the Fae races: gargoyles, unicorns, gryphons, chimeras, etc. Most primarily inhabit Otherworld, but some have Earthside cousins.

Dreyerie: Dragon's lair or nest.

Earthside: Everything that exists on the Earth side of the portals.

Elqaneve: The Elfin lands in Otherworld.

Elemental Lords: The Elemental beings—both male and female—who, along with the Hags of Fate and the Harvestmen, are the only true Immortals. They are avatars of various elements and energies, and they inhabit all realms. They do as they will and seldom concern themselves with humankind or Fae unless summoned. If asked for help, they often exact steep prices in return. The Elemental Lords are not concerned with balance like the Hags of Fate.

FBH: Full-blooded human (usually refers to Earthside humans).

FH-CSI: The Faerie-Human Crime Scene Investigations team. The brainchild of Detective Chase Johnson, it was first formed as a collaboration between the OIA and the Seattle Police Department. Other FH-CSI units have been created around the country, based on the Seattle prototype. The FH-CSI takes care of both medical and criminal emergencies involving visitors from Otherworld.

Great Divide: A time of immense turmoil when the Elemental Lords and some of the High Court of Fae decided to rip apart the worlds. Until then, the Fae existed primarily on Earth, their lives and worlds mingling with those of humans. The Great Divide tore everything asunder, splitting off another dimension, which became Otherworld. At that time, the Twin Courts of Fae were disbanded and their queens stripped of power. This was the time during which the spirit seal was formed and broken in order to seal off the realms from each other. Some Fae chose to stay Earthside; others moved to the realm of Otherworld; and the demons were—for the most part—sealed in the Subterranean Realms.

Guard Des'Estar: The military of Y'Elestrial.

Hags of Fate: The women of destiny who keep the balance righted. Neither good nor evil, they observe the flow of destiny. When events get too far out of balance, they step in and take action, usually using humans, Fae, Supes, and other creatures as pawns to bring the path of destiny back into line.

Harvestmen: The lords of death—a few cross over and are also Elemental Lords. The Harvestmen, along with their followers (the Valkyries, the Death Maidens, for example) reap the souls of the dead.

Ionyc Lands: The astral, etheric, and spirit realms, along with several other lesser-known noncorporeal dimensions, form the Ionyc Lands. These realms are separated by the Ionyc Sea, a current of energy that prevents the Ionyc Lands from colliding, thereby sparking off an explosion of universal proportions.

Ionyc Sea: The currents of energy that separate the Ionyc Lands. Certain creatures, especially those connected with the elemental energies of ice, snow, and wind, can travel through the Ionyc Sea without protection.

Melosealfôr: A rare Crypto dialect learned by powerful Cryptos and all Moon Witches.

OIA: The Otherworld Intelligence Agency; the "brains" behind the Guard Des'Estar.

Otherworld/OW: The human term for the UN of "Faerie Land." A dimension apart from ours that contains creatures from legend and lore, pathways to the gods, and various other places like Olympus, etc. Otherworld's *actual* name varies among the differing dialects of the many races of Cryptos and Fae.

Portal, Portals: The interdimensional gates that connect the different realms.

Seelie Court: the Earthside Fae Court of Light and Summer, disbanded during the Great Divide. Titania was the Seelie Queen.

Soul Statues: In Otherworld, small figurines are created for the Fae of certain races and magically linked with the baby. These figurines reside in family shrines, and when one of the Fae dies, their soul statue shatters. In Menolly's case, when she was reborn as a vampire, her soul statue re-formed, although twisted. If a family member disappears, their family can always tell if their loved one is alive or dead if they have access to the soul statue.

Spirit Seals: A magical crystal artifact, the spirit seal was created during the Great Divide. When the portals were sealed, the spirit seal was broken into nine gems, and each piece was given to an Elemental Lord or Lady. These gems each have varying powers. Even possessing one of the spirit seals can allow the wielder to weaken the portals that divide Otherworld, Earthside, and the Subterranean Realms. If all of the seals are joined together again, then all of the portals would open.

Supe/Supes: Short for Supernaturals. Refers to Earthside supernatural beings who are not of Fae nature. Refers to Weres, especially.

Unseelie Court: The Earthside Fae Court of Shadow and Winter, disbanded during the Great Divide. Aeval was the Unseelie Queen.

V.A./Vampires Anonymous: The Earthside group started by Wade Stevens, a vampire who was a psychiatrist during life. The group is focused on helping newly born vampires adjust to their new state of existence and to encourage vampires to avoid harming the innocent as much as possible. V.A. is vying for control. Their goal is to rule the vampires of the U.S. and to set up an internal policing agency.

Whispering Mirror: A magical communications device that links Otherworld and Earth. Think magical videophone.

Y'Elestrial: The city-state in Otherworld where the D'Artigo girls were born and raised. A Fae city, currently embroiled in a civil war between the drug-crazed, tyrannical Queen Lethesanar, and her more levelheaded sister Tanaquar, who is trying to claim the throne for herself. The civil war has escalated to other lands, and many races are taking sides in the fighting.

Youkai: Loosely (very loosely) translated: Japanese demon/nature spirit. For the purposes of this series the youkai have three shapes: the animal, the human form, and then the true demon form. Unlike the demons of the Subterranean Realms, youkai are not necessarily evil by nature.

And now . . .
a special preview of the next book
in the Otherworld series
by Yasmine Galenorn . . .

ΠIGHT HUΠ+RE88

Available from Berkley!

The late-April night was unseasonably warm, so I'd left the window open a couple inches. Just enough for a breath of fresh air to pass through. From the bed, I gazed up at the moon, which glittered a quarter-past full. A low bank of clouds—illuminated silhouettes against the sky—rolled through, streaking the moon with their long fingers of ink. I slid out from between the sheets and silently crossed to the window, padding softly over the braided rug that Iris had recently found in a little vintage store.

Lifting the window just enough so I could lean my head out, I peered into the shadows of the backyard. My sister Camille was out for the night staying with her husbands Morio and Smoky— a fox demon and a dragon, respectively—in the woods near Smoky's barrow. They were performing some sort of ritual to bring home one of our own. Trillian, Camille's alpha lover, was missing. We knew he was alive, but that's all we knew. He'd disappeared, and from all accounts, a goblin contingent nabbed him back in Otherworld, which spelled potential disaster . . . for both Trillian—and for us.

Menolly, my other sister, should be just getting home from work. She ran the Wayfarer Bar & Grill. The driveway wasn't visible from my window, so I couldn't see if her Jag was parked there yet.

I turned back to the bed. Chase was staying the night and he was sprawled out across the mattress, sound asleep, cover thrown to the side. The man was hot blooded, which made him very amenable during the nights when I yanked all the blankets away and curled up in them, leaving him naked. Speaking of naked . . . Chase was obviously enjoying whatever dream he was having. Either that or he was dreaming he was a sundial. I licked my lips. Time to wake him up in a very special way. If I was careful . . .

I slowly climbed back on the bed and leaned down to cautiously trace my tongue along the length of his erection.

"Erika?" he muttered.

I frowned and paused, tongue still poised against his skin. Who the hell was Erika?

"Delilah, come quick!"

The door slammed open. I lurched, Chase jumped, and my fangs scratched an inch-long razor-thin gash, leaving a delicate red line as a few drops of blood oozed out. *Oh shit!*

"What the fuck are you doing?" Chase yelled, his voice unnaturally high as he scrabbled away. The expression on his face was *not* the one I'd been hoping for, that was for sure.

"Chase! I'm sorry—"

"Oh, Christ!" His foot got caught in the quilt and he went tumbling over the side of the bed. He hit the floor with a *thud*, swearing a blue streak.

I scrambled to his side as Menolly snorted from where she stood by the door, wreathed in light from the hallway. Blood burbled out of her nose and dripped down to her lips.

"Can you maybe remember to knock next time?" I stared at her, shaking my head. "I take it you just had a nice long drink?"

She coughed and I caught the glint in her eye. It went against every instinct I had, but I managed to repress my own laughter. I felt bad for Chase—especially since I'd been the one to inflict pain on him—but I felt like Lucy Ricardo caught in the middle of one of her harebrained schemes.

I didn't dare let him see me smile, though. My detective had been going through a rough spot the past few days and his sense of humor had taken a hike. His job—or rather, jobs—were driving him nuts.

Not to mention that Zachary Lyonnesse—a werepuma with whom I'd slept one time, and who was constantly trying to woo me away—had been hanging around a lot more the past month or so since he got wind that Chase was too busy to drop over most nights.

Chase was furious, but knew better than try to push an ultimatum. I liked Zach and we *had* to work together as we formed the foundation for the growing Supe Community. I reminded Chase time and again that I loved him and wouldn't stray without talking to him first. But the fact that we'd only managed to have sex four times in the past six weeks didn't help. We were both pent up, frustrated, and feeling out of synch.

Menolly delicately stepped over the pile of clothes I'd dumped in the middle of the room. She plucked a tissue from the box on my dresser and patted her nose. As her gaze flickered back to us, her pale blue eyes—almost gray really—grew luminous in the dim light as she stared unabashedly at Chase. The tip of her tongue reached out to trace her lips.

I was about to give her a good what-for when I realized it wasn't his nether regions she was focused on. Nope. She could smell his blood. Menolly was a vampire and while she did a good job of keeping herself in check, when she was startled her steel-clad grip on her emotions could slip a little.

Chase noticed her intensified scrutiny at the same time I did. "Stop right where you are!" He hurried to pull the sheet over his groin. "If you think you're sticking your fangs in my . . . in me—*anywhere* in me—you've got another think coming!"

She reined herself in. "Sorry, didn't mean to stare. Just . . ."

"Menolly . . . remember where you are," I said, standing slowly.

She glanced at me, then back at Chase, and shook her head. "Really, I didn't intend to be rude. You okay, Chase?" Without waiting for an answer, she whirled back to me, and a goofy grin spread across her face. "You need to come downstairs or you'll miss it!"

"Miss what?" I scrambled for my sleep shirt and dragged it over my head. "What's going on? Do I need to get dressed? Are there demons in the yard? A goblin brigade marching through our kitchen? Another unicorn visit?" Knowing our luck, it could be multiple choice—take your pick, any and all. Or something worse.

"No, no brawls tonight." She clapped her hands. "I just got home. Iris is up—Maggie said her first words and she's awake and babbling up a storm. Most of it's nonsense still, but she really can say a few things! Iris is recording it on the camcorder. So hurry up."

As she shut the door, Chase pushed himself to his feet. He fumbled for a moment, then sat on the edge of the bed, staring at his penis. The blood had stopped, but the thin red wheal left a reminder of where my left fang had lacerated him.

I winced as I rooted around in the pile of clothes, looking for my slippers. "That's gotta hurt."

Chase glared at me. "You think? Ever decide to warn a guy first? We already tried that maneuver before and I've got the scars to prove it, thank you very much." He sighed. "I'm okay with forgoing blow jobs, you know that. So, Delilah, honey, what on earth gave you the idea to try it again?" He gingerly examined his wounded pride, shaking his head.

I let out a little growl. "You don't have to act so pissy. I wasn't planning on giving you a *blow job*. I was just teasing you awake so we could have a little late-night fun. We've barely even—" One look at his face and I stopped that train of thought. "I said I'm sorry. Let me get the antibiotic ointment." I stalked into my bathroom, which was right off the bedroom, and brought back a tube of unguent. He relented and let me slide a thin layer down his skin.

As I gazed into his eyes, he leaned forward and kissed me. Slow, deep, with tenderness. I was tempted to catch Maggie's first words on the morning video rerun and see just how far we could go without hurting him any further, but he abruptly pulled away.

"Come on, let's get dressed." He slid into a pair of burgundy boxer shorts and the velvet robe he kept in my room. "This is about the only good news we've had in a while. We don't want to miss it."

As I found my slippers and slid them on, he headed out the door and I scurried to catch up. Chase adored Maggie, that I knew. But for him to forgo sex for something like this . . . there had to be something going on. And whatever it was, he obviously wasn't letting *me* in on the secret.

Iris had the camcorder in hand, while Menolly knelt beside Maggie. Menolly had taken our baby calico gargoyle cub under her wing and played substitute Mama as much as possible. We all loved the little twerp, but a special bond had grown between the vampire and the gargoyle. Maybe because they were both out of their element—both adrift thanks to the demonic envoys that walked the world.

Maggie looked a lot like a cross between an imp and a large cat. Short, downy calico-colored fur covered her body. She had pointed ears and whiskers, but her wings were still far too small to support her so she couldn't fly yet.

The baby 'goyle could barely walk, actually. She'd taken her first steps a few months before. Maggie had a long tail, with a devil's point at the end, and it, too, was covered with fur. With Menolly's help, she'd gotten the hang of using it to balance herself. Now, she could stand for several minutes without leaning against the coffee table but when she tried to walk, her wings flailed and she fell back on her butt most of the time.

She gazed up at me with yellow-topaz eyes as I knelt in front of her. Would she speak in English? The Fae dialect we often used among ourselves? Or something else, I wondered?

I glanced up at Iris. "Well?"

Iris, a Talon-haltija who lived with us, shook her head. "She's taking a break, I think. I swear, the moment she said one word, she opened up like the clouds and she's been babbling on ever since. I wasn't sure whether to disturb you, so I waited till Menolly arrived home." She lifted the camera again and zoomed in on Maggie as I reached out for her.

Maggie shook her head at me. "No!"

Surprised, I sat back, waiting.

"No sit. No sit. Deeyaya no sit on me."

I stifled a laugh—Maggie had already proved extremely sensitive to anything remotely decipherable as ridicule. "I think she's got that backward but she's definitely talking. That's for sure."

Menolly sat on the edge of the coffee table. "Yeah, and she knows all our names. When I walked in, she called me Menny."

"Menny!" Maggie looked extremely proud of herself. "Menny, Deeyaya, Camey? Where Camey?" She glanced around, a confused look on her face.

"Camille will be back in a while," Menolly said, slipping her hands under Maggie's arms as she lifted her onto her lap.

"Who's that?" She pointed to Chase. Chase had spent a number of hours babysitting Maggie.

Maggie giggled and clapped. "He-man! He-man!"

I looked over at Chase. "What the . . . is she trying to say *human*?"

"He-man!"

Chase blushed red, right to the tips of his ears. "I don't think so."

"Then why is . . . oh good gods, did you teach her that your name is *He-Man*?" I snorted as he rolled his eyes.

"Well, it seemed like a good idea at the time." He appealed to Iris for help but she just pressed her lips together in a winsome grin and shook her head. "I didn't think she'd remember it—let alone repeat it."

Menolly arched an eyebrow. "We found out your secret, Johnson. You want to play superhero. At least we know she's developing somewhat normally. The demons may have treated her like livestock, but now we know she can grasp basic concepts . . ." She paused as a crash echoed from out back, then again, louder. "Delilah, come with me. Chase, Iris—wait here." Without another word, she handed Maggie to Iris and slipped out of the living room.

I followed her to the kitchen. She held up her finger to her lips and eased the back door open. Almost as silent as she, thanks to my catlike nature, I tiptoed out behind her. We paused on the porch to listen. There it was again—another crash, sounding like tree limbs being bent and broken.

Tapping her on the shoulder, I motioned for her to step back. As she did, I focused on my core, on the part of me that remained hidden most of the day. The world began to fold, the shadows deepened into grayscale as I spiraled into myself. Limbs and torso melding, blending, breaking apart to reform. The metamorphosis never hurt, though nobody believed me when I told them. At least, it didn't hurt as long as I shifted smoothly. Hands and feet to paws, torso shrinking, spine lengthening, all was a whirl of change and transformation. I rolled my head back, luxuriating in the feel of the magic as the waves rolled through my body, claiming me into a different form.

A whiff of mist, the scent of bonfires in the distance, but now was not the time for Panther. The Autumn Lord, my master, was still and silent. No, now was the time for Tabby to emerge. As my golden fur quivered in the wind, I flicked my tail and blinked, then raced out through the cat door.

In cat form, I could find out quite a bit without alerting whoever—or whatever—was playing havoc in the woods that lay boundary to our land. As I padded over the silent earth, the scent of late spring threatened to cloud my senses. It was hard to keep hold of my instincts when playing the tabby. Every flutterbug tempted me, every scent that might be dinner—or a toy—made me want to race off and explore. But I was on a mission, I reminded myself, even as I spotted a daddy longlegs and promptly smacked it with one paw. I sniffed it, then gobbled it up before racing over toward the noise that crashed into my ears.

In my half-Fae, half-human form, the sound had been loud enough to hear. Now it was almost deafening. I lowered myself into stalk mode and slinked forward, keeping to the shadows. I was downwind, so unless whatever it was had an extremely keen sense of smell, it might not notice me.

As I crawled through the grass, practically on my belly, I began to sense a presence nearby. One that I recognized. It was Misha, a mouse that I'd formed a semblance of friendship with. I still chased her, but it was all in fun and she said it kept her alert and alive. She'd saved my butt when my tail got stuck in a patch of cockleburs during the winter, and we'd managed to transcend our instincts and forge a weird but viable alliance.

Now she slipped out of her hole and came running over to me. "Delilah, there's something on the land that shouldn't be."

In my Were form, I could talk to animals, and understand them. Oh, it wasn't the same form of vocalization that I used as a woman, but there's a common speech among animals—a combination of body language and sounds.

I gave her a slight nod. "I know, but I'm not sure what. I haven't picked up a scent yet and I was just going to investigate."

She shuddered. "Nasty thing. Terribly nasty thing. Big and dark. It eats mice and rodents and other small creatures so you'd better be careful. Sticks them in its dark mouth and chews, chews, chews them up."

I paused. Maybe not such a good idea to go into this in cat form. "Have you ever seen anything like this before?"

Misha sniffed. "No, never. Terrible beast. It drools and it's gray. It is, and looks like a broken two-legs. Not so tall and not so wide, but ugly and hair stringing down its back, and its belly fat and bloated. It has fur, it does, but not in the right places. *Not Friend.*"

She scurried back toward her hole, pausing for a moment to look back at me. "Be careful. This creature could snap you like a twig." And then she vanished into the earthen lair, back to her children.

I waited until she was safely underground then crept forward again, one paw-step at a time. If this thing was capable of catching and eating small animals, I had to be careful. I could be killed in cat form easier than when I was hanging out on two legs. As I neared a bend that would lead me into the wood, onto the trail toward Birchwater Pond, I paused, one foot in midair. The sound of bushes rustling and boughs breaking echoed from up ahead. Whatever it was, it was a lot closer than before.

As I neared the source of the noise, the wind shifted just enough to sweep an overwhelming odor my way—dung, fetid and cloying like sickly overripe fruit. And testosterone—thick and musky. Atop *that* delightful mixture rode the scent of someone who delighted in administering pain. Animals can smell the intentions of beasts and humans, and I could sense this creature was cruel and reveled in torment. Misha had been right. He was vicious, whatever he was.

I brushed aside a stand of tall grass with my paw, silently peering between the blades. From where I crouched, I could see into a small clearing. Moonlight struck the ground, breaking through the wispy clouds, illuminating the dell enough for me to see the source of the disturbance.

A creature that stood about four feet tall was clawing at two prone tree trunks; one had fallen atop the other. I could hear a whimper come from between the downed trunks.

Wait a minute—I knew that sound! It was Speedo, the neighbor's basset hound. He occasionally got loose and wandered onto our land. As I tried to figure out where he was, I saw that he'd wedged himself into an opening between the trees and couldn't get out. But his woodland cage was also his saving grace. The creature—whatever it was, and I suspected Demonkin—couldn't get into the hole. While he could reach his long, twisted hand into the opening, Speedo seemed to have enough room to back up, just out of reach.

It wouldn't be long before the demon figured out that if he

moved the top log, he'd have access to what lay beneath. And in his eyes, Speedo was obviously a Happy Meal just out of reach. The hoser wasn't too bright, but even the dumbest demon couldn't possibly be stupid enough to ignore the obvious. Poor old Speedo was a goner unless I did something.

I sized up my opponent. Going in as a cat would never work—he'd eat me in one gulp if he caught me. I could probably take him down by myself but I'd have to shift fast. While in mid-transition, I was helpless and if the demon noticed me then, it would be over before I managed to shift back into my normal form.

I silently backed away until I was hiding beneath one of the nearby fir trees in a bushy patch of maidenhair fern and huckleberry. The thorns on the huckleberry would hurt when I transformed, but I'd been through worse. Thank the gods we weren't under a full moon or I'd be trapped in cat-form until morning.

Sucking in a deep breath, I envisioned myself metamorphosing back into my two-legged body. Golden shag haircut, six-foot-one, athletic, a few scars here and there from all the fights we'd been in over the past few months, emerald eyes—just like my eyes when I was a cat . . .

As I clung to the image I began to shift and willed the transformation to come fast. For once, my body obeyed me. With a dizzying *whoosh* I hit the ground and changed back into my clothes. It hurt a little—I had shifted too fast—but it wasn't anything I couldn't handle. Sort of like being spanked with a rubber mallet. As soon as I was sure I'd fully transformed, I ripped out of the huckleberry bush and shook off the fern fronds in which I was tangled.

"Get out of here, you ape!" I raced toward Speedo and the demon at full tilt, ready to kick butt. The moment I'd made the full change my sense of dread and fear had shifted into *I'm pissed off and you better make tracks!*

The demon lurched around, staring up at me with a bewildered look on its face, but his puzzlement lasted just long enough for him to raise his ugly claws and slash at me. I dodged the attack, but barely. The ugly brute was a lot faster than he looked capable of. I'd almost gotten snagged.

"So you think you're going to rip my new jeans, do you?" I'd just bought three pairs of the coolest indigo low-rise jeans from my favorite store the other day and I wasn't ready to punk them out yet. "Think again, Bubba!"

I pivoted on one foot, lashing out with the other to land a kick right in the middle of his grubby face.

"Crap!" My leg shuddered as it made contact. It felt like I'd just kicked a brick wall. Well, maybe not brick, but damned close. The demon might look like a little pissant but he was resilient. This was going to be more of a challenge than I'd first thought. Worried, now, I took aim again. Again, my foot bounced off him, this time from a kick to the stomach.

"Watch out!"

The unexpected shout startled me, but being used to combat situations, I obeyed and dove into a somersault. Good thing, too, because the creature opened his mouth right as I ducked under his radar and let out a long belch of flame. I heard the crackle of dry tinder as I rolled to my feet and spun around.

A small patch of debris from a downed log was on fire. Standing next to it was a tall man with pale skin and dark hair, wearing a leather duster.

The demon seemed to think that facing *two* opponents wasn't such a hunky-dory idea and he turned tail and went crashing through the woods, away from the path. He had to be heading toward one of the boundary lines that divided our land from a protected wetlands area.

"Roz, be careful! He's hard to kill," I shouted as I gave chase.

"I know, you twit," Roz shouted back as he raced past me. Very few creatures were faster than my sisters and me, but Roz—Rozurial—was one of them. He was an incubus—technically a demon—but he roamed in that nicely shadowed ethical region into which we'd all slipped lately. He was definitely on our side, but make no mistake—he was an incubus to the core.

Since he was helping us against Shadow Wing, the demon lord bent on taking over both Earth and Otherworld, we conveniently overlooked his cavorting with—and seducing of—nubile young maidens. And nubile older women. And non-nubile women. Roz liked women of any type, age, shape, size, or color, and his greatest delight was in seducing the ones who considered themselves in full control of their instincts. He loved seeing strong women capitulate to his charms. Apparently, he was good at what he did, but I had no intentions of finding out for myself.

I dodged around a burned-out tree stump, hoping to hell the

fire behind us wouldn't go anywhere except *out*, and then hurdled over a clump of three fallen trees. Roz took them without a single hesitation, his duster flying out behind him as he gracefully sailed over the moss-laden trunks.

After a moment, he stopped where he was and stared into the undergrowth. "I can't smell him anymore. The scent of cedar's too thick."

I sniffed the air. Yep. Cedar, it was. Cedar and fir, and the moist scent of soil still damp from the rain. Cocking my head, I tried to pick up any sound. My hearing was keen, like a cat's, though in my half-human, half Fae form, not quite so much. Small creatures were rustling through the tall grass. A jet soared overhead in the darkness, and somewhere in the distance, the faint sound of rippling waves from Birchwater Pond indicated an incoming breeze. But no sound of the demon.

"Damn it, we lost him." I looked around once more, trying to decide if it was worth giving chase. But chances were he was long gone. He might be back, maybe not, but there was no doubt in my mind he'd broken through Camille's wards. She wasn't here to alert us, though. We had to do something about that. Create some sort of warning system so that if she was out, the rest of us would know they'd been breached.

I shook my head, disgusted. "Can't even kill a simple demon. I'm getting soft," I muttered.

Roz moved to put his arm around my shoulders but stopped when I shot him a warning look. He knew the rules—he was welcome in our home as long as he kept his mitts off Camille and me.

He'd put the skids on his pursuit of Camille after a run-in with Smoky. All it had taken was one misplaced hand on Camille's ass while the dragon was watching to squelch any more attempts. As a dragon, Smoky could crisp Roz with one belch, but even in his six-foot-four wantonly gorgeous human form, Smoky was stronger than the incubus. He'd grabbed the demon by the scruff of the neck and dragged him outside where he proceeded to beat the crap out of him. It took Roz two weeks and a lot of ice to heal up from Smoky's thrashing.

But Roz still flirted constantly with Menolly, and she flirted back. Kind of. He'd tried to get in my pants a few times until I threatened to give him a nasty bite where it counted most. Now, he left me alone except to act as a buddy.

"Don't chide yourself. That was a bloatworgle. You couldn't have killed him without help. They're lightning-fast even with their potbellies and scrawny-looking limbs." He motioned toward the trail. "Come on, let's go make sure that fire's out and then get back to the house to report."

"A *bloatworgle*? Demonkin, I presume?"

Roz nodded. "Yes. Mainly grunts. They tend to congregate over here Earthside, a lot. Several nests of them were hiding out when the portals were closed against the Subterranean Realms and they've kept the line going, it seems. But they're usually found in deep caverns and barren mountain passes, so I'm not sure what the hell this one's doing here."

What the *hell* was right. Great, just great. Yet another monster I'd never heard of, and the thing was still on the loose. What had it wanted?

Regardless of what Roz said, there was no doubt in my mind that the bloatworgle had been sent here. Either another Degath Squad of Hell Scouts had broken through, or the demon lord Shadow Wing had something else up his pointy little tail. Either way, it looked like we were headed right back down the rabbit hole.